JOURNEY
to the
FAR WEST

A Young Irishman's Journey in Search of Freedom

Steven Sears

TABLE OF CONTENTS

The events and characters in this book are fictitious. Certain real locations and real figures are mentioned but there words are imaginary all other characters and events described in the book are totally imaginary.

This book is dedicated to Arlinda who has taken me on many journeys and we have agreed to pursue other journeys together. Writing was one of those journeys and I am at last free to pursue it and will do so for the remainder of my days as I have found a format I like in the novel.

Arlinda thank you for this journey that we did together.

Writing has been in my heart for a long time and in hers. Reading novels is part of writing novels and reading and writing are like two fingers twisted together you can't have one without the other.

May your journey be a dangerous one.

CHAPTER 1

JOURNEY ACROSS THE SEA

Colmcille O'Toole Journal

Monday 19th September 1831

I thought I would welcome the silence of the sea, but only a short sail and now becalmed on a vast sea I think of my family and our squabbles.

I face the breadth of the Atlantic with Cape Clear of my dear Ireland behind me. It seems a puzzle I am standing on tons of a sailing ship floating on the ocean, but I am and not a flap of wind to move her.

Some three days ago I had sight of sweet Dublin for the last time. Out of Liverpool we sailed and past my family and all who are dear, twas only the stone of quay and buildings of Dublin I could see as we sailed past her. Tis nearly two weeks since I saw my family last and I fear for them more than myself at sea. Does Dublin still suffer from the Indian Cholera Morbus? I fear an infected person will enter the bakeshop and pass the curse onto them. The English are much afraid it will penetrate her ports and news while I was ashore was about the measures to keep it out: the quarantines, the flagging off infected ships by the Bureau of the Marine. The meeting in Parliament and town halls, the smoking and soaking of mail in vinegar from infected countries, the doctors and health officials reading and recommending while thousands perish of it around the world from war-torn Poland to India. Tis said to be on the shores of the Baltic, in Denmark, Holland, the Hanse Towns, Prussia and Russia.

I'm leaving her and I have barely seen her. Twas my first sight of the harbor of Cork, and the mountains of Wicklow, standing on these very planks. Past Old Kinsale where the Captain told how the British sloop of war Albion dashed upon the iron coast in a gale so violent it rendered the masts and sails and fouled the anchors swallowing 200 English. Tis the vengeance of St. Brendan my Da would say for the English trying to drown General O'Connor in Scottish waters. It might have been a miracle that saved the General, but it seems a bigger miracle is needed to save Ireland from the English. I'll record the story here before I leave the waters of Erin behind for if this story had turned out different I might not be upon this ship.

I WAS TOLD HOW LORD Castlereagh tried to rid England of the threat of O'Connor, for tis the legend that since King O'Connor lost Ireland to the English in the reign of Henry the II, there would return an O'Connor to free her. But our General O'Connor was captured in the uprising of 1798 mostly due to the faltering courage of a Mr. Emmet. It could have been like the States, for the General had the French army ready to land and assist us in getting our country back. But 'twas the luck of the Irish to have a weak man in a strong place and our General was captured. Lord Castlereagh couldn't execute him without causing more troubles, so in the cunning way of the English he set General O'Connor and his brother on a leaky sloop towards a prison in Scotland on a tossing, stormy night captained by a man unfamiliar with the rocky coast. When they started it was blowing a howl and the captain tried to put in the bay where the British frigate lay, but it would not let him enter, turning their guns on him and so into the howl they sailed and soon they were off the black rocks of Scotland a fair mile off, but closing in collision. O'Connor's brother called for him to join in throwing themselves at the mercy of the sea, rather than be dashed upon the rocks. The captain said all was lost and to prepare their souls for in minutes they would all perish. Then just as the General was moving to the lee side of the mast so as not to be crushed when it splintered, the wind dropped like a rock. Like a miracle it 'twas, but they were without rudder and drifting towards those selfsame rocks. The captain cried out they would yet die for he could not steer and barely had the words dropped from his mouth afore a breeze sprung directly from the rocks, billowing the sails and filling all on board with astonishment at their salvation. They fell to the deck in thanks. That 'twas the miracle and O'Connor yet lives.

The English being thwarted by the Almighty they then let him rot awhile in prison, but his countrymen forgot him not and so the English told O'Connor he must go to exile and he would not, so in the diplomatic style for which the English was famous they made him watch as they began one by one to execute his friends until they broke his poor heart and he relented.

Now he lives in France a friend of La Fayette, married to the revolutionary Condorcet's only daughter, Condorcet having perished under the bloody rule of Robespierre's faction. The General is said to be an intimate of the British Prime Minister Earl Gray. Tis ironic since summer of last he lives under the rule of a king again, none other that Louis Philippe the richest man in the world.

So Ireland does without its O'Connor and the seventh generation of Irish live under the fist of England. My Da thinks we shall be free before the end of his life and my uncle Bres thinks not for another eight generations will all of Ireland be free. But I shall be free of England and I shall see a new and free land and I most certainly will return to see my Ireland in whatever state she shall be in. I shall return and when I do I will bring these words with me, for I have the grand dream of setting down all that I see and experience in the new world in my journal.

Tis tears that flow with the ink today for my heart does not seem fully informed of my decision to sail away…away from the faces that have been before me for all my days, my family foremost, but tis curious how I miss those people with whom I had daily intercourse—Mr. O'Leary in his checked vest, hat and cane, coming in the bakeshop with a new joke every day and buying a loaf every day, even though he lives alone, so where the bread went and the jokes come from shall forever remain a mystery to me. All the good mornings and hello's and ta's and hat tipping and smiles were given to me with the calm expectation that I would always trod and sweep the cobble of that Dublin street…and that the O'Toole lad would become an O'Toole man and that there would be another O'Toole boy with broom in hand some day greeting them. I recall Mrs. Kennedy comin' in for a *wee bit of sweet*: her so prim and proper and her boys such bullying louts—them I'll not miss. The Sullivan brothers I will miss for they were the salt of the earth, but so big and with such big hearts. Once they loved you they watched over you. I miss the strength of their silence and their love of adventure for they knew there way out of all matter of scapes. I am fortunate to have an older brother in the states. It's time I put my face and heart to the west for that is my destination.

20ᵗʰ September 1831, Tuesday

Oh the wind does howl today. The gangway stairs screech and groan and the stateroom doors are banging and creaking, spray is coming o'er the bow, near which a brave passenger from steerage is standing naked getting a cold salt bath, his arms out, face clenched, his body jerking with each flick of Neptune's finger. From calm to chaos I have been so busy watching the sights these first days that I neglected the details of this ship. I am employed as a cooks mate and steward I am engaged to wait on the cabin passengers at mealtimes which are break fast at eight O'clock, lunch at noon and dinner at four o'clock and tea at one-half after seven. There are two cook's, two cook's mates, three stewards, four waiters and three boys mostly to serve cabin passengers. I do not get a wage, but there is a collection taken at the end of the passage by the cabin passengers for the kitchen people and we split it. The other cook's mate told me that it amounted to ten pounds for him on the trip to Liverpool, so I may expect that as my wage for the forty to forty five days journey. The sailor's wage is thirteen pounds a month. And that seems more difficult as the worse the weather the more they seem to work and the more difficult the work. The sailors are a mixed lot with Swedes, Hollanders, Norse, French, English and a few from the States. The cabin passengers pay one hundred fourty pounds for passage.

I hear that wages in the States are much higher and costs like rent are much less than England and much less than France since that country is at a stand still since the troubles of last July and that these low prices and high wages are due to America having no standing army, no pensions, no national debt, no royalty, nor palaces nor national monuments to support like most of Europe. Russia and Poland are at war. France is in a continual flux from mob rule to Republic back to having a king rule as it now does. This has upset trade and caused the streets to fill with beggars and her wharfs to sit idle. Now that the Cholera Morbus rages trade is stopping and prices rising. I'm glad my parents have put in a store of flour at the bakeshop.

The ship has many in steerage going to the States. I am told that there is more cargo than people on the return trip to Liverpool with cotton and flour being the common cargo of this ship. In steerage is mostly German, Swiss, French and a small number of Irish—them being protestant.

In cabin there are several students returning: two young doctors, one from South Carolina, both returning from medical schools in Paris. There is a twenty-six year old man who is returning from five years in Paris having studied at the School of Mines. Several gentlemen French and English who are traveling for their health and a number of lawyers: American, French and English. It is said that France has more lawyers than any other country and more need of them as it is infested with rules and inspectors.

I met a Mr. Dagget a young American returning from three years of business in Paris, and a Mr. Concord also in his twenties returning from a trip of pleasure and amusement. A Mr. Billingsley, a middle-aged Englishman traveling to the States for his health. A Mr. Viscount a lawyer returning to Quebec.

The crew numbers thirty including sixteen seamen and captain Wayne, first mate Mr. Axle, second mate Mr. Norby, a carpenter and the rest of us serving the cabin and steerage. Nearly half the people in the cabin have servants engaged.

The sea here is an overall darker color than the sea near the coastline of Ireland. After break fast this morning I walked the deck and spied a number of blackfish and porpoises and there are still birds to be seen flying over the sea. The deck has a clutter of cages holding live birds, there being over three dozen ducks and a couple dozen geese, dozens of chickens, tortoises swimming in a hogshead and another hogshead full of oysters and a milch cow and a couple of sheep all to provide crew and cabin with fresh meat and milk.

21 September 1831, Wednesday

First day of fall the winds have fallen to a stiff breeze and a glorious sun has appeared over the shimmering ocean—the first of the trip. The ship is sailing at seven knots. I watched at the first mate measured the speed and he explained the mystery of the measure. First he tossed a three cornered piece of wood with lead attached into the sea, this wood being attached to a marked line which is wound round a roller held by a seaman. When the wood is tossed a glass of sand it turned this measuring a minute of time. The amount of line unwound in a minute is measured and the marks or knots on the line are used to calculate the speed in knots.

Curious how Mr. Dagget referred to fall beginning on September one do they not know of the equinox in the States? I feared to question him on it as I know him not well enough. He seemed quite curious about me writing in my journal when he came upon me on the deck and questioned me intently about my schooling and seemed quite amused at my description of our hedge schools.

There is a French couple in cabin. He is middle-aged and she seems in her early twenties and has beautiful long black hair, rounded brown eyes and the most graceful movements I have ever seen—she flows across the deck while I cannot help but to step too hard or too light with the movement of the deck. It is comforting to watch her flow over the deck. I have not spoken to them yet only nodded to greeting them. She strolls the deck every day, most times without her husband and seems to bring the seaman out even when they've no duties at the moment. She is not the least bothered by us watching her and seems intent of her twice-daily walks.

Today looking over the side I see millions of little needle-like fish or worms about a half-inch long, wriggling in the water like they are fascinated with the wooden bow of the ship.

22 September 1831, Thursday

Very foggy today we are making only three to four knots. Last night I saw the sea light up around the bow and sides of the ship with phosphine—tiny creatures that lights the foam created by the motion of the ship. What mysteries there are below that we do not know.

Today after break fast I was on deck making entries in my journal and Mr. Dagget approached and asked if I had ambitions to be a writer and I was surprised to find I had not considered it. Not because I didn't wish it, but because it wasn't even a calling that seemed one from my station could consider. Mr Cooper and Captain Marryat—two successful writers are writers who had family wealth and position. There are many Irish poets with barely enough peat to burn, but I felt a strange sensation at the question. He said he kept a journal and did some publishing in America. He proposed that I assist him in recording some evening conversations that he had taken to having with some of the other gentlemen in the cabin. It was a form of amusement to help with the passage. He explained that he talked to the captain who had agreed to lend me to the group after I had completed my evening duties. I served this group at meals so I have some knowledge of them. Mr. Dagget explained that they sit around the table in the cabin drinking port discussing news, politics, religion and theater. He explained that he wanted to preserve some of these conversations. I explained that I did not have the skill of a clerk expert in such matters, but he waved me off saying only that he needed the gist of it all. He offered to pay me and that sealed it. Upon reflection in my hammock, I became quite excited at the prospect of being a professional eavesdrop to a group of gentlemen. I've often wondered about the world of gentlemen, while serving them in our bakeshop. Surely it will be useful.

23 September 1831, Friday

A high sea with dense fog and some rain with the wind roaring the cracking cordage and the rapping sails making such a din that the captain made his commands through the brazen trumpet. The winds did ease as darkness fell, but the fog kept our world closed all the live long day. To not see, even it tis only the vastness of the sea gives me the feeling I'm living in a hole.

The captain hosted a feast this night for the cabin passengers. First we had a course of turtle soup followed by a rich white soup made from two fat fowl and onions, turnips, celery and potatoes. That was followed by roasted minted mutton, boiled ham with a raisin sauce and boiled tongue, roasted goose and duck and fowl boiled in a curry sauce. We had oysters, pickles, rye, buttered wheat bread, pies of oranges and lemon, dessert of oranges and almonds, all served with a white wine. We also had Madeira wine, porter and Newark cider along with Saratoga water and port wine. Quite a mess was made and work enough for all and plenty of picking left over. It was certainly more grand that boiled potatoes and mutton.

24 September 1831, Saturday

Still foggy with a fair wind we sail under reefed topsails, and we make good headway. There is a young French man, sickly when we set sail, consumption they say, but some fear he may have the Cholera Morbus and keep their distance. He has only been able to make the deck but a day since we set sail and now requests that he be left in peace to sort though his thoughts upon what he believes is his last day. Tis a sad place to be in a hammock in the middle of the sea, far from friends and family. What man could conceive dying amid a vast sea? All my dying fantasies are full of bravery and pity and surrounded by family and friends. Tis the failing of the Irish my Da says to be full of pity—too many spend their pity on poteen, quaffing their pity instead of rapping the English. But nothing but pity I can feel for the poor Frenchman.

Tonight was my first reporting for the gentlemen:

Mr. Dagget: Gentlemen: I wish to introduce Mr. O'Toole I know you have met him in his service to you all. But I wish to gain your approval in my scheme of having this young protégé make some scribbles upon the subjects we discourse. Alas, do not fear your words will be used against you. This is a venture in which Mr. O'Toole may raise some knowledge to help him in his striving in America and by which I may organize my notes for a piece on the Natural Laws that I am much interested in.

Mr. Billingsley: Would this be one of your leveling schemes, Mr. Dagget, by which you hope to make America one vast mob without the proven safely of class?

Mr. Dagget No this is recording what we say so that I may extract an article from our conversation.

Mr. Billingsley You Americans think you can do away with your social obligations, by turning the country into one vast merchant class. But the educated among you know perfectly well that class is simply functional and absolutely essential for the well-being of any society that is to be civilized. (Nodding) Mr. O'Toole—for in this room are all so addressed, I welcome you as our scribe and hope you are up for the task. You seem young to have command of the letters. Where were you educated?

Mr. Dagget: He was tutored. Private tutors. He's from a merchant family in Dublin. I wish to keep our words going across the table and make Mr. O'Toole simply a comfortable presence—that is if there are no objections?

Mr. Billingsley: On with it then. Mr. Dufont and Mr. Dagget you both spoke of the troubles in France: I wish to hear more of those troubles?

Mr. Dufont: A most sorry situation for a once great nation. Perhaps it is the temperament of the French to sing loudest the praises of a republic while wallowing in anarchy and then tyranny. After the fighting ended a year ago July all the priests were turned out and monasteries taken over by the state for Catholics received the blame for the country's failure to achieve democracy. The country is filled with beggars, for the monasteries did cater to the poor and the richest man in the world: King Louis Philippe, has no institution to minster to the poor. All the while the custom spy's sit along the coasts to prevent smuggling, but of course no ships sail for so little commerce is conducted since the troubles. As I was leaving this July there was fighting in Paris with the young Republican Cadets wanting to plant the tree of liberty on Bastille day while the King's guard prevented it with bayonets to their bellies. This year the great banker Lafitte has not employed citizen soldiers to fight for he is content to let the King put down the rebellion. There is no confidence in the government and they say the

King cannot last, the factories are shut down—there will be no calicoes out of Rouen this year.

Mr. Billingsley: I say they well be rid of the Papists! The Roman Catholic religion has been the agent that has turned that nation into a nation of free thinkers.

Mr. Dagget: I should say that my experience in Paris and the countryside was similar. One cannot move in France without being accosted by beggars. There was said to be four thousand beggars in the countryside is Rouen alone. Families were living in holes dug in the ditches with only a pail and a bit of straw for comfort. They were peeling the bark of certain trees to eat even if the tree was on your property. The government employs agents to regulate and mark all the trees. They couldn't stop the starving people from stripping the trees so they call gensd' armes and both poor and gensd' armes were being killed in the clash and as the bodies piled up the soldiers soon refused to risk their lives to save the trees.

Mr. Billingsley: It is the population out of control that is the cause of it. Like all Catholic countries they breed like vermin and they are even eating the trees. Ireland is getting the same way—more every year living in holes in the ground. Mark me there will be troubles coming from there as well.

Mr. Dagget: "So you think a tree is worth a man's life?"

Mr. Billingsley: "No of course not."

Mr. Dagget: Government is not eloquence. It is force. And like fire it is a dangerous servant and a fearful master." That was said by our first president, George Washington I think it naïve for any to take government as benevolent, for power always and I must emphasize always contains tyranny, it is only a matter of time for abuse to appear if the populace is not peering over the shoulder of those in power with there hands on the reins. Must every generation have a Napoleon to learn that? A tree will grow again. We must all be secure within the garden of our land and the government should stay out of the private sphere.

Mr. Dufont: "If one is privileged to own land…"

Mr. Billingsley: Americans revolt over a tea tax, the French over a salt tax, the corn laws of England now cause much dissent…lady liberty seems to spring from hunger taxed.

September 25, 1831, Sunday

Nearly calm with dark clouds sailing by us dropping rain which runs down the sails in sheets and then the wind will snap the sails and water will spray off the sails unto the deck. Today I saw a sunfish, a fish as flat as a tabletop and just as large.

I tried a mocha coffee today having prepared one for Mr. Viscount. It was much more bitter than tea but it was agreeable.

The captain allowed a Mr. Fry to conduct services in the round house. Mr. Fry is a quiet polite American who does not take part in the evening port sessions. He read from Revelations and from a published sermon of some American minister. I'm given to understand that publishing sermons is quite common in the States. It is curious that Protestants have no qualm in holding a service without any church official present. It seems any Protestant can get up and tell the world about the Divine, but at the same time many are intolerant of those that drink, gamble or play cards. How they get intolerant of drink based on the life of one who created wine out of water I'll never know.

Evening port session.

Mr. Dagget: Since this is the Sabbath I thought is apropos that we have a discussion of religion and natural law. It seems many believe natural law to be one and the same with God's law and others perhaps those with scientific training believe the natural laws stand on their own merit without God's direct hand.

Dr. Northcut: Stand on their own maybe, but natural law was surely created by our creator the trouble lies in that the methods of science follow a rather strict course, which perhaps results in a narrow outcome or answer, but one that others may follow to the same answer. Having a priest declare that answer immoral or against God's will strikes at the very bedrock of scientific process. How can one reconcile this conflict among the masses?

Mr. Billingsley: Perhaps the masses should best be left to the Priests and that science caters to the educated.

Dr. Northcut: If all of society becomes educated?

Mr. Billinglsey: Ho! That will surely never be. And if it does there will always be those who chose the path of ignorance are you proposing that this, gossiping, quarrelsome, thoughtless masses whom are ruled by passions will sit to be educated?

Mr. Dagget: If all Americans had education would we become a nation of merchants. Who will till the soil and serve at servants?

Dr. Northcut: Is betterment not what the church and state seek.

Mr. Dagget: Think of a nation of all citizens educated. Democracy will flourish. A well-informed citizen's will demand an open and honest democracy.

Mr. Billinglsey: I do not see it as possible to educate everyone.

Dr. Northcut: There are those that advocate a public education system in America. They would have all Americans knowing their letters. If the masses don't accept science, science cannot serve them nor their governments. To return to the question, natural law follows but one course and it is for scientists to uncover that course to make it useful for mankind.

Mr. Billingsley: Science is but a new vanity. Men competing to be the first to publish like a penny paper scribble and the first to profit. What does it matter that one can go 40 miles per hour on the Manchester railroad? If science gives us a machine that goes ten times that speed what have we done but surpassed the speed of a falcon that has enjoyed superior speed and flight for thousands of years—so we have surpassed a bird what of it? If we learn to fly across the Atlantic we will do no more than what a tern does.

Dr. Northcut: Not all ride on the Manchester rail nor will there ever be enough railways to all of mankind to ride.

Mr. Dagget: But we would not be like the falcon, nor any animal if we possess immorality… and it is nothing less that what we have been promised by the church, is it not?

Mr. Billingsley: I say if it rids us of the priest we shall kneel at the altar of science! Me, I seen enough, I don't wish immortality not as a capricious youth nor as an insufferable old man. Immorality is not natural law—that I know.

I am dismissed at this point.

September 26, 1831, Monday

Perfect calm as the sun breaks over the horizon. Break fast is interrupted in the cabin by one of the seaman shouting porpoises! Porpoises cutting the surface, leaping, spouting and having a grand frolic amidst schools of blackfish that looked to weigh a ton each, surround the ship.

The Frenchman died last night. I couldn't help by note that he died while I made notes on immortality. He only made age 26. I believe I will live to a ripe old age, I suppose he did too at age 25.

The captain had a short service held around the body which was wrapped in sheets with ropes about the feet and a bag of ballast rocks tied within—that being the total expense on behalf the ship for his internment. It felt like the captain had done this service before. When the captain nodded after blessing his soul, two seamen tilted the board and he hung there for a second as if to resist the cold Atlantic sea. He then fairly shot off the board like a Congreve rocket without the smoke, making a neat almost splash less entry and not slowing down as he shot downwards into the dark cold water his body feeling the pressure of the deep. The captain thinks it could be several thousand feet deep here. I know the Frenchman feels nothing, but I could not shake a shudder at the thought of him sliding through the inky cold that kept getting darker and darker with more and more pressure. It's hard not to imagine your warm body in place of a dead one. Does his family now feel their son is pointed like a rocket towards the deep Atlantic? Does even a cold shudder pass them and they know not why? I've seen those that know when they have no earthly way to do so.

September 27 1831, Tuesday

Small winds today, the wind has not favored us on this trip. I'm told the voyage to Liverpool took only twenty-four days, but it is always a better sail to Europe.

I watched the Frenchwoman again today and felt entranced, but I have not yet discovered the cause. Tis a bit like watching flames lick in a fire. Yesterday she was there for the funeral in what I took to be a black silk mourning dress. It had large sleeves puffed out greatly from the elbows and then gathered at the shoulders. Around her waist, which looked like the hands of a man could close was a wide silk belt of which the ends fell to the side of her hips hidden in the pleats of material that fanned out finally ending just above her ankles that were clad in tiny pointed beribboned black shoes with her leg clad in black cotton stockings. A muff hung from a scarf round her neck into which her white hands rested out of view so the only the flesh of her very white face showed. Her head is covered with a hat rimmed large in front with black lace hanging on its edge, silk ribbon for the band and two large soft black feathers breathing in the breeze.

This afternoon the Frenchwoman walks in a black dress belted at the waist of the same length, but her shoulders are covered with a short cape of the same material, her neck wrapped in a long fur scarf that drops to her thighs and her hands are in a beaded-embroidered muff. The hat is a bonnet type, but with a round crown topped with feathers. He face rests in a high white lace collar.

September 28, 1831, Wednesday (12 days out)

Port Society meets again.

Mr. Dagget: Gentlemen! A Mr. Fry suggested that he address our group in a temperance meeting, which has become a popular meeting form in America.

Mr. Billingsely: I heard it has been well tested in the States and now some agitate for such meeting in Britain. Another crazed American religious scam in my opinion. Pass the port, sir.

Mr. Concord: Temperance? I've heard the term, but not the explanation for it. Is it to learn to drink more modestly for the whiskey drinking Americans?

Mr. Billingsley: Why is Mr. Fry so full of fervor to flagellate us for our port and philosophy? Only people with some new religion in their craw want to go around jamming it down another throats. Every year it seems a new form of salvation appears and every year the world will end if we don't stop doing something. I'm still waiting for the year we can do something. If you people from the States want to do something why don't you ban slavery like good old England.

Mr. Dagget: Slavery is only allowed in the slave states and the slave ships are to be banned…and any child born to a slave in the North is born free.

Mr. Billingsley: So you are telling me that a Negro male in New York City can vote, own property and enjoy all the legal rights you do?

Mr. Dagget In law yes in practice no. No public clerk would allow a Negro to vote.

Mr. Billingsley: You Americans are too cavalier with your laws. We have never granted those rights to the Irish. They know they can't vote nor own property, unless they turn protestant.

Mr. Dagget: And what about this Nat Turner business? It seems he has the entire countryside full of Negroes murdering decent people.

Mr. Concord: That's my point, no sane white man will ever feel safe with the idea of freeing slaves who could get hold of guns and murder them. The only responsible way to deal with freeing slaves is to have it handled by those who are slave owners who free only those who would not be a danger to society.

Mr. Billinglsey: So you believe it part of natural law for one man to own another?

Mr. Concord: A son honoureth his father and a servant his master Malachi chapter 1 verse 6. The bible says that slavery is a natural condition of mankind, that is the way God has ordered our world and so I believe that the Negros must have committed some great offense against God to be put in such a position and it has always been the natural law of the conquered to do what they wish with those they have conquered and our Constitution does not forbid it and it fact endorses it for it says that no man shall be deprived of his property without due process.

Mr. Billingsley: Leave religion out of it. It's your dam laws in the south that allow slavery. Own up to it. It sounds like a big fight is brewing over this issue if you southerners don't smarten up and drop slavery. It's a foregone conclusion you will lose the fight with the industrial north.

The port society ended in a huff.

September 29, 1831, Thursday

A horrible pitching storm began early this morning and rages still. Lightning is crashing all about us, and the waves turn confused and seemingly hit us from all sides. I could not sleep the entire night for my hammock swung wildly and I began to feel sick below deck and then upon arriving on the deck somewhat unsteady I was nearly washed overboard with the thunder of a wave o'er the deck at the same time the ship pitched to the side, I was hurled against the caboose and that is what saved me. The sails are reduced by three quarters, but how the wind howls through the ropes like a pack of banshees. There is water everywhere and it rolls below deck as well.

I still have a copy of the *Adventures of the Columbia River* by my neighbor Mr. Ross Cox. He is now at the Dublin Police Office. Tis a newly published book about his adventures with the Astorian expedition of 1811 and he gave me a copy just before I left. He had told me many stories in the pub about some of his adventures. Reading the book has ignited a fever in me to see the American Far West. I read passages from the book every evening by candlelight and must find a way to see this land inhabited by many people and animals so very different from the people in my world.

September 30, 1831, Friday

The storm rages on it is damm frustrating for the bowls tip and the doors swing at one like a madman and yet we try to feed the cabin passengers although few have an appetite.

October 1, 1831, Saturday

This has shown me that a life at sea is not for me. Tis cold all is full of water there is nothing to see but large waves looming over us and then a precipice into which we dive, over and over again.

I have been thinking about what Mr. Ross from Dublin told me about his adventures of the crossing the Far West to the Columbia River and Pacific Ocean. He told me that he couldn't even describe some of the sights he had seen to his own satisfaction, and he was questioned by his publishers as to where he was stretching the truth, which he claims was not the case at all. What is it like to have an adventure where the truth seems like fantasy? Oh how I wish for the same adventures and I'll scribble every detail so that some day I can write my story like he has. Seeing him walk the cobble as a policeman, you would never think he climbed those high mountains, fought battles and learned to trap and trade in the Far West.

October 1, 1831, Sunday (15 days at sea)

The storm broke last night. Tis amazing what this ship can do, still foggy.

October 2, 1831, Monday

Tis still cloudy and the winds are only fair and from the southwest so all sails are out and we go slow fighting the wind that was too much only yesterday.

Today the captain ordered that even the cabin passengers are not to use the fresh water for bathing, only drinking, as we have to preserve the water. The captain related the story of large slave ship out of Rio Janeiro, which sailed for Mozambique and took on 500 kidnapped slaves these slaves having been kidnapped for profit by a rival African tribe. The ship had a crew of 40 hands and off they sailed round the Cape of Good Hope and having used up the fresh water which stood in barrels on the deck they went below to tap the main stock of water. The puncheon had been emptied for ballast as is the practice and this mate whose business it was to fill them with fresh water had been changed in Africa. No water in the middle of the Atlantic so the throwing of humans overboard commenced and there arrived in Rio Janeiro nine men: Seven white and two Negro. That mate killed 531 people by what he didn't do.

October 6, 1831, Wednesday

The sea turned rough and so did my health. I don't think it was the sea-sickness, but it felt similar, as I've been down with a doubled stance and woozy head. I'm back to my duties today, but a bit unsteady.

October 9, 1831, Sunday

We have been becalmed for the past three days. I've been very busy with extra duties due to my sickness.

October 12, 1831, Wednesday

The French woman spoke to me today! "What do you always write so earnestly?" She asked in a slightly accented, clear, nearly deep voice. I was elated she spoke to me and has never spoken to another on deck. I felt my chest swell and could see the seaman squint their eyes at us.

"It is my diary of my trip to America. I am going to record everything and then sent it back to my family to read in the pub."

"It is good that a boy is so earnest with his letters."

My chest pricked with her words. I am a mere boy in her eyes. Here I am on my own, sailing across the sea…but only as an earnest boy. She smelled of lavender, which is a godsend as the ship is befouled with smells from the water that sloshes below deck and from the sickness in steerage. Her eyes and skin are clear, her breath like a morning meadow, She smiled and seemed to float away. She has the magic of a fairy about her.

October 13, 1831, Thursday

A pair of Grampuses appeared today and went round and round the ship. It is said that they weigh five tons. I was enjoying this view, watching them spout and imagining that they were delighted in our company when one of the seaman launched a harpoon which stuck with the whale disengaging it and then a seaman fired a ball into it and both our visitors departed to the deep. I do not understand why this was done. I saw no way they could land such a large beast. Why do such a thing if one is not to profit with food it was an American seaman who did the act, but I'll not hold it against the country.

October 14, 1831, Friday

A shark appeared today and the seamen fear it means another shall die.

Ah the sun shines bright and rose over the sea, deep orange while we sailed in a light breeze. The cool night air got colder as the sun cleared the sea, so fast did it rise those first ten minutes and it is always a fascinating surprise to witness. Then the wet deck began to steam and my woolen clothes warm under her rising embrace. And so at the stern I did stay watching her for an hour before I had to hurry to serve those breaking fast.

October 15, 1831, Saturday (30 days at sea)

A frantic morning, Mr. DeLaurie disappeared last night, After a hurried search a seaman who had been on watch and coming off at 4:00AM had been sleeping while we searched for Mr. DeLaurie It was reported that Mr. DeLaurie was on deck last night about 3:00AM walking about. The seaman reported he heard a splash off the stern and rushed to look, but could see nothing in the dark. Only upon waking did he realize that Mr. DeLaurie had never passed him from the stern when the seaman had rushed to look. It just never occurred to him that a gentleman would throw himself overboard. The captain declared it a suicide. Mr. DeLaurie is the husband to the French woman I have been writing about. It seems a shock to us all.

Port Society Meetings

Mr. Dagget: A bit of a somber meeting tonight, but from my experience in France it seems not an unusual occurrence.

Mr. Viscount: Sadly so I visited the morgue in Paris—I passed it one day and would not have noticed had I not seen all the clothes hanging in front of the building, a curious sight for the clothes were arranged one piece atop the other as if one were wearing them and one set of clothes were wet. It seems when officials find suicides, drowning or random murders they hang the clothes out in hopes that someone recognize them. They hold the bodies laid out on slabs for 48 hours and then bury them. There were six bodies in there when I stopped and three were suicides and one was a bludgeoning murder.

Mr. Dagget: Sad, but true so many are to full of despair and toss their lives away. I was below Paris near St. Cloud where a weir is built across the river just to catch the bodies of those who throw themselves into the river. They say up to four bodies a day are taken off the weir. I spoke with your American man of letters Mr. Cooper who told me of incident were he witnessed two people jump from the Pont Royal bridge, one of whom was saved by the spectators and he was told four had jumped from the bridge that week.

Mr. Viscount: James Fenimore Cooper? Yes I heard he had a residence in Paris.

I did call on him and had break fast with him and his family. Rue St. Dominique No 59 is his address and I would say it costs him $5,000 a year to keep that address. He tells me his books are printed in five languages simultaneously. Quite a lively gentleman; interesting subjects to publish for a man of his family background, however did he manage to venture among the savages. I'll never know for he seemed quite a gentleman of the world in Paris.

Mr. Billingsley: I daresay it is Europe that honors that copyright laws and that is why Mr. Cooper is publishing there.

October 16, 1831, Sunday

We are on the Eastern edge of the great Newfoundland banks at Latitude 47N. The winds still blow adverse and it is cloudy and cool.

Mrs. DeLaurie was on deck today walking in her mourning dress. She did not look up or acknowledge me, but it seemed all looked at her with different eyes. One of the seamen who spoke French said he had overheard her speaking to her husband in a belittling way and another said he thought she was a silk seeker—one only interested in what her husband could buy. He said only beautiful women he can honor are those from uncivilized countries where they hadn't learn to make men pay for beauty.

He thinks Mr. DeLaurie paid with his life for her beauty and that she was like some beautiful but inedible fish and just as cold.

I felt a strange mix of feeling at the seaman words. He carried envy and his judgment of her seemed harsh, but she has never acted open and friendly like so many other people on the ship and held herself aloft and so she was easy prey for their dark thought after the tragedy.

October 17, 1831, Monday

Cloudy with adverse winds.

The area we pass though is one that holds dangerous ice floes and so all ships must be vigilant in their passage. The ice moves down from the North into the warmer waters of the South.

October 19, 1831, Wednesday

We pass the eastern edge of the Grand Banks and it is full of fishing smacks of French, English and American flags—I saw nine today, but alas I missed a ship that sailed for Liverpool while serving break fast and missed a chance to send mail to my family. I'm somewhat mollified that those who tired to pitch some letters by potato to the other ship failed and the fish is reading their letters. They say there is enough codfish on these banks for every human being in the world. They fish with large hooks with a piece of pork on it. The Americans go the French Island of Miquelon to dry their fish. Many more birds are appearing. The water is a lighter blue, as it is shallow.

October 20, 1831, Thursday

I witnessed a sounding today, which they have commenced doing since we have entered the shallow water of the banks. They take a round bar of lead nearly two feet long and two inches around attached to a cord

120 feet long with markings on it. But down it went and no bottom did it find.

October 21, 1831, Friday

The wind is up in our favor.

44 degrees 36 minutes North Longitude 53 degrees 40 minutes west. The captain puts us about 400 miles directly east of Halifax in Nova Scotia and 800 miles from New York.

October 22, 1831, Saturday

The swells are different with dome waves coming across others and with a different frequency, sometimes it seems nearly a half dozen types can be happening at once. One of the seaman claims he can tell where we are in the ocean by studying the swells.

October 24, 1831, Monday

Saw many birds today including two flocks of geese. We are nearly 200 miles from Halifax.

October 25, 1831, Tuesday

I hope this is my last week at sea. I've always wondered about the land to the west of Ireland and dreamt of sailing this sea and now I feel weary of her.

October 28, 1831, Friday

Clear with a strong breeze.

We are on the western edge of St. George's shoal only 300 miles from New York.

October 29, 1831, Saturday

Each degree of Longitude in 45 miles and we passed two degrees in the last twenty-four hours.

October 30 1831, Sunday

A weak wind.

At sunrise we are two hundred miles from New York, the New England coast is before us and we are only twenty miles off Nantucket Shoal and eighty mile from Boston. I have never been so excited in my life. Will yer look at that land! This is the strange new land of the west.

October 31, 1831, Monday

A glorious day with the sun up and shining on Sandy Hook as we sail past her

we move southwest of Montauk Point on Long Island. If I could blow more wind into these sails I would for I can't wait to taste this new land

CHAPTER II

THE UNITED STATES OF AMERICA, PORT OF NEW YORK

WHERE'S DENY? FORTY-THREE DAY OF frothy seas and my brother doesn't show, now isn't that just like a brother?

Maybe Deny is at another wharf? He could be working. He wrote and offered to pay half my fare so I'm sure his intent was to be here. I may be his younger brother, but he'll not shun me on a new shore.

Barrels, boxes and bales in no apparent order dictate a disordered path for me over the cupped and worn wharf. The noise of wind and rattlining sail is driven out of my ears by the screech of barrow wheels, the gritty sounds of sliding bales and the grunt and grievances of stevedores.

I felt as high as the mast coming down the gangway and now I feel of bilge water. Tis the first time I've been without my family and friends these long weeks at sea and I so looked forward to a family face. It never occurred to that Deny wouldn't show. I should have made some plans in case this happened and now it has. I'm sure this is a land not so unlike Ireland; people are people are they not? Such a truth does not seem to loosen the fear in my chest and it is fear I don't understand and can't quell.

I take to a bale to wait and think and find I can't order my thoughts, so I watch the stevedores backing the barrels down the ramp and wrestling the bales into the handcarts. The Wharfinger is standing atop a set of bales yells' out instructions though an unruly black and gray beard as to where the cargo could and could not be moved. He's a curious looking fellow he speaks rapidly and has such an accent I can catch but a few words. And bellow like a bull seal at the stevedores. A great rounded belly he has banded with red and white stripes. And wav'n those short arms—why his forearms are the size of Mrs. Kirwan's calfs. And his face look'n as if his body is pumping steam. He turns his eyes upon me and glares as if he's hearing my thoughts. Seems it's time to search for Deny.

These wharfs wrap all about the end of the island. The next wharf I come upon has fewer ships and less bustle. It's possible that Deny went to the wrong ship. I see another British ship anchored there. The custom officials are long gone.

The evening chill is now coming off the sea I better have a look around as I'm not going to spend the night on this damp wharf. I'm grateful I just have me soft bag slung over my shoulder. As I go about my business my ear is bent to the many different tongues swirling about my head. I slow to marvel and fill my ears with words that come out of the mouths, deep guttural noises out of the back of the throats, trilling and a sing-song tongues that sound as if they know no consonants. I've heard a few tongues in Dublin, but this is like a jungle of birds—some even flap their arms like birds while they talk.

"Haay laddie! Just come ashore have ya? Have ya secured a place yet?" Inquired a rotund red-faced redheaded man.

"I've not."

"We 'ave a fine place full of your countryman, that we do and we can find ya work too! Oh! Excuse me manner. Me moniker is Joseph O'Neil and who might ya be?"

"Git."

"Now, what have I done to deserve such a rude reception?"

"No it's my name Git…Git O'Toole."

"Well I know the O'Toole that's a familiar one. But Get is a strange one isn't it? Did you Da have too many drops of poteen?"

"I named myself."

"Ooh! Come out talking did yer? I know the people have the gift of gab, but I never heard of a wee one coming into the world and given orders and such."

"If you must know it's the name I gave myself when I can ashore. I left the old one on the boat."

"Could you be persuaded to tell the one that still over they're on the boat?" He said nodding his head with his eyebrows raised.

"I believe it bad luck to do that."

"Tis no such thing lad! A man makes his own luck in America, dat you'll learn soon enough—you make your own opportunity in this land. So out of with it lad…I'm curious as a leprechaun as to what name you left on the boat."

"Colmcille."

Colmcille! Colmcille yer say. Tis a great name! One of our greatest poets: St. Columbra from the Golden age of Ireland. He too left his coun- tryman to live among strangers and was a great traveler. Dere's no shame in dat name. Although, I grant yer in this country they won't be able to put there tongue around it and there's no history here dats both the shame and the salvation of the land. Are you sure you not needing a flat? I see a gag- gle of our countrymen struggling over there and I'm not earning a pence talking to you, luck of the Irish to you, lad."

A bit overbearing he was. This looks to be the last wharf. Deny is nowhere to be found. He must be working. I head down that wide street. Oh my look at the ladies in this city covered in silk with ruffles and bustles of which I can't name. It's like London here I had no idea. Even some of the shops are same as London.

This is grand wide street the building aren't as fine as Dublin's, but a wider more busy street I've not seen. I'll have a look at the sign of this fine street: *Broadway*. Oh my such a rush of life surging past me with such pur- pose, such determination, most are not slowing or tip'n their hats they're not greeting a soul as they hurry past.

And I thought it was noisy on the wharf with the construction going on here. The walk is a maze of barricades and scaffolds. Bricklayers are shouting to scurrying tyronics among the legs of the scaffold while they keep up a drawn-out rhythmic scraping of the iron trowels on wet mortar. I step into the street and become smothered in streets sounds; the hollow rolling scrunch and screech of steel meeting gravel as burdened barrows roll by balanced on blue-veined arms. Hoofs clop-plunk and ricochet down the red brick canyon with wheezing horse breath, switching tails, jingling halters, rustling leather interspersed with the occasional jarring splatter of horse piss on cobble stone. I thought I was so familiar with city life but nearly two months of flapping sail has softened me.

"The damm little Teagues are everywhere these days."

I feel myself being pushed off to the side and I turn to catch a dark suited fellow turning back to his mate after pushing me out of his path. I feel like running behind him clipping his back heel so he'll trip on his fat yapper. As I stand there burning it hits me that I don't even know were to run and hide. The anger flows out of me as I think it would be a sad fate to a grand dream if the first place I landed in this new land is in jail. My cheeks burn red at the remark. How did he know? I don't have the red Dublin hair. Mine is jet-black. There must be more blue-eyed people that aren't Irish? I'm a wee bit slow, then I look about and I don't see any others passing by wearing brogans and short pants and wool socks coming up to meet them. And my cap doesn't seem to be much in style on this street. I feel a fool thinking that I am blending in with people on this street. How could I not see? Oh Lord, open your eyes and don't be such the fool. How will I make it in this land if I can't even see what's about me.

I stop at the hitching post and close my eyes to gather my wits. How will I find my brother in such a place of confusion and size? It's a wonder to see it but it's a fright to be lost in it and not a soul even knowing you are lost as yer rubbin' shoulders with them. I don't know if this is my fear, but I've never been in a place where I'm, all alone among strangers—people are everywhere and I seem to be nowhere. To be in the woods alone is a wondrous thing for I know what to expect there, but here I can't run back to my neighborhood or family and there is no shade of an oak for me to curl myself under and feel safe while I sleep. I believe I now understand why people pay so much to stay in a hotel, tis more fear than fancy. I do not have that choice.

Mr. Dagget told me that if I have any trouble finding my brother or work that he was staying at the American Hotel on Broadway and to look him up. I feel some shame in doing so, but what choice do I have? My Da says start with what you have or what ya know and you'll be surprised where it will lead ya.

Mr. Dagget is all I know.

Unbelievable piles of luggage and trunks sit on the boardwalk, the porters heedlessly heaping one atop another. It's a babel of voices and a clattering of hacks, shays and cabriolets waiting, arriving and leaving. Groups of gentlemen standing, leaning and spitting outside the double doors I see more men inside the open doors lounging on settees and reading newspapers. I feel in the way of this energy. So I walk about the corner. Women are entering a side entrance. I go back determined to wade though all those American gentlemen, which I do without being able to observe much on my way. I finally reach the pillared and carved front desk tended by a tall, slim man with enormous bushy sideburns and long hawk-like nose.

"Would a Mr. Dagget be staying here?"

"If you've a message, I'll put in in his box. I suppose you've no writing instrument?"

"Yes sir I got a quill."

"Here is the paper. Over there on the table in an inkwell." He points without looking at me I turn and stare at several long tables along the wall.

He motions me with his nose to a standing writing table. The inkwell is dry. I return with it and he rolls his eyes and reaches under the counter and uncaps another well and hands it to me silently.

I wrote Mr Dagget that I had not located my brother and that I would call on him in the morning. I did not want to put my plight on paper for the clerk to read. I waited for the ink to dry on the paper before I folded it and handed it to the clerk.

I walked head down for the next three blocks until a reaching a public well. Elation fills me as I fill my tin cup for the spigot. When I tip the cup I see that the water is as murky as a bog after having horse set though it. I rest it on the stone to settle. This end of the street doesn't have near the people running about it. Mostly women and they're not wearing any silk. And a few of them appear to be my people. What if Deny doesn't show I managed the ship I'll manage this country. Mr. Dagget may be able to get me work. Wouldn't that be the cat meow! But it feels grand to be able to watch all the curious people move about on the street. I could stay and listen to the squeak of the well and people's voices for hours on end but the sun falls behind the buildings and drinking so much water has it consequences. As I hurry down the street I see the sky is clear, so nature is smiling of my first day in the States.

I make my way back towards The American. The pace of the street has changed fewer people are about and those seem more composed and relaxed, less driven, their faces contain more pleasure, contentment. It appears some are strolling, some anticipating perhaps going home, perhaps some evening frivolity at a local pub? How many are alone like me. It's dark in Dublin and the sun will be setting in New York. I have no family to go home to, but I am free to sleep when and where I wish. This place smells different from Dublin with its tea dust, biscuitmash and the lingering order of porter on every street. Here tis more odors and more of the kind that makes ya turn down your mouth…more mineral-like smells coal dust and rancid oil intermixed with preserved pork and fish smells.

Alone I feel it best to find a place by the Hotel so I can set out and do some exploring in the morning with my bearing straight. I'm such a clay brain that I neglected to check my timepiece. I didn't note the local o'clock. I will simply have to be there quite early for Mr. Dagget as I do not know his routine.

My bag feels heavier, my body burdened and yawns overcome me several times on my trek back to the hotel. It looks so grand tis made out of fine pinkish stone. I have to circle the block looking for a courtyard or alley., but this block seems to be all business buildings with nowhere I can slip for the night. The third block away I find a narrow alley and it is a welcome sight as I need the relief the dark alley provides. The alley ends in a small courtyard. I hurry back to the wharf to see if Deny is there. Tis quieter now, but men are still loading. Up and down I go, but no Deny. I sit and rest with my back against a bale.

Thud! I jump and see a wooden crate in front of me, and a stevedore walking away. It's dark I've fallen asleep. My Bag! Oh it's here. My time-piece...it's here. It's cool, the stars are shining and more that half a moon is shining over the harbor, a steamship puffs, sails riffle, lapping noises and distant voices nibble at my ears. I see amber lights glistening and only then do I really remember I am at the wharf. I like the view, but I feel too exposed here. I grab my bag and walk I feel heavy footed and disoriented I feel a bit fearful on these unknown streets. I round a corner and two large fellows are coming straight at me. I don't run but make a step into the rutted street like I am intending to cross and I see out of the corner of my eye that they keep to their intended path. I round another corner and find a man naked next to an alley. He is holding his head, which is bloodied and muttering in a sobbing singsong voice about losing his clothes. I feel fright at the sight and run.

Panting, I slow down as the darkness of alley finally surrounds me. My breath quiets, but my heart does not. I let my eyes take on the dark, rolling them and never looking directly ahead as to see the path ahead better. It smells a bit stronger in the night air than I remember the damp air is thick with smells of stone, brick, rotting wood and boiled cabbage. I think of Crones and Cluricaunes waiting in the nooks with hooked canes. I choke down feelings of drear and fear and evince a good show of bravado by standing straighter with my chest out. I wish I had a shillelagh in my hand to swing, the heft of it would give me more courage, but I grab the handle of my skain instead. I stop at the inner court. I let the breath out of my mouth slowly and I swing my eyes over the courtyard. I can hear the muffled brays of horses and hollow clopping sounds coming over the top—it looks to be three stories tall. I find a spot between a coal bin and woodpile and set my bag there, the woodpile even has a small overhang above so I'll be dry in case of rain, for I don't know the patterns of rain in this land. I fall down upon my bag and search out the twinkling stars through the corridor of building surrounding me I look for the North Star, but I don't have enough stars to find it nor do I have any idea of direction I pass under the veil with the rocking motions of the ship and visions of Deny waiting for me.

Horses neighing and metal banging bring me about. The sounds fade away I lay unmoving, curling my knees up, hands between my thighs. I roll my eyes about. Light, but no sunshine is visible. No one seems to be up and out. A steamship whistles. I wonder what its like to be on one of those smoking beasts. They seem so strange with two pipes instead of sails, so off with nature, shunning the winds that most days are freely given.

I stretch and pad myself for my timepiece and skain. Leaving my bag I step to the corner of the courtyard and unbuttoned myself, feeling my first relief of the day, breathing the damp air my water steaming in the morning cool. As I finish I look up for some reason and find a young woman staring at me out an open window. She has a look of fierce concentration mingled with something else I can't name. I finish my business and shake the dew off as my Da says ignoring the woman above, but as I do I hear her giggling and I look up as I button up. She seems quite amused with me although I am doing nothing but my own business. Then she is gone as quick as a leprechaun.

When I enter the street the pigs are busy cleaning up the garbage that people have tossed into the middle of the street. They toss the contents of their chamber pots for the pigs to eat. The further I go from the wharfs the stronger the city smells. Although I not witnessed it yet I figured that some privies are on are on the ground floor of those three or four stories building, some in back of these buildings and some have none. I am careful to lookup when I walk.

The air has the sweetness of the morning dew with a small stretch of wooded and green land that I cross between blocks of buildings. My head fills with vision of the countryside in Ireland: the green grassy hills, the clear streams and the woods. London is like New York City only with much more coal dust in the air and in the time I was there I never saw the sun. At sea I was topside with the sunrise and nearly every day there was sun. It was rhythm that seemed to balance me on the rolling sea. I miss seeing the sun this morning and I feel my soul hiding waiting for the sun to bring out. I love the first morning hour when the colors are rising and the blues hold the lead before the reds take over while the mists are hanging and the birds are singing the loudest to claim their branch for the day—that's the one hour to be alive if you've only one to live. If two hours take the other one at sundown when the sun takes all the red away at sunset. I've always yearned to follow that orb to see where it goes and I have and now know a new place it sets. Last night was Samhain the end of summer and the beginning of winter. And me, without fire or feast. I wish I was at uncle Bres farm. I wish I was in the countryside where I spent so much time rousting about the clear rocky streams and the soft green grass on my bare feet, The taste of freshly caught fire-roasted salmon. Last night would have been a grand fire and much feasting, singing and dancing. I could have used the feasting; ship biscuit and a bit of stew on the ship was all for me.

The worst thing about a strange city are not knowing who is friend and foe, and where one can go. I havn't seen any public jakes, maybe they don't have them here. I have to inquire. I'll take this path between these building it certainly stays dark between these tall buildings. Oh I'm in luck a shant in the courtyard and a bit of the sheet left here. The first news sheet I seen here in the States. Ah, well I suppose there'll be more this sort of news, so I don't feel bad in wasting this paper. Step 'n out, the door hinges screech like a banshee, never noticed it so loud going in.

"Hey there...you!"

I spot an old spleeny full-bearded man in red flannel nightshirt raising his cane filled hand and lookn' angry with me as he rocks side to side in his approach.

"Ya thieved my news didn't ya! I was saving it special for this morning and you sulking necessary thieves took my morning pleasure again!" He waves his gnarled cane about in the air as he come near.

"I'll crack ya the side of the head for filln' my necessary with your no-good shit and thieving my penny paper!" I stand unbelieving that a man would begrudge me the use of a jake.

"I dug it myself and I'll not have another ass upon it unless yer pay'n me. Oh ya likely can't even read ya little ignorant Paddy."

As he came close he looped his cane at my head, I ducked under his arm and scooted behind him. I felt sorely tempted to boot him in his fat, soft arse and propel him into his precious necessary, but twas all too strange and even funny so I lightly skipped out of and his reach and then turned and said: "I used chapter three of Captain Marryat's story to wipe me arse—I think the British stories make the best asswipe. Don't you?"

I laughed, thurst up my arm and give him the digitis impudicus and skipped away leaving him waving his cane calling me names his skinny white legs shaking under his red flannel night shirt.

The stillness of the cool morning was breaking up as more people rushed about afoot and ahorse with a few knots gathered in conversation. I must check the wharf or the Battery as they call it. I fear I may be too late, what if he works beginning at sunrise? I take to the streets as there are not many carriages around so I can lope to the wharfs.

Deny, Deny where are you? He's not here I wonder if I missed him. I have to come before sunrise tomorrow. We wrote him about the ship he should know. Could he believe I wasn't on her? Has he given up on me? I don't have his measure to know. Deny seemed so much older when he left four years ago. I was eight he was fourteen. He was always working at the bakeshop. He didn't have much time for me, his friends he called them his gaffers took up the rest of his free-time. I can't judge it. But I'm his brother he has to show he just has to. Maybe something happened to him. He could be ill. What if he's gone? He is my only relation here in the States, Lord have mercy as Ma would say. I'd better ask about him and leave word in case he is working. I'm loath to but I suppose I should interrupt the fat warfinger.

"Pardon sir? Beg your pardon sir? I wave my hand and smile Pardon me sir!"

"I ain't got time for wharf-rats, be gone. He said with a wave of his big arm."

"Sir I 've lost my brother and—"

"Get this elf-skinned mewler out of my sight—you Sullivan Get the barnacle off my wharf."

I am lifted from the deck tucked under a massive arm and carried away from the wharf around a building an out of sight of the wharfinger, set me on my feet with both arms ahold my shoulders

"Lad you stay out of his sight If yer lookin' for your brother din lookin in the customs house over dere. And don't be talking to that Joseph O'Neil he's a Gombeen man, I saw you with him yesterday. He works for a Postestant thief who owns the buildings, once you're in dat place they find yer jobs that'll barely pay the rent there are few getting out dere. Yer have to be very careful everything is enslave you in this country, it's all about the money for the bosses and rich. Now go on and luck to yer lad."

He gave me a gentle push and stood watchin me until the wharfinger bellowed at him and he jumped and ran back. This can't be true. No I don't believe it. There are no lords who own all the land in this country. No royalty. He got a grudge. I would too working for that wharfinger. Not one letter from the States that all my relations and neighbors sent have ever said a word about such a thing. One sour man that's it! There are bad men everywhere, so O'Neil may be a Gombeen man. I'll take that advice, but I'll wager that the stevedore is an ignorant and uneducated man.

To the customs house why hadn't I thought of that before? Maybe Deny left word. It is certainly not nearly so grand as the Custom House in Dublin. Ah there looks to be an official for he has a peculiar hat and is putting stamps on boxes.

"I'm looking for a person, a relation he may have left me a message, can you direct me to someone who my have such information."

This is customs we collect tariffs on goods not people, although maybe we should on them that's too numerous: talk to Mr. White over there by that doorway, sometimes he keeps tracks of such things.

"Thank you kindly sir."

"Pardon me Mr. White? The fellow over there told me you might be able to help me in locating my brother."

"Well that man says many things most of which can be ignored. Don't know your brother."

"His name is Deny O'Toole I was to meet him at the wharf here yesterday, but I've not been able to find him.

"Don't know him. O'Toole you say? Nope. Sorry. I'll let you know whether I hear from him sorry I can't help you."

"Thank you kindly sir."

Deny hasn't been here Maybe he was held up by work or sickness. They've heard the name and will remember it at least until tomorrow. Maybe Mr. Dagget will have an idea where I can start to look for Deny. I've nowhere else to go. I have a great hunger somehow I'll have to get some food. I wonder if the American takes Pounds.

Ah heres a pub maybe I can get some viands here. It 's a bit dark in here.

"A grand morning to you. Would you be having any mutton stew today?"

And I suppose you'll want a pint to go with that?"

"I would if the price is not outrageous."

"Piss off ya little hedge-pig. We don't serve pints to little potato heads in this country—ya likely don't have a pound in yer poke anyhoo."

"I'll just have the mutton then sir."

"We don't have the mucking mutton, Ya'll come here straight fron the bog expecting us to feed ya rotten mutton. We're pork eaters I tell ya."

"Then I have the pork and I have pounds."

"You'll nuthin you rogue. Now outahere!" He waves his arms and moves towards me.

That's the diffence between the states and Ireland. Pubs in Ireland are family gathering places with the exception of the women. The children are served beer based on the father's guidance. The food in generally good, not here in the states no family allowed I can't even get a meal in a pub here in the states.

A bakeshop is what I need a big brown loaf with some butter. It seems that white bread is particularly favored but it isn't filling. To me the white bread tastes fluffy and flat and doesn't sit long in your stomach. I don't know of a bakeshop so I go to the American and wait for Mr. Dagget.

"Hey Irish catching a dream are ya!

"Pardon? Oww me dozed off."

"It's just as well that you're fresh."

"I looked at him puzzled then I leaped up. "You mean I have work!"

"I've recommened you to the chef so mind you manners I know you're industrisous. It's a bit up from ship work, but I think you can learn."

"I've a good ear so I can pay mind you see."

"Yes will you come with me? Your bag? So you not located your brother yet?" When did you last hear from him?"

"Nearly two months ago."

"Yes a long time…many things can happen. Come inside and I intro- duce you. I send someone to the wharf at sundown you will be engaged at that time. You will be working twelve hour days like everyone else and

I'm told the bakeshop shift starts at four in the morning. I will be here for a fortnight yet if you need any more assistance. I will return to stay from time to time and I will look in on you. Do you have any money to secure a room?"

"Yes I have serveral pounds and some thirteen's. Can I use them here?"

"Yes even better than American money—what's a thirteen?

"Tis an Irish shilling."

"That will do I know a widow who rents she may have a garret where you can stay. It's a bit run down, but I expect it will be sharp and hold you until you find your brother."

CHAPTER III

MY LIFE IN NEW YORK

Git O'Toole Journal

November 14, 1831 Monday

I miss Uncle Bres farm. The city is exciting and there is much to see and do there is an emptiness behind all this brick and cobblestone and a sameness that never happens in the country. Walking ten paces in the wood or moors contains so much more suspense, so much more life so much more history. In ten paces in the woods I can see last night tracks who was that animal? A sudden movement up ahead. The sound of a bird what kind is that? Stopping there are ants and beetles on the earth and grass, soaring birds above. What are the grasses and trees that my eyes take in. And this rock with a glittering pieces on it what is that called. Even going slow I cannot possible take it all in. I feel that I cannot ever learn all that surrounds me in the country. I want to see this country, this continent to see all the strange creatures that live here.

The bustle and hubbub of the city make sit seem as if something new is always about, listening reveals a repeating cacophony. Most of the buildings are the same inside with simple flourishes to make them different. The shops are interesting and always amusing to see what is new, but unless one has riches and a large place what is one to do with all the fine things now being made. I see a fine carriage with painted sides and gleaming brass and I admire it and am glad I'm not the one to guard it and keep up the paint and polish the brass along with keeping the ornate harness oiled.

The street is cluttered with every kind of posting for goods. Boards hang every few feet out front of the shops. And people are putting up signs about not allowing pigs in the street and not allowing carriages to stand. One is either accosted by a hawker or a beggar and the beggars multiply daily it seems and I ashamed to see some of my countrymen among them.

Last night I had a fright. I had to take my skain out and slash at a fellow who grabbed my arm trying to rob me. I feared what could have happened if I had hurt or killed him. Now I must find a new path home. Everyone seems a stranger in this city so I know not whether he works alone and has family to defend him and I fear what the police would do to me with no witness on my side.

I heard a man, a military man talking in the hotel of going west to establish a fur trading business. He has good knowledge of the Far West as he called it. He was obviously getting financial backing for the men at the table. He talked about the high price of beaver skins and how he will save labor by taking wagons. One of the fellows at the table is a man who works for Mr. Astor. I want to go but I have no trapping skills. Maybe I can cook. I shall inquire of this Mr. Bonneville and ask for a job.

MY DAYS ARE FILLED WITH work. Twelve hours and more as there is a constant shortage of workers or rather workers who do not show on their appointed day. Many work, collect their pay for the day and are not seen again. This is a vexing problem for those of us who remain to work. But the owners have been generous with us compensating us with extra food and allowing us some personal items that customers have left like blankets.

The kitchen is large but so many work that one has barely room to move. The seating in the ordinary occurs at eight in the morning, twelve-thirty in the afternoon and six-thirty in the evening. This puts our energies first preparing the foods, then we are engaged in serving it, followed by cleaning and then back to preparation for the next meal and the cycle repeats itself. The food is served in the French style so there are many dishes. Here there is known as American foods, but every since the Prince of Soups Monsieur Brillat–Savarin opened up the famous restaurant called Julien's here in New York City more than a generation ago many hotels have hired French chefs to make French food.

Our chef is a frustrated French chef. It seems that only a few Americans really like French food, preferring pigs head and feet and all in between; pudding pies and the popular beef cakes, oysters even for breakfast, cabbage, potatoes, beef stew and sausage, soup or consommé and American's prefer masses of lightly spiced food to petite portions of exquisitely flavored delicacies. Our Gallic leader runs around and screams a lot while most of the work is done by a Mandan/French man called Chomper and a Canadian called Ménard our chef doesn't much like Ménard because Ménard was able to get the hotel to add one of his dishes to the menu. It's called Tourtiére which sounds elegant but tis a sausage meat pie with potatoes, onions and bread crumbs cooked in a cast iron pan called a Tourtiére (what we call a bastable oven) and Americans love it. But we serve more elegant dishes to Americans and to many who have traveled to France.

Most of are staff call our esteemed chef Fame Vetel behind his hackled back, referring to the high-strung chef during the time of Louis XIV by the name of Vetel who impaled himself on his sword when the fish did not arrive in time for a royal feast. (Of course the fish arrived a half hour later in true Gallic fashion and no it wasn't swordfish.)

Our latest kitchen amusement comes courtesy of Mr. Graham. The name of this fellow can turn Vetel the color of raw liver. *Graham crackers* he screams, the name is a screaming name. Mr. Graham makes a brown cracker with most crackers being white. He claims his crackers a new manna that will cure all ills and eliminate meat from the diet. It only takes a request from the ordinary, usually from a woman for an order of Graham crackers to get Vetel rushing around beating a ham hock or a whole ham against the walls. He screams to the rafters that he has never seen such insane people "a people who grow up with unnatural love of eating only undigestible grains." He whacks the bricks to emphasize his point that these people should have four stomachs, as they are clearly not human, "they are vaches!" (cows) "Vaches of tastelessness, vaches of vapidity vaches of vulgarity!" this insanity of American's he is convinced comes from deranged livers from eating too many grains and drinking no wines. Of course we look serious and agree with him while we yell Viva! And then under our breaths Vetel.When he is not there all oatmeal orders are shouted out *viva Vetel Oat-mal*!

Most of the people who work here understand French, myself the least.

Visions of my being able to bake pastries hasn't come to fruition as there are few pastries made here, mostly pies, cakes and puddings—Americans have a real love of sweets. I'm told it's because of all the salt pork they eat.

My main baking task is making corn dodgers and hoe-cake which is the primary bread eaten here. I do make a rye bread one that has corn meal in it, and a soda bread and a barley bread using pearl ash and on Saturday I make a yeast bread, which means I have to make the yeast on Thursday. This is made with wheat, which is very expensive here and comes from Russia.

Most of my time is spent in cutting and peeling and carting. I have recently been given charge of the sauce box. I make the sauces that go in the box as condiments at the table. I make catchup, which is a mushroom sauce in which I use the juice of mushrooms that I have packed with salt in a stone jar which I boil and add black and cayenne peppers, ginger, cloves and mace. I also make a walnut, a lemon and a English catchup and, of course, a mustard. This sauce box is put out at the ordinary to allow diners to spice their food. I help in making our ginger and molasses beers as well as our cordials and brandies and we mix a few punches such as ratafia, orgeat, sangaree and negus.

The kitchen is new and well-equipped we have a larder which is a room three steps down into the earth where the salted meat in barrels is kept and where the sausages and cheeses hang as well as where the eggs are kept in crates full of sawdust. We have an icehouse with a large thick wooden door for storage of fresh meat, fish and shellfish. We have our own well in the tin sink and it drains in the alley behind us so we save much labor by not having to haul water. There is a large brick oven for baking and a cast iron stove for frying and boiling as well as an open fireplace with a removable tin oven.

I've not had to purchase comestibles as I get all I need at the job and that is most fortunate in that food is very expensive in this city and we have no fireplace in the garret in which to bake our food and bread and even if we had a fireplace we would have to buy firewood which is priced dearly. Bought bread costs nearly thrice what pork does, but meat must be eaten the day it is bought. The country is blessed with meat and tis a wonder to serve it at every meal we make.

I am able to save most of what I earn, I have expended some of my coin for cotton pantaloons and tunic; it was way more expensive that wool and linen clothes I have, but I bought it at a ready-made shop so I saved by avoiding the tailor. Most of what I own is wool and although very service-able it was becoming quite warm in the oven-heated bakeshop room. This is my first experience in wearing cotton and I find it very light and soft on the body but cold on the skin in the evening air. The most expensive fabric in the tailor shop is silk and it costs ten times cotton. I now have a different view on all those silk dresses I see daily.

My indulgence is that I have found a library where I pay a subscription fee to use books for a week at a time. My duties end in the late afternoon so I have a few hours of daylight in which to read. I purchased a reflector lamp to read by, I am abed, but a few hours after sundown as I rise very early to tramp the dark lonely streets with the squeaking farm wagon and pungent fishmongers.

I have experienced many moments of embarrassment upon opening my mouth, which I am inclined to do, but I have lately fallen to listening and nodding my head. I am called upon to help serve in the ordinary at the time of the seating. I hear much conversation from the crowds gathered awaiting the seating. There is much talk of President Jackson; he seems to elict strong feeling either way many of the upper crust are appalled that a mere military hero could be President they still talk of the entire resignation of his cabinet this past spring and all the scandals, especially of the former Secretary of War's young wife and even the background of the President's deceased wife.

Serving at the ordinary is very interesting for a newcomer like myself as it serving in the bar. I've heard discussions about the death of oratory and references to those great American orators Webster and Clay. There is discussion about how the Federalist party that is mobilizing religious leaders to "check that rampart freedom which is so characteristic of the American People!" Many ministers are outraged that mail is delivered on Sunday and are trying to get the government to honor the Sunday Sabbath. Others say the government should stay out of all religious disputes. There are many conservatives who have vigorously opposed the Jeffersonian deism as a threat to the social order saying that religion is necessary it restrains the brute appetites of the lower orders, but of course not necessary for the upper classes as they are civilized and keep their appetites in check. I've never seen Protestants so riled up about issues not to do with the Catholics or the Pope, but hatred of Catholics still runs deep fueled by many pamphlets from England published since the Parliament passed the Catholic

Emancipation Act, which many in England violently opposed. Now they are stirring up the Americans against the Catholics and emigrants. Mr Sanuel F.B. Morse the famous American inventor is one of the leading anti-Catholics voices here. He has written two pamphlets that are circulated here at the hotel. I have read one called, *Imminent Dangers to the Free Institutions of the United States through Foreign Immigration*. He says that the Monarchs of Europe are allied with the Catholic Church to dispatch their minions disguised as immigrants to America until they are numerous enough to seize control of America "affecting the conquest of liberty." He wants to close the shores of America to immigrants to save America. There is also a weekly newspaper called The Protestant that is devoted to articles about "Popery" and "Female Convents" with stories about of the "Secrets of Nunneries Disclosed". One of a big fears heard often from Protestants is that the Pope is going to move the Vatican into the Mississippi Valley with the help of European Monarchs who are anxious to stem the flow of democratic ideas from the States.

A woman called Fanny Wright spoke at the hotel in defense of the common laboring man and spoke out against the elite, religious run education system in this country. She has the most arresting, fine musical contralto voice full of enthusiasm. She looked at angel with her big blue eyes her fair skin surrounded by long curly chestnut red hair. She stood and moved with grace and spoke with conviction and logic combined with an elegant, vivid prose.

There is but little time for exploration mostly I try to find some amusements on my daily journey from work in the late afternoons daily I pass the Centre Market on the way back from the American. The area is not ony a market but a place for many to orate. Tis an area with long benches facing a box and of course, many people like myself who stand to listen as they pass or pause in their market chores. The market is full of stalls of fish, meat and produce and there are all manner of items sold there.

Of the political issues of the day there are several that keeps the soapbox warm: temperance, hard money, slavery, union and debt laws. There seems to be no lack of people orating about these issues, including women.

In Dublin I grew up with someone always orating on the corner about the British Penal laws or Catholic Emancipation or even expounding on theories as to why the Irish are such a degraded, poor miserable people compared to the British. In Ireland, the Catholic Irish have nary the rights that most Americans possess—the Protestants having taken most of our land, denied us an education, the vote and we can't hold office nor even own a horse worth more than five pounds while a white man here can vote it he owns property. Now some of these laws have been rescinded, but little has changed.

Both England and France have new Kings and it doesn't look like either William IV or Louis Phillip will make any changes in the freedom of their countries. What is odd to me is that there has been so much printed about freedom and natural rights of mankind and reason and the Republics run by the people for the people and of democracy—the American and French revolutions supposedly change the world, yet I come to this land of freedom and find people even more enslaved than mine. And France still has a king!

Before I left Ireland, Daniel O'Connor, "The Liberator" was overwhelming elected to the House of Commons for County Clare, but he could no take his seat because of the anti-Catholic laws. In other words the law allowed him to run for office, but not to stand or hold the office. That was the last time I saw my Da pounding the table and shaking his fists at lawmakers. He used to frighten me when I was younger as I thought I had enraged him, but then I began to see it was men far away that enraged him.

One other curious thing about the States is that they have filled their jails more than any other country due to their debt laws. People are speaking out about this and some states are beginning to change the laws. It seems that over three-quarters of the people in prison are there for debts of less than twenty dollars according to some newspaper accounts I read. The business community opposes the repeal of these laws citing the sanctity for the Rule of Law and fidelity to contracts and honor for property.

Chomper who works in the kitchen with me is the Mandan/French man who I mentioned before. His name is Edvard Du Champs. He came to New York City as an interpreter for some Tribal members that the War Department brought to the East on a tour to impress upon them the power of the U.S. Government. Something happened and he refused to continue his duties. He had eaten at the American Hotel and was so taken with the taste of some of the foods that they couldn't keep him out of the kitchen and hired him when he came back. He will only do certain tasks and will not let others do them for him. They kept him for they didn't have to pay him at first he was so into learning about, "Big white man food."

But he found about being paid in coin and he is paid like the rest of us. Now they need him as no one debones meat like him and he loves to make the bread pregnant as he calls it. He can't get over how sugar tastes for he has never had anything sweet like it in his life he being raised in a Mandan Indian village on the upper Missouri river. He is a very clever man, although he seems so naïve about some things. When he found out I had no place to live he brought me back to his garret even though I had one to look at myself and he accepted no coin for rent. He loves my sweets I bake for the kitchen staff and now he watches me intently. He has been telling me stories about the Far West as it's called here it is the land west of the Mississippi.. He tells me about his village and the crops they raise and the food they cook.

Last night I returned to our little upstairs hovel passing dour-faced Mrs Speyers setting on the steps reading her bible. I tipped my hat and bade her a grand day as I entered and she smiled and blessed me. We are fortunate in that she in one of the few landlords that resides in her own building, her husband having died and now the income from the building supports her. Many of the building on the street are owned by men who do not live in their buildings using them for investments and that means cramming as many people in them as possible.

I hid my coin wages in a hollow that Chomper carved in a beam. I held out the Spanish silver Real to examine further as it is my first one. The gentleman who gave it to me for special baking duties per his order said tis worlth twelve and one half cents in Santa Fe, but was likely worth fifteen to twenty cents here now. He showed me the Doubloon that had been cut into wedge-shaped and represented two dollars or one eighth of the coin. He also had some copper coins from Chihuahua called Jola and Cuartilla the last of which is supposed to worth one quarter of my Real, but he said they are worthless. I should like to possess a Doubloon, but it would take me nearly two weeks wages to get and I don't know where except from this gentleman. He told me stories about Santa Fe, which means Holy Faith. It is a trading town drawing Mexicans from Chihuahua and California and Americans from Missouri as well as many different aboriginal people from the prairies and mountains. The Mexicans are descendants of the Spanish and native people who revolted like the Americans, but Mexico have only been a republic for ten years. The Mexicans are allowing American immigrant to establish communities in Tejas in the hopes of ridding themselves of the constant Tribal attacks. This gentleman is going to a place he calls Tejas with some other settlers. I have seen French, Dutch, German and English coin passing hands at the Hotel. I would like to have a sample of each as tis exciting to have so many coins in one place each from a different county.

I settle down to read the from the little light that was left of the day. I had rented two books yesterday, Thomas Paine's *Rights of Man* and fearing that volume might be too much preaching I rented Samuel Taylor Coleridge's *The Friend*. I found it exciting to know that part of Paine's work was composed in a French prison under threat of guillotine and he wrote it in part to stay the progress of atheism, started in the anti-monarchy, anti-priest chaos from the Revolution. And the fact that he was raised a Quaker is curious to me as well since I knew little about this American Protestant sect. Coleridge, I knew would be interesting in his essays and his philosophy and I had no doubt I would enjoy him.

I had barely cracked Paine when Chomper returned. I did not expect him so soon. I could see he was in a foul humor.

"I wish to go back and kill him!"

"Vetal?" I asked

"No, Not-Her-Husband. I was called into the ordinary by a black-robe, only he didn't wear a blackrobe."

"A priest?" I asked

"That's the name. He was interested in my tribe and had me sit to join them, his sister, named Elsa and the other man who is named Not-Her-Husband. This man who questions me is named Jack. His heart is good. I anwer all his questions and he wants to come to my village to tell his stories. I tell him yes for he tells good stories. He asks me what I want. I ask him if Elsa is wife to the man sitting next to her he says no he is engagé—he did not look like a trapper to me, but I did not question. It is Jack's sister so I know he can speak for her. I ask Jack, I say I want to see more of her skin, for since I have been here the white women have been covered like it is winter and I have never seen the skin of a white woman. Not-her-husband makes a bad noise and rises with a pistol to shoot me so I push the woman into him and knock him to the floor...the woman with him. Jack jumps over the table on to Not-Her-Husband. He takes the pistol. I have my knife out. He cannot hurt me Jack helped me. I say, "She has no skin!" They look at me like a man full of whiskey. I point to her legs they are open and her big cloth is up on her waist, but her legs are covered with more cloth—like your legs, the pantaloons, it is a very fine cloth."Her legs have no skin?" I say. They look at me like I am spirit. All the people in the room look at me like a spirit. I feel myself for I think I must be spirit or Not-Her-Husband shot me and I do not know it, but I do not leak and I do not hurt. An old woman makes a shy gesture and she says in a loud shaming whisper: "He said leg!"

Then the people are angry, but they are angry at me not at Not-Her-Husband who pulls a big weapon to the feast table and who tries to kill at the feast table, he should be killed for such an act. They start war cries and come towards me, not the man who should be killed for such an act. Jack is brave. He puts his body in front of me and he tells me we must go and we go to the kitchen and out the door. He tells me to run here and he will come later.

I sat there with my mouth open not knowing what to say.

"I have told you the truth. Why do you sit with no words?"

"Chomper...Not-Her-Husband is going to be her husband—"

"So he was going to kill me because I asked her brother instead of him? But he is not married to her."

"True. The offense you made was not who you asked or didn't ask it was *what* you asked."

"He looked at me puzzled. I used only words. I asked what I wanted because he offered me a gift of what my wants were. She was watching me women do not watch men unless they want the man to catch her in the woods. I did not know if I wanted to catch her, for I was afraid that she had no skin like all the white women I had seen. If she showed me her skin I know I could take her."

"Chomper I'm new to this land, but I found out you can't say leg and the women do not show men anything unless they are their husband and I'm not even sure they do to their husband.

"Do the white women all have sickness of the skin and ears."

I laughed. I'm too young to know the skin of women, but I do know that they will never let you touch it and their ears are easily offended. As my Da pointed out to me—he did this one day when we alone in church, he pointed to the statue of the Virgin Mary; she's our female God. He said to me: "do you see how her eyes are fixed?"

I said, "Yes she is looking up to heaven."

"Tis not true, he said, They want you to think that, but she looking up to the the lace Irish, Colmcille, he said, when you find one who isn't looking up grab her and marry and hope she has no sense of direction and you'll be a happy man, but don't be doing that with one who looks down for she is a serving woman and will always have to serve other men. So that is my education about women.

She looked neither up nor down she looked right at me like one looks at a new animal.

If I am an animal to the English, I'd guess you're an animal to, this white women, hell you have dark skin, long hair and earings.

He looked at the skin of his thin arm. "Does she fear my skin?"

"Did she talk to you?"

"No."

"So all she knows is what the others have told her and what she sees. All I know is the look of fear from those who have lorded over me, and my family all my life. I see the fear and hear the words: I'm an ignorant, lazy, tricky, lying Irishman who only wants to sing fornicate and drink who would stab my betters in the back given the chance, that is if' I'm not singing, scewing or drunk."

"They want your skin too?"

"No my skin hold no prize for them for tis not different. Tis everything else about me and my countrymen that they fear and hate; you and your brothers they don't know and they don't need to know —they have your skin tis a good place to start till they get some fine adjectives to attach to your skin. Oh tis a confusing world, but you'll not long have your skin if you stay among them that don't like it."

"All white men have always been friends of the Mandans: the French, the English and now the Americans. Why are these men now my enemies?"

"They are not all your enemies some are because they don't like Indians. Just because my skin is white doesn't mean I understand it better than you. We know that this man is now your enemy and we know that they will talk against you to the people at the American."

"Is this a law I've broken?"

"If you haven't broken one a broken law can be found."

"Will the blue seizers come?"

"The soldiers? Tis certain if they do you'll sit in a room the size of a jake till it's convenient for a judge to hear your side of the story."

"I must go."

"You can journey in the winter?" I asked

"It is hard and I may not be able to make my village, but I have friends among the Pawnees and I can make it that far up the river."

"I will help you. I can ride and shoot and I can work hard and I'm hardy."

"It is full of danger with many enemies."

"But isn't is more dangerous alone?"

"That is true with no guard for the horses the sleep is light and the day long. I have not traveled with you. He said this with doubt in his voice."

"Chomper, there is a large area of settled land you must pass through getting to the Mississippi and it would be safer if you traveled with a white person and even safer with someone young like me for we would not been seen as a threat. Listen I will follow your orders."

"That is true, but a man cannot be taken on how he flows words, that may work for men of the city but not for men of the Far West. A man's true heart shows itself when there is great danger of losing heart. This I do not know about you and yee yourself do not know. I know it is better to travel with a white man though their country."

"Did I not brave the great water without friend or family?"

"Hey you did that…"

"Chomper, my land Ireland means the land of the west and my people have always told stories about the land of the west. Tis the only direction for those of us who seeks a journey whether a journey of spirit or body we have stories of people getting in their round skin boats and sailing west."

"These boats are made of skin?"

"Yes stretched over a wicker or stick frame…it's called a cockboat."

"You have buffalo in this land?"

"No we have cattle, horses and sheep and we have all the creatures of the sea for we are a great Island with many rivers, but we are all not like the white people here: we have our families, our clans and we celebrate our gods with dances around fire and feasting and contests."

"We have boats like this. Do yee not go into the building of the black robes to talk to your Gods?"

"Oh yes, but some still do the fire festivals as well and certain trees and springs are still sacred and there are many spirits besides the Christian God that are honored, spirits that live in the forest and underground and even spirits that play tricks and steal children's souls."

"You are a different white man. I want to see your land. I need my pipe so I can smoke, then we will talk."

CHAPTER IV

Journey Through the West

Edvard De Champs Journal

November 22, 1831, Tuesday

A new moon has started and I will leave my heart here in this city and I will bring a new one with me. I have made three cuts on my leg and I bleed out the three moons that I have lived in this place—a place of great medicine and evil.

I am troubled by the journey for I know not the way and I have no friends and the Cold One is near. I am heartened I have the coin to trade for goods. If I had a journey during the cold time I would like my buffalo robe. I am told the white man has killed all the buffalo until many days journey past the Great Father River.

I have seen much too much to tell it would not all be seen as the truth: the smoking ship steams runs it, I do not understand how, but I will mount one one day to see. And the railroad carriage and the great straight waterways and large stone buildings three of four tepees high and the people more people than live on all the prairie. But the eagle, white bear and buffalo do not live here. They flee the white man.

I have learned much about the white man but his heart and spirit I do not understand. The white man is the greatest of builders and knows how to find the secrets of the metals of earth and knows secrets of how to travel over the earth and great water in his sail and smoke machines. The village of New York is a people of stone. They make square stones and they make their building and some of their roads of stone and likeness of people stand in stone and they put stones on the ground were they bury their dead.

The white man's heart is troubled everywhere he goes he must change the earth; he cannot live among the trees, the long grasses and the wild animals. The white man has many animals like our dog—pigs, cows, chicken and sheep and he eats them all.

There is much I have not seen. I never watched a white man dance. I hear some pretty songs, but not to honor to humor. I miss the joy of my people. Only with firewater did I see the white man full of joy. He offers nothing that I could see in his God…he makes no sacrifice. His women are lazy and full of pride. They do nothing by paint themselves in dull colors and wear pretty covering and the men honor this! The men have many goods but can only buy one wife.

These people have no clans, no societies no celebrations and few ceremonies. They couple have children and then try to break the spirit of the children casting them off to other people in what they call schools where they are Harangued all day. Some have honesty, few have honor and all are takers. I must leave before they poison me.

"CHOMPER!" I NEARLY SHOUTED. "I have a map from a coun-tryman on the whole eastern country."

"Maps I do not know maps, do you mean drawings?"

"Yes tis a drawing by an Irishman man named Carey showing all the roads through the west from here to the Mississippi. And Shelaigh's brother says he has traveled through the Pennsyvania and Ohio country and marks our route since this map is from the turn of the century, they have built canals since the map was made and bridges."

"This drawing will show us the way to the Mississippi?"

"Yes we will go down the Ohio river if it isn't iced up and come out below St. Louis and I calculate you will know the way from there."

"Much of the land west of the river is known to my people. Hey let me see this drawing."

"Yes here it is. In this book the drawing are folded inside, see there are many I think twenty drawing or maps."

"We will need guns, powder and balls; we will need horses and trade-goods. Chomper replied at he looked at the map I had unfolded. We make drawing like this on the earth he said as his fingers followed the lines."

"I found out we will be going through the country where they make rifles and muskets. We can get them there. We have to cross the water and get off this island first and then we can follow the rivers and canals to the west to the Mississippi. I have all my wages and some from Ireland so I can buy my supplies, I said expectantly."

"These are Northwest guns—my people only use Northwest guns."

"That I can't tell you having never seen one, but I can tell you that I'm told all the best rifles made in America are made in this country we are going through and I hear, the price is better then one can get in St. Louis."

I will wait. I can trade in St. Louis if they have not Northwest guns on our journey. What about yer brother?

I think he is gone, I don't know, but I can't stay here. I have to go to the Far West! If not with you, I heard of group leaving in the spring from St. Louis. Chomper I can go as far as the Mississippi with you and if you don't think I'm worthy then you can go on without me. I made my way in this city so I can in that one as well.

Chomper looked at me sternly from his crossed-legged position of the floor and then a smile broke on lips as he said, "It is settled you will guide though the eastern land with your map."

"Yes! Yes to the Far West. When do we leave?"

"Tomorrow. Winter is at hand we may not reach the Mississippi if we follow the water the hand of the Cold One may harden the waters."

"I'm ready, I will fill my bag now and we will go to the Battery to find a fisherman to take us across the water at sunrise tomorrow."

There is a knocking at the door as we were putting our kits together. It is our landlord, Mrs. Speyer and I had a sinking feeling that maybe she was there to prevent us from going but I could see no reason why other than rent due and if unpaid we could pay it. I'd heard her talking downstairs with several deep voices.

"Mr O'Toole and Mr. Du Champs I've several guests waiting on you downstairs. You'll have to come down to see them," she said, as she turned to go with a dour face.

Not knowing why they couldn't be shown in, we are puzzled as we followed Mrs. Speyer down the stairs. Waiting for us was Elsa's brother Jack and an older man wearing a preacher's color both looking grave and outside the open door is a soldier stading with his arms folded. Chompers said nothing and for a moment I thought he would bolt upstairs as I could see anger on his face. We stopped at the bottom of stairs and Mrs. Speyer's simply said "Here you are then," to the preacher and turned into her room. It seems a long silence but finally the preacher spoke.

"This does not concern you boy. Our business is with Mr. Du Champs."

"My business is with Mr. Du Champs as well, I replied. We are partners I will remain with my friend."

"As you wish, but it is no concern of your and I will not brook interference. He looked at me as if I should agree with him. I simply folded my arms and kept my eyes on his."

Ignoring me he said: "Mr. Du Champs my daughter and her financé has given me the most distressing news that you have abused her and I am here to seek satisfaction on behalf of my daughter."

"You wish to dual?" Chomper asked in an amazed voice.

"Then you admit such abuse?"

"It is I who was abused it is I who had a pistol pulled on me at a feast table. I will duel Not-Her-Husband.

The blue-coated soldier leaned in the door and saying, "They'll be no dueling or any form of fighting unless it is done by me, do yer understand?"

"Yes my man. I think we can handle this another way. Mr. Du Champs these as serious charges and I can have you detained by the courts until this matter can be heard by a judge and decided and that may take many months as they have quite a backlog of cases I understand."

I was afraid Chomper would leap up and break the Preacher's neck, but he did not move. It smelled of a trap.

"Do you understand what I am saying, Mr. Du Champs?"

"Yee, what is it you wish?"

"That's certainly more of what I had in mind. You see I know my daughter can be a bit high strung and at the same time she is very doting and it can lead one to believe you are the only being on earth in her world. Up till the incident you have always conducted yourself well, as well as it not better than most white men I know. I know you are determined to return to your people. I have some cloth for your women to cover themselves and small useful object like needles to sew with. Would you be so kind as to accept these gifts?"

Chomper replied looking pleased: "If you wish to send gifts to my people I will carry them, but I am afoot and have not means of transporting many goods."

"Of Course, I would not impose on you. My son has gladly consented to bear the burden of these gifts and accompany you back to help you distribute them and spread the proper word of God amongst you. You know my son Jack. I am proud of him for he has forsworn the spirits and turned his life to reaching out to save sleeping souls. I have faith that he will do well in the Far West…away from temptations. I have the goods outside, Jack will stay the night with you so as not to delay your departure, which I assume is to be in the morning. Is this satisfactory to you?"

"I am free to go and your son is to carry the burden?"

"I will be happy to carry such a burden to your people and do whatever I can to assist you in your journey!" Jack smiled and gave a slight bow.

"What my son says is correct", he said as he bowed slightly towards his son.

"I am sorry my relations with you have been marred by this incident with my daughter, but I can assure you that I have always had the highest respect for you and, of course, your people even though I have not met them. Forgiveness is the highest Christian virtue and it must be, of course, balanced with justice. I hope you understand that as a father there is nothing more precious than my children and it is my duty as a father to protect my children and it was with that sentiment that I came here today. Soldier! I believe we will not need your assistance as we have come to an agreement have we not?"

"We have." Chomper asserted

"Sir I'm willing to see it though in case events take a turn." The soldier stiffly said.

"No thank you we have an agreement you may leave. Do we not Mr. Du Champs?"

"Hey we do!"

"See there he's said it several times and I have always known him to be a man of his word. Thank you my man and Mr. Du Champs I thank you as I see you are a man who allows his reason to rule and I offer you my hand to seal our agreement."

"It is agreed," said Chomper and he shook the old man's hand vigorously.

Now everything is bustle and friendly talk and there are many blessings and the Reverend gave Chomper a large plug of tobacco and a new Bible. Myself, I become let down from the high hopes and spirits that I had experienced upstairs and then crushed by the Reverend's words and Now I could feel my spirit being smoothed by his words, but I felt wary even though I could see no reason for it.

Jack lifted his pack up to our room and it did not seem very big pack for what it supposedly contained. Jack spent most of his attention on Chomper in praising him and acting very excited to get started on the journey. We soon retired so as to get an early start. I wanted to talk to Chomper, but it was impossible with Jack there, for I did not really know Jack having met him only twice. I did not know if this was really agreeable with Chomper, but it seemed we had no choice...as least for a while.

I could not sleep. All I could think of was going to the Far West and I could not believe that I was going. I was worried about all the things that would stop my journey, but I was not worried about the river or the snow or the weather I was worried about the Reverend about all the unseen power from the streets of this city and to all cities that we must pass on our way to the Far West. Nature felt sometimes dangerous, but in my experience almost always gave a warning before she struck. The Reverend struck without warning and he seemed to posses such complete power, at least with bandits one could draw one skain to defend oneself, but with a Reverend or a merchant with a constable or soldier at their side one had little chance…

I bolted straight up on hearing a noise. It was Chomper gathering his possibles. Fright followed with the thought of him leaving me. I was so startled that I had fallen asleep I couldn't seem to get up fast enough and spun not a few circles until Chomper laughed at me.

"Is that the way yer be leading me through the west Irish?" He said as he chuckled.

"I'm scouting. You—like you told me how you have to circle the area of camp."

"You may have to make some larger circles than that. Will yer look at Jack. He appears to sleep the sleep of the spirits. Shall we leave him?"

I didn't know what to say and I didn't know if he was testing me or joking with me.

Ha! He laughed. "No need to answer Irish, I don't wish to be stopped before we are off this island. We had better wake him and be on our journey."

Jack took a while to get his wits about him, but when he did, he is all smiles, trying to be as helpful as possible. We slung our bags and headed out onto the dark cobbled street covered with hoary white frost, down Broadway, down the slope, down to the Battery, where the masts of the ships slowly waved their tops and finally we arrived at the sound of lapping water.

Behind us the street is silent but the wharfs are filled with creaking wood, yawning ropes, clunking crab pots, overlaid with shuffling feet and furtive scratching scampering sounds. I suggest we split and inquire whether anyone intends crossing to the Rariton River. We do and I quickly locate a fisherman who is willing to take us across. I had baked some breads, Johnny cakes and smoked meats when I went back to the American to give notice I was leaving and the fisherman was more than willing to take some fresh bread in payment as he was going across. I raced down the wharf to find Chomper and Jack. As I raced I thought of how many times I have trudged wharfs looking for my brother. Is he in this city? Is he alive? I have heard no word from my family. I will step off this wharf and perhaps never return, perhaps never see him again. But this city is not for me and I fear no city will suit me…good-bye Denis, whereever you are Good bye brother.

The inky water it still so we are put to the task of rowing. The fisherman sits on the bow mending his nets in the dark as we row and Jack grips the tiller under command of the fisherman. As we slide away the false dawn shows first the church steeples and then the squares of the secular city began to appear in our wake. Another island I leave, but this journey is short. The liquid slurping of our paddles and squeak of oarlock speak for our unspoken thoughts.

A blessing! A blessing on our great adventure! I am so joyful that I am to accompany you Chomper. I should have blessed us on the wharf. Jack cries rising at the rudder. But it is better to be over the waters with a fisherman…like our Lord was when he started out with the Apostles. Yet we start of water and we end on water from the Atlantic to the Missouri. From Manhattan to the Mandans! The three of you here in the boat reminds of Paul's Epistle to the Galatians. Paul said: And when James Cephas and John who seemed to be pillars perceived the grace that was given unto me they gave to me and Barnabas the right hands of fellowship; that we should go into the heathen and they unto the circumcision.

"What is circumcision?" Asked Chomper in puzzlement.

Jack looked at him in puzzlement with one hand on the rudder and other in the air. His arm dropped heavily to his side as he gave a big sigh and answered in a slow voice. "It's a holy rite done by the Jews on the new-born babies—"

"Done to them? A chant?" Asked Chomper as he rowed.

"No they cut the skin of the baby cut off some skin…like a sacrifice to God." Answered Jack with a look of inspiration of his face.

"Ah! This I understand. We cut the little finger and sometimes the next for the spirits to take pity on us when we mourn." Chompers added holding up his left hand to show his little finger missing at the second knuckle.

Jack looked at Chompers hand with a look of revulsion and then recovered. "Well it is not that drastic of a cut. It's not really losing anything, it's actually supposed to be a good clean thing to do and it's not disfiguring like losing a finger."

"If one can not see it, how do you know yer have made the sacrifice and how can yer Spirit…yer god see it, where is it one can hide the loss of flesh?"

"It's …well…it's a little confusing …it's not a sacrifice one shows and I'm not saying Christians do this some maybe…Jews do and well…it's on your manhood."

"Chompers stopped rowing, looked at Jack, but Jack was suddenly looking behind and then Chomper looked at me and said: "It this true?" Yer telling me that it does not scar or mark one to cut one's manhood but it is bad to cut one's little finger? I know of no nation all across the Plains and into the Shiny Mountains and even to the Great Ocean to the West where a people cut the part that imparts life. The part that gives the greatest pleasure that which makes a man. I know of no Gods that ask such a sacrifice. This seems a most terrible thing to do to a child, for a child cannot make a sacrifice until they have reached the age of understanding. This sacrifice is wasted! My people all the peoples of the plains would not consider this a sacrifice…it is what you people say…a mutilation. Chomper held up the stub of his little finger. I willingly gave my body and my blood to the spirit. He as a part of me and because he has a part of me he pities me and helps me. But it is not the end. The spirits want more. And I want to please them I will give them more. I do not understand what kind of spirit accepts the manhood of newborn babies. What kind of power comes from such a spirit who does not ask me to give of them selves but give babies. Chomper hung his head and said: "There is so much I do not understand about yer Gods."

"God, Chomper—there is only one God. The circumcision it in the Bible, but I don't know that it is actually explained in the Bible; I mean who started it and why they do it...the priests or the rabbis is what they call their priests do the cutting. Jack isn't that correct?"

"Yes it is the Jew who practice it still and it is in the scriptures."

"Who are these Jews and are they part of yer tribe." Chomper asked with a puzzled look.

Jack looked at Chomper with frustration and said, "No they are a different tribe, a Semitic tribe and they come from the Eastern land of deserts across the ocean with other Semitic tribes."

"This Jesus, yer God you always speak of...was he a Jew or of yer tribe?"

"He was a Jew," Jack answered.

"So the white man's sacred book, is written by a spirit man from another tribe? And the white man doesn't follow all the sacred ceremonies like the circum-cutting sacrifice."

"Yes, but there are different books that the different tribes follow," said Jack, who seemed to not want to pursue the subject as he turned his head back towards the city.

"Jesus did not write the Bible our sacred book he wrote nothing and only some of the Bible is written about him, much is written about his father and his father is God," I answered as Jack seemed not interested.

"You said you only had one spirit man now you say he has a father. Who wrote your sacred book and why do yer believe it if the Spirit-Man did not write the sacred book?" Chomper asked with a puzzled look.

"I was wrong it is the Father , the Son, who is Jesus and the Holy Ghost who is...a...ghost. As to who wrote it. About three dozen men over a hundred years wrote—"

"We believe Jesus put the words into the minds of these men! Jack said as he looked off over the water. We know this because the men wrote it told us that the words came from Jesus.

Chomper Rowed. "My people have no spirit book, but we have sacred objects, sacred bundles and sacred places. We know these things to be sacred bcause we see the deeds, we see the medicine with our own eyes. The medicine man calls and Buffalo come if the spirits listens to him or the rain falls or our enemies are defeated. Our Gods bring us dreams as well. Everything about our Spirit-World come before our eyes or does not come before our eyes as the Spirits will. I came to this village to see the deeds of yer God. I have seen great deed so yer people , but I am not sure they are from the hand of yer God. It seems the same God to me, but every White man tells me his God is different and I must need his God and only his God. What I have not seen is will yer medicine men yer black robes bring the rain when the ground is cracked? Will they foretell when our warrior shall slew our enemies? Will they bring the buffalo when our caches are empty—for these are the deeds of holy men who are honored by the sprits."

"If it is God's will, it will be done." Jack replied.

"I accept. Tell me where and how many enemy I will kill?"

"It does not work like that. God does not want you to kill the Sioux and other tribes . And you must accept all his teaching and live a Christian life and give up killing others and must settle down to farm."

"Do you not know that our women raise the corn, sunflowers, squash and beans and hold the sacred right to our fields I cannot farm, it is not permitted! I am a warrior. I protect our fields, farm as you call it."

"Yes but we don't make other tribes like the Irish our enemy and kill them whenever we see them." Jack said. "We defend our property usually against those who would steal it or harm us."

Chomper looked puzzled. "We do not defend the dirt, that is foolish. We defend our corn our women and children. And we know who to kill— it is the Sioux unless they come to smoke and trade. If they do not it is to kill, so we kill. As men it is what we do. It would be foolish to send women to kill, as it would be foolish to send men out out with hoes instead of bows. Sometimes your words are wise and then comes only foolish words, such as telling us not to fight our enemies. We would follow such words soon there would be no Mandans to listen to you words."

Jack seemed to contemplate Chomper words. Purple and orange rose behind the receding city we rowed on with the eerie screech of the oarlocks blending with the screeching seagulls who seemed to think we had something to feed them. Chomper seemed lost in his thoughts. The fisherman had paused in his repairs to listen to this intercourse and now resumed putting his hand into the intricate movement of repair. As the sun rose the wind began to riffle the surface and we entered Raritan bay. The fisherman unfurled the sails and took the keel and we move up bay towards the river.

The river is alive with low flying duck's, shorebirds and black scolding birds perched in the tall rushes. Rustling and splashing sound emanated from the edge of the rushes, but all I saw was the ripples left by what disappeared under water. Rough wooden houses on stilts began to appear as the morning wore on we passed several villages. We headed in a south easterly direction and then the river turned south and we had not gone very far when the fisherman shipped ashore next to a small wooden house on stilts. He told us this was as far as he went. We tired to help him tie up, but he knew his business well and moved without speech and with purpose so we were left with only the task of our bags. We stepped off onto a muddy path that led to the house and there stood a woman her dark hair framing her brown face with a shawl over her head which she clutched with one hand while the other supported a child on her hips who was feeding from a swell of milky flesh white soft looking compared to her face and her coarse, dark homespun cloth. She watched us without a smile and without a frown. The fisherman directed us to a path on the other side of the house that he says lead to a road that went west to Trenton where we could cross the Delaware or take a boat down to Philadelphia. I gave him his bread. He stood in the doorway watching us breaking the bread stuffing large hunks in his mouth. The bread moved up and down with his jaws, his woman shifted the child to ther right breast pulling her folds back so the her heavy whiteness shone in the rising brightness of the morning, the child cries reaching us before it found what it was looking for.

"The air is clear here and a good path we will make," said Chomper "we have nothing to fear here?" He asked me with a furreowd brow.

"No we have nothing to rob and this land is occupied by farmers."

Chomper seemd to approve of this and set the pace with his long stride of putting one foot nearly into the step the other Jack took up the rear being of shorter stride with his compact body and perhaps having a bigger burden to carry. After an hour or so Jack began singing some Christian hymns and helped shift our attention from our burden to our ears, even though Jack had a difficult time keeping in tune. After nearly two hours at that pace Chomper called a halt. It was now early afternoon. I wanted to make some tea and have some bread but Chomper insisted we push on and I agreed after examing the map that showed us some eighteen miles from the Delaware. We kept pushing on as we had a road and was sure it would lead us to the river.

The day was pleasant and clear one with a good nip in the air, but our pace warms my nose and fingers. Darkness fell as on we trudge for we have a road. Several hours after sundown we hear the water ahead and trot to the banks of the river. The road we had taken led to not a bridge and there is a ferry tied to the opposite bank with no one in attendance. I quickly gather some wood, while Chomper explores the banks of the river and Jack sits and sucks on some hard candy. I have the tea steeping in the small tin kettle when Chomper returns. I pour the tea though a screen into our tin cups for I do not like the leaves in my tea like some do. We are just laying out our wool blankets on a bed of willow branches when a boat with a oil lamp on front comes down the river We hail it and it heaves to. It is some type of riverboat loaded with livestock. The owner tells us he's headed to Philadelphia as he has a buyer for his cow, a few pigs and some crates of chickens. He welcomes our company as he is feeling a bit sleepy.

With the current we flowed, perched atop the small cabin as the animals are in the bottom of the boat. The farmer held a long pole back to the rudder. He inquired of our destination and seemed quite curious about how we happened to know each other. He kept referring to us as the boy , Young Reverend and the Indian. We passed the night listening to his exploits with domestic livestock and his stories didn't quite measure up to the *The Cattle Raid of Cooley* as a story.

There are still lights to be seen in the city even though we came upon it in the middle of the night. We float on past the main part of the city as the farmer has his customer on the outskirts of town, so we pass the Schuykill river and set down on the other side of it, which worked fine with us as we felt safer on the river bank that we would have in such a large strange city, although Jack claimed to know some folks there, but didn't rightly know where they lived.

The farmer nosed into a muddy point and we pushed him off and then stumbled in the very dark night to some thornless overhandging bushes on a ridge of dry land where we curled up without a fire in our wool blankets for we were too tired to struggle finding wood in the dark.

The sun drew the cold out of the ground and into my back and put warmth to my face. I felt tired and the air too cold to loosen my blankets but I resigned myself to be awake to the insistent sun. I could smell smoke and looked about to see Chomper gone his bag neatly closed up. I rose shivering in the cold morning air. I followed a path out of the bushes to a small ridge and found Chomper squatting before the fire and looking out over the river. He smiled and said nothing as I came up. The fire had burnt down to flowing rounds coals. I headed to the river and filled the kettle and we had tea in silence watching the moving river with the boats and birds on it. The warmth of the fire is so welcoming. Chomper went back in the bushes and I heard a scream from Jack and Chomper come out of the bushes with a smile, Jack trailing in a stumbling stupor.

After Jack finished his tea we headed up the bank and wandered through pastures and woods for perhaps an hour before we came to a road. I used my compass as I had little idea of direction at the time the sun being under clouds we being in a thickly wooded area. And the other two were at a loss as well. We took the road in a westerly direction. We had been walking perhaps two hours when we heard horse behind us, first at a trot, then they broke into a gallop and we turned to see three young fellows, perhapst a few years older than me bearing down on us, whipping their horses. When Jack realized they were aiming for us he scuttled into the trees he being the hindmost and the lead rider veered towards him to cut him off. I darted to the opposite side of the road. There is a large tree close the road and I sought it. I looked back to see Chomper still standing the road, his bag on the road, facing the rider his left foor forward and I did not fear for him because he looked so confident and he watched the rider bear down on him.. The rider was whipping his horse with a quirt and yipping at the top of his voice. When the horse was nearly upon Chomper he raised his hands and made a high-pitched screech and a wave of his arms caused the horse to veer to the left throwing the rider further over to the side he was leaning to and the rider pulled on the reins to regain his balance and shifted his attention to staying in the saddle he passed Chomper and Chomper snatched the quirt out of his now flailing hand and in one motion struck down hitting the horse in the flank near the tail causing the horse to spin to his rear and to the left, further upsetting the rider who put all his weight on the reins in an attempt to stop on the horse and horse followed the reins carrying the rider off the road right though a brush thicket where the rider flipped off the back of the horse as it leaped though the thicket. His companions had both turned off the road and had slowed to watch his attack and now they rushed to his rescue. We could hear his horse crashing though the woods with the rider disappearing into the bottoms of a thicket. Chomper motioned to me and I ran out on the road with Jack arriving at about the same time. Chomper took off at a trot down the road and we followed. We ran for about a mile when we came to a wooden covered bridge over a creek and we went below it to hide and rest.

"Chomper I feared he was going to run over you."

"If it had been a buffalo it would have but horse will rarely do so and only if they cannot avoid you. Why were those men attacking us? I thought this was safe white man's land."

"I don't know I think they were trying to frighten us."

"Why?"

"We are strangers and they are young and full of mischief."

"It is mischief to run down another white man? They are not your tribe?"

"Maybe they saw your black hair and that is why or maybe they saw we were unarmed so they took advantage of our position. They were not Irish. How were you able to stand so firm in the face of a horse charge."

"He had no bow or rifle and I cannot outrun a horse...running only make other men brave. One's only chance if you cannot reach cover is to stand and face your enemy and study him closely for weakness. He wanted to strike coup on me, not run me over so I waited to try to unseat him, but his grip was weak on his stick and I did not unseat him his horse did for he rode with his saddle instead of his legs. We must get rifles if we are to travel without fear. They may recover the horse and pursue us so we must be alert. Irish, you lead and Ill take the rear and we will disappear to our right into the woods on my whistle."

We set out again and after about an hour Chomper whistled. Into the woods we went. Shortly he emerged and motioned to us. A wagon was rolling down the road. It appeared it was going to pass us as they saw only Chomper, but when Jack comes into view with his black hat the wagon slowed.

"I expect you folks together?"

"Yes sir, said Jack. We're headed to Lancaster and then to Harrisburg."

"We'll I got room in de wagon if'n you'd like a ride. I fixing on going to Lancaster likely be dark afrore we make it, had some trouble with a wheel back a spell. We'll git up here and we'll hear what yore stories be. *Hi, go-land, jiddy jiddy, ally loo!* He hollered to his mules as we started out."

"This here a Conestoga? Jack asked as he twisted his head looking back down the line of the curving frame."

"That's a fact. Made in dere Conestoga valley o' Pennsylvania. He patted the seat as he said it. Ten tons she'll haul don't have near that much on now, you see I only got four mules hitched. Not a finer dern wagon made. The curve yer eyeballing keeps the load from slipping to the back… keeps it center and shur maked it easier to float across a river. My Paps had Conestogas and I guess my sons will too. That's a darn fact."

Where you fellas headed after Lancaster?"

"We're headed to the Mandan tribal village."

"Where's that?"

"Upper Missouri River area."

His name is Larned and I don't recall his surname I think it is a German name. He is one of these fellows that keep asking questions and hardly listens to the answer before he's at the next question. He spent the whole afternoon at his questions and into the dark we rode with him interrupting our answer with another question. I don't know if he was trying to learn something or he just thought the way to talk was by asking questions. When we came up on a creek name Pequea he told us Lancaster was about six miles further and we decided to make camp on the creek so we could make the town in daylight.

Chomper made him a gift of the leather quirt and he was so pleased with it as it was a finely made one that he didn't question the gift.

We made a fire and ate the last of our breads and dried fish we had it with dried fruit. The night was cold and the fire a great comfort. Chomper had arranged thick branches around the fire and we would wake from the draught of the fire dying and reach over and push the branch further in the fire to warm outselves again. I woke as the sky was going from purple to dark blue, pushed the remaining branches into the fire and put the kettle on. Chomper was up at my movement and Jack lay in snoring slumber.

Chomper and I was both eager to get to town to look over the rifles that they made there. We believed we could get a better price than in St.

Louis due the shipping cost, plus we might get a wholesale cost at the gun-smith's shop.

With frost on the grass our breath in the air, our eager feet crunched the cold ground at a light step as we anticipate having new rifles by day's end. This would be the first rifle I had owned, the first in my family except for my uncle and his, an illegal one under British law.

We toured up and down the main street viewing the shops. We passed *Conestoga Rifle Works* and *J.J. Henry Gunsmiths* and then a place simply labeled *Guns*. I asked Chomper if we could look in the guns shop as I thought we might get an idea of the local selection rather than looking at what was available in a specific shop. He agreed and we entered. Jack said he was going over to a shop that sold English weapons. The Proprietor a kindly short man with a bushy gray beard was very friendly, but was engaged in a conversation with another man. I walked around and listened to them as follows:

Customer: "Well I calculate it's first-rate, but this damp air hear-abouts don't favor certain wood stocks, I reckon."

Gunshop owner: "It's a lovely piece with elegant steel."

Customer: "It looks right good, I expect. (The customer looked out the window and picked his teeth with a splinter for several minutes.) I shouldn't mind giving eight dollars for it." (He said this still looking out the window.)

Gunshop owner: He kept looking at the fusil for more than a minute, while the customer stared out of the window. "I had to work mightly hard on it, but I shouldn't mind eight dollars if'n you want to trade that knife on your belt."

Customer: "Do you think of taking eight dollars?"

Gunshop owner: "Well…I hadn't ought, as it's such an elegant piece…I could wait a bit."

Customer: "Could be that wait could be from November to eternity."

Gunshop owner: "I reckon I could go the whole hog, but it's a right down good piece."

Customer: "I'll jist do it, if you'll hold fast on the eight dollar."

Gunshop owner: "That's a right clever price and that's a fact."

Customer: "God Damm let's go it then."

Gunshop owner: "Gotta feed the little responsibilities and costs more to be raised up nowadays dammanation."

Customer: "That's pretty considerable much the darn truth. Here it be and I hope that piece turns out to be as right down good as it appears."

Gunshop owner: "I's be in an unhandsome fix if it wasn't. I swow it's good made."

Customer: "I thank yee sir."

Chomper An English rifle made by J.J. Henry had the fox in the circle indented on the stock, which Chomper showed me.

"This is English?" Chomper asked the shopkeeper.

"Yes English, but made in Pennsylvania."

This seemed to puzzled Chomper who kept asking if it was English, as he seemed to think the only gun of quality had to be English. I had fear of the quality of American rifles as well since I had only used an English gun and they were known to be the best in the world as was their steel.

The shopkeeper handed another rifle to Chomper. He said it was also a Henry, but a new Steel Mounted one. It was a fine rifle and Chomper like the look of it, not as well as the silver and gold inlaid rifle with a rubbed red wood stock on display, but he liked it, although he was still concerned it wasn't English. I couldn't get him to consider anything but an English rifle. I suggested we look further. He agreed and we left and entered the Conestoga Rifle Works. Chomper explained that any rifle that any of his people had used other than English rifles did not last. He explained that the fox stamp and the dragon drawn on the rifle showed it was English.

Chomper immediately found the rifle he was looking for. It had the dragon on the side plate and fox on the lock and stock. It was a 32 guage or .53 caliber and was stamped H. E. Leman. I decided to get the same so that we would have the same size balls. Chomper also urged me to get two pistols. I got a pair of the same caliber pistols and a powder horn. Chomper brought an extra set of pistols that he said he could trade.I paid twenty-two dollars for my equipment which include ball mold and wiper. Chomper bought extra balls and powder. I was excited to try out our new weapons.

Jack was waiting for us he was holding an engraved leather cowhide case slung over his shoulder and a handsome powder and shot bag.

"What did you trade?" I inquired

"An English flowing piece."

"No rifle?"

"This fine piece has a double barrel so I will have two shots to your one."

"But it shoots shot, Jack! It's for birds, why an enemy would have to be within six rods for you to use it."

"Yes and I have two barrels and it is made of the finest watered steel, besides I could put a bullet in it if I wish."

"So without rifle grooves in your barrel maybe you could hit a man standing still at thirty paces—"

"But if I miss I still have another shot, Git it's all about firepower, besides, anyone I face will see the two barrels and know that another one is coming. Firepower is power, Git, no one will want to face a full barrel and when you shoot yours that it. The jig is up Irishman! Ha! Ha!"

"You forget, Jack that I have two pistols and that my rifle can kill a man at three or more times the distance that you fowling piece can and that my rifle has more range than a bow, whereas yours has nearly the same range."

"But it can't match the firepower of my piece, no you will see, keep your rifles with the one heavy ball and I'll lower barrels to deliver hundreds of small balls that no man or beast will be able to penetrate."

We proceeded up towards the Susquehanna River and reached the bank by early afternoon. Chomper proceeded to load his rifle and I also loaded mine, being eager to try it. Chomper moved down a game trail into some woods.

I caught up with him and we walked down the path and began our target practice. It seemed a fine rifle, a bit heavy for my small frame, but it didn't kick as bad as I feared. Chomper got off three well-aimed shots to one of mine, so inept I am at reloading. In my excitement I poured powder down the barrel without swabbing it with a the wet cloth and singed my hair when the powder fizzed and brunt out the barrel, ignited from a small ember in the barrel. I could have been burnt much worse if I had not been turning my head to retrieve a ball and wearing a cap. Chomper laughed at me and I felt so childish and even worse, felt he would not allow me to enter the Far West with him. He warned me to sure my ball was seated tight and deep as he had seen several men who had exploded their rifles by dropping the ball down the barrel without a patch to hold the ball tight against the powder. He said some men tired to hunt buffalo by carrying a few balls in their mouth, which they would spit out into the barrel after pouring power while riding horseback and then lower the barrel to shoot the buffalo and the ball would roll part way down the barrel before the powder caught with the result of the barrel blowing up. Some men lost fingers, eyes and even died from exploding barrels. That is one reason all the men in his tribe use the bow in hunting buffalo, the other being that powder was too expensive to waste on buffalo who didn't shoot back.

When we returned, Jack was sucking on a piece of his sugar candy. We resumed our journey towards Harrisburg following a path along the river. We camped at dark and Chomper brought in two rabbits. I fried the rabbits along with the liver, kidneys and chopped heart and then browned the rabbit with salt, pepper and some dried ginger and then added a bit of water to simmer it soft.

The next day late in the afternoon we arrived in Harrisburg. There is a long covered wooden bridge, the longest I have seen in the States across the Susquehanna River. Here Chomper wanted to get horses and Jack argued for waiting until he got to the Ohio—it would be more expensive putting horses aboard a boat, he explained. We soon found out that there was a canal boat that went to the mountains. Jack agreed to pay most of the cost of the canal boat out of his missionary fund.

It began to rain and to turn cold as we lined up to board the canal boat. It looked to be a large barge with a little house on it. The deck was full of luggage and barrels and wooden crates were also stocked on the roof of the cabin and covered with tarpaulin. We stowed our guns with the captain who assured us they would be safe. There was a cast iron stove in the center of the cabin and row of small tables down both sides of the cabin. The cabin was mostly men, some families and a few women—well over two-dozen people. The trip was to take two or three days and it wasn't clear to me how were we were to sleep. Meals were provided with fare.

After loading of more crates and then an uneventful wait, three horses were attached to the towrope and we swayed, then creaked at the slow pace of the horses of the path. These horses are hauling ten times the weight and bulk that horses overland could haul. The cabin is so low that Chomper has to bend over to move about. People are strewn about the stuffy cabin, a single small window is still closed, some have their heads upon the table sleeping other try to walk in the cramped space, some stand talking and spitting their tobacco into the middle of the floor, some try to hit the stove making a steamy splat that gave off an earthy stench.

At six O'Clock all the small tables are put together to form one long table and after the women are seated the men sit down the to a full spread of *fixings* as my neighbor called it and indeed as hungry as I am it certainly looks grand: Salmon, shad, liver, ham, chops, sausage, potatoes with milk and butter in them pickles, black pudding, brown bread, coffee and tea. Some use their two pronged forks others just their knives and of course all in consumed very quickly with a minimum of words. Then there is much scraping of chairs, picking of teeth with knives and sticks, and plugs of tobacco produced, followed with a few lighting of pipes, but most soon retired to the deck after one of the women protests the smell.

I had to get out of such a closed space with so many people. It is still raining lightly, but the rain feels cooling on my face. I am standing looking at a small swirl of our wake when I hear the man at the helm call out "*bridge!*" I look over my shoulder and see a bridge that appears two feet above the cabin. I have to duck. It is soon evident that there are many bridges. I stay on deck and listen to the plod-clop of the horses, the creaking of the leather and wood and songs of some birds I do not recognize. It is rather pleasant as there is none of the jog and jostle of a carriage nor the rise and fall of a boat, with only a slight sound of watery swirl behind to remind me we are on water.

"Where ya headed?"

I turned to see a ruddy fellow, clean-shaven with big brown eyes topped with arched, bushy brows and thin lips addressing me while he held the lapels of his jacket over the round of his pork-belly.

"To the Far West."

"St. Louie?"

"Beyond."

"To Injin and buffalar country, eh? Used to be buffalar round here….north of Harrisburg, in the wild of the Seven Mountains and up to White Mountain."

"You take care out in the Far West as them buffalo are a murderous bunch. Here, have a sup of hard cider. This here cider is made o' the fine Baldwin apple, one of the finest in all of New England. Been visiting my brother up there and he learned me some 'bout the cider apples. Believe this jug got some Northern Spies apples in it too. A little dry with a sweet edge don't ja think?"

"I haven't had hard cider. It's like wine…even lighter."

"Don't have as much kick as wine, but is sure makes for some good sippin'. I got me six barrels I'm taking back. Have another sip; one can't taste anything with one touch of the tongue. Nothin' finer than New England hard cider Oh ther some good cider in Normandy and in England but the early frosts of New England make it the finest cider in the world in my hunble opinion.

Darkness and fingers of cold crept down the valley as my informer returned below. I have only seen drawing of buffalo and Chomper told me here were no buffalo left east of the Mississippi river nor any in the state of Missouri. He had been told by some old Delaware from the east that the buffalo had ranged down into North Carolina and up to Washington D.C.

I returned to the cabin to see the master of the boat surrounded by a crowd who is drawing numbers and I thought it a game of dice until I see men holding pieces of paper and walking along the wall. I look about and see boards hanging by chains all around the side of the cabin with numbers by them. So this is to be the sleeping arrangement. I get my number, finding that the beds are very close together, three up and that some are already full of sleeping men some of their clothes dropped on the floor next to the beds. There is a red cloth tacked up towards the back of the room to shield the women and children. The spitting continues from the beds. I notice that one of the husbands of the women is in our group and then I realize that the families split up, with the men on this side and the women on the other side of the cloth. The family has an African slave and he is up on the deck where I believe he is to stay for the night.

As soon as I lit on my board I am asleep amid the damp noise smell and noise.

At five-thirty in the morning, movement of others wakes me and I go first to the stove with a few others to warm and then to the deck. There I find the toilet area. A tin ladle is chained to the deck, which one it expected to scoop water from the canal and to use what they call the jack-towel, which means common towel along which hung a common brush and comb. There is a tin basin to pour the water into in. after waiting in line I wet my personal bit of soap in the icy water and use my own wooden comb which seemed to surprise the fellow behind me and I'm not sure why.

It drizzles all day. Chomper and I sit at the bow and watch the slow passage of scenery The Reverend Jack is holding forth on need to bring the word of God to the savages. He came up at one point to crow about the fact that he got some donations to help in his quest to tame the Wild Red Man. He said all agreed that it is best to start with the civilizing influence of farming first and then teach the Indians about God.

Chomper listened to some of this passivlely and then then said: "My people are the Mandan not these Wild Red Man you talk of and we farm as you call it. We raise from the earth much more than I have seen on this trip. I see forest cleared leaving blackened stumps. Why the white man does not plant in the meadows I do not know. The forest animals have left with the trees and pigs and milch cows stand chewing in their place. I see lonely lodges with only a family, I used to think that these were the people who had committed an evil deed banished from their village, banished from their tribe. But I have seen the white man is a people without a tribe and these people fear to share the fields with other White-men. This sight makes my head twisted." Chomper held his head then let go and went on. "Why does the White-man wish to raise one grass? It is not wise for what animal eats only one food? What year makes all foods abundant? Maybe the years on one hand counted out of six? One food brings many six-legs many foods do not. We have seven types of corn, three of squash, we have sunflowers and three beans our squash climbs our corn, our sunflowers separate the types of corn, our beans grow up the corn stalks they are in mounds. The land rolls on beyond a thousand eyesights and the White-man plants his crops shoulder to shoulder in a small square and I have seen miles of such squares were no wild plants grow. This will sicken the land. We let the prairie provide for us by growing turnips and all our fruits and many cures for sickness. We do not try to plant every food we eat for that means these foods would own us there would be no time for the spirits if we planted berries and all the food on the prairie. The prairie raises the buffalo, deer, antelope, bighorn and elk. The prairie does not always meet our needs and somethimes gives us too much, but that is as the spirits decree that is the prairie. The buffalo is much better meat than any animal the white man raises that I have tasted. The buffalo has a great spirit and your white horns have a spirit so poor they will live in the same house as the White-man. That is not good such a weak animal spirit will weaken the white man. As for your God you know we have our Gods, but that does not mean we do not welcome yours if it protects us better. If it brings us more strength as a people just as we welcome your metal for it make better arrows than our stone."

I passed the day watching the countryside and listening to various conversations. Most have a rhythm of a constant exchange of question and answer as most people are strangers and eager for news and information about other areas. Evening rose and we return to the table of silent heavy gnawing punctuated by the occasional head turning to spit. The mood at the table felt as if someone dictated no talking only the task of eating was allowed and our full attention was upon it. It seemed frightening to me that everywhere I went in this land the tables were like this. No talk of the delights of the table or the day, only will you have some o these fixings? It was like cattle at a trough, they had learned not to jostle for position. Except, that when seating begins there is much talk when women are present. The men fall all over themselves to get the women the best seats and there is much commotion in this ritual before the silent gnashing begins.

The next day we reach the base of the mountain and are pulled one car on rails while another car is let down opposite from us. It is the Allegheny Portage Railroad we take. Of course, everything has to be loaded onto the cars. A fixed steam engine pulls us up in stages and horses are employed as well. We descend the same way and board another canal boat. We pass settlements some looking newly built and others like they have been rotting a while. Some of the windows are boarded over or patched with bits of tattered calico. Many have clay ovens outside and the windows and steps are lined with pots and earthen jars. Most have pigs inside sheds as sturdy as the house. The fields are filled with hundreds of rotting blackened stumps surrounded by the straw of the past season's grain. There are tangles of trees everywhere lying where the settlers fell them some partly submerged in the water. Many times the family stands staring at us as we pass; children with fingers in mouth, parents with drawn faces, arms at sides or scratching nether parts.

The next morning the smell of coal reaches my nose as we see openings high up on the bluffs into the coalmines, but as we near the city the coal veins showed to be lower and lower until one could see them passing below the river. We come into Pittsburgh with its clanging sounds, with it dark haze, with it soot blanket giving industrial equality to all. We retrieve our rifles and wait while many of the best-dressed ladies and men tug at Jack's sleeve and wish him well. He returns to us full of smiles and determination to rid the earth of evil.

The reminder of the day is used in trying to secure a keelboat as we find the steam passage too expensive for deck passage is filled and only cabin passage is available. We fail to find keelboat passage whether we are too many or armed or just the final of the season before freeze up I don't know. Chomper finds a Choctow and he trades him some whiskey for his dugout canoe. In the morning we carve another two paddles and set off down the Ohio to the Mississippi. We are flowing with the current and flow of the river. This is the river the divides the North and South meaning the Negroes on the north bank are legally free and those on the south bank are slave. One would think a swim across the river would be well worth it for those on the South, but alas the Rule of Law here in America sinks any such hope as it decrees that men who swim for their freedom are runawasy property once in the North and not free men even though Ohio is not a slave state. This shows the reach of the southern states in congress in this country. It seems the only way to freedom is down the Ohio River and beyond the reach of the law in the Far West… and this is our path.

For four days we paddle with the current and have few portages and most days we start before sunup. On the fourth day it rains then sleets and my feet get very cold but my hands stay warm working the paddle. Chomper tells me we need moccasins. That night I kill a deer as we had not eaten anything the day before. I am quite thrilled for it is my first deer.

But I let on like I had done this before. Chomper seemed quite pleased at my hunting ablity, although what happened was that I had stopped to rest by the creek that emptied into the Ohio while hunting and a doe came walking cautiously down a path to the water. I froze and when she looked behind her at some noise. I raised my rifle to my knee as I was sitting with one knee up.

Chomper immediately set to scraping the hide with his knife showing me how to do it, but warning me that this is a task for women as is cooking. I feel elated as this is the first time he has mentioned the village to me since our journey had begun. I determined that I would do what I had often thought about at night in New York. I would talk to Chomper about the Far West . Whether with him or on my own I wanted to see the Far West.

Chomper quickly got frustrated using the knife on the deerskin having cut though it in a couple of spots while scraping the hair and flesh off the hide. He has me save some of the hair and stuff it in my brogans to keep out the cold. We cut most of the meat from the bones. He cut the back leg joint freeing it and showed me where the sinew is along the back of the leg. After boiling it he let it cool. Out of his possible bag he pulled out a small piece of metal that looked to be part of an old barrel ring. He pounded it flat and with a small file rounded the corners and then made a slit in the top side of the knuckle of the thigh bone with his knife and he inserts the metal blade he just fashioned and wraps it tight by the edges with the sinew. By tomorrow it will be ready to use he advised me. He did a curious thing by going back to the gut pile and taking out the bladder of the deer showing me where it is in the slimy mess.

He then split open the deer head and took out the brains and put them into the bladder. He said tomorrow when he is tanning the hide he will show me how to do it.

If we see bits of rope or wire or any type of metal on our journey Chomper insists we stop and retrieve it. We stop at a canebrake and Chomper selected many straight piece of cane to use as arrow shafts. He tied these in a bundle with sinew and hung the high over the fire at night. He said we would be coming on some good wood to make bows. I had him show me the proper canes and I cut some for myself, although several became curved lying in the wet bottom of the boat. He showed me how to straighten them by heating them over the fire.

The next day we reached Cincinnati. As we approached the city we see droves of pigs in the valleys and along the shore were men butchering pigs. Any parts not used and it appears most parts are used are tossed into the river for the catfish to eat.

We hid our canoe in some brush and prevailed on Jack to stand guard over our rifles in the canoe. Chomper and I agree that the best protection we are to get from Jack is from his mouth. In the boat he seemed to have more energy as he has a strong upper body. Jack told us how the Far West is going to be the refuge of all Indian tribes as the government is moving the Eastern tribes to the west so that civilization will not corrupt them. There will be no whiskey there to tempt them. The government is encouraging missionaries to bring civilization to the tribes. That the men of God are to be vanguard of civilization the leaders of a new world order. He saw himself as a Christian soldier marching into the wilderness. I think he looked to us to cheer him on, but we are more interested in observing nature.

Cincinnati is a pleasant city for its wide cobbled streets and brightly painted houses, much more red paint than in New York it has rather more pigs on the street than New York as well. We bought flour and a cast iron pot. I also purchased a Sheffield butcher knife, as my skain didn't prove to be such a great knife in cutting up the deer. Chomper brought serveral dozen Sheffield blades explaining that he could trade these British blades at the village and they would be easy to transport in the small wooden box they came packed in.

We came upon a curious poster on the side of a building for the rules of the theater. There are five rules all about what not to do to disturb one's neighbor. Fighting in the theater is one of them as well as thowing apples into the pit. It seems Americans get quite boisterous in their theaters.

When we return we set up camp a little beyond the city and Chomper uses his scraping knife that he made yesterday to scrape the rest of the flesh and fur from the hide. He staked it to the earth by stretching the hide and staking the edges. He used his new instrument like a hoe to scape the flesh and remaining hair off the hide by flipping it and restaking it. He then boiled the brains and when they turned white he spread them with his hands over the hide rubbing them on both sides of the hide. He left the hide that way overnight.

In the morning it is clear and cold. Clear ice sparkles in a jagged line a hand's width along the shore. The fire died to embers and we hold the hide over it to warm it and Jack and I hold one side and Chomper the other side and we pull and stretch the hide pulling white streaks across it where we stretch ti. We load up for the day and off we go to Louisville, which is a bit short of two days travel. Chomper has dried some of the deer meat on a scaffold of branches above the fire and we still have fresh meat left, although not much. We paddle hard all day until full dark and then camp and raise a fire and have roasted meat and biscuits as I am too tired to make bread.

We pass Louisville late the next day and don't even stop there being nothing we need and the many rapids occupy our attention so I can't tell you what the city looks like. We are forced to stop at some rapids to portage and that slows our progress.

We have four days of icy rain before we reach the Mississippi. But it cannot dampen my joy at seeing the end of the Middle West. We pass Cairo and surely it is misnamed for it is a city surrounded by a swamp, which we do not want to enter. We are so tired that we rest a day as we fight the current of the Mississippi up to St. Louis.

It is a dreary place to camp with stunted trees, old cut stumps, low muddy banks and a few scattered log cabins on stilts. It looks to be a sick and dismal place in the heat of the summer with mosquitoes and flies in abundance. The town of Cairo is on the north bank of the Ohio. The Mississippi looks to be three hundred yards wide and full of floating logs

and trees. I am told by a passing boatmen, that the river is low and the current slow perhaps three or four miles per hour. Steamboats make the journey in two days and we are likely to be five days toiling against the current
to make St. Louis. We have dried meat and biscuit to eat for the journey.

We set out early up the Mississippi and soon find that a constant
effort is needed keep from being swept backwards and many time we lose
forward momentum in trying to avoid trees and snags and soon we find
the slowest current our eyes seek sand bars, fallen trees and the inside of
bends. The river is full of sandbars and islands the water muddy unlike
the clearness of the Ohio.. These obstacles require us to go from one side
of the river to the other all the while fighting the current so there is little
direct progress.

By noon we are so tired we land on the east bank or left bank as they
say here referring to the source of the river being to one's back. We find a
path along the river and tie the canoe to two ropes in case one doesn't hold
and we are able to pull the floating canoe along for a couple of miles before
we run into tas trees between us and river so as to make it impossible to
pull the canoe any further. Back to the water we go. A steamboat passes us
and I certainly want to toss it a rope to tow us to St. Louis. We row until full
dark and then camp on a sandbar with willows. We make a fire with grey
chunks of driftwood found higher on the banks and boil tea into which we
add our dried meat and dip our biscuits and it tastes as good as I imgagined
consommé would.

I have two light wool blankets, which I obtained at the hotel. I believe
they are two pounders. Even digging into the sand, which makes a comfortable bed the two blankets are barley enough as a north wind is blowing
down the river. I doubt that we made more than twenty-five miles and
maybe ten miles in a straight line what with all the bends in the river. At
this rate is will take us a week to reach St. Louis. I am excited to be so close,
but so tired I can barely make my wishes known to the half moon hanging
over the river. I fall off with the sound of the mass of water besides and
rattle of wind in the willows behind me.

It is cold but clear when the sun breaks though the bare branches. Small pools of water are clear and still and sparkling on their hard, clear surface. It is now the thirteenth of December and our every move is to an increasingly colder land. Chomper has finished making the case for his rifle and of course he has the fire roaring. We have tea and I take a walk and find a rabbit sitting to the side in the grass thinking he is concealed so I slowly raise my rifle and my ball finds him before he can flee. We boil him in our iron pot.

"We will have more rain and snow now," Chomper said as we sat round the fire eating our hot breakfast. "That is why I made a cover for my rifle. We must keep one rifle dry. Wrap yers in blankets and it will keep dry for some time. Did you see that I smoked the hide before I fashioned the case?"

"Yes, but I thought you were coloring it with smoke?"

"That happens, but I am making it repel water and the smoke makes the hide soft again after it has been wet. It yee do not smoke then yer hide will turn stiff once it is wet. Hey I will make a rifle cover for you once yee bring me another hide. And those pants, he nodded at my pants will catch seeds and burrs more than good buckskin so yee may want new coverings."

I have my wool pants on and they did pick up every burr, which the river bottoms are full of. But my brogans bothers me the most as they are coming apart in the daily wetness thank the saints for my wool socks.

We set out with the sun four fingers high as Chomper says. Jack has been doing most of the talking along with singing for most of our canoe trip and I have tired of it and want to speak to Chomper. Today Jack has been put in front as we found he has strong arms and has now been shown by Chomper how to read the logs and snags. I am put in the middle. There is a west wind today so we hug the west bank when we could so as to not fight both wind and current.

"Chomper today is the thirteen day of the month on the White Man's calendar. My ancestors used to count 13 months per year and count by the moons isn't that what your people do?"

"Yes I don't understand why the White Man uses months instead of moons. In New York I saw that the great sea moves by the moon a fisherman told me how it happens. The White Man knows this and yet ignores the moon. What do you name yer moons."

"We, of the old Irish ways name our moons after trees. Each tree is sacred in a different way and has different powers. I see many of our sacred trees here: Willow, Oak, which is our most sacred tree, the Ash and the Birch. Some of the others I have not seen yet."

"Catholics don't have sacred trees," sneered Reverend Jack

"I'm not talking about Roman Catholic I'm talking about the old ways of Ireland that go back before St. Patrick. What you may call superstitions legends or even witchcraft although it has little to do with any of those things. Tis just ancient teaching that are recorded in our stories, poems, song and festivals. Look at the look on your face Jack! I can see you are getting all worked up to do some preaching. I've never understood that. If it's harmless medicine for the country people why the need for the inquisitions."

"It's the devil's work."

"There was no devil before the Jews and Catholics stole him form the Greeks. Those old ways had no devil that you speak of so how can a devil direct them? I know only a little for I am young, yet at my uncle's farm since I was a wee boy we have celebrated and talked of our ancestors. I have many fond memories of Samhain bonefires."

"You mean bonfires," Jack interjected

"No it was bonefires that's what we called it as the old bones on animals are burnt in the fire as it is a fire that ends the year and begins a new year. Makes a good fertilizing ash too my uncle claimed."

"Did you ancestors build churches like those I saw in New York?" Chomper asked

" Yes some did. Dublin has many churches. Our ancestors believed that sacred places are found not made one can recognize them by their power and so it was rare to build a place of worship where the spirits lived. Maybe a little stone seat or cover over a sacred spring. There was no grand heaven to go to there was no terrible end coming it was just other worlds above and below and they weren't one good one bad they were just other worlds."

"My people see a similar world. We do have a sacred medicine lodge, but it is more for protecting our sacred objects and their powers. Objects have power only for the care of the bundle owner and it come from the spirits not the object. We honor places of evil power that we avoid and these are found places just like sacred places where we leave offerings. But there is not big evil place to go like the Christian hell, just many evil forces to avoid."

"What were you doing in Ireland running around in the woods casting spells?" Jack said over his shoulder.

"What are spells," said Chomper

"Magic talking to the the spirits making the devil do your work," Jack said

"Why do you talk to an evil spirit. Do you talk to your great God?"

"Chomper yes they do and it's called praying. Jack doesn't understand these ancient ways. He's been taught that they are evil because they are not his way or his God's way. Jack, I did not hear of anyone casting spells. Our festivals were celebrations at the cusp of the seasons and connections to help our clan and farm and to honor the past and pray for our future. At Samhain we would bring all the stock from the hills for the winter and butcher all the animals that weren't used as breeding stock or we sell them at the fall market. So we did so much work as well as feasting.

The last of the fruit was picked and what didn't get picked by Samhain had to be left for the animals and spirits of the woods."

"What animals were you butchering you did not have buffalo," Chomper asked.

"No we don't, our sacred animal was the Irish Stag now gone from our land forever. Deer is stocked on many estates. Most of the animals we kill and preserve by smoking and some we feast on are beeves, sheep, goats and some fowl. I wish it were wild animals like here, but Ireland is a land of many people and so the wild animals live only in the most remote areas and or big estates and the animals are owned by the English or Protestant landlords. Most of the the wild animals we ate we had to poach."

"Poach?"

"Steal, usually at night."

"People own animals in your country?"

"Indeed they have for hundreds of years."

"You have horses?"

"Yes some fine horses, but Catholics under the Penal laws weren't allowed to own a horse worth more than five pounds. That law was repealed several years ago, but not much has changed at the time I left."

"The English make these laws?"

"Yes"

"You poach with rifles?"

"No too much noise we use bows and snares."

"You have no guns"

"Legally no. All Irish Catholics were outlawed from owning any weapons, but we had a neighbor who turned protestant and he had a rifle that we used. He wasn't really Protestant, but that was the only way he could own his Da's land so he pretended to be Protestant. Many Catholics thought he was a traitor but we always treated him well and so we learned to shoot."

"These English have always treated us well and trade guns with us," Chomper mused.

"Yes they are good traders as are the French, but they don't occupy your land nor consider your religion to be a threat and you live far from their land so it is a different matter here in America."

We carried on talking all day and we paddled the current. Jack seemed less threatened and more amused by our conversation as the day wore on so I went deeper into some Celtic rituals than I had originally intended because I got so excited at some of the similarities with our rituals and the Mandans. Chomper seemed excited as well and I felt even more excited to be able to journey to the Far West with him although he hadn't indicated that I could accompany him.

That evening Chomper shot a deer and we feasted well and he started on making a gun case for me.

We continued this routine for the next four days until we finally arrived in St. Louis on Saturday December seventeenth a rainy and wind-swept day.

CHAPTER V

St. Louis, State of Missouri

Git O'Toole Journal

16 December 1831, Friday

From the Black Pool of Ireland on the river Liffey I did sail across the sea. The Raritan, the Delaware, the clear Ohio has now brough me to the murky Mississippi. I wish to see the muddy mighty Missouri and at last I will be free.

Soon I will be in St. Louis and soon I will find a way to the Far West. There are people leaving that city for the Far West all the time. I do so want to go with Chomper to his village, but I know not whether he will take me. I will find a way to the Far West.

I have a small amount of coin left whether tis enough for a horse I don't know but I have my rifle and pistols. I'm not sure I should have gotten the pistols as they do not seem to be of much use in hunting except at very close range. If my mates could see me shooting that deer and see this vast, vast country of which I have not seen but a corner of with nearly a month of travel.

There is not a soul telling me where to be what to do. No landlords, priests, parents, or soldiers. Only the weather and the journey beckon me. The Far West beckons me the wild animals the wild rivers the great mountains. I can roll my blanket under the stars and drink from the pure rivers eat one of the million buffalo and fish during the day and not feel I am a thief and sneak. I can enter a village not as a Roman Catholic not as a despised Irishman, but as a free man and man of the West where there is no parliament, no penal laws, no commandments only those of survival. I shall learn the laws or survival and I shall roam the land from end to end with all of my wits and this land shall become me.

No imagination, no word, no painting can convey the immensity of this land. I've not yet crossed half of it Already we have crossed land that more than a dozen different tribes occupied. I'm told there is many hundreds of tribes and those in the Far West are not reduced to poverty and begging like the tribes we have passed. The buffalo once roamed in all of the this land from Lancaster westward and now not a single one remains east of the Mississippi. What would Ireland be like with many different tribes or Europe where the tribes are measured in the dozens to find a place on earth with this many different people living with all these languages all these different clothes differ-ent religions and amongst all these wild animals surely this is what paradise was meant to be. Everything that mankind has ever been seems to be here hunters, foragers farmers and toolmakers. Maybe not the toolmakers that Europeans are, but the Europeans are not the hunters and foragers that the Tribes are. The Europeans have none of the dash the boldness, the passion and the sheer pageantry that the Tribes have.

It is truly a New World that I now trod and I want to witness all I have been told.

IT IS A MISTY MORNING through an area low and swampy we paddle cutting though the foaming current and tis our first sight of St. Louis, but tis not the town we see but steamboats keelboats canoes and all manner of craft all aslant on the mud shore Wooden slopes and slatted ramps scattered askew serve as a wharf. No steam noises just the clunk of wood on wood from the few boats about and some ravens fighting. The twenty-four star flag is fluttering about the mast of of a schooner. The last star representing the state we are in.

We hear the pitched call of the Patron on a keelboat pulling away with a full load headed downstream. *Tomber les rames* we watch as their oars lift from the water. Then the ellipsical outline of another keelboat comes out of the mist for upstream angling to the levee the Patron commands *Laisser aller Laisser aller* we watch as their oars bite into the water and make whirlpools.. The cabin of the boat is a round shape made from willow branched with hides stretched over it. The boat has a rough appearance to match the appearance of the men in it

We slip into the downstream side of town the bank is greased from use and ready for our canoe. I nearly fall when I step out so slick is the bank but tis easy to slide our craft out of the way of the hungry current. The top of the levee is anchored with faded once whimsical wooden structures seemingly being pushed by square brick buildings warehouse buildings marching from the north. The face of the city from the river looks to be no more that dozen blocks wide with a few church steeples rising above the warehouses. Chomper espies something and runs over to the strange craft about thirty feet long twelve wide tipped face down and a little deeper than a canoe. It looks more creature than boat, like a large seal except it has longer fur. Dark brown color and a rounded bend up the shallow side Chomper tips it easily with one hand to reveal a frame of willow branches inside.

"Is this like yer Irish boat…yer cockboat?"

"Yes, but this is so much larger and shaped too long for ours is round and this is nearly the shape of a very large canoe."

"Oh these are made by the trappers and traders to carry bales of fur. Ours are small and round also."

Next is a canoe rudely chopped out of tree next to that two canoes of the same material with planks fastened ato the tops of the canoes and a platform on top.

"The Americans call this a dugout Pirogue by the French. These are made out of cottonwood." Chomper said pointing to the rudely chopped vessel. It is over twenty feet long. Another small boat nested next to it catches my eye nice curving lines coming from the high pointed ends and bowing out in the middle much more design to it than that dugouts. Chomper catches my eye.

This is a bateau or little boat he says patting the curve of the gunwale with delight.

A two-pound swivel gun canted on the bow. It looked like a rowboat blown out in the middle at the sides. The bow and stern are curved up equally high but the expected keel is not there. It is flat bottomed like all the boats here. I want to examine more boats but Reverend Jack is impatient with such watery matters and insists we hasten into the city. We shift bags and rifles and walk to **the (add the)** top of the levee to Front Street.

Old French wooden house once bright and gay with high gable windows protruding from the roofs and old warped galleries in front of double doors look forlornly over as us we eye them from the levee. The streets narrow with many small barbershops, dram shops, boarding houses and nighttime cafes shouldering each other. Burning Arabian beans mixed with twisted chicory roots flay our nostrils garlic twisted with thyme and oregano wind it way from unseen cauldrons that surely hold foreign fowl and autumnal roots these smells reach deep to caressingly squeeze my empty entrails. Open doorways emit smoky heat and cloying lavender drawing our eyes to languorous, porcelain women sipping coffee as black as their hair while quaffing us over their raised china like lean costermongers.

Silently we walk the muddy street returning smiles slyly diected our way by some of the porcelain faces from behind the delicate porcelain cups. The Reverend Jack emits a audible sigh at the sight of the the sharp-edged clean red brick of the warehouses looming or beckoning at the next block. The sharp damp December air cannot compete with the lingering stench of the hidefull storehouses full of the plunder from the clear mountain streams. At the corner of Vine and Front stands the American Fur Company warehouse open doors shows the beaver and buffalo hides flattened, pressed and tied in sinew stacks of big square bales. Passing it we turn to the next street named Laurel and soon end that block and begin one with modest mansions. Chouteau labeled the first with an elegant gate and then more modest house comes the name Clark in the front of red brick house with a large square building attached to it. Chomper told me this is the home of Red Hair the white chief who speaks the wishes of the white tribe to many tribes on the prairie.

"Red hair wintered in our village.. He was the leader of a group of American blue coated seizers that went to the Stony Mountains now called the Rocky Mountains and on the great sea beyond."

We pass a faded sign of a summer past:

THE CITY OF ST. LOIUS PROHIBITS THE SALE OF FRESH PORK, WATERMELONS, GREEN CORN, CUCUMBER AND OTHER VEGETABLES CONSIDERED PREJUDICIAL TO HEALTH

"I told you pork is bad for you, don't you agree Jack" Chomper said.

"I never had it as a child but I rather like it now," said the Reverend.

This making Christians will raise the price of hogs: if we grow all to be pork eaters, we shall not shortly have a rasher on the coals for money.

"What are you talking about?" Jack says as he looks at me with some anger.

"Shakespeare. The Merchant of Venice"

"Why did you pick that play?" He asks suspiciously.

"I don't really know except that is the one I remember about pork."

"I don't know that I believe you."

"Well look it up yourself."

"Not the words, your motives."

"I don't think Shakespeare talked about watermelons or green corn; even now Europe is not much given to eating such foreign food."

"Why is this village not allowed to eat green corn?" Chomper said. "Hey there is nothing better that the first green corn of the season."

"Cholera. The city health officials believe they are all responsible for cholera," said Jack.

"But we have eaten green corn since before memory and we have not had cholera in our village it is a white man sicknesses not a corn sickness."

"If nobody eats the corn who's going to know. That makes the health official right doesn't it. Anybody doesn't die they've saved," I replied.

"You can't prove a negative that never happened," Jack retorted.

"There are so many of the black white men here," Chomper said was he eyed them.

"Tis true that most of the stevedores we passed on the levee are Africans. Are they all slaves Jack?"

"Most are, I imagine, but I hear ther are some free slaves in this city. *A son honoureth his father and a servant his master*: Malachi Chapter one verse six the Bible says that slavery is a natural condition of mankind that is the way God has ordered our world and so I believe that the negros must have committed some great offense against God to be put into such a position, but I believe that the day will come when they will be released from their sins."

"Isn't that just in the Old Testament"

"Oh no for it is in Revelation in talking of all the fine merchandise of Babylon…*and horses and chariots and slaves and the souls of men*."

"Do the black white men make slaves of the white men?" Chomper asked.

"That has not been God's will or the natural order," Jack replied. "Here is the public house are we going to board or will we continue to live the savage life?" Jack demands.

Chomper looks at me so I say: "I am low on coin and need to get a horse so I would like to continuer our life in the woods." I still didn't know if I would be continuing on with Chomper.

"Look it is only a dollar a day or five dollars per week at this house. We can recruit here in a week and then continue on," Jack says with a smile.

Yee may stay the week and do what you wish on your own hook, but I must hurry to my village. Today I am here to trade, but I leave at sunrise. Let us do our trading and meet in front of the Missouri Hotel at sundown?

Jack sullenly agrees

Chomper turns back up the street and I follow him We came back to Red Hair's house where we meet two Indians. Chomper says something in Mandan to them and one answers by a, swift movement towards his nose followed by pressing both hands with finger tips extended and touching just above and across the forehead. Then their hands started moving so fast back and forth that I couldn't follow. After about ten minutes of signing we continue on our way.

What did they say and who are they?

They call themselves Chopunnish, whites call them Nez Percé or Pierced Nose and they came with their war chief and with a Salish those two are both dead. They come from the Rocky Mountains. They all came seeking someone to teach them the white man's medicine from the book.

"You mean the Bible?"

"Yes they heard of the black robes and the book with marks that make magic."

"So they want to become Christians?"

"What they wish is trading goods: guns, powder, cloth tools, mirrors and such. They have been told by some Iroquois that lived with them that the white man's medicine can be learned from the White Man's holy book and so these two named Rabbit-Skin Leggings and No Horns on His Head as been talking with Red Hair and he promised to send them Black Robes to teach them. I told them that the Black Robes don't do much trading, but they thought I am trying to get the White Man's medicine to my village first. I have not reason to do that. The White Man has been to our village for over five generations we know that such things do not come out of a book. I told them I had visited a place where White Man makes guns and they did not believe that either. I think there is such a place here as I saw signs like the place we visited. I have no time for foolish men who do not want to hear. Already two of your weeks have passed since the moon when the river freeze has come. Those other two both died of white man disease."

We did trading at several places and Chomper told me to buy various items like flint, balls, powder, knife blades and some glass beads made in Italy. He said I could trade those Items for a horse, as there seemed to be few horses for trade in town and those quite expensive. I also bought a heavy coat, a striped, worsted Petersham made of knotted wool and a pair of sattinet trousers filled with wool. My bag was now too heavy to carry, but I followed Chomper back to the French section and we entered one of those shops full of perfumed women.

Chomper went up and began to talk trade in French, but I couldn't see what he is trading fas there is nothing but coffee and whiskey and I know he doesn't drink whiskey. He calls it fools water because it makes men who drink it look like fools. There is one green-eyed women with full rounded breast tops exposed who is doing some fine needle work and who smiled at me, I smile back feeling embarrassed. Chomper went through a door and told me over his shoulder he would be back soon and pointed at me and whispered something to one of the women. A couple of the women came and sat at my side and began to talk to me in French so fast that I can barely understand as the accent is not one I know. One pinches my cheek, which I hate and my face reddens in embarrassment. Finally, a dark-haired woman a head taller with matching swollen upper and lower lips hollows in her cheeks and fine smooth arms and hands grasps my hand and leads me though the door Chomper had entered, promising to show me something extraordinary. We pass small rooms smaller than a larder with a bench bed across the far wall. She calls herself Francine. She leads me to a room and there is Jack drunk with women laughing at him. Jack sees me and his face turns red. Apparently he is done with the sex part of his encounter. I thought she was leading me to a brothel. I am relieved to laugh at Jack.

When I get back Chomper is sitting a settee drinking coffee and laughing with three women. Just then Jack emerges from another door and stops flat-footed with door in hand. He smiles crookedly and lurches into the room.

"Well ain't this the most confounded congregation ya ever saw!"

The petite dark women behind him is rolling her eyes at the other women while making a quick motion with her hands. The women all laugh at Jack and he thinks tis his charm they laugh at and so he joins their laughter and causes the women to erupt again in another chorus.

"Yer been drinking whiskey," Chomper says with a puzzled look on his face.

"It's that little hellion's fault. Jack points to the petite dusky woman named Elizibeth who is moving away from him. I only take a small drop in my tea to satisfy my company… but she gave me some darn Kentucky whiskey, it was all whiskey…and she keeps talking about herself."

Jack slumps into the settee and seems to be done speechifying. There then ensues a parley between Chomper and the blonde women on the disposition of the snoring Reverend Jack. They wish us to take him out and

Chomper wishes to leave him as we have some more trading to do. Finally they agree to keep him it we put him in one of the rooms in the hallway, which we do.

I told Chomper I am surpised to see Jack in there based on the way he has talked about women I thought he had no taste for them. I told him Francine took me into Jack's room.

Out we go and we pass a place with a doctor sitting out front of his sign whittling and spitting tabacco whitle he talks to a fellow leaning on the porch post. He ignore us as he talks and finally with looking our way says:

"What kin I do far you fellows?"

"You have medicine?" Chomper asks

"Well that seems to be a matter of opinion. Yoo fellows look to be stout to me, but ifn't you smart ya'll let me inoculate against the pox, especially you there you Injun. Jest be a little scratch on the skin and ya might feel a little febrile fer a day or two, but it fix you up and keep the pox off. Step on in."

"How much is it?" I ask

"Bit expensive out her in der West. Four dollars…each."

"Four dollars! I don't have that! Chomper I got a four pounds if you want that."

"You say this is to stop the pox?"

"Why have the the traders to my village not spoken to us about this?"

"Well I expect they could. They jest gotta buy it. Don't reckon yer people would be willing to do much trade fer a scatch on the arm. What say ye? Could save your life?"

"What medicine man makes this?"

"Don't know his name this here medicine is made from a cow."

"The medicine comes from beeves? How can such a strong medicine come from such a weak animal? I think it is a trick for such an animal can only make a man sick, not strong. I wish to watch you do to one of our people so that I can see if the medicine works."

"Well that's how it works the very thing that can kill you can save you in small amounts. Pox comes from cattle ya know and so does this medicine. Don't matter to me who I do it to as long as they have four dollars. Don't know how long I have this though. Could be gone soon and then I don't know if I'll be getting more afore spring. Might do a trade with that rifle?" He nods his head at Chomper's rifle.

"Without a rifle, I will be dead I thank yee"

"Chomper you should get it if you have the coin. It may save your life."

"All right I do it and do Git too."

As we leave Chomper tells me we need a mule to carry our trade goods. I give him my coin and off he goes. I wander along the docks asking questions about the fur trade. I stop and take off my sock into which I had sewn a pound coin, my last coin.

Chomper returns with a young mule with big brown expectant eyes and a high step. He has on a packsaddle along with a headstall. He said, "we will get horses from the Pawnee or Kansas up the river. A mule has more strength than a horse," he remarks. We load what trade goods we have and then Chomper leaves to trade for more. The mule looks at me with calm brown eyes then walks over and gently rubs the back of it's head against my shoulders. I hook my hand behind his headstall strap and walk alongside him while I continue to find out all I can about the Far West pestering everyone I can with questions. He stands quietly beside me making snuffling noises and looking about.

Chomper finds me at the American Fur Company warehouse. The packs are full so we head back to the brothel to pick up the Reverend as it is nearing sundown. It takes some doing to wake him, but the one women seemed skilled in that art the green-eyed one and we soon have Jack blinking and weaving on the street.

When he sees our mule, he smiles and goes to put his pack on her. The mule turns his head with a quizzical look at Jack and his pack. We start out but the mule pulls me up short with her front legs locked.

"No he is full. He is for trade goods. Chomper says to Jack. I will take you to a place to trade for one. They cost little more than the women you traded for and they will do more work. And if you want work and pleasure we can get you a hinny." Chomper says as he smiles at me.

Jack takes the pack off and mule makes a sign though his lips like he is relieved he doesn't have to do something about the imposition. Then he looks at me expectantly and I go over to scratch his ears. I soon find that he loves for me to run my thumb up and down the inner edge of his ear he turns his head into my hand and makes slow rhythmic heavy exhalations though his nose and his lids get heavy. When I quit he nudges my arm with a gentle upward motion and his eyes are expectant.

But was rebuked for his iniquity the dumb ass speaking with a man's voice forbad the madness of the prophet. Peter Chapter 2 verse 16 intoned Jack

Chomper and I look at each other with wonder.

"I am surrounded by iniquity!" Jack whales as he shoulders his bag. "You are right, we must go were the land and air is pure and without sin except Original sin and were hearts are pure and souls ignorant and I must bring the Light into the darkness."

"Jack you walked into the brothel on your own two legs if that's what you mean by wicked, I was the ignorant one. And what does you being with a prostitute have to do with an insane prophet listening to an ass speak?"

You are both hopeless. You hear not the true words, because your hearts are dull to faith, they beat not in belief. I can only believe that you two were put on earth to test my faith and tempt me from my path. I will prevail you'll see both of you will see the Truth I will not waver in my mission. But now I must find water.

We watch his waddling ungainly gait. The mule turns his head and watches Jack then does a rolling shake down the length of his body. Sighes and paws the soil into little puffs that drifts towards the departing Jack.

"These words he says in that weak chief voice, they are other chief's prayers? Why does he not have his own words that his God sends him if a man owns his world he cannot be weak."

"Chomper I agree that a man's words should be his own, but I have known few men who could claim that and never a priest or preacher and few men know that they own their world and it is but one life we live.

"I have known many! My people speak their own words and they do not try to make others speak for them. Every man's dream or vision is his own he does not make others see his vision nor speak his words. It is true that some sacred words come from the spirit world and they are passed down from father to son, but these words are used only at sacred times and never to shame or in pride. I admire many things about the Christian God but I do not understand the ways of the priests."

"He is not a priest."

"He lies to us?"

"No a priest is only for certain types of Christians he is Protestant and they are not called priests. They are called reverend or preacher."

"Oh so Reverend Jack is the priest word? I believed it as his name."

"I prefer preacher as that better describes what they are."

"Preacher Jack? I have been trying to understand the White Man's ways of the spirit and I seem to learn less every day." Chomper says as he shakes his head. "I lived in your village and even that I do not understand. I saw only trading. Every White Man spends his days trading or as a slave to another man so he can get coin to trade.

"America was formed because of a trade dispute with the British that you so favor wanted more coin that their colonist wished to pay so they killed each other until it hurt the British so that they gave up and

America was formed. Your father's country France really made it all possible. France is an ancient enemy of Britain and far more of a threat than America to Britain."

"So America broke away from their tribe the British?"

"Yes."

"So this is why Americans are so jealous of the British traders that come to my village."

"Yes and vice versa I imagine."

"That is why Red Hair came with the soldiers and others after him. He is like the Nadouessioux the Sioux and Arikara who do not want others to trade with us they want to control all the trade that comes up the Mighty River so they become the most powerful tribe. If that happens we will be destroyed. This is not good for my people. The British have better trade goods and they come from the North where the Sioux cannot stop them. The American are strong, but the Sioux get stronger each year. Come I must speak with Red Hair. He must have a smoke with our chiefs. For many years now the trade our people have done with other tribes: the Assinboins, Crow and Cree and others as been less and less. Many more tribes from all over the plains and the Great Shiny Mountains traded with us Mandans. Our hands reach north to Hudson Bay down to the Spanish land. Red Hair must help our people. He will see how the American traders have taken our trade. Every year they build trading forts and every year fewer tribes come to trade with us for the forts supply their needs. Last year they build Ft. Clark next to our village and there is Ft. Union on the Missouri by the Yellowstone and Ft. Techumesh down on the Bad or Teton River."

Chomper set off pulling the braying mule behind him the mule looks at me out of the corner of its eye.

"Chomper! General Clark...er Red Hair works for the Americana traders!"

"I do not understand? He stops, the mule seems relieved. "He works for us for all the tribes...does he not bring our cares and wishes to your chief the President. Does he not?"

"Yes, but all the traders must get his approval to trade and the forts he approves them too. That rich man in New York...Astor he owns many of those forts. And the liquor and sugar that makes your fools of your people he allows them on the boats."

"This is true?" Chomper swirls and comes at me the mule lifts his head slipping out of Chomper's grasp. The mule watches expectantly with ears cupped.

"Listen Chomper, I have asked many people in New York and here. He doesn't really work for you, only your people can represent you. The Birtish have done this very thing to the Irish for generations working for our best interests since we aren't capable of doing it on our own at least that is what the British think. Red Hair...William Clark works for the War Department and the War Department helps the traders. Do you remember when the Arikara attacked the Ashley and Henry trapping expedition?"

"Yes seven or eight years past, he replys while folding his arms rigidly in front."

"Did not the American soldiers return to attack the Arikara?"

"Yes, but the Arikara's were our enemies then."

"Red Hair sent those soldiers. Red Hair is not going to help you get your trade back he is going to send more and more American boats up the river and he is going to have more and more trading forts built. There is even talk of a steamboat going up the river this spring to Ft. Union. Do you not think he knows about the whiskey that goes with the traders out west?"

"Irish you are my friend," he says his hand touches his heart, "but Red Hair has always been a friend to my people. We have always welcomed all white men first the French then the British and now the Americans never in the past one hundred years has a white man died by Mandan hand. But now since the Americans have come we have lost trade with other tribes, but we had dearly loved the American's and did not think they wished to take trade from us but it has been so, as you say."

"Chomper thats it! I have heard the men on the wharfs and streets and they believe the American traders will soon control all the trade all the way to the Pacific Ocean.

Some even say the buffalo will replace the beaver as the main trade item."

"The British do not want our buffalo robes for they are too heavy and we are not good in trapping beaver so we rely on trade with other tribes to obtain more beaver and the Americans will trade our winter buffalo hides. I must speak to Red Hair. Take the mule. We will meet at the Mighty River Hotel."

Chomper ran down the street. I slowly walked over to the mule who looks at me with curious eyes. I ignore him and grab the reins and turn to go, but I'm drawn up short. The mule stands and looks with its neck stretched out. I jerk the rope and it snorts though its nose and leans back. Soon we are in a tug a war until I am out of breath and I find myself pulling the rod out of the rifle. I stop and nearly sob. What am I doing? Am I going to beat this mule our only mule? It looks at me with determination, but has no expectation of harm I might render him. It hits me that he has never been beaten he has only had the most gentle of care. But still he will not move as I try to coax him. He stands firm. I want to leave him. I stand stymied. I can't even get the mule to move down the street how am I going to see the Far West?

I sit in the half frozen mud. This seems to satify the mule and he walks on by me giving me a snort. I jump up and follow and try to lead, but he stops every time I go in front so I have to walk by his side the whole way to the Hotel. I tie up the mule and pull my wool blanket out as the sun has set and it is getting damp and cold. I sit the bench and wrap the blanket under and over me. The mule stands looking at me and his eyes are getting heavy as he seems ready to doze on his feet.

CHAPTER VI

The Shillelagh

Edvard Du Champs Journal

Saturday December 17, 1831

I am troubled. For if what Git says and others speak is the truth then Red Hair has many faces and I believe only the face of a friend to my people. Yet he is a leader in a trading company that sells whiskey up the Missouri. I am heartened when I meet him for his words are true. It is troubling to know what is the heart of a white man, for some seem to be the hardest friends of my people and the next white man it the hardest enemy. I have lived in their village and I cannot tell their hearts for so many are so clever at hiding their hearts they say love with their lips, but their lips cannot stop their own hands from doing bad.

So much power has the white man in his steamboats his rifles his wagons so I know the spirits honor him. But are these new spirits? Are these the spirits who killed the buffalo from the white man's land? I cannot know why this would be so? The beeves are there now and I cannot believe that the beeves have a stronger spirit than the buffalo. Why is the white man so powerful with such weak spirit animals? Why would a powerful people choose such weak spirit animals?

The white man's spirit men…Preacher Jack do not seek the power that I know spirit men seek. The preacher care not for power over animals and over the clouds, he does not wish to be a brave and honorable man, he does not seek power in deeds, he believes in the power of words, power of written words and power of haranguing. He does not seem interested in the power objects like a rifle. My people will not believe that a white spirit-man do not want power objects and I cannot tell them why, for I do not know, nor do I know what power Preacher Jack has, for it seems little to me, but I fear he may be a trickster.

I followed in the footsteps of our old chief to Washington who came back with Red Hair. He retuned to to our people a hero and soon became a fool for my people did not believe much of what he told them. But I have seen that he spoke the truth, but I will be a fool if I speak of all I have seen. My people did not believe so many white men live and they live in lodges stacked one atop the other and so may other truths. I know them to be truths, but my people will not. Maybe they will listen to white man I bring. Maybe if the old chief had brought white men back with him to talk he would be honored today.

I WOKE TO SEE PREACHER Jack's large nose and bushy eyebrows and moving maw. As my head clears I caught up his words.

"He's not here. It's sunrise. Something must have happened. Chomper isn't here I tell ya."

"Yes, yes I relpy. He went to Red Hair's. We'll go there first. No, first the mule. He hasn't been fed let's take him to the stable and then go to Clark's place."

I pick up his rope and walk off, still sleepy. I am pulled up short. I look back at him and his big brown eyes look at me like I have the problem. I sigh and walk back to him petting his neck, scratching his ears and he snuffles and walks. I take my place beside him, hand on his neck and accompanied him to the stable. He brays when he smells the hay, which is a street away, and now he is overcome with a need to rush and I have to run to as to not lose the rope. So tis with surprise that a bit of hay I offer him he sniffs and turns his head away with a patient look. I go find the freshest bunch of hay and after several tries he finally consents to eat making little grunting noises as he noses and sort though the hay pulling out and dropping some offending grasses. I tie him off and we go to the Indian agent's house. Looking back he is chewing and watching me with his eyes and great ears.

We go to General Clark's house.

An African answers my knock. "Is General Clark in?"

"I'm sorry sir, but General Clark is presently away on business. Could I be of assistance?"

"Yes my partner, Chomper you see he is a Mandan he set out last night to see General Clark about trade in his village."

"Sorry sir, but there have been no Indians calling there this past week. We do have two Indians as guests, but no one called on us yesterday."

"Hmm, that's queer, he's not one to be sidetracked. Well I thank you sir and good day. I nod and make my way out the gate with Jack who has stood by my side during the exchange."

"Didn't sound like any Negro I ever knew. A bit haughty too, don't you think?"

"I don't know Jack, he's only about the third African I heard speak in my life as one of those had a British accent."

"Well you've been keeping some uppity company for a kitchen slopper."

"Jack that sure sounds strange coming form a fella who seems to favor those uppity people when you need money for you mission."

Jack gave a broad smile. "Don't be a fool , Git, the Lord gave those folks guilt with their abundance.. Do you really expect these uppity people to give their money directly to the savages. No it must go to a trusted fellow white man with few earthly needs, but most importantly he must be a man who is not afraid to mix with savage's or negro's or even the Irish."

"Preacher, I seen enough of you to know that you are more at home among us people of the earth than those who live in stone towers and I believe you feel you are better than those uppity people you talk about because you are more pure and live according to you principals rather than according to capital."

"Git, I am not a cynical man. I live my life according to my principals…you can see I have very little, oh maybe I indulge in some rock candy and sometimes the ladies catch my eye, but my mission is my life and will remain my life."

"That I don't doubt, but yer mission is one concieived in the clouds and yer what my uncle calls a public man, which is a man who lives by what he sees in other peoples eyes. My uncle taught me that most public men are not what they seem, for such men soon lose sight and live within the shine of the eyes of others. No matter what I really have on my mind is Chomper we must search for him. I am at a loss as he has always followed his word and and his intentions. That made me think that he has been prevented somehow or detained somehow. What do you think we should do?"

"Git I believe to the depths of my soul in my mission—"

"Jack! I'll not be converted by words that serve you and I've not an ear for usher talk this morning. Tis Chomper on my mind is you going to help me find him?

"Yes I here to help. Perhaps he returned to the brothel."

"No he said not a word about it and his thoughts were on our journey."

"A dram house? Maybe he met a friend and he is now sleeping it off."

"Fool water! You know he won't touch whiskey he thinks it's a white man trick to turn him into a fool."

"Well that harlot at the brothel certainly turned me into one."

"Perhaps she had help. Jack, I will go down to the wharf and to the warehouses and you go back to the French section. We'll meet at the Missouri Hotel."

No sign of Chomper at the wharf or anywere on the streets. Jack is standing in front of the Hotel when I return. "I see that you didn't find him either. What is to be done now?"

"I am at a loss, but I did get an invitation by some wealthy couple to explain my mission to the upper Missouri."

"I looked at him crossly. There likely won't be a mission without Chomper. Did you check the jail?"

"Why no."

"Come! We must get him out if he is in there. Reverend Jack I think you should go in it will look better and they are not likely to pay much attention to me. You can tell them you are escorting him back to his village from out East or whatever you think will work to get him out.

"You want me to tell a lie."

"I didn't say that! You are going with him to his village."

"All right, I shall return soon."

"Is he in there? Couldn't you free him?"

"No calm down. He's not there."

"Why the delay what were you doing in there."

"The sheriff asked to me to help a few fellows seems they are going to be hung soon."

"No word on Chomper?"

"Sorry nothing. Seems there is nothing more to do today. Are you going back to the hotel to wait?"

"Yes, where are you going?"

"To that boarding house I seem unusually tired it's been a very trying day. If he shows up come and fetch me. I'll stop in the morning."

I watch him go then turn and head to the stable. What am I to do? I have almost no coin left. I pay the stable hand and untied the mule. I walk out of the stable thinking what am I going to do. I am nearly two blocks gone before I realize the mule is following me. I had forgotten about him! I turn and he snorts and raises his head as if to say keep going, so I do. I arrive at the edge of town, pause looking back and the mule keeps going so I hurry to catch up. Down the road we go with me following the mule. He is ten paces ahead and when he comes to a grassy valley with no fence he turns off and wades into the grass. I stand on the road asking what is he doing now. With his ass to me his head turns around he looks at me with his big brown eyes with a look of patience for I must have other redeeming qualities. I look about and see no huts or houses. The day will soon end. I sigh and set to unloading him. I tie a rope between two trees make a loose knot around it on the line for the mule. He seems content, satisfied that all in order. He watches me and chews and switches his tail while I pull my blankets out and make a bed between the packs. He looks at me, and then the rope betwixt the trees as if to say the rope in really unnecessary. I hear horses coming down the road then voices. I stand silent and stiff, but they pass without seeing us for we are behind a nice curve of oak trees. I top my pistols with my rod to feel the dull thud of ball, satisfied that they are still loaded. I sit my blanket chew some dried deer meat swig some water watch the evening star burn bright in the darkening west. I am tired, but it seems a long while before I sleep and then tis fitful as I dream of Chomper meeting my brother Deny and of them hitting it off and going down the trail together leaving me in Missouri.

I jump awake in the grey-blue dawn upon hearing Chomper voice. I sit but his voice is gone. I am shivering. I had lit no fire for fear of attracting someone and the cold damp air is in my bones. The mule is above me looking at me like I've been drawing on the poteen all night. My breath clouds the air. I pull the blanket over my face and breath my warm air into the blanket to warm my nose and face. Chomper has spoken to me, I am sure. He is telling me to wait and he was telling me he wanted to see if I could listen. I feel confused. If I was hearing him of course I could listen. He was in a room full of smoke, but he didn't seem afraid so I wasn't afraid for him. The sky is turning orange but I don't want to rise I want to go back to my dream and see Chomper. I hear a wagon creaking on the road above and distant hoof beats. I stare at the bluing sky and I rise with my blanket around me and stand to the side of the mule. I lean against his neck which is warm, then wrap my arms around him and hug him for warmth. I see the white of his eye and he slides his eyeball back to look at me. He smells a leathery, moldy wet hay smell mixed with clay dust. I want to get on him, but I'm not sure he is broke for riding. Instead I talk to him.

"You are quite the creature you know?"

"He looks at me and flubs his lips as if to say *I know*."

"Are you going to help me load these packs?"

He looks away at this question and I keep saying Creature, Creature to get his attention, but I know he is purposefully holding his head away from me.

"All right I'll figure it out by my lonesome, but I bet you look when I say *treat!*"

His head comes round and his ears perked and eyes are shining bright. I had gotten some parsnips in town and oh boy did he love that, sniffing me all over for more. I had my fun with the Creature and now I had to face my tasks.

I consider hiding the packs in the ravine. I hope these trade goods will give me more freedom some day soon for now they are but a burden and my first act of the day is determined not by my will but by the trade goods.

My fingers keep getting numb, one wood from the pack falls on my shin my blankets that I have wrapped around me keep falling off and my teeth are chattering, but finally after an half hour during which I have warmed some I have the packs secure. The creature stands patient the whole time looking back to see how I'm doing. When I cuss and make angry noises his ears flatten back and he hunches his shoulders as if I am about to hit him. His action causes me to talk in a soothing voice explaining that tis not him I am angry with and I talk till his ears rise and he steals a glance back at he. I am so frazzled that I am on the road before I remember my rifle and I feel my face redden at such a feeble mistake and I run to retrieve it calling to the mule to stay though I have tied him to a shrub. I feel embarrassed stupid, tired and hungry and tis only the beginning of the day.

I am so glad the sun is shining on the road as I leave the valley for it warms me and I began to warm as I walk back to town. I feel as if I have been cold for weeks my body starved for the orange heat of the sun. In hell I would never see my breath and that seemed a comforting thought. I could hear the church bells ringing for Sunday Mass and the only part of St. Louis visible to me are the church steeples. I wondered if Reverend Jack found a pew. Do preacher's scope out the competition attend other services. I know priests would never enter a Protestant building.

It occurs to me that I may be walking out of St. Louis this morning and into the Far West. I pause on a hill above the city. The city is only about ten blocks deep to the river for tis a city that feeds off the river. On the outskirts I pass several dram houses and they get more numerous as I near the city. Even on this cold Sunday morning several of the doors are open and I see men seated at tables gambling and serveral sleeping on chairs and the steps outside, There are many of these places in town by far the most numerous business. A curious thing I pass a building with a sign reading *Hibernian Relief Society.* No one is about at this early hour, but it is a sight for my poor heart to see. If Chomper doesn't show maybe those folks can help me. I do have a mule and supplies so I could sell it all and board somewhere until I find a job. But my heart sinks at the thought. I don't want to live in a stinking stifling city I want to see the Far West. I want to live free in the open air I want nature to be my guide for it has not greed, nor judgment to be satisfied. I want to use my wits and follow nature rules. I want to fend and defend myself and not have do-gooders and nay-sayers eyeing my every act.

"Irish! Heya Irish!"

I look around for the familiar voice. I see Chomper leaning out a second story window of a whitewashed house.

"The smoke is done, Irish! I have found you a job!" He yells down at me. "Come! Come! Tie up the mule." He waved both hands at me.

I tie the Creature to a post in the yard, he makes a snuffling noise an watches me ascend the stairs no doubt wondering if I was hiding any more parsnips. The doors opens and dark-haired man with blue eyes and an unlined face steps out. When he smiles I know him to be one of my countrymen.

"Hey laddie. Come along now let me have a look at ya. I'm told you're a friend of Eagle Hand and so you're a friend of mine. Thomas Fitzpatrick, he says as he holds out his hand."

"I'm so please to meet you sir, would you be the Fitzpatrick form county Kilkenny?"

"No County Cavan from just down the land from the Sheridan's. And were might you hail from?"

"Dublin sir, but I've relations in the countryside."

"Come on lad come in leave the morning chill out and have some tea with us."

"Irish! Chomper cries as he comes down the stairs two at a time. Did you meet my old friend Fitz."

"Yes he did? Laddie did you come over with family?"

"No sir by my own self."

"Ahh a bit young aren't ya? I came over when I was sixteen. I've just returned to St. Louis from eight years in the mountains. Your friend here tells me you are eager to take to the mountains can't blame you for that, I'm headed back in the spring, likely in late April we'll push up the river and leave Independence with a train sometimes in May."

"There's a train out here?"

"Ha! No a train of horses and mules. I expect to have sixty to seventy men heading to the mountains. I hear you can cook?"

"I grew up working in a bakeshop cooked my passage and worked in a kitchen at the American Hotel in New York."

"Not much baking gets done in the mountains we're usually out of flour by the time we hit the mountains. Be better if ya had another season on yer bones before ya headed to the Far West."

"I crossed the Atlantic by my lonesome so I figure I can make across the plains of the Far West. I sure like a chance to cut my stick with ya sir."

"Ya would would ya? I'll grant you it's no easy task across the water, but it takes more wits to avoid the scalping knife and the charge of the grizzly bear. The only way I could take a flatlander like you is with an expe-rienced man. Maybe you can get your friend to go? We've a new company: The Rocky Mountain Fur Company and we can't afford to have so many flatlanders running around like Mr. Astor can. Enough of that, I want you to meet Major Sanford he's one of the agents for the Upper Missouri Tribes."

"The Major in his stiff wool uniform stands next to several tribesmen bedecked in buckskins, beads, shells and feathers. There is also an African standing slightly behind him. The Major shakes my hand stiffly gives me a slight bow and smile and turns back to speak to another man in uniform. The Major doesn't seem inclined to speak to me so Chomper guides me over to the tribesman."

"Chomper who is the African?"

"Oh that is the Major's slave, his name is Dred Scott. Irish, I would like you to meet a great friend of mine of mine he is the son of the chief of the Stone Band for the great Assiniboine tribe who hunt the land north of our village and who come to trade with us every year. His name is Ah-jon-jon he is known to the white man as The Light."

Chomper signs and says some words to the man. I extend my hand , but his hand slides past grasping my upper arm and pulls me to him hug-ging me and talking to me and holding me by the shoulders an shaking me while laughing and talking to Chomper. He has a very charming way of looking at one of touching and signing so that I feel he understands me. His demeanor is one who is always laughing and smiling. He points to Fitzpatrick and to me and makes a circle and puts us in it with his signing which I took to be a question of whether we belong to the same tribe. I nod my assent and he seems very pleased. I touch his shirt and sign for a deer, but he shakes his head and makes a slightly curve horns. I asked Chomper what animal is that and he says a White Mountain goat.

Chomper then introduces me the Eyes on Both Sides known as Broken Arm. He's a famous warrior who broke his left arm in battle and continued fighting with his other arm killing serveral enemy and counting coup on several more. He is of the Plains Cree tribe who also hunt to the north and west of the Mandan village, but north of Assinboines. The top half of his face is painted vermilion and he has more delicate feature than the Light. He wears a thick elaborate choker covered with blue and white glass trade beads and drops of silver on a ring though this earlobe. He has shorter hair than the Light and two strands of beads and tubular shells known as hair pipes strung on each side of his face. There are two other Tribesmen in the next room, but Chomper whispers to me that he doesn't like them. One is plains Ojibway (Soteau) and the other a Yanktonai Sioux. There is also a Frenchmn named Loupon Frenier who came with these men as an interpreter.

Major Sanford is taking these men to Washington and on a tour of the East to show them the power of the white man. Mr Fitzpatrick says to me, then in a hushed voice he says this is being done because Mr. Astor is attempting to break the British trade with the tribes of the upper Missouri with his American Fur Company and to beat out my Rocky Mountain Fur Company by making Astor Company appear to have the full force of the American government behind it. But they can't trap worth a dam he says with wink and smile.

I am not introduced to the man Major Sanford is talking to but he seems a distinguished gentleman. The man is talking loudly about a passage to Asia and to India across the American West. What caught my ear is his talk that the human race had always moved westward with science, civilization and rational power. Soon American pioneers will complete the circumambulation of the globe! He declared. He went on to talk about how the gold and riches of the Orient would soon be coming across the West the feed American cities in the East.

I notice a boy sitting quietly in the corner I asked Mr. Fitzpatrick who he is.

Mr. Fitzpatrick broke into a warm smile and his eyes lit up as he called to the boy. "Friday come meet my countryman. Git, you say? Well Git meet my foundling Friday. He is an Arapaho boy I found wandering around the desert near the Cimarron on our way to Santa Fe. Weak from hunger and his teeth chattering in the bushes I found him. He told us he got separated form his tribe. I've just put him in school here and he has even learned a few words of English already."

Friday is younger than me by several years but seems very interested in everything that is happening. He says heya to me, and points at the Major's sleeve and makes a circle and points at himself. I know he is telling me his name, but I am puzzled by his signing. He covers his eyes and pointe to Mr. Scott again.

Dark? I ask as I point to him. He shakes his head no. "Black?" I ask. He nods vigorously. He keeps making the circle with his hand on his shirt. "Circle?" I ask.

He shakes no and then points to a dark spot on my shirt. "Spot?" He jumps up and down points to himself. "Black Spot!" I say. He already is understanding English sounds. I feel jealous that I know not a word of any native language and he is much younger. Black spot keeps pointing to a clean shaven white man with a boyish face and thick brown curly hair. He makes motions like he is drawing.

Thomas Fitzpatrick sees his foundling motions and comes over . "He's trying to tell you that the man over there is a painter, his name is George Catlin. He has already painted The Light and now is working on Broken Arm portrait. He hails from out east and will be touring the Far West this coming spring to paint as many tribes as he can visit. Come ladd I'll introduce you. Mr. Catlin excuse me, but I'd like to introduce you to a fellow countryman of mine whose burning desire nearly equals yours to see the Far West."

"Well lad I'm afraid your right you had better see the Far West before it is gone. I myself am embarking on the adventure and passion of a life-time I shall record everything about every tribe in the Far West or I shall die trying. Lad you are entering one of the truly great ending in all of history. Never again will we see so many different peoples so many different ways of life—can you write?"

"Yes sir I love to write and read too."

"Draw?"

"Some, I've not been educated to draw."

"Nor have I, son I taught myself gave up the practice of law so I could practice my passion, for the law will be trudging along when I am long buried, but the Far West will be gone except what is saved in painting and words. If a man has passion and patience there is no dream he cannot own. Do you keep a journal or diary?"

"Sir?"

"Why you must keep an account of your days, your life. So few educated men go where you're going. Fitzpatrick he's an educated man but I fear he will use it for business and not for history that is what most Americans do for they have no sense of history, they would rather chase the impossible dream of riches all their lives and die as ignorant as the day they were born. Me I may die poor, but I will die having created something more substantial than a castle and a carriage. Come with me, lad."

I follow him into the next room. He unbuckles a leather case and digs about until he comes up with a small leather book.

"Now listen to me lad, this book is filled with blank pages and I want you to pour your life into it and turn it into a living history, a history of your life in the Far West."

"Thank you sir, but no one will want to read the story of a poor Irish lad's struggle in the Far West."

"Nonsense! Take that fire in your eyes and put in on the page. I 'm telling ya ya'll not regret a word of it. And what of your family are they in Ireland?"

"Yes all but a brother who's lost in New York."

"Well there you are! You're the only story that your family is likely to get. And those Indians you met are they going to writing their story? No! We must write their story, because they don't know their story is about to end."

"Why do you say that sir?"

"You are too new to see what has happened to the tribes east of the Mississippi. One by one they are being destroyed by the states or federal government encroaching on their land why look at what Georgia is doing! It will not stop at the Mississippi. Already the wealthy from the East are moving their tentacles across the plains and destruction always follows in the businesses footsteps. Are you earnest young man."

"I am determined to see the Far West. I've thought of nothing since Chomper my Mandan friend described his life in his village. I want to live that life, a life of nature, of freedom, a life next the the sky and with dirt between my toes and cold running water dripping down my chin."

"Then by God do it lad. Do it and write it as you may be the last men to experience such a life. Take this fill it and fill another and another. Good luck to you. Lad and I hope our paths cross again. I will ask you about your story. Now I must return to General Clark's to continue painting Broken Arm."

He looked a quiet man, but in speech he was almost overwhelming with his passion. I thumbed the blank pages and smelled the leather case.

After all the exicitment I finally get my tea a very good Chinese oolong tea.

I feel my spirts dancing at the rooftops. Meeting these people is exciting and finding a countryman who is so experienced in the mountains makes it all seem so real. And Mr. Catlin giving me the book is like another omen that I will soon be in the Far West."

Chomper sits by me putting his hand on his knees. "Did you get the job from Mr. Catlin?"

I look at him with my face scrunched into a question.

"I told him you write and he said he would give you a real job of writing."

My face stayed scrunched.

"He says he will have you write a history story. He said that all stories are history, but that most men are blind and he seemed to think you could see even before he saw you."

"So in a county obsessed about money and trade I have the only job that doesn't pay? I shan't mind for at least I live in a time when the land will support my art."

I suddenly know what I have to do, what I should have done before. I slurp the last of the delicious tea and head out the door. Unknown to me to at the time I had spotted what I needed on the ride into town. There is a meadow acoss the street and so I lead the mule to it and let him eat while I trot down the road with my chest full.

Tis gray, weathered , but strong and dry with a knot on the end. I think it oak wood, but I can't be sure without seeing the leaves. The leaves are long scattered by the wind I returned with my wood and sit on the stoop and begin carving. The mule grazes and looks over his shoulder at me while he chews and switches his tail.

I am at my task nearly an hour when the door bursts open. Irish! What are you doing? Chomper asked.

"I'm cutting my stick. We call it a shillelagh. It is a tradition when we Irish leave on a long journey we cut new stick."

"Is is a war club?"

"Yes and a walking stick. Traditionally made from the Blackthorn wood, which I cannot locate here in this country."

"Now what you need is a wah kee."

"A wah kee?"

"A shield to go with you war club Shi Lay lee. He holds his stomach and covers his mouth and laughs."

CHAPTER VII

ACROSS THE PRAIRIE

Git O'Toole Journal

18 December 1831, Sunday

Of course I am inspired by what Mr. Catlin said and am grateful for his beautiful leather bound book, which is much finer cover and paper than my own. I don't know why I didn't tell him that I have been keeping a book of my own, he seemed so excited and determined that I shrank a bit under his passion. But he has instilled in me a renewed purpose to my writing. I shall pay more attention to the details of everyday life in the Far West. They seemed not important to record before, but is what he says is true or becomes true then I will be able to look back with not only fondness at the record, but with astonishment at ways of life no longer lived.

Just look at today! All the people I met. And look how I started out all gloomy, cold and angry and at my ignorance of packing and balancing a pack tree. Now I sit by a warm fire with ribs of a whitetail sizzling. Chomper is hobbling the mule and Jack is either drunk or reading his bible. Tomorrow we head north our first steps into the Far West. Chomper tells me that game will be scare for days because it has all been killed or left when the white man came with his whitehorns. We'll have to live off of small game. But we have been given part of a deer the front quarter and neck should last us a few days. We will all have to pack some goods as the mule is overburdended with trade goods and now the meat. But this type of burden I wish to carry may I never have to carry buckets for the kitchen again.

Tomorrow is a new moon so I feel it is right that we start our journey. My Shillelagh is nearly done. I wish I had some paints to put symbols that would protect me from evil spirits. Soon it will be the winter solstice and Bel will begin his slow banishment of the cold winter and Bride will be pregnant with the life of a new spring. I wish I had some milk to pour onto the ground for Imbolc. It is good that I am entering the Far West at this time of awaking this time of promise and hope for spring will be only months away.

My heart is filled with pride in meeting Mr Fitzpatrick. It shows that the English are wrong about us Irish. He is one of the greatest leaders in the fur trade of the Far West. Of course he's been well educated so he know not only the ways of animals and tribes but he can handle ledger and correspondence that's what I wish to do. I wish to read animal tracks as well as the classics. I wish to feel myself grow into this land to know that my feet stand on a land that is free to feel my legs strengthen and fill with energy of this wild land. I wish to race across this land for the sheer joy of touching land that is free from the domain of any ruler other than nature a land untouched by deeds, rules, or kings claims. I want to be a man not a subject, not a poacher nor a trespasser but a man who can stand and dig his toes in the soft earth of the prairie.

WE LEAVE BEFORE FIRST LIGHT, Chomper declares. We will stop to eat when the sun is two hands high if a good camp can be found. In a weeks time we must change our ways for we will be in enemy country.

"Are these enemies of the white man," Jack askes as he gnaws on the side of rib.

"These are the tribes that the white man has moved form the other side of the Great River, the Mississippi they have not buffalo to hunt and few deer and most do not know how to raise corn so they raid tribes to the west and create more enemies they drink firewater and steal to pay for it. Without food nor honor they become dangerous for any men who are not strong."

"I have the Lord as my protector. I don not fear to walk in valley of death for I have my double barrel." Jack says as he smiles and pats his scattergun.

"We shall see whether you are woman or if you spirit protector is stronger than the spirits of others. Preacher Jack. Irish I have sage we must do a cleansing before we start on our journey. We do not have time for a sweat, but I do not wish to journey with you if you spirit is bad or has been hurt for it will attract wandering spirits who may do us harm on our journey. If my dreams about you are bad about you tonight you must stay until you are cleansed."

"Chomper I feel fine, my spirit is strong—"

"I have put a blanket over those willows go in there take your clothes off and paint your face with this."

He hands me a small piece of wood, the hollow filled with grease and ashes. He had made a tripod of branches and wrapped a couple of blankets around them like a teepee. I take my clothes off being careful to land them on branches as Chomper told me to never leave clothes on the ground as one never know what has happened on that particular piece of ground. Something may have died a bad death and the spirit is still there and will jump into my clothes and then into me when I put them on. I sit naked with my face painted black and wait.

A low singing voice circles my tent along with a clattering metallic rattle, which I am sure is his schischikué his rattle is made of iron that looks like a small kettle with a wooden handle. When Chomper comes past the opening I can see his body is painted his arms and legs have diagonal red lines of paint and he is wearing only a breechcloth. The upper part of his face is painted red the lower black. He has a long bone whistle hanging from a leather lace around his neck and he is carrying a stick ornamented with raven's feathers. I shiver with the cold and apprehension. He circles several times and then enters holding a club-like bunch of smoking sage wrapped in twine. He moves it up and down my body, blowing the smoke and singing as the goes round and round me. He whiffs it in my face, makes me breath it in. I choke on its harshness and cough, which he ignores. He has me rub the smoke in my hands and he cups the smoke and strikes both my ears with his hands. He has me stand and lift my feet to take the smoke. I jump when he grabs my sac and chants something and waves burning sage so close to me. He has me sit and puts his hands on the top of my head and presses down while he chants. Then he leaves without a word. I sit shirvering for some time before he hollers at me that he can hear my teeth chatt and he wondering if such a chattering nosie is a strange Irish way of speaking to the spirits. The fire is warm he says and he would like to listen to it sizzle, instead of me rattle, he says laughing. I clothe myself and sit by the fire. Chomper has his pipe out and he smokes and passes it to us. We do not question him for he seems very serious. He holds the pipe while we smoke and then puts it beside him. He stands and addresses us:

"I am not Chomper. That is a name for the white man's village and a white men's name. I am not Edvard De Champs. It is the name my father taught me to use with the white man. We leave all that behind. No one who knows me in this land knows that name except a few white men. It is a name that offers no protection. Like many white names it carries no power, no history and no honor the white man starts with a name not his own with his father's name and tries to make it powerful and trys to attach honor to the name or trys to live off the honor his father has made for his name. The white man wants to name everything, but he does not want to accept a name from the spirits. With my people the spirits choose our name based on how well we please or displease them. I have a spirit name that is only known to the spirits. I have a name that is known to my people and you are now part of my people so you will know my name. I am Eagle Hand for I have plucked the Eagles from the sky with my hand and I have done it without the Eagle pit. You call me Eagle Hand and honor me, and my spirit bird. You shall have names when the spirits touch you or ignore you, but until then I will call you by you white man names."

Eagle Hand sits. He is still painted and in his loin-cloth, his long hair touches the ground in back when he sits. I cannot speak, the fire pops and hisses.

"No offense, but I prefer to use Christian names—"

"You dishonor me by doing that and dishonor my people and includes the white men in our village who call me Eagle Hand. You want to call me by this Christian name to honor yerself. It is the name I earned. My Christian name has nothing to do with the spirit world and with the power that world has given me.. You may call me any name, but I will only answer to Eagle Hand."

Eagle Hand rose pulled his bedding out donned his wool trousers and tunic. He slides a long stick a few inches into the fire and puts his feet towards the fire and his head to the east and closes his eyes. Jack sits opposite me. He looks at me and rolls his eyes. I do not blink or respond. He then makes a disgusted grunt and pulls his blanket near the fire. I sit my log staring into the fire with my arms tucked under each other. My breath floats off into the still air. The night is lit with only stars and planets. The new moon is up there, but hidden by the earth. I tried to will Eagle Hand good dreams so that I could at last begin my journey to the Far West. I hear the who who whooo who who whooo of an owl to my right. Who indeed, I thought. Who am I? And what am I to become? I'm afraid I won't find out unless I get to the Far West.

"Git! Git!" Whispers the voice in my ear. I find myself on the deck of a ship. I jump up. I am sailing out to sea. New York is receding. I leap and the cold green sea rushes by me. I swim and swim under water for I feel the need to get as far as I can before I rise to fight the waves. I dive deeper and my ears hurt and my chest squeezes and I feel as if I have more air so I kick harder. I want to stay deep under the waves, but I need to get somewhere and can't remember where so I kick and kick and I look up though the green to the light and I know I can't stay so with a big kick I rise and my chest expands and I break the surface into the cold air looking at New York over the waves.

"Git! Git!"

A dark face looks down into mine. I am dripping wet. Has this talking face saved me?

Cold rain pelts my face. I am cold and I move towards the fire but it is out. The Preacher snores and mule answers him pawing the ground. I stand up and squish my leather hat on my wet head. I look over at Eagle Hand. Eagle Hand is packing the mule. I can tell nothing. I roll up my wet blankets. I can't tell if I'm shaking or shivering. I feel miserable from my dream and tears mix with rain as I kneel trying my blankets with rawhide. I look over at Eagle Hand as he leads the Creature over to us. He wears a light colored capote with a hood over his head. I pull out my India rubber cape from the pack and put my head through the opening and the water makes loud pelting noises shedding off my shoulders.

Eagle Hand come around from the other side of the mule and says in a very serious voice: "Take two rocks and smash them together next to the preachers head." Then he smiles from within the hood.

I leap in the air, spin around and grab two rocks and start smacking them like a fellow having a fit. Jack bolts upright and yells "Attack!" at the top of his lungs. Eagle Hand and I hold our stomachs as we bend over in laughter at the sight of Jack sitting bolt upright with wiry hair sticking out at all angles and his eyes as huge as the mules. The Creature makes a great heeing intake of air and snorts it out in a loose lipped flubbing noise which makes us laugh even harder.

"Time to go Jack the Preacher," Eagle Hand says and he leads the mule and turns out of camp.

I follow. There is only the squishing sounds of our feet and from behind the scambling, mumbling, sounds of Jack-come-lately.

To the Far West! This cold miserable rain cannot dampen my feelings. We are going west in the last western state of the United States and within days we will leave this state and enter the Far West or Indian Territory as some call it an uncivilized land as most white men call it. But to me it is not an un tis leaving one civilization to enter many others for I can't believe a land with so many different people could be defined as not-something. Columbus did not sail to seek a un or a not and I do not leave civilization to become les savage like the French say or turn savage like the American's say for I am not turning my back not rejecting for all those words imply extreme arrogance about what Europe and America thinks of itself that type of thinking reminds me of the superior attitude of the British how they go about with their nose in the air, as my Da says how they seem interested in you culture, but one soon finds our the interest in purely in finding divisions so that they can set one against the other. For that is how they conquer and rule. It seems than Britain and now America believe that going to church and making thousands of the same baubles and foforraws makes people civilized. As my uncle Bres says *If one man honors the sun and the other a bauble who is the noble...who is the savage?* I have never been able to find anything on this earth to surpass the awe I feel for the sun, the moon and especially the vastness of the stars at night. I am but a bauble under such a sight. So it seems to me that tis into a new world I go and tis a world that honors what I love and respect the most: Nature. So I leave baublization and enter the Far West.

I am entering a place where people have been part of nature for thousands of years, where nature nurtured man and murdered man. I am about to enter a land where tens of thousands of men know every hill and stream and I know not one. I am about to enter a land that has Gods and creatures that have not an English name yet fall off the tongues of men of the Far West in hundreds of different sounds. I am about to enter a land that holds millions upon millions of animals and yet one can walk for days without seeing one and then for days seeing millions. I am stepping at last into the Far West of North America. For me nature is a civilizing influence that brings out my humanity and love of fellow man and those who live close to nature live close to my heart.

The valley we move though is mostly cultivated and by early afternoon we reach the Missouri river opposite St. Charles. We cross the river in a flatboat and continue beyond the village where we halt. The rain has stopped. The area is dense with farmhouses so there is no place to loose our mule and we are forced to buy some corn and cornstalks for the Creature. We are able to get some corn-hoe or johnny cake to go with our deer meat. We spend the solstice next to a haystack and Jack makes it clear we won't celebrate any type of pagan ritual and I try to get him to understand it is nature the sun and seasons I want to honor but he will have none of it. And I wonder what is it about nature that so threatens so many Christian men. I am so tried from our journey that I give up and slept deeply on the shortest night of the year.

On December 22 we enter the eighteen-mile prairie east of Franklin. The countryside now has fewer and fewer homesteads and we can have a nice fire on the Franklin prairie that night for tis a cold night. After Franklin we cross the river again near Mount Vernon and enter Liberty. We leave Liberty and cross the Missouri again on Christmas Eve. We enter a limitless prairie with trees lining only the ravines of small streams. Every time we come to a stream the Creature refuses to cross unless we unload him. This because he slipped on some rock crossing a stream. Eagle Hand even tries to twist his nose, but the mule refuses to cross all but the shallowest of streams. This, of course, slows us down are all panting from having to load the packs across ourselves. It is difficult to cross especially in mud with a heavy pack on. More than once one us goes down onto our knees or hands. The days have been sunny and windy so we are able to dry quickly.

The day we enter the large prairie it begins to rain and then sleet. The wind picks up force and blows into our faces with a terrible stinging force. This all happens within a hour and we are on a level part of the prairie. Eagle Hand looks worried and shouts to us to hurry that a big storm is coming and that we will die if caught on the prairie. We head for a low line of trees more than a mile distant that we are able to spot in a lull of the sleet. We have just started to trot, and even the mule senses trouble as he leads us in a trot for the first time when large very wet flakes of snow fall melting as they hit our faces and the ground. It is such a relief from the stinging sleet that I let out a yell, which elicts puzzled looks form the other two. The wind continues to pick up speed to the point we are leaning forward into it. And within minutes the ground turns white. The treeline has disappeared from sight. In fear I fumble in my possible bag for my compass for I have heard of whalers wandering in tight circles upon the ice in blizzards when their ship is less then a mile sway and freezing to death. I take the reading where I have last seen the treeline. Northwest is my reading. We are now enveloped in whiteness and surrounded by the howling wind. When I next take my reading we are going northeast and I shout at Eagle Hand and shake my head and point to the left. He looks at me puzzled not knowing either what I am saying or how I know the correct direction. I show him my compass and he understands. I am now quite frightened as the wind is getting colder and colder and it is getting difficult to breath. The ground has a wet and sticky gray mud that clings to our feet making it feel as if we have on lead shoes. The mule is kicking his feet to keep them clear of mud and has more success than I do as the mud seems to be freezing to my leather. I keep taking reading and we keep having to correct and I hope that I made the first reading correct for I really wasn't sure I had seen the trees when I took it and to be walking in such weather with doubt seems a perilous thing to do.

A howling white world closed around us forcing Jack and I to grab a strap on each side of the mule packs as Eagle Hand led the mule for two steps back we would be lost in whiteness so thick is the air with snow. Walking and holding on I can only occasionally see Eagle Hand's heels or his hand appear of the mottled whiteness that closes us into this tight space on the prairie. My face is numb, my toes and fingers hurting. I stumble over a bush and nearly lose my grip of the mule my heart jumps as the wind is howling so loud my screams will never be heard if I fall. Never before have I felt such wind, such cold, but there is no doubt in my mind that if I let go the mule that I will end up a curled up frozen lump on the edge of the Far West. On we go leaning into the wind and I now have no faith in my compass reading, but have no other choice but to follow it, for to stop is to die. My body is shaking and my calves are stiffening and each step the howl of the wind…is less…are we going down? I nearly walk into a tree and I am so happy to find such an obstruction. Each step downward improves our sight until I can see nearly a rod in front. Eagle Hand stops us in a stand of trees and shouts for to get all the rope out which we do. He ties two pieces of rope to the trees and then ties them around my waist and Jack's. He tells us to fan out and pick up all the fallen wood we can and that he needs some long poles with forks on the ends at least twelve feet long if possible. He says that one of must stay tied to the tree near the mule and the other could ties off at the end of the other's rope if we run out of wood. He disappears into the white veil.

As we bring sticks and logs back by the mule he chews off some of the bark on the cottonwood branches thinking we are doing this all for a meal for him. He begins to bray as he wants the packs off. So I sideline him and take his packs off. He hops about testing the rawhide tied between his front and rear legs and looks at me like I had committed the original sin but his hunger soon overcomes his humiliation. Even though it is morning one cannot tell it is even day. It is not black like night but there is no direction to the dim light and it seems as if the snow itself glows with a light more like moonlight and certainly one can see much farther in moonlight than we can in this swirling snow. Eagle Hand appears out of the whiteness with a fallen tree upon his shoulder dragging it to our pile and then disappears again. For over a hour we gather wood and logs within reach and we now have a good sized pile. Eagle Hand comes back and selects a smooth twelve-foot log the size of a man's trunk at the bottom and motions for us to erect a similar branch with the Y in his log. We then erect a third branch the same way and begin to lean smaller branches around the tripod. Eagle Hand sees that we have the right idea and his dark outline steps back into the white void. He keeps reappearing with great rounds of bark from cottonwood trees piling them up next to us. I think it for the mule but the mule ignores this pile of thick bark.

The work has warmed me up a even though gust of wind come sweeping down the ravine they are nothing compared to the constant onslaught felt on the prairie those winds fought you for your breath making you feel that it is a Banshee that is constantly trying to steal your breath while it dulls your senses with cold and constant howling.

For several hours we trudge back and forth in the snow that came in wet in large flakes and then turns into smaller and smaller and harder and harder flakes until it is like a fine powder. The temperature kept getting colder and colder.

Eagle Hand comes back and kneels on the ground and directs me to get on his shoulders with my feet hanging over his chest. He lifts me up and then directs Jack to hand me the rounds and strips of bark. He has me place the bark around the upper parts of the shelter sometimes making me stand on his shoulders to reach the upper branches. We also put cedar tree branches outside Then he sets me down and directs me to lean branches together outside the entrance making a low entry to the opening of the shelter. He begins bringing wood inside the shelter and directing us from inside where to fill the gaps and spaces in our shelter.

Eagle Hand starts a fire inside while we tie ropes between the trees to make a corral for the mule. We tie a rope to his lead and around an iron ring on our corral rope. There is no feed for him outside the cottonwood branches. He seems content to eat from the pile of bark and branches that Eagle Hand has stripped for him.

It is now really turning dark. Going inside is amazing. It is warm and bright with the fire and there are logs to sit and the floor is covered with fragrant green cedar branches so it smells wonderful. I can hardly believe a storm rages outside except for the gusts that shake the top of our shelter and makes a low hollow whistle overhead.

"Yer have built your first war lodge. Not as big as the ones we build along the Missouri when we go west to take horses from our enemies or avenge a men's honor. We stay it these lodges when we go eagle hunting or scouting for buffalo. Some build a lodge like this in the river bottoms for a winter homes."

"You have different home in the winter?" I ask as he takes out a small amount of venison and props it against a teepee of sticks on the fire.

"Yes."

"But you told me your homes are covered with earth on top and all the walls are made out of great timbers. Would that not keep the people warm with a fire inside in the winter?"

Eagle hand took up the split and debarked limb of a tree with a yellow-orange center to it and began to peel off the white outer sapwood with his knife. "Did you not just fight with the wind for your breath?" He asks

"Yes"

"Only the river bottoms offer protection when the Cold One comes and blows his breath on us and only the river bottoms have wood for our fires, there are no trees on the prairie bluffs. You will not find our enemies the Sioux on the prairie either. They will be in the river bottoms. One cannot move far on the prairie in this weather. I had brought some willows in and I show you how to make snowfeet for I fear we will not be able to travel without them. Now the mule or even a horse become a burden for there is only feed around the streams and rivers and mule will not be able to walk as far as a man in this deep snow for a mule has smaller feet than a horse but it has feet that cling better to slippery land. We can hope for the sun to take away this snow, but when the Cold One is this fierce in his first visit the snow may stay. And we cannot stay here long."

"Why not? This seems a cozy place and quite fit after all our labor," Jack said brightly.

"We only have a few meals of meat left and this land no longer has buffalo or any large game for this is land that the white man hunts."

"Well if that's true how does the white man live? Jack asked.

"The white man brings his tame animals with him and so he cares not for wild animals. He eats whitehorn beeves and pigs and wheat grass."

"To be a shepherd is in the Bible and chasing buffalo in not," Jack says as he spears a chunk of sizzling deer meat.

"All white men who live in our village and all who visit, hunt and eat the buffalo."

"I don't guess they have any other choice do they?" Jack says, as he cracks his bone with the end of the knife against the rock. "My father helped bring some beeves to a Shawnee village for they were starving. It had a bull in the herd and he explained to them, how they need to keep a portion of the herd for the future. They killed off every last one, they said it was a feast or something and they were starving again within the month. Now that don't make a bit of sense to me."

"Your father gave this gift to the chief did he not?"

"Yes."

"The chief was obligated by his laws to distribute this gift to his people. It makes no sense to me why you father was not generous in his gift so that the chief would have beeves left to multiply."

"He gave them to him! Free!"

"And he would have had much more luck and power if he had been more generous."

"How much more generous can you get than free!"

"I don't believe I have ever understood this word free. We have not such word. The white man moves the Shawnee to land that the white man has hunted out until there are no buffalo, elk or deer. On such barren land a tribe with a choice would move to better hunting grounds. But the white man says they can't or they will make war. So the Shawnee stay, the white man brings some beeves and then stops bringing beeves. The Shawnees starve and the white man doesn't for he still has beeves. So free means giving one time poorly after killing all the food and blaming it on those who starve while the white man still has beeves. We share until there is nothing left to share. It would have been better for those men to die in battle with honor."

"Don't you see they starved because they wouldn't become shepards. They starved because they ate all the beeves."

"They were hungry. Why was the white man not generous? The Shawnee honored the white man's wishes in living on barren land and the white man was obligated to share his beeves form that day forward. One does not ever refuse food to the hungry on the prairie if one is a friend."

"The white man did not kill them. They did it themselves."

"The white man did not honor the Shawnee. I do not know the Shawnee, but I know that all men except some white man know that if one has food it is always shared. If your friend is starving you are starving, if I feast you feast. All know that but we do not know this word free. Eagle Hand stood up. Git your pointing device is why we are warm you have the eye of a crow. I have been caught on the prairie when the Cold One blankets it in snow and blinds us with wind and we had nothing but buffalo chips to lie on and our robes to protect us. I lost a great war-horse that way and did not think I would ever see Father Sun again. Preacher Jack does you God speak of snow in his Great Book?"

"No No I don't believe he does. Lots of fire and heat, but no snow."

"If he made this world why doesn't he speak of something that covers it for more than half the year?" Eagle hand says as he takes up a few stake-like branches. He pounds two stakes on one side of the bow he has carved down to the yellow-orange wood and ben bends first one end and stakes it and then the other.

"Guess he had more important things to talk about."

"We consider what a man doesn't say to be as important as what he does say. When a man is silent while other speak of their war deeds he speaks louder than those beating their chests. I fear your God does not understand our land."

"He knows all. It is not for us to question his word."

"Why does he not question us? Does he not want to know our ways?"

"He doesn't have to question he knows."

"I like spirits who speak. Today I heard the white man's bird the one that sqeaks like wood on stone. The big bird that flows where the white man settles. The Pawnees tell me when they see the bees and hear this bird then they know the white man is near."

"Turkey? You heard a Turkey?"

"Yes, that is the name. It sleeps. I mark the tree. We must be under the tree before the light shows if we are to eat."

"Eagle hand then took up another stave of wood and began carving that for a bow."

"The Osages make their bows with this wood. It does not grow in my country. They have shown my Pawnee friends this wood. This makes a strong bow even if one does not have sinew to back the bow it will not break. Our wood called green ash by the white man needs sinew to make it strong,

But I have sinew and I have put hooves in the pot and will make a glue to hold it on the bow. I will make one for you Git and show you how to shoot. Preacher Jack does not wish for a bow as he has his big two scatter gun."

Eagle Hand has both carved staves staked to the earth before we wrap ourselves in our blankets for the night before the warm fire.

Tis Christmas day today and into the dark morning we go. I check on the Creature and he is quite content sitting down in the snow and licking his front legs his back legs are covered with snow. He yawns and looks at me like it's too early to rise. Eagle Hands tracks of last night are a slight indentation in the foot deep snow.

I fill my rifle with shot and fresh power before leaving the warm lodge. The snow has a slight crust on it and we have to move slow and follow in the same footsteps along the floor of the ravine. The wind is down but is still puffs and rattles the dried oak leaves on the hills above us. We make our stalk behind the cover of some green cedar trees. We hear the squawk that sounds of fingernails on slate. And we freeze. Eagle Hand goes to the edge of the cedar and peers around. He motions us up while he kneels and takes aim. I move beside him and Jack is behind me. Fizz goes Eagle Hands scatter gun. The turkeys make an alarmed squawk and I fire at the dark shapes moving off the branches seeing two fall while several make a racket of alarmed squawks as they flyoff. Jack fires his barrels one, two and all the birds keep flying, but bark flies off the trunk of the tree above us. One turkey is still flopping in circles in the snow and the other is nowhere to be seen. How can I lose such a big bird? There are no tracks and we did not see it fly. I grab the flopping one by the neck and twist it sharply as I lift him and he continues to flutter for a short time before falling limp in my hand. Jack and Eagle Hand circle and then Eagle Hand points to a hole in the snow goes over to it and reaches in pulling out a dead hen.

The snow continued that day at first light the wind shifting to the south. We saved the wing and tail feathers for our arrow fletching and plucked the larger feathers. It was an easy pluck as the feathers came out easily. The plucked birds looked like Thanksgiving. We put hot rocks in the cavity and suspended the turkeys on our tripod above the hot coals to slowly cook we sewed the turkeys up with the hot rocks inside. We cut out the backbone to make the turkey's flatter to cook more evenly.

Jack proposed a Christmas service and blessing of our food and we heartily agreed. After explaining to Eagle Hand that this day honored the birth of our God as a man we settled by the fire as our clothes steamed and Jack began his service.

"The Lord has provided this abundant food to feed our depraved bodied and this warm fire to regenerate our souls and the howling cold outside to remind us of his need for our faith, for our love for our fidelity to him. He has honored all today Christian heathen and pagan alike for he offers free grace and salvation to all who repent their sins recognize the depravity with which we are all born and he wished us all to be born again in a pure state like the Chirst Child was on this day. Save us from our sins oh Lord and deliver us from all evil for only those who believe will be saved. Amen And she brought forth her first born son and wrapped him in swaddling clothes and laid hin in a manger; because there was no room for them in the inn. Luke Chapter 2 verse 7. Thus was born our God the Lord Jesus Christ. Now let us feast."

"What is a manger?"

"It's a trough form which the cattle, sheep and donkeys eat," I reply.

Eagle thought about this awhile before he replys: "Yer God was not born in the best lodge. He was born among your dog animals I will tell you that yer God being born with such animals is not a good story for my people to hear. You have other more powerful stories."

"Yes, I have more powerful stories."

"Good."

Jack began to sing Silent Night and other hymns while we ate our turkey and this seemed to please Eagle Hand.

The next day the wind blew less and so we moved to try to get nearer to the land that had game. We did not get far as the drifts are thigh high and much of snow is mid-calf and it is hard on top from the wind so we have to constantly break though the crust. We do not have furs on our hands or to line our shoes. We cut up the extra blanket and wrap pieces around our feet and hands. We spend the evening around a fire in a small lean-to sewing mittens and fashioning wool socks that hopefully won't keep balling up as we walk. I wish for the war lodge, as the lean-to doesn't keep the wind is from whipping around the corners.

The next day we struggle though the snow and tis difficult even thought the wind and snowfall stopped. Eagle Hand spots a rabbit in a hole in the side of a drift and instructs us to keep walking for if we stop the rabbit may flee. When we had gone past the hole he turned still walking raised his rifle and then he stopped he fired. I see nothing but smoke from his rifle. He walks to the hole and pulls the rabbit out. We continue on towards some distant trees.

The dark form of a small rough-hewn building with smoke coming out a stone chimney greets us as the day darkens to night. Jack rushes ahead, slipping several times in his haste waving his arms like vanes of a windmill his feet dancing like an invisible devil is nipping his ankles with a bullwhip. He is rewarded upon reaching his goal when a dark bearded man greets him at the door and Jack waved to us with a broad smile as he enters the house.

Eagle Hand leads the mule to a lean-to with a horse and hay waiting. I pull off my pack on the small porch and am about to turn and help Eagle Hand when the door opens and it startles me and my feet sail out and I land full-rump in the snow. A dark-haired women stands there smiling and looking at me. I am caught with my mouth open. She laughs and asks if I have a special fondness for snow.

"Come come," she cries in an excited voice using both hands to motion me in. "It is warm in here and a broth is cooking. Please join your friend we've not had visitors for weeks."

I feel guilty about not helping Eagle Hand, but know he will not be long in pulling the packs off the mule. I enter the damp warmness of the house. I am surprised to see another young women slighting older than the one who greeted me leaning over a pot hanging in the fireplace of glowing logs. The master of the house is seated with Jack at a plank table in the center of the room.

Ere ere! He cries as he rises. Come put the chill and snow behind you. Berbonna how dey broth doing. Welcome young feller. He stuck out a huge hand. Name's Trask and these here is my youguns: Berbonna and Hipzabah. Both women gave a slight quick bow and pull at the side of their dark wool dresses. Get yee over dere Berbonna won't bite now whare sa other fellar? Bed the mule? Ha! Ha! Berbonna Git that broth on de wood afor dese fellars—

The door swings open and Eagle Hand steps in surveying the room. Trask stops with mouth open when eagle hand shakes his hair out out of the rabbit fur hat and swings the wool blanket off his shoulders. There is a moment of silence and I make a move to talk, but Trask beats me to it.

Get the mule bedded? Har har! Well you're a friend of the parson here so set yourself to the side to dis wood and have a broth. Berbonna! Another bowl! Ever since my wife Nabby died of the fever the girls have had to fend for themselves. Berbonna taken to all the chores and Hipzabah is trying to follow her but she more the artiste see those samples on the wall dere all done by Hipzabah. Don't suppose it wouldn't look good in a parsonage, eh parson? I could have it sent back to the Missus Parson people goin by here all dey time. I expect that dere cross she stitched would be a fine one.

"There is no missus," Jack replies but before he can say more Trask jumps in.

"Hear that girls not a missus for the parson we could have us a nice congregation people could come from miles around Har har. But I wouldn't be able to give up my girls, har har."

Trask looks over at Eagle Hand who is still standing by the door.

"Lookit here Mr.? Don't believe I caught yer name?"

"Eagle Hand"

"Mr Hand gots us a hare Berbonna critter for stew on the morrow! Better dig out a few pertaters and turnips for the stew, Berbonna."

"Mr. Trask—"

"No! No! No mister out here name's Trask everybody on equal foot'n in America hell even the heathen Injuns got rights Jackson gonna pay them civilized tribes in that Georgia land dey found gold on. Gotta have rights to sign a treaty I say, otherwise dey just run em off, but not her dis is the land of equal foot'n the land of leveling. No sir don't even have to be Christian now you tell me whare else in the world dey treat heathens that way. I got's nothing again savages and heathen hell dey been that way for thousands of years, but I have to learn me a few things and I'll tell yer from here in dis breast dat dere can't be no minglin. No sir dere common Christian jest can't take no minglin with any heathens like mixn whale oil and whiskey it ain't gonna mix and its gonna stink har har. Get that sample down for the parson to look it Berbonna. Yes sir equal foot'n and we got no idear what dem heathern be doing outta our sight. Could be hav'n anunther Gomorrah. See that fine work. Hipzabah got's an eye she does. Sure am glad yere keeping an eye on them parson teach'n im some morals. Man ain't a man without morals to guide 'im. They could be doin that Sodomite thing. Dat's why it don't mix cause it jest ain't natural and it ain't natures way. Equal foot's a fine idear but heathen and civilize man don't' mix any more natural than whiskey and whale oil. Suppose since yer doing the work of civilization I let yer have it for only a quarter of a dollar?"

"That's right kind offer, Trask and this is one pretty piece of work I'm not sure I seen the likes of it in all of New York."

"New York!" Hipabah leaps off the plank at the word. "You been to New York!"

"Yes 'em I lived there."

"Do ya hear 'im Daddy! He lived there! Oh do tell us all! What were the ladies wearing and what news do you have?" Hipzabah beamed as she sat close beside Jack and implored him with her brown eyes and her hand on his forearm.

Jack swelled as he told of the glittering carriages and the large brick homes, the formal gardens the restaurants and even the theater, which surprised me as most preacher's considered the theater a corrupting and vile place. Eagle hand sat in front of the fire mending a set of moccasins and making rabbit fur toe socks for us.

My head started nodding to the droning of Jack's voice and I saw Eagle Hand sitting before the fire with his head on his chest. Trask's booming voice caused me to jump.

"There there nuff 'citment girls Fellars just spread your blankets afore the fire. If I had any we could sit and liquorize, but I ain't that's that. Ladies abed we go Night t'all."

We gave our good nights as they all went to the back of the house where two beds were built one in the corner and other a few feet away on poles going to the ceiling. They pulled a calico sewed to a horse hair twine across their bedroom. I reveled in the warm fire and dry wood floor under me and felt I wanted to sleep for days.

Har! Har! Up with you all! Har! Har! Trask stood in his woolen underwear his big jovial face looking down at me. Come men out with ya time to yellow the snow Har! Har! Out with ya time to let the ladies ride their pots, Har! Har!

We shuffle out to the gray dawn stand in line facing the crack of yellow light opening under a line of clouds. My steaming revelty interrupted by Eagle Hand's voice.

"You cut like the Jews."

"By Jove your right Injun the preachers got the noodle of a Jew. Look's like Moses got to him. Har! Har! Doesn't look like you had much to cut off. Har! Har! Maybe you could borrow some form the savage he's got plenty to spare. Har! Har! The Lord giveth and taketh you preachers aren't into doing much root'n and rogering anyhows so thar's the wisdom of the Lord's allocatin of de flesh. May be that why you preachers' is alwsy haranguing agin da sins of dah flesh yous the fellows without the flesh. Har! Har! Well da Injun and the Irish make up for it, Har! Har! But don't be getting no idears on my young uns. Har! Har! Let's git warmed up with the wood cutting we'll earn our breakfast."

We split and cut wood and then had rabbit stew with turnips taters and a bit of salt pork, which helped flavor it as there was not any other spice in it. Hipzabah was at Jack's side plying with questions during our meal and seemed sad to see him go looking at him wistfully. The day had cleared, and so we set out following a ridgetop blown clear of snow.

We load the Creature and he is miffed at not being included in the group last night. He thinks he can go in houses and see no reason not to go where we go. Of course he won't move when we want to leave and I decide to leave him and we all walk off. He stands watching us until we get to a hill and disappear over it and he trots up to the hill to keep us in sight and this continues until I tell him I have a treat and he trots up to get the carrot gobbles it and sniffs me all over to make sure I don't have more then satisfied that I made amends he joins our group like a normal mule.

We travel several hours, but Eagle Hand is nervous traveling on the exposed hilltops where there are no trees so it is a tense journey, a journey filled with the huff of our breaths the crunch of leather on snow and the slipping sound of our feet on the hillside. Several times we halt as Eagle Hand raises his hand in silence his stilled footsteps awaking us from our reveries and worries. He would very slowly walk up the hill sometimes crouching and pausing for many minutes to survey the countryside before he would let us be skylighted. Much of the time we traveled several feet down on one side of the hill with Eagle Hand up front slightly higher so he can just see over the top to the countyside yet untraveled. Our heading is Northwest so the left leg in tiring from always being on the downhill side and our feet keep slipping in the snow making the distance seem three times what it is.

We are forced to descend a hillside to cross a frozen stream and are nearly at the bottom when over the top of of opposite hill a donzen horse come charging mounted by men uttering unearthly pitched screams. Eagle Hand is ten paces in front of me Jack is right behind me leading the mule. The mule screeched reared twisted and turned and left Jack flat on his back with Jack's fowling piece secure in the pack on the mule. Eagle Hand leaps back towards where there is a small mound. He screams *down!* We had talked of such a situation before and he told us we must try to hold onto the mule for that is what most men take and sometimes the only protection in laying the mule in front of us as a fort. I dive behind the mound and imitate Eagle Hand I lay my rifle on the mound. Eagle Hand grasps my ankle pulls on it and shouts *Do not shoot unless I do.*

I feel utterly exposed as the mounted men are above the hump. I try so desperately to flatten myself. They are perhaps one hundred yards away although they feel nearly atop us with their screams and thundering horses. All the stories I had heard of my ancestors making their sceaming naked charges downhill with swords raised could not prepare me for this sight of a mere dozen men ahorse with rifles and bows raised high. I put powder in the pans of of rifle and pistols. We have six shots if all ignite and that leaves us with six men ahorse if we are steady enough to shoot true. That is our brief advantage we can be steady in each shot while they have to fire from a moving mount. I lay my pistols on the mound in front of me with barrels pointed towards them and I cock all my flints. Without taking my eyes off of them I slip the loop holding my shillelagh from over my neck and drop it over my right arm as I put my club beside me. I check my skain at my waist and then put rifle to shoulder, but I didn't sight as they are still out nearly fifty yards I watch them come. I felt this might be my last sight of earth I feel a sad pity for myself that I would not see all the wonders of this land nor feel what it was like to be a full-grown man and my fear of pain and of humiliation and most of all my fear was dying helpless in the grip of fear. I wanted to die brave and without pain and I did not want a horrible wound. I did not want to see an arrow sticking out of my body. I did not want to see my body jerk and jump when a ball ripped into it. I see only the men coming at me painted faces that would be curious if they weren't trying to kill me, mouths open emitting horrid high pitched screams their bodies are strangely steady on the churning horseflesh and flying clods of snow and grass. A man with a red painted face with a strip of bright red hair standing straight up in the center of his otherwise shaven skull with a white tipped feather bouncing from it, he is leading. He has white marks like hands on the chest of his horse. I think about those hands pressing into the pulverised rock paint, maybe this very morning those perfect little prints from hands now holding a shield, bow and arrows his mouth in a full scream though two arrows his white teeth hold. I see the hand marks as I raise my rifle to to sight the man. He sees my move and lowers himself behind the horse and the horse neck. Fear shoots though me knowing he is watching me. I cannot watch all of them, but with us two bunched together we are easy prey for them. My stomach sinks I no longer see six dead men scattered on the ground. I'm taunt as a drumskin waiting for Eagle Hand to shoot. I fear they will be upon us and I will have one shot. They split left and right and with yipping calls they all ride hidden now behind the horses. Though my fear I feel confusion. Now I have a dozen shins, feet and ankles to send my carefully husbanded balls to.

Eagle Hand leaps up and raises his rifle above his head while he yells. I do not understand. One of the riders rights himself and raises his lance and yells out words over the yees and yips of the rest of the riders. He turns his horse and charges straight at Eagle Hand holding his rifle. Eagle Hand returns the high-pitched war like yips. The rider rides nearly atop Eagle Hand before the horse without any hand or reins turns away at the last moment.

The horse stops prancing in place the rider lifts his leg over, slides down the horse's side, landing softly on the ground planting his lance at his feet shifting the rifle to his left hand and extending his right with a broad smile on his painted face.

I feel a nudge on my shoulder and tis the Creature who has figured out there is no danger so he is returning and insists I scratch his ears and I feel too nervous to do so, but he insists and soon I am calmed by his presence and by scratching him.

CHAPTER VIII

SKIDI PAWNEES OF THE LOUP RIVER

Git O'Toole Journal

29 December 1831, Thursday

I feel embarrassed. When the Pawnee warrior leaped off his horse I realized we were not being attacked. Later eagle Hand told me that it is traditional to charge as if attacking when coming towards friends. My body did not know that and my mind took some time to know that even Eagle Hand did not seem to know it at first. I was shaking so much that I was afraid to hold my rifle in front of me so I clasp it under my arm and against my body. I was so thankful that Eagle Hand was greeting his Pawnee friend that he did not notice me and to be sure I moved between the Pawnee horse and Eagle Hand. The others ran several circles around us yipping shrilling and screaming and some fired their rifles in the air. My legs were shaking and so I sat down and I felt I was being disrespectful so I stood on shivering legs. I hoped they were too engaged to notice, that they thought I was shivering from the cold. I hope anything, but that they would not know the truth of my fear.

I felt even more shame when Eagle Hand told me how brave I had acted. I never felt brave I only felt I was doing all I could think to do at the time even though there seemed to be no thought to my actions. I felt consoled that I did nothing foolish and so I took that as a compliment from Eagle Hand I was sure he knew how frightened I felt and he was only trying to make me feel better. At least I wasn't flat on my back like Jack but then he really had nothing to fight with.

I soon lost my fear to curiosity for the warrior had faces of red, white, black and green in the manner of a fierce mask. I had heard stories of my ancestors painting their naked bodies green before charging into battle screaming like banshees, but this is the first time I have seen men painted for war. Their heads were shaved except a swath of red errect hair down the middle of the top of the head and down the back about three fingers wide. They were adorned with necklaces of shells, bones claws and metals and had similar smaller objects in their ears. Most had a buffalo robe around their trunks secured with a belt around the waist. And fringed buckskin leggin's with moccasins that had long tails of fur streaming out from the heels in the wind as the warriors rode in circles around us. Most had no saddle other than a blanket strapped to the horse and braided hair rope for rein that was wrapped through and under the jaw of the shaggy long tailed horses they rode. A few had a full high saddle that I had see some of the Santa Fe traders use in St. Louis. With foot high pommels in front and back. The horses has bigger heads and smaller bodies than most American horses I had seen and they were painted with all matter of symbols some of which I recognize like lighting bolts and stars and others I have not seen before. The horse ranged in color form dirty white to dark brown. With some being spotted.

Eagle Hand Journal

31 December, 1831 Saturday

It has been too long since I felt the warmth of that lodge too long since I have felt the welcome of a woman beckoning me to sit near the fire. Too long since my hands were warmed with a ash bowl filled with steaming chunks of buffalo and kernels of corn and too long since I have lifted such a bowl to my nose. The moons since I have been beside a fire of men who understand me the moons since I have been offered a pipe to smoke have not been long, but the distance stretches from this frozen earth to the clouds of the spirits. That is what my journey to the white man's world feels **like.(add like)** *It has been too long*

I am with the Pawnee people who are on the warpath against the Kansas. These people are my friends. These people are related to our neighbors the Arikaras. It is the Wolf band of the four Pawnee bands, the traders call this band the Skidi, but I don't know what that name signals. These are a great and powerful people, but they have been made smaller by the white man's disease over the past two generations as have the Otoes, the Omahas the Wichitas and the Missouris. These people live in lodges like mine and grow maize like mine…it makes me pine for my lodge. These are a people who are great and fearless warriors who every year are fewer and fewer and every year face new enemies such as the Delawares and other tribes that the white man has brought to the old Osage hunting grounds and now even the Dakota fight them for they see the Pawnees getting weak. I have been told that the Pawnees are a people who have driven the Apache from their hunting ground near the black hills. A people who roam the hunting grounds from the Niobrara down the Red river who leave their villages on foot and cross into Mexican and Comanche lands and come back riding horses these are a brave people.

My people once had many times the village we now have and we too lost many to the disease of the white man. The pox the cow disease. I know this now but my fathers did not know it. I do not know if it is the spirit of the white man that created this evil disease or the spirit of the beeves that live with the white man. Perhaps the beeves spirit is angry with the white man for putting it in fences. But why does the disease attack my people and we have no beeves. Many white men do not die, but many in the tribes do. The buffalo will kill a few of us every year as they fight us, but never have they or the buffalo spirit killed off entire villages never has any animal had such power. I do not understand why the white man fears the buffalo but not the beeves that kill thousand times what the buffalo does.

I am afraid of the white man's medicine and I'm afraid our medicine is not strong against this cow-pox spirit. I have dreamt about this, but I cannot write is here until I fast and sweat and find the meaning of my dream, but I am troubled and my breast feels heavy.

THE PAWNEES ARE TAKING US back to their lodges several days distant at the Wolf or Loup River, which empties into the Platte. We travel quickly as they have extra horses and so we all ride. I have not ridden bareback for many years and found my inner thigh muscles barely adequate to keeping me mounted. Jack seems to lie on the horse and grasp its neck and ride more with his belly than with his legs, but he did not complain, as he seemed happy to finally reach a tribe. The weather agreed with us and we had no more snow and little wind and the land was flat in between the numerous creeks and the ground frozen with snow only a hand deep so our horses made good speed, likely better than if the weather was warmer as much of the soil seems full of clay. Even with the weight of the snow some of the dried grass in the valleys brushes my dangling feet so I imagine that it would be even taller and thicker when green and lush. Much of the grass has thin dried vines criss-crossing it, which I am told is a type of wild pea. We crossed numerous creeks and many were either froze or very shallow so that even the mule would cross with little coaxing and I believe the mule moved better in a large body of horses. I found the horse kept me warm with my head and face the most likely to be cold. I had never experienced such cold in Ireland and Eagle Hand tells me it will get much colder as the winter wears on. Clearly I need better clothing if I am to survive and I envy the warriors their buffalo robes

I am disappointed that we have seen no buffalo, but they are further west and south according to the warriors. We see some deer and elk, but we are moving quickly and quietly and the warriors have dried meat and cornballs. I ride with Jack to the rear of the party and Eagle Hand rides towards the front, but he does not go out with the scouts who start before us and ride the country on each side of us and forward of us. Eagle Hand tells me that the Omahas say the name Pawnee means red feather crest and they are so named because they dye their hair red. I found they also add dyed deer or animal hair to the crest on their heads. It looks very impressive and I observed that they spend time keeping their hair and paint arranged by using mirrors, tweezers and their knives.

We are up before the sun rises each day and the first two days we have no fire as they believe there are enemy war parties about. So it is cold getting out of my blankets in the morning. Two of the Pawnees are only a few years older than I and they have the camp duties of the taking care of the horses and any needs that the leaders have. They have not struck blood yet and are being tested in how well they meet the needs of the warriors. On the third day the Pawnees deem it safe enough for fires and they make one but it is much smaller fire than any I had yet seen and they made it near a steep wall of clay in a ravine but it warms us all better than a big fire as the heat bounces off the clay wall. That night they all become more easy and joke and talk much more and stay up late into the evening telling stories.

Some of the talk around the fire is in the Pawnee tongue and I find it difficult to tiring to try to follow. After some time I need to move away from the fire and so I walk the ravine. The land above me tugs at me so over the top I go. I feel weary, but it is not of my body I am still seeing the movements of hand and hearing the strange rhythm of the Pawnee tongue. The moon is nearly full with an uneven ring surrounding it. The light has a bluish unearthly glow that cast grayish soft shadows onto the white snow making it look like it glows. The snow has a crust on it that makes loud crunching noises as my feet break through to coarse powdery snow underneath. When I stop I feel I am in the eerie soft scene where silence reaches out and grasps me in her soft handle. Tis a night with no wind, no birds, no rattling leaves…no sound. Even my breath becomes a distraction in this soundless world so I hold it. As I hold my breath my heart thumps and the silence roars about me. I find it difficult to describe a total silence of a snow-covered prairie for it is more silent than the words you read on this page. It is a blank white page that you must stare at in a state between almost sleep and almost awareness but even then you will not hear the roar of a silent snowy prairie night in the Far West. It is so queer that it feels me with fear. The sight of my exhalation feels like redemption, like a return to life, but I find myself curious about the silence and stop my breath again and again. All I can say is that if you cover your ears you will hear a rumbling silence generated from the engine of your body…the silence of the prairie is both more silent and much louder.

Exhaling and bending over I see the heavy seeds heads of the grass bent over at my feet they have made weeping furrows in the snow crust in an east west line. Looking at the row of lines it looks like our early Celtic alphabet as if the grasses are writing a message to the gods and birds. Our ancient alphabet the ogham is based on trees scratched onto twenty different tree shapes a primitive alphabet. Strange that I find this land of few trees scratched onto the prairie snow by the prairie grasses. Crouching to examine the message of the winds I sense a presence: a slight chill waves down my body as all my senses become alert. I let my body go as Eagle Hand has taught me he keeps telling me I am trying to see everything with my eyes and head and not allowing the body to see. If one allows yourself to see you will respond without knowing.

I find myself turning to my left focusing on a rocky hill that appears to be fifty yards distant. First I see puffs of breath and then a slight movement I make out the silhouette of a head with pointed ears. I have seen some of the scouts wear a headdress made to look like a wolf head and is my first thought. This person is clearly looking at me. I have my rifle with me as Eagle Hand told that I must have it with me at all times in case of a attack and to keep it from being taken. I do not want to pull the hammer back as it seems the click will carry across the silence of the prairie and alert the watcher. I fear there could be more watchers behind me. I fear they would fire on me if they heard me cocking the rifle or taking aim. I turn my head to scan the horizon but find nothing and have difficulty finding the watcher again up in the jagged rocks. He has not moved and seems intent on me. I move my head around as if I am looking around but keep my eyes on him. I finally realize the slight movement I am seeing is his ears. It is a wolf not an enemy scout! From his rocky perch he is able to watch our camp. I eye him at he watches me with only his right ear turning toward camp and then turns forward towards me. Without the bright moon and the light hair edging his ears I would not have seem that. He is waiting for us to move on and leave him our scraps he is the cleaner of camps patiently waiting to do his job. Out here he is honored by the tribes and rarely killed for they identity with the wolves and use some of his tactics in their hunts. Out East I heard terrible stories of how wolves eat small children and are a vicious evil force. When I told Eagle Hand some of the stories he laughed at me and told me how wolves never attack men until they have a sickness. As I move back towards camp the wolf watches me. Approaching camp I can hear the gravely crunching sounds of the horses pawing the crusted snow to get at the grass underneath. Do they know a wolf watches them? From out of the herd of horses I hear this half-baked whinney ending in a ah aw sound and I know it is the Creature ever alert to my smell and movements.

I return to the fire. Hands move rapidly, heads nod, feeling dance across the fire flickered faces, punctuated with words of affirmation, sounds of glee , sounds of surprise, querous and quibbling sounds punctuated with pantomimes of bravery and tomfoolery. All round the fire the men seem to sign at once my eyes cannot focus, not in time to follow what the hands are speaking. I do not feel I should ask Eagle Hand to interpret for me, although he does occasionally lean over to tell me some funny mot someone said or explain the general gist of the story being told. Their hand movements are very expressive and I do seem to understand some of what they are saying, but I do not know the context of their stories nor do I understand anything about their culture so I concentrate on understanding certain phrases and themes to their stories and hope that I can get Eagle Hand to explain some of it to me when we reach their village and we have more time.

I did pick up a few more signs watching these men. I find the sign for anger curious: it is a fist to the forehead pulled out and twisted and means mind twisted. Soldier is closed fists held together in front of your breast and then violently separating. And think is holding your right index finger against your heart then moving your hand straight out palm down about a foot. I like the idea of a people who think with their hearts and anger with their minds.

Jack seemed to understand more than I do and I am mystified as to how he can do so and I am jealous that he seems to be able to enter into some conversations with them while I can only answer and make simple requests and questions.

We are being led by a man called The Medicine Horse and his chief scout is The Bird That Goes to War. They talk a bit more than the others and order the young men to fetch things like firewood and water, but seem more like equals with the other warriors. There seems to be no clear line of command and subservience like I have observed with soldiers. The young warriors act as it eager to prove themselves rather than being fearful of retribution in serving the elders.

The Pawnees all sleep with feet towards the fire except a few young men who opt to sleep out on the prairie and they sleep in twos or threes under a single buffalo robe.

Tonight I trade two fire steels, two awls, two knife blanks, a mirror, a tweezer several tobacco knots, vermilion and a handful of fancy brads for a buffalo robe. Wrapping it around my body with my two wool blankets brings me to the warmest and coziest feeling yet in this new land what a wonderful trade! My mind dims to sleep with the hiss of logs and the last sight I remember is the diamond colored twinkle of Jupiter rising in the east.

The crackle of cottonwood and willow branches fueling a stew of dried buffalo meat and corn balls wakes me. Tis full light . Two of scouts are just returning they bring the smell of the cold prairie air with them to mingle with our smokey sleep saturated bodies huddled round the fire. One of the scouts talks with his hand to us: he says that he rode, he says this by holding his left hand in a vertical knife position while mounting is with his right hand , index and middle finter over his left hand like a man astride a horse, his hand rode to the northwest and he makes the sign for ascend by holding his left fist up and pointing to his fist with his right index finger He then makes the sign for bear. He is excited and wants to return with others and tired to coax us, but Medicine Horse and the others around the fire make it clear that he can return, but they are pushing on to their village. We side with Medicine Horse I think the warrior didn't want to pursure the bear most likely a white bear or Grizzly on his own as he is poor in trade goods not owning a rifle like Medicine Horse and several others.

Today the pace is more relaxed and everyone takes much more care in preparing their paint and arranging their clothes. Eagle Hand tells me we will reach the village that afternoon. He also tells me that the horses we are riding have been taken from the Kansas. I ask if they fought the Kansas and he tells me they found them all sleeping even the guards. They had watched them dance most of the night over a scalp it was not a Pawnee scalp. Bird That Goes to War crept into the camp and untied all the best horses leading several out of the lodges and the rest of the horse grazing outside were gathered quietly and led away Bird That Goes to War will keep the horses he took and rest will be given away by Medicine Horse as it was his vision that brought this war party about. He dreamt of the horses and that no warriors would be killed on, either side and it has come to pass and it is proof that his medicine is strong. There will be a great celebration tonight when we return to the village.

The mood is high as we travel even the horses can sense it prancing and holding their heads high prancing to the side and willingly giving out more energy than needed to travel our path. Several hours later we come across an increasing number of tracks and the leaders pause on the ridge ahead. I ride up and see smoke rising out the ground on a bluff along a tree-lined river. Then I make out a palisade along one side and see that it is earthen mounds that the smoke comes from. More and more forms move between the mound and some come out to the palisade. We are at least a mile away and I assume the warriors will do their swift charge but instead they arrange themselves like ladies meeting a beau and spread out in a long line along the ridge and pause a long line of very long horse tails swishing in anticipation. One warrior rides his horse back and forth and makes his horse rear. I see increased movement in the village below and soon horses and riders are charging out of the village and racing across the hills towards us. Appearing and disappearing into the ravines their yipping and whistling sound rising and fading with the line of the land. Sooner than I expected they are charging at us with lances raised and again I feel anxious even thought I know their intent. Some turn aside and others ride through and they have infected us and our horses with their spirits and we prance down the hillsides horses barely contained while they ride around us and race back and forth in front of us. The women, children and elderly are lined up near the palisade entrance and we ride between them as they cheer and touch our legs and our horses. Several people hold up both index fingers with thumbs clasped to the remaining curled finger and keep crossing their index fingers. When one holds up a beaver pelt I figure that he wants to trade with me. I wave and shake their offered hands all the way into the center of the village. Everyone is excited and talking and yipping all at once and running besides us.

The captured horses are first presented to several families and to older women and then led to a pasture by the river. We slide off our horses and they are taken by boys younger than I. All is chaos and embracing and racing about. Medicine Horse leads us to his lodge as he grasps hands and arms in greeting. Eagle Hand explained to me that it is an honor for Medicine Horse to house and feed us as they brings him esteem in the eyes of the others.

The sides of the lodges are made with cottonwood logs packed with dirt the roofs are well beaten dirt. The lodge entrance has more that a dozen logs the roundness of the trunk of a just weaned child There is a screen of wrist thick willow branches at the end of the entry serveral feet inside the lodge and we move to the right around the screen into a large round room with light coming thought a hole in the center of the roof which rises more than nine feet above us. A fire pit lined with stone is below the hole with another willow screen behind the fire pit in back. Near the walls are beds raised on pole about a foot above the ground and covered with robes and several storage benches built similar to the beds. There are four poles in the center supporting the round peak of the roof and many utensiles and weapons hung from these supporting poles. The place has a steamy warmth suffused with the smells of horse, cooking meat and dried green things

Medicine Horse's women it seems he has three wives rush ahead of him into the lodge after embracing and greeting him. They are fussing and patting the smooth skin on right side of the fire directing us to it. There is an iron pot hanging down from a stout branch between two upright branches on each side of the fire.

Medicine Horse takes his place at the back of the fire on a cane chair with no legs the bottom resting on a smooth polished earth the back braced with two sticks extending back to notches that allowed adjustment of the chair back.

Medicine Horse is one of several types of chiefs in village he being the war chief. Many of the other chiefs and warriors are still on the winter buffalo hunt. Getting the thick warm hides used as robes and and winter bedding and even more importantly as trade items for rifles, powder and balls need for defense of their people against the many other tribes who raid and plunder them.

That night around the fire I ask serveral questions about the history of the Pawnees and Medicine Horse tells me his people are called the Skidi and that he would now tell me how they come by that name. When he speaks all are silent even the children and the women working behind us. Eagle Hand translates for me:

Medicine Horse says that first I must understand what has happened to all the Pawnees and their hunting grounds. He says that long ago the Pawnees were more than fifty villages and some of the tribe had split off and moved north settling on the Missouri North of the Niobrara at several places along the river. These people are called the Arikaras or Rees or Starrahe and that they had over a thousand lodges and four thousand warriors before the first white man's disease hit them over three generations ago These cousin's to the north did more farming than hunting but have lately returned to the hunt since they cannot defend their fields against the Sioux raids like they used to. Only since so many Arikara villages died has the Sioux been able to move onto the Missouri nor did they dare venture in Pawnee lands. All of the Missouri was lined with lodges like the Pawnee lodges and all farmed and hunted buffalo like the Pawnee and some were friends and some enemies. At that time no Delaware Cherokee Choctow or even Sioux roamed our hunting lands when Red Hair came up the Missouri the Sioux had been but a generation on the Missouri. If you travel up the Big Muddy he told me you will see it lined with the lodges of dead villages and now the tribes that live in skin lodges live where so many have died of the white man's disease.

Medicine Horse thinks it was around our year of 1760 that the first pox hit and worst time was around 1790 when it reduced the Rees to only three villages and less than three hundred lodges. This disease hit their own village and had similar results. Since then the disease has hit each generation. His people and relations once controlled all the hunting land from the Big Bend down past the Arkansas River. There are still three more Pawnee tribes living south of him now plus his cousins called the Wichitas or Pawnee Picts by the white man, but everyone and every tribe has suffered every generation since 1760 and now they are barely able to hold even their own villages against other tribes that the white man has pushed out of the land of the East. Medicine Horse's great grandfather fought the Padoucas or Prairie Apaches and had never see a Sioux. It is said that it was raids the on the Padoucas where the Pawnees first captured horses. The Spanish would not trade guns with the Prairie Apaches, but the Pawnees traded the French for guns and with those guns the Pawnees pushed the Apaches west and took the Apache horses. The Apaches had lived from up by the Big Bend to way past the Salt springs out to the Black Hills. The Comanches and Utes came out the Rocky Mountains and the pushed the Apaches south. Now the Pawnees are being pushed west and south and all their friends are too. With the French guns we ruled this land and when the French lost to the English the disease came and now we are brave but our number are like two fingers out of ten, the chief told Eagle Hand. He said that he has much harder time getting rifles and powder for there are only some English rifles coming out of the north and a few American rifles from the trappers. They miss the French sorely.

Medicine Horse says that his people had the most powerful medicine of all the peoples of the plains, but that many of the white men feared their medicine and kept trying to trade with some of the chiefs to get them to stop using such medicine and use the white man's medicine. He said it was Black Robes and Seizers who most feared their medicine. Some of his people were afraid of giving up their ways as they thought it would destroy them but others thought the white man's medicine was more powerful. It was not like the day of his childhood when all knew and feared and honored only the Pawnee holy men.

Medicine Horse says he will now tell the story of how his tribe came to be called by their name. "He said that many winter ago in a winter not unlike this one his ancient grandfathers who were then young and supple and living in this world had set up a winter village on a river which was further north that any had lived before. It was colder and there was more snow than they had seen before and they were beginning to think they had made mistake moving so far north in search of food. They were discussing this very subject in council when scouts reported buffalo moving towards them from the north. They rejoiced and waited for buffalo to cross the river and they killed many and fires were happy and the juice from the loins of the buffalo hanging in every lodge and the people wrapped themselves in the warm winter robes and their skin shined with the fat of the buffalo and all worked at skinning and drying until every cache in every lodge was full and still the buffalo come and so we took only the skins for trade so that we could be strong against our enemies and we spoke of how many French guns we would obtain and still the Buffalo come and still we kept taking the skins."

"Soon in the moon of the early thaw the frozen river was covered like a village with the shapes of the skinned buffalo the wolves stood in the pools of melting ice water feeding off the meat we could not eat. They fed day and night and every day more wolves came. The nights were filled with the sounds of our warrior's and women dancing in thanks and if one stopped outside the sound of our drums the night was filled with the joyous howls of the little and big wolves."

"Then one day a hunting party from a brother tribe arrived. They were thin and lean like the little wolves of the prairie, They told us they had found no buffalo all winter and that their village was starving and they looked in awe at the meat we had for they had never seen so much meat. They asked how it could be and they were taken down the river and they saw as far as their eyes would of the naked buffalo and the wolves standing in pools of water upon the ice beside them. The wolves were so full they could not run so they just turned to watch us. Our brothers were given all the dried meat they could carry and they returned to their village an told others of us and of our medicine that brought us buffalo while they starved and they called us the people were the wolves stand in pools of water Skidi rah ru. We have been by this water every since and we are called the Skidi Pawnees."

The talk and smoking by the fire went on very late and I found my head upon my chest as the voices moved in a circle around me One of the wives led me to a bed along the wall behind some robes. I laid down on the stretched skin and pulled the heavy shaggy robe over me and I have never felt so tired and so comfortable. I entered another world just as fantastic as the world going on around me only in this new world I could not smell the smoke of wood and tobacco.

I woke once at the end of night but before the glow of morning. Medicine Horse is chasing one of his wives around the center of the lodge and she is laughing. I woke again to the sound of Medicine Horse's rasping breath and his wife's breathy exhalations. I could not see them they seemed to be ghosts hovering among the heavy cottonwood logs above me.

The next morning I am up by the time several young men about my age are leading the best horses out of the village to graze. These horses are kept in the lodges at night or tied up outside the lodge to keep them secure from nighttime raids. Some of these boys are bringing in firewood, not quartered logs like the settlers back east, but stacks of dead limbs for they do not even carry a hatchet. Some of the village is waking and some lodges seemed dead to the world with hardly a puff of smoke rising out the lodge hole. I walk though the village meeting mostly young men like myself, and women. Most seem to hurrying to some task. The unshod feet of horses make a muffled thurping sound against the hard packed frozen earth of the village floor and the soft leather shod feet of the men and women at their tasks raises an occasional puff of fluffy snow without a sound. The voices of greeting fill the air mingled with the distant caws of crows and the snuffling of horses punctured with dogs barking. The shrill clang of things metal and the seams of wood wheels protesting is not in this morning air. Not even the jingle of halters as most in use are rope from twisted hair. Some people look at me with curiosity but all who pass me greet me with words and smile. I pass one lodge where a beautiful young women walks out of the lodge naked and glistening with steam rising off her smooth brown skin. She carries a clay bowl with both hands. Her eyes widen at the sight of me. She stops as if offering the bowl in her upturned hands averting her eyes from mine, but she makes not a move to cover herself. Her blue-black hair falls loosely about her shoulders and nowhere else on her body does she have hair yet her breasts would more than fill my hands. I turn away in embarrassment, although a part of me wants to stop and take her bowl and wash her feet so compelling is her beauty and image. She looks the sight of a saint like an aura as she stood so confidant, so connected, no so natural yet she was naked without shivering in the cold winter air. She looked at me with the same calm curiosity as the young men I had just passed before she caught herself and averted her eyes that being the custom of both men and women of this tribe to look to the side of you when talking or down but never directly in the eyes. I know not what my face told her. I do not really know what it is the be a man at that moment in my life, but that moment gave me a picture of creation and I have always thought of that woman as Eve of the Far West. I saw the vision of her every night in that Pawnee village and many nights to follow in every corner of the Far West.

Eagle Hand approached me while I am wandering taking in all the sights.

"Irish, Medicine Horse has asked me to trade you to him."

I look at him puzzled. "Well I know many of my countrymen and women have been sold in America and the West Indies as indentured servants for hundreds of years, but I never heard of us being sold in the Far West."

"No servant, he wants you to be part of his lodge. Do you not see the young men bringing in horses and firewood? Eagle Hand asked me."

"Yes, but it seemed their duty."

"That it is, but they are owned by the men they serve. Medicine Horse thinks that I own you and he wants to trade you. It will make him look powerful to have a young white men serving him."

"But you don't own me!"

"You cannot tell a man who feeds and house you and who wants to buy you that you are not owned."

"Of course I can! I'll be blasted if I do it. No man owns me."

"You do not understand. We are guest in his lodge. To refuse those who lodge you is an affront."

"I'll not stay in the lodge of a man that wants to enslave me! I started for the lodge and Eagle Hand caught my arm and held firm."

"You cannot leave his lodge without offending him and we cannot leave this village for we have not given our due to these people."

"Bog the due! I—"

"Eagle Hand shook my arm. "What will you do if you are turned out of this village? You will die with your freedom on the cold prairie. A man does not die for what you call freedom. There is not honor in that."

"What? Eagle Hand what am I without freedom? Without my free will what am it if I only do the bidding of another man?"

He laughtes a deep laugh. "Git If I had not seen how you did the bidding of every person and how you had to pay everyone for every action, for every what yer call freedom in New York. In New York you were never once feasted or honored by another man not even your own tribe. You gave yer days to the Hotel and they gave you metal and me metal and we were forced to give our metal away to live without a fire. You lived without people who honor you without even being able to see the sun rise until it is high above the buildings of the city. Here you have a warm fire and bed yeer belly is full and you are safe and they have not has asked for yer silver **for** trade and not one is angry with you for staying. Yee life…yee freedom means nothing when yer under the care of another man. Honor and respect come before your feelings yer what you call your freedom. There can be no freedom with honor and respect. It is a man's heart that rules. Have you seen how these people all respect and honor each other. I do not understand what you name your freedom. Is it freedom to live without a tribe in a square of logs with the filth of hogs and beeves? Is it freedom to be able to walk inside a fence of forty acres? Is it freedom to walk outside where the city father's can lock you behind iron bars if you do not understand their commandments—commandments more numerous than the grasses. Git you are like the Americans they know nothing of freedom those with the smallest understanding talk the biggest. Git you owe the Skidis you can only stay alive and to be free if you stay under my protection here on the prairie."

"Yes, but that is only because I choose to come with you and I wouldn't have come here without your protection and permission."

"No you do not understand. If I own you I can refuse to trade you."

"Oh…so you won't sell me?"

"No…I cannot refuse his request."

"What do you mean? You can't sell me I am going with you. I like these people, but I want to be with you. They don't speak my tongue. Why can't you sell Jack?"

"Jack is a medicine man or they think he is and they would not take the chance on buying a medicine man as he may cause trouble."

"Tell them I am a medicine man!"

"They can see you are not. Words do not change the world. No I have no choice I must trade yee. But I will take you with me when the first thawing moon arrives."

"If you trade me how can you take me back? Will you buy me?"

"He will offer you to me and I will accept."

"How do you know this will happen."

"I know."

"What if something happens to you? Will I spend my life with the Skidi?"

"I cannot answer that. That is not a concern of mine. That will be decided by your power. If yee had powerful helpers and spirits yee will go where your power leads you. Tonight I will smoke with Medicine Horse and see if his wish is strong to own you. Tomorrow you will know."

He left me and disappeared down the path between two lodges. I stood there with my palms out. He can't sell me he doesn't own me. How can this happen. I travel thousands of miles to be sold to a man who doesn't even know what money is by a man who is my friend and who doesn't own me. I look around and find several boys looking at me for I had been speaking out loud. They ran off when I look at them.

I sit to the left of Eagle Hand Medicine Horse sits at twelve o'clock in the circle around the fire his back to the west. Some elk ribs rest on a flat rock sizzling. Our faces and hands are shining with the juice of the meat. The meat is crisp on one side and tender on the other side. Medicine Horse keeps urging all to eat more. I have never tasted such good meat. There are several other Skidi's that I don't know around the fire. When all have turned their bowls over, Medicine Horse wives spear the remaining ribs with their knives and move behind some robes to eat them. We all lick our fingers and some rub their hands on their leggings as Medicine Horse pulls his pipe out of the quill-encrusted scabbard. He makes a short speech and tosses some dried herbs on the fire. After filling his pipe with some small dried flowers he reaches into the fire and plucks out a small ember and drops it into the pipe bowl. He blows smoke to the six directions and passed to his left. There is no talking. The pipe goes around the room and he taps it clean. Medicine Horse addresses Eagle Hand and Eagle Hand responds and is doing most of the talking. Since they are doing less signing I cannot tell what they are saying although I know I am the subject of the talk. It strikes me as strange that I am in the circle yet I am to be a slave to this man. I can't imagine an Irishman being at the table of an Englishman who is buying him.

Soon all are standing and Eagle Hand is presenting me to Medicine Horse and he embracing me and bidding me to accept a set of earring and a necklace. When he finds that my ears are not pierced he motion one of his wives over and she rubs something on them and it numbs them and she pushes though what looked like a sharpened thorn through and they are pierced and earring are tickling my neck. Eagle Hand tells me as he leaves that he has gifted me to Medicine Horse and so I go to bed under my warm buffalo blankets a slave.

CHAPTER IX

My Life As A Slave

Git O'Toole Journal

11 January 1832, Wednesday

I am certainly the only slave who is scribbling about his fate on paper in this village. 'Tis a strange fate that has befallen me, all my life I've heard stories about the natural rights of man, of the peoples of France and the States have risen up against the ruling elite, against the king to create new Republics and although the French made a bloody mess of it. The States beat the British. For the enslavers of my people to be beaten was a balm to every Irish soul and gave up hope which everyone I know nurses still. So how strange it is that the British have banned slavery and America has embraced it. Not once did I give any thought that the natives to this land were also enslavers.

It's no simple matter this slavery of mine for I can't draw a single barbarous act form my experience. My body is still pure and intact despite my spending my first night of slavery weakened sleepless and taking far too many trips to the field outside the palisade. My spirit is flagging, but not from any treatment from my masters more from idea of me being beshackled and so I've been beside myself not being able to walk the trail of my chosing. But I wake with dread but I spent no waking hours in dread.

And master is hardly the word at least in the sense of having someone you utterly dependent on someone who worked you for his profit, someone who begrudges you your personal time. Such a thing hasn't happened. I've been barely spoken to except in greetings. It seems I'm expected to simply follow the lead of the others my age who have duties of herding and caring for the horses. I can't be sure as Eagle Hand is not here and I not very good at signing yet.

I know that pity is as useless at a titty on a bull as my da used to say, but why is Jack free? He spends his time showing off some magic tricks he knows and talking in sign about his powers. He is already seen as powerful and my only power is that I own a rifle, which someone tries to trade for every day. Cross the index fingers back and forth back and forth and pointing at my rifle. *That's a sign I see every day. Yesterday one fellow offered me his wife for the rifle, but I wasn't sure if he meant marry her or sex here. No I'll keep my balls in my bag.*

I shall endeavor to learn all I can and jump into this life fully as I am free to learn and if I do perhaps I can learn to survive on my own and then I know I would be able to leave, but I do not have a village or family to hold me so I intend to explore this land.

IT's THE WOMEN WHO STIR first putting faggots on the fire, fetching water, filling the pots and skins and bathing. The boys stir next and so I rise and put my feet over the pole to the packed earth below. They motion me out the dark tunnel of the doorway we go. I clutch my buffalo robe the warm fur rubs my neck, but the boys were nothing but their skins. Two boys turns to three then four and we are half a score before we reach the palisade. I linger behind and they look back talking about me of that I'm sure. The village is moving in the cold morning air with puffs of breath everywhere. Women with stacks of branches on their backs women scolding dogs dragging travois of branches up from the river bottoms women gurgling by us with skins of water teasing, greeting and laughing at the gaggle of boys leading me out to the horse pasture and the young women always with an older woman flits, flirts and giggles at the boys as the boys show off and very little girls always playing or holding puppies. Most of the young girls avoid my eyes and I feel like I stare overlong at everyone for no one meets my gaze steady only with a flicker.

Not all the horses are at the pasture. Several boys lead war-horses the prized horses out from a night spend in a lodge they take few chances with the best. During daylight when the danger of thievery is low these horses graze, my companions guarding them and it appears it is my job too. I am one of the few with a rifle among these boys for young here like in Ireland possess few items that they cannot make with their own hands. Most of the rifle and smoothbores are in the hand of battle-bloodied braves who were able to trade robes or horses for the weapons.

There is no guard at the palisade entrance there no gate just an opening wide enough for two horse astride to pass. Off the blufftop and down the gentle slope we go. I smell the horses on the gentle south wind before I see them in the purple light. One of the boys let our a gentle who who who whooo which is answered at some bush to to our left. The boys do not speak once we leave the palisade. Each of the boys carries several braided ropes. They move into the herd with purpose leaving me standing. One comes out leading two horses with ropes knotted in the lower jaws he hands me the horsehair rope and turns back to the herd pulling a coil off his chest and over his head as he disapearers into the herd. I see someone standing in front of the bushes watching me. I feel awkward holding these strange looking horses with their patchy skin shaggy hair small stature and big heads. They are unlike the horses of Ireland and they seem unsure of me as I do of them. They look at me and sniff me I do not have the thick meaty slightly sweet smell of bear grease on my skin or hair like so many Skidi's do.

One of the horse's I hold raises its head pulling the rope through my hand. I feel fear and I won't be able to handle the horses so I find myself reacting quickly jerking down the rope. I grip the rope and wrap it around my hand and jerk the head down and she looks at me and I see she decides and I ease up on the rope. She follows me. The Skidi's are more brutish to their horses than us Irish and Americans. I watch some Skidi rope both legs and tighten until a wild pony fell, the then he covered both eyes and breatherd and whispered into its mouth until the pony is calm enough to follow him with just a rope wrapped around the lower jaw. I have never seen a horse tamed so fast.

Back and forth we go gathering horses and leading them to the various lodges and tying them up there. I follow them blindly going where I am pointed.

After the horses are back we enter the lodge it is now full daylight. We are served a steaming bowl of delicious stew with meaty kernels of colored maize and beans and prairie turnips in it along with what looks to be marrow meat. The little boys play naked off to the side of the fire rolling a leather ball around. Everyone seems to tolerate the cold better than I do. The boys motion me out and we start down the passageways with high-spirited lopes and much chatter. Across the almost blindingly bright hillside we run I follow their lead. They have bows and quivers with them. I long to to learn how to shoot as well as them, but I dare not put my rifle down for fear of losing it. They shoot without seeming to pause to aim. They raise the bow and shoot in one fluid motion cocking it at a twenty-five degree angle pushing the bow out away from their bodies with the left hand while bringing the string up to their chin with the right. Within fifteen yards they are always within a fist of where they aim and many times they will hit a small bird out of the air. Every day they try to get me to shoot, but I won't waste the balls on small game. They get angry with me and don't seem to understand. Most of our day is free with our horse duties coming at the beginning and ending of the day with some occasional help of a grandmother in wood gathering.

We return to the lodge in the late afternoon and bowls are filled for us. Warm food is almost always available and if it is not then a Parfleché case is opened and dried meat is taken out of one of pemmican bags that hangs from the poles the Skidi verison of sausage is taken down. These bags of corn or beans that are not stored underground in caches come from strings that have a rectangular piece of rawhide halfway up the string this piece of rawhide serves to keep the mice from climbing down the rope by tipping under the weight of the rodent and throwing them off. There are not rats here. It is nice that with the low fire going all the time a pot seems to be on all day and into the night so there is no formal sit down ordinary like at the hotel. One eats when one is hungry, although the women do not eat with the men the same as the ordinary. I like this way better than the hotel and the fare is better.

After I have eaten, Medicine Horse's father I don't understand if he is blood father or brother of blood father as all are called grandfather and regarded the same at blood. Grandfather come to me and sits looking at me so I know he wishes to talk. He asks me with sign and a few words of French and English what I saw out there today with the horses. What birds what animals what was the snow like did it have a crust on the hillside and what was it like in the willows? I am confused by his questions but try the best I can to answer.

A small group of men left at first light and now they return so we take their horses and lead to the night pasture. My head is full of Grandfather's questions so I am looking at everything as I walk. We join the other boys who are scattered about on the outskirts of the herd. A few build fires and look to be settling around them for the night. This group is all boys and nearly young men and there is much jousting laughter and loud voices. I came out with Boy Who See Far. I sleep in the bed next to him the bed of his brother Steps High who had been killed and scalped guarding horses a few weeks ago. The war party we met arose from that incident. They think he may have discovered the horse raiding party, but before he could give the alarm he had been clubbed the side of his head caved in and his scalp removed and his steel knife taken.

I am distracted thinking about Grandfather's questions. I don't feel I did myself any honor with my answers. I walk around the grazing herd carefully looking at the little valley with the trees along the edge many with curled light-brown leaves still curled and clinging and at times making a dry rustle as a wisp of air come like a hand gently shaking the tree. He wanted to see what I see. He was trying to see how my eyes and my mind saw. He told me one can strengthen the eyes, but now I think he meant train the eyes for I am now seeing things I missed yesterday. These things were before my eyes and my ears and I was too involved in my own thoughts my own pity and that covered my senses. Tis magic that Grandfather sat with me now I am seeing so much more. Just his care and attention bought this all about I've never been nudged into an education before.

After taking in all the sights I can with my new eyes I take up to a small fire with my lodge mate. The moon is rising and tis past full but bright so we don't expect any trouble as it is nearly like daylight with the snow on the earth. In the group is a very proud, tall fellow who seems not to like me as he makes sneering faces towards me whenever we cross paths and I can tell he is talking about me to the others. He now stands in front of the fire looking down at me. I glance up at him and return my eyes to the fire. I feel Boy Who See Far freeze next to me and fidget as the tall boy stands looking down his nose at me. I have the same feeling meeting him as meeting Thumper O'Brien our neighborhood bully in Dublin. There is nothing one can do in the long silence of a bully trying to decide how he will strike. I have my rifle across my lap sitting cross legged. This boy has many older brothers to defend and avenge him, hurting him will get me either hurt or killed. I know I have the advantage of sitting close to the fire for it keeps him from standing directly in front of me. I put the outside rims of my feet into the ground so I can rise when he makes his move. He makes no move. I just start to relax, I suppose he sees it in my shoulders for he swings down with a loop of braided rope and catches the end of my barrel pulling it out of my left hand, but I squeeze hard behind the trigger guard with my right and I rise following the barrel. He uses his right to move the rope and he grabs the barrel with his left and yanks up so I follow his motion spinning the rifle though his move and thank the saints pull of the earth is with me as he has the awkward hold on the barrel. I jerk downward. My action loosens his hand and he jerks it away. I see blood. He must have caught it on the metal ring holding the rod. His face flashes in anger and his hand shoots out open until he has his fingers wrapped around the stock and barrel and he pulls back with his long arms. I have just time to plant my feet or my rifle would be gone. Lucky for me this is a contest of the arms for I notice that most Pawnee men do not do any heavy work with their arms, so even though I am smaller I have worked with my arms my whole working life. But his pulling at my rifle fills me with rage that he is trying to steal my rifle. I spin the rifle crossin' his arms for he is determined to hold on so I push towards him into his pull spinning it with all my strength and it comes up close to his body catching him on the chin with the stock. You would a thought I swept his legs so fast he found the earth. I stopped with the rifle held high over my head. I could see fear in the eyes of Boy Who See Far, but after a few panting breaths, I realize that he thought I was going to kill the tall crumpled bugger at my feet. He looked frightened of me and I could see in the eyes of the others standing there. I don't want to be there when the bully comes to his senses. I walk off though I want to run, but I did not want to show fear. I walk towards the peacefully pawing and grazing horses. When I get past the herd I stand near a line of trees puffng and with my legs trembling whether it is anger or fear I can't say. There is no way I going back to that fire even if I freeze, of course I have my buffalo robe. I find a snowbank between some tall grasses and I dig out a comfortable chair in the snow bank. I watch the horses graze about fifty yards in front of me and slightly below me. I sit and stew about how can I possible survive alone out here without losing my rifle or worse. I didn't believe sleep would ever touch me.

I wake to sounds that would frightened a banshee: horses screaming thudding and slipping it looks like large waving birds are attacking the
horses pushing them past me from right to left up the draw. The shape of
men's forms behind the wings and one comes riding sceaming and waving
a blanket on my side of the herd . I cock and swing and I nearly pull the
trigger on the man's chest, but I become frightened that I can't tell distance
in the dark so I swing down in front of his knee hoping to the hit the horse
and the most brilliant flash goes off in the dark and I think surely every
attacker sees me like a lantern on the hillside and I leap behind the bush
fumbling for my ball pouch grabbing one and nearly forgetting the powder.
I am keeping my eye on the rushing horses and riders. The horse I shot
went down in a cloud of snow and I see the man bouncing and sliding
down the hill. Three or four men afoot suddenly sail though the air and
are mounted and I can hear twangs and some soft whistles in the air above.
I tip the horn in spit the ball out of my mouth cup the barrel pop the ball
with the heel of my hand and push the ram home. I swing on the closest
man but he is now more than hundred yards and out of range, but I swing
on him putting it in front of his left shoulder as he laying against the horse
and I fire and see nothing but the flash, but I hear the thwack and I know
I have connected with flesh, whether man or horse I can't tell for no form
hits the glowing snow. I watch where the herd went for the Creature is in
that herd and I don't want to lose him.

The boys come rushing down the far ridge at the same time others
come rushing out of the palisade. The air is filled with the high sounds of
fear and bravado as I frantically load again. Looking down on the field of
now emptied of upright horses one lay on his side kicking and throwing his
head back and desperately neighing to the heavens sounding more like a
scream. I can see the still dark body of the man contorted on the snow. I am
frightened of what may be behind me. Someone ready to rescue or revenge
the man on the earth., but the safety of the numbers below me draw me
down. Maybe these hills contained the Aes Sidhe like the hills of Ireland? I
certainly feel there are ghost around me. I pray to the Celtic gods to protect
my backside. I hie down the hills with mustable steps on the snow made

more precarious by my constant backward glances at the tree lined hilltop while the Boy Who Sees Far descends the slope at a forward tilting, careening and heedless pace his hand filled with a knife and an axe. He didn't slow at he approaches the man on the ground he raises his axe tries to brake but he slides stiff-legged towards the contorted man. Fear fills me that the man is waiting for him. Boy slides by and he swings. I cannot see if he touches him but I hear the hollow thop of the side of the axe hitting followed by his whoop. He is down clawing at the frozen ground in a snowy frenzy until back up by the man just as another boy approaches who swings a stick slapping the man.

When I reach them the Boy has the man's black hair wrapped around his fist. He looks up at me saying something and jerking the head up. I nod and point at him not sure what he means maybe that I shot him? The dying horse makes a frothy gurgling sound blackness seeps from underneath the horse. The snow under the man is clean. I look at his chest with shallow breathing. Cheyenne is the only word I can make out form the excited boys. The Cheyenne reaches a hand down to the ground as if to help support his upper body, his lashes flicker. He stills wears his knife. His mountain lion quiver lies in the snow the bow beside it twisted like the tail of a lion. He groans Boy looks at me with a hard nod. His knife spins and flashes in the luminous blue moon light. He puts his foot onto the man's back. A papery ripping and smacking sound cuts though the distant yips and yells followed by the appearance of a white skull cap on the crown of the man's head. Boy leaps around the circle holding the cap of hair. I am amazed at how white the man head looks. The man groans still propped up on one arm. He reaches for his knife with his free hand. One of the other boys kicks the back of his arm and keeps kicking frantically up the side across the back the man jumping from the kicks as if he is moving and another boy sceams and starting to whacking at his head with a stone wrapped club the hollow thunking noise penetrating though all the sceams and trilling noises of the boys and approaching warriors.

Deny's face come to me I wonder if he is alive. I feel alone, I feel no hate only fear. The horse side heaves. Nothing. I watch the horse. Nothing, dead too, I think. A deep heaving breath. Her eyes are still open the moonlight reflected in them. I walk to her head. I stand, looking into her eyes I do not see what one sees every day in eyes. I can't describe it but I know she is gone. I feel my image standing above her in the moonlight I feel the noises behind her going in those big glassy horse eyes and not coming out. Another breath...but it is a breath apart from her eyes, a breath that believed it should just keep filling those big lungs it was not desperate maybe not even determined but it was the last part of her to leave and I watch it float out her nostril rise in the still cold winter air full of her heat as it drifts down the snowy hillside that she grazed. She makes no sound as she moves across the prairie breaking up under the moonlit night.

The sign for Cheyenne is made by holding the left index finger in front of the heart and putting the the right index finger on top of it at the first joint and then making slashing motion several times downward and across for this tribe has a custom of making cuts on their wrists and arms.

Three summers ago a war party of Cheyenne was discovered sneaking upon the Skidi horse herd. They were surrounded and every Cheyenne killed. The Pawnees cut up their bodies so they couldn't go the spirit world and return and kill them. They threw the Cheyenne pieces in a creek. Another war party of Cheyenne discovered the pieces. The following summer a large force of Cheyenne including women and children along with Arapahos and even Sioux who had not yet dared attack the Pawnee alone these three tribes followed the Platte to the South Loup in search of the Skidis. A group of Skidi buffalo hunters ran into this large force and were chased back to camp where they gave the alarm.

This was a great mounted force arrayed against the Skidis. But the Skidis and all the Pawnee tribes have a history of fighting to the last man against great odds. I was told several different stories of Pawnees going deliberately on the war path afoot with as many as fifty going afoot in search of horses usually to the south into Comanche country or to the west into Cheyenne county some of these parties were discovered by their mounted enemies and wiped out men on foot fighting men on horses. Yet to this day there is no shortage of warriors willing to wage war in such a manner.

The Skidis were not going to flee the Cheyennes they prepared to fight this massive force. Both sides consulted their medicine men. The Pawnees have a reputation of having some of the most powerful medicine men on the plains who can perform fantastic feats like piercing their cheeks though and leaving no visible hole when the lance is withdrawn. I have not seen this yet, but I have heard stories.

"The Cheyenne followed by the Arapahos and Sioux lined out across the prairie and advance at a trot, being led by their great medicine man a man named Bull he carried the sacred Cheyenne Medicine Arrows tied to the end of his lance. These arrows were taken out of their sacred bundle and had been in that bundle ever since anyone of the tribe could remember and they along with the Buffalo Cap were the most sacred and most powerful medicine the tribe possessed. The allied northern tribes marched across the prairie towards the Skidis with Bull in the lead.

"On a prairie between these two armies sat a lone sad figure. He was sitting on the ground amid the prairie grasses turning brown with the late summer heat. He was a Skidi awaiting an honorable death. He had been sick for some time and was very despondent as no cure could be found for his illness. He could not even walk well so he had his friends carry him out onto the prairie before the army advanced. One lone man who was going to make his last stand who sought an honorable death in front of his whole village."

"The Cheyenne medicine man Bull was several yards ahead of the warriors he sat tall proud and sure of victory. His face curled into a sneering smile when he saw the single Pawnee sitting on the prairie in front of him he spurred his horse and let out a high pitched curling scream lowered the lance with the sureness of drawing first blood and of inflaming the charge of his people to annihilate the enemy."

"The Skidis watched the lone sick man waiting for the lance, he did not move. The fearsome charge of Bull and his war-horse closed on him throwing clods of dirt and dust into the air the hooves of the horse thumping like a drum. Cheyenne voices rippling behind Bull fell silent as he neared the Skidi. Some Skidis called for him to stand, but he did not. The lance is lowered and all brace for the impact. The Skidi leaned hard left at the last second. Bull had leaned into his lance over the side of his horse in anticipation of the impact into the man's chest. The sick Skidi right arm shot out like a rattler and closed around the lance like an eagle claw. Bull stopped his horse looking down at his empty hand his fierce face had now fallen. A great look of misfortune and disbelief passed down his face and slumped his shoulders. He turns his horse walking it back towards the massed warrior crying making mourning sounds. Some of the Cheyenne warriors of his clan rush forward but the Skidis had rushed forward at the instant the man grabbed the lance their voices rising in a loud crescendo of awe, joy and power. The sick man rose to his feet and ran towards his people screaming he had great medicine. His people surround him and surged past to protect him from the Cheyenne warriors who had rushed forward to recover the lance. They clashed with the sounds of horses and men screaming hooves beating the twang of bowstrings the drumming sound of clubs and arrows bouncing off buffalo hide shields and the crack and smoke of weapons mixing with hoof dust and dried gasses whirling in a vacuum, men whirling trying to get enough advantage to keep living and for a short time there was a fierce battle, but many of the Cheyenne held back and those fighting were full of fear. The Cheyenne's lost all heart when they saw they could not recover their sacred arrows and they withdrew without putting all their forces to battle. Soon the hillside was filled with the rumps of Cheyenne, Arapahoe and Sioux horses their tails not even bothering with the flies."

The families of those men killed in the creek still try to avenge them but the Cheyennes have lost all heart in trying to move against the Skidis as a tribe only small parties like the one we encounted.

As the Cheyenne is dragged off to the village and his body stipped of clothes I see there is no bullet wound. I hit the horse and he was injured by the fall. The rest of his hair disappeared with people reaching down to cut off chunks left. One of Medicine Horse's wife runs up and the crowd parts for her. She is the oldest wife I don't recall her name it was her son who was killed . She held up her knife and pointed at the moon and called out some oaths and then bent over grabbed the Cheyenne privates and in a flash she is holding his manhood above her head screaming and is joined by others who crowd round the Cheyenne slashing at him. I am pushed away and can only see people carrying pieces of flesh. He will be another Cheyenne denied entry into the other world denied for an eternity being linked with his loved ones. His death was honorable but his spirit dishonored.

There is a dance tonight but as there are so many missing from the village it is an affair of young boys and old men and many women. There is a procession of men on mules though the village. There is too much excitement to give me signs of what is going on. Jack refuses to take part calling it savage and sulking in his lodge so I do not get his insights, which I sorely needed.

The next morning dark clouds from the west and the winds turn from the south to the west and keep going to the north and clouds bump under clouds darkening the plains. Medicine Horse, Eagle Hand, The Bird That Goes to War, The Man Chief, The Big Chief and Ill Natured Man returned from the hunt. They arrive just as darkness surrounds us, and large flakes of snow swirl and twist about us. They are pushing the horses and mules we lost yesterday. There is much excited talk but Medicine Horse refuses to be engaged indicating that they need to eat before they talk. They killed a few buffalo but did not locate the big herd. They told us more warriors are on their way back.

We took the played out horses to the ravine where we had moved the rest of the herd. They would have plenty of cottonwood bark to eat as some of the grandmothers told us the snow would be too deep. There is no sign of enemy nearby and the storm will protect us. I am no longer left behind the other boys walk behind me. My rifle has gotten me a new respect. Eagle Hand had been somber and said nothing to me merely handing the horses to us. I feel a bit lost. The other boys tried to give me attention and honor but I feel closed. I fairly race back and find Eagle Hand cleaning his rifle. I cannot hold back with my need to talk and understand.

"How did the scout go?"

"It was not a good vidette. We moved south for the other party was far west beyond where they found the buffalo last season. Little buffalo sign mostly sign of other tribes looking for what is not there. Medicine Horse had fear of this his dreams spoke of thie and the past two seasons have been poor during the winter hunts. He wants to smoke tonight on this I will be at his lodge tonight and I will tell you his words. The horses we recovered was just luck. We came across them and recognized the horses. We gave chase but our horses had too much day behind them and enemy made fresh mount out of the herd. The horses are back. I hear you killed a Cheyenne."

"Yes I knocked him off his horse but it was luck I hit the horse he hit his head on the frozen ground and Boy Who Sees Far and the others finished him off."

"You will get the kill, Boy will get the coup. It is your scalp. It must go on your war shirt. But you don't have one do you? He smiles at me. You are young to draw blood It is good you don't know their tongue. It is not good to get too proud too young. There will be another scalp dance tonight to celebrate the return of the horses. This is your first blood I'm proud of you. The Cheyenne hunt the lands of the Black Hills out to the Yellowstone and up the Little Missouri. Four Bears has had many fights with Cheyenne. I must sleep now for it will be a late night."

"I thought I make biscuits for the feast at our lodge?"

"Medicine Horse will be honored but the women will be amused."

"Why is that?"

"Some things you will have to find out."

I am puzzled, but if there is to be a feast I want to make something for it. And flour is a rare treat. Also I want some delicious stew with a biscuit. I took some of our flour, salt and saleratus from our panniers and the women looks at me strangely coming up to stick their fingers in the flour and soon they are giggling and putting flour spots on each others nose and the children are doing the same.. I have to shuss them away. I have a hard time getting them to understand that I need some fat and they finally take some buffalo fat out of a beautifully painted parfleché bag and then all stand around intently watching me melt the fat and mix the biscuits. We have a fold-up tin oven that I put over some heated rocks on the coals. There is much talking and pointing going on during this process.

I thought of the dead Cheyenne as I mix biscuits. It all happened so fast I have a hard time believing it happened. It was strange but it felt good that my ball did not hit him. He is dead by my hand I keep telling myself. I wonder about his family. The Cheyenne's don't have big permanent lodges like these I'm told. They live in teepees and brush lodges on the river bottoms during the winter. I thought of him leaving with high hopes of coming back rich and honored. Now he doesn't exist. Now a teepee is filled with women cooking like this lodge and they will go on eating sleeping and working and he will not be part of that life. There will be no good byes no last touch of his body no comfort for his mother or sister to wrap him in his finest clothes. There will be no wake like so many I attended where stories are told and where everybody connected to him would help him into the next world and he would help them stay in this one. I've observed that a dead man's name is never spoken after he is dead so I don't know how they give a dead person a sendoff here on the prairie. They seem to fear the spirit so they don't want to call them. I will have to ask Eagle Hand about that. It seems sadder that they can't even speak the name of a man who ceased to be. I can't speak for it I don't know it.

The celebration begins with a feast and much talking and the food seems plentiful Squash, corn, bean, turnips aplenty, but I was told the meat is running low. You'd never know it with the people stopping by to bring gifts of food so the lodge was full and many were outside around fires with food cooking there as well. The biscuits disappear almost instantly and I would not have had any had I not reserved some for myself. I watched the women uncover the caches for the first time. These are deep holes eight feet of more in the ground dug in the floor of the lodge. Inside they are shaped like a vase with the bottom bowing out all round and it is stacked with cobs of corn and skins of beans and strings of dried squash. They use a notched log as a ladder. I had not even known this cache existed as it is covered with a layer of logs and branches with dirt on top.

Boy Who See Far dances for me and as Eagle Hand explains his acts. When one does a worthy act one paints oneself with certain colors but with much freedom of design and then he dances his dance that shows the people what brave deed he did and he sing his deed for the people and the spirits to thank them for his safety. And those who witness it dance what they saw. It seems a frightening number of skills to use that I do not have but twas wonderful to see the creative way that Boy Who Sees Far moves his body and makes us understand every important event that happened his sound and motions of the horse running even the quirt the Cheyenne hitting the stolen horse I could feel it happen all again and it seems the many watching can feel it as well. The drums follow his actions and seems to know just when to punch a dramatic point an when to go low and slow as when Boy Who Sees Far show the Cheyennes' sneaking into the herd.

Some chiefs and warriors such as Big Ax Big Elk and Black Chief a very swarthy man with a reputation for bravery and Soldier Chief and Spotted Horse and Bloody Hand return that night. It is my first sight of them and are fearsome looking men, but handsome too with their neatly shaved heads sprouting the roaches of red hair making them look even taller, their ears pieced up the outside rims full of metal rings and colorful ribbons. Their necks hold many necklaces of beads, bone and claws even their wrists hold bracelets. Some have paintings around their mouths and on their chests dark horns and ears of the buffalo.

The chiefs and medicine men had a smoke and decide that a ceremony and offering has to be made to Ready to Give so that they can find the buffalo their people need. The priest will not eat at they begin fasting for the ceremony to be held in the medicine lodge. The women are busy packing for the coming trek.

"Ready to Give? What kind of God is called Ready to Give? I thought they were beginning to understand God but now they shoo me off telling they must fast and wait for visions."

"Catholics have a long tradition of fasting, Jack. I sure they find the name God just as strange. Ready to Give is their God of food quests...like Saint Columba is the patron of travelers."

"Thats Papist not Christian. They do have a supreme God near as I can figure called Ti rawa and these people are related to the Arikaras who have a village up near the Mandan's They seemed real interested in God. I think these people will go with the most powerful God you just have to somehow prove that to them which I haven't figured out how to do just yet, but the Lord will provide the guidance I need. You killed an Indian?"

"Injured he was still alive when I got there."

"I heard you shot him off his horse."

"I shot the horse and he went down with it."

"Why do you get involved in their petty wars? You know it just encourages them to see white men murdering just like them. How do you expect to make them understand our ways to make them civilized if you act like them?"

"I didn't come to be a white man or turn people from their ways and their Gods I didn't come here to turn tribesman into white men mostly because I've never been treated like a real white men so I guess I just too dam ignorant to do all that teaching for you. I'm here to learn their way of life and live that way"

"You were raised a Christian that's all that's necessary when dealing with savages."

"How do you know I'm not a savage?"

"A Christian even a fallen one cannot be a savage even if you want to be. A savage lives like animals and belives in the animal world and is half animal. I'm not sure that the depravity can ever be taken out of a savage, but if his children are raised as Christian it might be possible."

"I'm real sorry that I can't ever be a full-fledged savage."

"Oh yeah, How slavery?"

"Confusing but the work is easy. I don't think the Skidi's have it down like the white man. Don't seem to have much motivation they don't need to exploit labor since the guy who gives the most has the most power and they don't seem interested in converting me to their religion so that about covers the slave issue. It feels strange to be a slave with a rifle never even read about that in stories."

"Sounds like you moved up in rank with that dead indian."

"I thought it was my biscuits."

"You mean I missed them?"

"Jack-come-lately. Why didn't they pick you for a slave?"

"Perhaps you need a higher power. Nothing is an accident, you know."

"So a few more prayers and I'd be a free man? Wonder why all those African slaves haven't been freed after singing all those songs to the lord all day? Thought you said it was God's will that they are slaves. But an Irishman can pray his way out?"

"I didn't' say that, you needn't presume you know the mysteries of God's ways."

"But you do?"

"Why do you accuse me? I have not enslaved you. I'm only trying to help you understand and I get rewarded with you skepticism and unbelief."

"Sorry...I try to see reason in your words and when I do you turn to nonreason for answers. It sounds patronizing. I've listened to nothing but patronizing English in our shop since I could hear and somehow your words remind me of them."

"Didn't realize I had such an accent."

"It's more the way you say things."

"Perhaps it not me so much as the Lord's words that bother you all that Druidish mumble jumble drivel your from your uncle may have addled you soul."

"Actually I love the Roman Catholic religion because without it there can't be sacrilege heresy and perversion tis one of the teaching of my Uncle Bres that I remember. Beside you preachers wouldn't have a job without us sinners. Then you might have to take up sin yourselves if there was no one to watch doin the sinning."

Jack laughs. "Watchin' is almost as good as doing but it ain't a sin like doin. I suppose if the world were full of preachers we'd spend all our days out on our porches watching each other to see who would sin first. But there seems to be enough savagery in the world to keep that from happening. I'm going over the Bird That Goes to War lodge he promised to share some of his sleight of hand knowledge with me. Professional courtesy you know. Jack winks. Maybe I can allow him to have you watch as well if you wish."

"I love to I haven't done that since playing hide the nut on Dublin corners, but I promised Eagle Hand I would go with him to a smoke".

Thum thum thump the drums have being going all night as the Priests work their medicine and travel over the prairies in a dreamy search for buffalo. Thum thum thump! I had gone to sleep with the thumming hide of buffalo booming into the cold night air calling their living brethren. Closing my eyes under the warm caress of the buffalo fur I can see the booms and silent plumes of smoke from all the lodges of the village enter the ether and call for sustenance of a people cry out of the vast rolling land around then to have pity on them. I can see their pleas travel over the vast prairie surrounding the village…I see their hunger ride the cold winds undulating over the hillocks and icy water-cracks in the sea of sleeping grass. I see their need alive moving over the whiteness slithering over every curve their cries like puffs of life coming off the ridges in ghostly ragged flags their need like a nimbical blanket moving over the plateaus illuminating the night prairie in smokey streaks and swirls of whiteness…all night they move over the prairie while I slumber while the Aes Sidhe the Celtic gods of the hills peeking at me from every motte every stream and wondering what I am doing here.

The priest's cries ring though the village buffalo, buffalo. They are calling Medicine Horse crying A-ti-us Ti-ra-wa the Spirit Father heard has heard us.

"Arosha Arosha," voices are demanding horses. They want their horses it is a mad scabble for us to round up the horses and the horses sense the excitement and make for an unruly bunch to gather. The men carry moccasins full of the a meat-fat-berry mixture called pemmican and the colorful leather cases called Par fleches packed with dried corn and the skin of small animals sewed shut bulging with the hardened buffalo or bear fat. Travios are being lashed to horses and dogs. The buffalo are reported to be to the southwest.

"As the chaos of assembly is happening a procession of Enchanters painted in vivid reds and blacks dance, rattle and sing in howling, yodeling voices. These are the caster of lots, the sortilegium, the soccercers that saw the bufflalo, that sought out the buffalo, they are the men that found the buffalo with their vision these are the men who can see all of the prairie from the sky, like giant bird high above the earth these men will lead us to sustenance.

The warriors normally so calm and clement rush about with not a whit of patience giving orders to us boys their wives and even the grandmothers who they always speak to with respect and deference and not one person seems to be listening to the other. The women are sceaming at the dogs, horses and children. The children are sceaming with delight or with hurt or at someone younger. Waves of words what sounds like curses ripple down from the Chiefs to infants. Horses neigh, whinny and whirl in nonsensical circles thowing off half secured packs, dragging empty travois between the lodges bouncing the poles off the dirt walls and scattering all in their path. Many of the warriors erupt in laughter at the sight of a women chasing after a braying mule who kicks off his pack leaving a string of pans bags and tools on the trampled earth. Finally the chaotic antics of the dogs horses and mules chafing at the excitement and flinging goods all about has the warriors laughing so hard the the tension is released and the men begin to move with more calmness.

Medicine Horse leaps onto his palfrey horse and I hand him the hair rope to his buffalo horse. He looks at me and signals for me to come. I am going on a buffalo hunt. I am given a horse and a charge of several more of his horses. The enchanters lead us out of the palisade rattling as they go afoot followed by the warriors. I look back and when we are nearly a mile down from the village and I see a long string of people walking, riding and still chasing horses in the surrounding fields.

As we are riding out of the village Eagle Hand comes riding back smiling at me, "We go to the buffalo Irish! There is nothing in your world like it. No white man has ever told me of any sight like the buffalo or the prairie hundreds of thousands of buffalo rumbling like thunder creating their own clouds as they race across the prairie. His face is lit up." Never have I seen such a face on a man about to slaughter a pig or beeve. "Your trains and steamboats are nothing compared to seeing thousands of buffalo." Eagle hand has painted some red and yellow marks on the flank of his horse. "It makes my breast swell for you to be able to hunt in this country, he says as his hands sweep the land. "The buffalo have been scarce but this land has more buffalo than any other land and that is why so many tribes hunt these lands. We are going towards the Flint-Knife River named the Arkansas by the white man. I see you have new moccasins they will be good in this cold. Your Irish covering were not made for this land." He laughs and gallops off to the front with the hunters leaving me back tending the horses with several other young men.

214 JOURNEY TO THE FAR WEST

The march has men riding way ahead and out to our flanks where they appear on distant hilltops from time to time. They signal by riding their horses back and forth and wave a blanket. Most of the boys from age five or six up to my age run about in groups beating the bushes for game or surrounding a brushy area while other beat the bushes with clubs to frighten out any game. A group of boys jumps a covey of prairie chickens and they carefully watch where they alight. Then they walk and then slowly creep and soon there are several shillelaghs spinning though the air and fewer birds lift off than landed and one of those that lifted has an arrow in him. They come running back with their chests all puffed holding the birds. These birds are plucked and roasted whole in the coals with the most of the entrails left in them and they taste better than any stuffing as they feed on berries and rose hips in the winter and their crop makes a natural stuffing.

I cannot join all the jabber floating past my ears and tis difficult to get anyone's attention to sign. I am following a woman who is big with child, but she has not looked at me. Suddenly she veers off looking hurt. I slowly watch her. No one else is paying attention to her. I'm sure she is in distress. She disappears over the hill. I follow leading several horses. One of the young boys apporaches keeps talking to me, but I cannot make out what he is saying and his hands don't make any sense either.

I come over the hill the woman is squatting beside her par fleche case in some willows. Her side is to me and she has her eyes closed in what looks like pain. He skirt is hiked up over her butt and tucked in her belt. I stop, thinking I have blundered into her doing her toilet, but I have never seen a woman in a partial squat with her dress hiked so high. She had both hands between her thighs and the snow is spotted pink below her. I know I should leave, but I cannot. Her hands fill with flesh growing out of her and before I have taken a few more breaths she has a wriggling infant in her hands. There is no sound except one long sigh that escapes her lips against the distant tumult for the march behind me over the ridge and then it just the quiet of the willows rattling and the rustle of dried grass stalks. She has a skin on the earth in front of her. She lifts the baby's belly to her mouth and then I hear his cries and see his breath rising in the cold clear sunny air. She puts him upon the skin pulls out a bag and cover the umbilicus she had just severed with a fine powder. A dried puffball mushroom falls out of the bag. I have seen these growing in New York. Then she reaches into another bag and pulls out the head of several cattail plants I recall the Pawnee name for this since it is so easy to remember *hawahawa*. She strips the brown head of the cattail and made a big downy pile of the cattail next to the baby. White fluffy clouds of of the fine seeds swirl about her and over her. She sets the child in the puffy mass, closing the child's eyes with her fingers. He hands work over the baby and soon the bloody birth is cleaned off as she rolls the wetted seeds off the baby. Then she takes out her breast. I think she is going to feed the child, but she pumps her breast with one hand while holding the child with the other its face near her breast. The steamy milk hits the child in the face and she wets his face and then wipes off the remaining white fluffiness from his face. The child is moving but not crying. She wraps the child in a fresh skin turns her head notices me and begins to harangue me and wave me off in anger. I sulk off feeling full of shame knowing I have broken some taboo, but the feeling of awe fills me more than shame.

I am amazed not so much from witnessing the birth for I have seen many animals born, but from the fact that it was done all alone, without ceremony without the use of a medicine man or midwife and done quickly and without even the use of a tent or bed. Every other act of these people seems full of religion yet the most creative act of life is done without ceremony and indeed seemed to require solitude, but no special place or assistance what an amazingly strong sight it was.

Late that afternoon we reach the Shallow Water called the Platte River about fifteen miles to the southwest of our village. They call the Loup River the Kuddi or Many Wild Potatoes River. It took nearly two hours for everyone to reach camp after we arrived. By that time the high spirits of the children had fallen to the far side of ill nature. The dogs pulling the travois are snarling and yelping and the men are yelling and again no one is listening. The women have the teepees erected in minutes. Many of us boys had gathered firewood for our teepees having arrived early and knowing that we would be sent off to do we did it ahead and were ready when the teepees were. One thing I noticed about Pawnees is that they rarely chop wood for fires even though they do have some trade axes. They prefer smaller dead branches to chopped logs the size that can be broken off by hand. They feel it entirely too much effort to chop wood when one can walk or ride a little father to gather wood. They say the wood on the ground is right for the fires the living wood on trees is full of water. Even longer branches were not chopped if the could be fitted around the fire and pushed in.

The water is open in some spots and horses broke more open with the hooves. When we arrived we drank washed our hands and face with some boys taking off their clothes to strip in the hole in the ice as they played and washed themselves/ The tolerance for cold among these people is way beyond mine maybe growing up here begats that, but I have observed naked children playing in the snow and now some are playing in the icy water with delight.

The village chief The Big Elk is not with us having gone out weeks earlier with another part of the village. Medicine Horse and some of the other chiefs have selected this spot and now sit and await the women carrying the chattel. Eagle Hand sat by me and we were talking and he told me that the way I was taking about the chiefs has shown him I did not see the true way of the Skidi nor his people.

"Chiefs are not like he sees with the white man who have many people who rule by force I have seen that all your laws require force and that the few rule many. The people of the prairie have no jails to force people into. His people injure others like all people but the one injured and his or her family deal with the offender directly and village watches sometimes counsels but does not interfere by force. Most times the offender gives gifts or payment for their offense sometimes they leave the village to live with others, but this is not ordered by others. No chief has the power to compel any man to do what he does not wish nor would any such chief be tolerated for long. Some chiefs who have had powerful families many warriors have tired to rule by force in the past but as soon as they were weak they were destroyed. People always resent people who stand over them with the force of power. Resentment weakens a people and encourages betrayal and revenge. Force is not the way to rule either men or children. Force always begats force there can be enough people who can long live under threat of force without trying to use it against those who so threaten. A chief is a man honored for his wisdom and power and his brave deeds and his generosity and many villages have many chiefs some who have the wisdom over the village life and others who have wisdom of war. The prosperity of the people depend on the wisdom of many and a good chief is one who hear his people when their hearts are in the right place and waits when the hearts are not. No man can ever stand for all the people and the men who believe they can, will fail. We have many chiefs and sometimes they can speak for some of the people, but no chief speaks for all the people. A man can be a chief today and nobody tomorrow."

Medicine Horse has made a tripod to hold his shield and personal items and is sitting plucking his his eyelashes. He has a trade mirror hung by a rawhide strap the mirror is called *solid water* for that is what they used before the French brought mirrors in trade for skins. Most of the men pluck all the hair from the face and I'm told the eyelashes are plucked so the paint they use on their face doesn't stick to the hair. The paint is applied by mixing a powder with bear or buffalo grease. Black the preferred color for war is charcoal and grease. Vermeil or vermilion is the most popular color used by men on the face and bodies and by women who color the center part of their hair and sometimes to make round rubs on their cheeks. Vermilion is a big trade item but they insist it be Chinese Vermilion for I made the mistake of buying some cheaper American Vermilion and they wouldn't trade for it. The men use more colors and spend more time applying it than the women.

"How many you posit there are?" Jack is chewing on a stalk of grass as he looks at me and then at the straggling spectacle.

"Five...six hundred."

"More than that I say near the thousand."

"That's a lot of mouths to feed. It was a bit crazy, but I don't know how many white men who could get a village of white men to move within an hour quite amazing really, he says as he walks off in wonder."

The tent is up and Burnt Thighs one of Medicine Horse wives and all his wives are sisters is making ground beans my favorite these are not bean that are ground but beans from the ground that a meadow vole collects for they are hard to gather always growing under a canopy of bushes that the runner climbs while some stalks sink into the ground below the bush the stalks are the one that bear the beans. The women find the beans in the hole of the vole and puts in corn to replace what she takes and that is considered a good trade. Only a handful of beans is put each stew pot but they are a rich filling bean and I seek them out an Burnt Thighs teases me that I will bloat like a calf skin for eating too many of them. She is referring to how the skin the unborn buffalo by mostly pulling the skin off in one piece and then they sew it with sinew the holes created by the feet and nose and the skin can then be filled with air or water.

Medicine Horse is of high standing due to his war exploits and hunting ability and is therefore wealthy and can afford more wives, It seems the custom is to marry your wife's younger sister after she comes of age which is shortly after her menarche. It is supposed that sisters as wives create more harmony than unrelated women. It does not seem as odd as one supposes. There are far more women than men due the men dying in hunts and on warfare so the custom of having several wives addressee this imbalance. Can you imagine the number of spinster there would be in every village if they followed our custom of one wife. It seems when a women is pregnant her husband does not mount her and that is a time when another wife is taken. The wife who gives birth has the child with her constantly including in her bed. I have seen childen as old as six come to their mother and take hold of her breast to feed. The husbands don't resent this attention because they have another wife. They never see white men with white women so they think it odd they don't have wives. Men get married when they have some war honors or have learned some profession and of course the better hunters have the means for more wealth and getting an esteemed bride means a man must have war honors or wealth preferable both so in that sense our cultures are not different.

CHAPTER X

THE PAWNEE BUFFALO HUNT

THERE IS NO SIGN FOR Indian there is only the English word. There are signs for each and every tribe, but no sign to include all tribes under the word Indian or under any word inclusive of all tribes therefore the idea of Indian does not exist among the tribes it is wholly an idea of American's to put these tribes together under this word. The sign for Pawnee means wolf. The right hand is held in front palm out slightly above and close the right shoulder the first two fingers are extended like ears and the arm is moved forward and upwards while bringing the arm and palm nearly parallel to the earth.

There is no sign for the word meat just for the signs for the individual animals. Dried meat is the sign for cutting up and the sign for the animal. Here on the prairie animals and people are individual.

The sign for white man is hat, meaning people with hats and that means all who are not of the soil of the land or prairie. So we are people who come across the land with these strange things covering our heads. When I see it through their eyes I wonder what we are keeping from our heads it seems we wear these shields from something above us. I imagine them looking up to wonder what it is that we are shielding or hiding from. It is our hat not our skin that makes us stand out it is our hat not any other part of our clothing that makes us stand out. It is our hat not our guns that name us. There are some tribes who have been trading with the English who call American long knives to distinguish the two types of white men. The French the Spanish and the English being the white men most tribes of the plains saw first.

The sign for white man is very similar to one of the few signs most whites know the slashing index finger across the throat, just make the sign across the forehead at eye level and you have the sign for white men.

The drums beat all night, every night. I have been too weary to stay up each night to witness all that goes on with this drumming. We move further down the Platte after our first camp on the Platte and then we strike south camping on the Little Blue River and finally last night we made the Republican River. The scouts are out for this country is likely to have buffalo.

As far as I can tell the Pawnees do not use the sun nor stars to guide them, but rather rely on memory of the landscape consulting others in the tribe when they are unsure. Maps are drawn in the dirt with sticks and stones used to represent objects within the map. Most of our travel has been along riverbeds or on buffalo trails between the rivers with the rivers generally running west-east and flowing to the east into the Missouri. Given a choice they always choose the lower land or the ravines and valleys for travel rather than exposing themselves on hilltops and ridges. There is no caution taken with the large group I travel in as all the land around us is being constantly scouted with men riding back and forth all day to inform the leaders of what they see. This is not to say they won't use the sun or stars as they seem to be keenly aware of the position of the stars in the sky and have a ceremony honoring the Morning Star it's just that they have a more reliable mapping system with their memories.

Today there is much excitement in the camp as buffalo have been reported so the Priests are holding meetings in the medicine lodge. There also is much smoking and purifying of weapons with burning sage. The hunters are being selected and a force of soldiers is appointed with special paint and clubs to keep order and ensure all stay in camp. No big fires are allowed only those with twigs and the dung of buffalo. Only small drums are allowed and the horses are kept close the lodges.

All day the meeting goes on. The buffalo have been spotted south of us and a bit to the west. In mid-afternoon the village crier informs us ther will be no hunt that day as the signs are not right. I sought out Eagle Hand to learn more about the buffalo and the hunt.

"You will learn more when we get to my village, but know that for all the tribes of the prairie the buffalo is part of our hearts and in all our spirits. No one can remember a time without the buffalo. Our clothes our tools the lodges around us the containers holding our food and water our beds and even some of our games come from the buffalo. The buffalo were with us before the horse. All animals have power that can help us but the buffalo breathes life into us."

"I want to know about the hunt," I ask.

"Since I have been to see the white man hunt in the land of the east I must tell you that is not a hunt like you know. Many white men kill well and go with the excitement of the hunter, but they kill with a spirit that frightens me. The white man hunt and try to take away the animals spirit before they kill it. I do not know how they do this magic in their hearts, but I see it. I fear this will make the buffalo angry not angry in fighting angry but in spirit where they will try to hurt my people."

"Do you feel I will do this?"

"I do not know. Maybe it is like I do not honor your God and so therefore I cannot offend him and so you cannot anger the buffalo. To hunt with me I need your heart in the right place for only then will I feel safe with all the spirits there are too many spirits in the world to risk offending them. When your hearts opens in the heat of the hunt it need to be pure so that you do not draw bad spirits. First you must know this is about your spirit so that you can protect it".

"I would like to do this but you must tell me what I am to do."

"It is not something to be told it is something to be felt. I will tell you about the buffalo so that you have a place to anchor your spirit. I do not know if is white man fears the spirit of the buffalo or thinks his spirit is greater than the buffalo. The buffalo is like us she has her little ones at about 10 moons. Right now the unborn live within cows and soon in the months you call April and May they will be born These unborn are a great delicacy. You see we only kill cows for meat especially this time of year when the meat is getting poor. The bulls are killed for the hide for robes, shields and trade. The buffalo eats the sun for the sun makes the prairie grass grow and so we eat the sun when we eat the buffalo. That is the circle of life and the buffalo know this just as we know it. The buffalo wants us to respect them and to honor them and they give up many of their lives for us in turn."

"A fellow told me that every part of the buffalo is used…nothing wasted?"

"True if you include all the peoples of the land: wolves, fox, raven. The man uses foolish reason. Have you seen the hoes made from the shoulder blade of the buffalo?"

"Yes."

"Have you seen the hide scrapers the women use made from the leg bone?"

"Yes."

"We may kill 100, 300 or 500 buffalo on this hunt. Who will need 200 hoes or 500 hoes? The White man prides himself on his reason yet he doesn't see this. What would we do with 500 scrapers when all the women have scrapers and a scraper may last many years. **If** we have killed enough cows for the meat we will not take the meat of the bulls only the tongue and hide for the hide can be traded for guns to protect us from enemies."

"So you waste the rest?"

"We take what we need we do not understand this word waste."

"It means not used, useless no profit."

"I know nothing of this way in the world. Everything is used do you not respect that ravens little and big wolves and even the flies and hardback six leggeds and the grass itself all use as you say the buffalo? If I do not need a buffalo for my body my shelter my comforts I do not take but others do. Waste useless is not in our world it feels like something out of place like fish on land but I do not see such a thing in our world it is something out of the mind of a white man."

"From what you say I see there is no waste, but I think the white man means anything he personally does not use is waste or anything he personally can't profit by."

"Most white men who hunt the buffalo the first time kill a large old bull I have not been able to see to what purpose. They seem surprised to learn that the young cows are the best meat, but they know this about their beeves why they all lose reason. It seems that the white man thinks that the world and everything in it is made just for him for how else can this world have waste. How else can he lose his reason."

"If you chase the buffalo on a horse how do you reload at a full run?"

"We hunt with arrows for it tells us which lodge the buffalo belong each man's arrow has his mark. Our horse are trained to the twang of our strings so that they leap to the right when the arrow pierces the buffalo for many buffalo will turn at the pain and try to kill the horse for we ride within a lance length of the buffalo. It is difficult to load a rifle at full gallup and some hands have been lost to those who do not keep the ball to the powder and some horses lost to balls that found the head of the horse instead of the buffalo. The bow is the best weapon. That is why you must begin the arrow games with the boys so that you can hunt buffalo. Now you must use the rifle but is not good. Do not put your ball into the head of the buffalo I have seen white man's balls bounce off the head and only anger the buffalo. All shots are made behind the ribs forward into the muscle that pushes the lungs. When that muscle is cut the lung is also cut and buffalo will lose first his wind and then his life. For you to get close you must have a buffalo runner no horse not trained will approaches the buffalo close. I will speak to Medicine Horse to see if he has such a horse and you must go with the boy to see how to approach a buffalo on such a horse. It is better if you wait for summer. In the summer we train the by letting them chase the calves for the calves will fall behind in the chase that is the best way to learn how to get close to a buffalo. But the most important is that you follow what the clubman says is the one time that a man is not allowed to act on his own all else in life you may do as you wish, but you cannot go in front of the clubman. I will say that a place for you would be to hold the packhorses for the run the buffalo in no easy thing and there is much danger without skill. You should learn as our people do for you will have more skill and respect."

I was saddened that Eagle Hand did not wish me to run the buffalo, but I understood that I know little about it. Even less than I thought.

There was dancing and drums that night with men wearing the horns the tail and the robe of the buffalo with men whose face had horns of the buffalo curling up from the corner of the mouth with men from whose chest glared the image of a buffalo. *Tomorrow we eat. Tomorrow we feast.* Those were the words I remember out of that night of strange noises.

We move out as the sun rises the south side of the hills with ridges of hard snow sparkle below the diamond sparkle of hoarfrost on the leafless branches. The valleys are cruncy with snow thrice or more frozen. The scouts ride back from a night of watching the herd, consult with the hunt leaders. The clubmen are up front and to the side of the hunters. Most men ride a horse and lead their buffalo runner. I stay towards the back with the boys who bring the pack animals. Behind us the women gather to follow. It is orderly compared to our first morning and quiet. For all the babies there is not one crying. I noticed that the women early teach the babies not to cry by anwering their every need with close attention and occationally they pinch the nose when the baby does cry to discourage it.

After a slow walk we come to range of hills between two creeks there is a high bluff overlooking a valley. We are northeast of the forks of the Solomon River. The buffalo are down in this valley and it seems there are several herds spread out as far as the eye can see in a generally north south direction. The hunters are moving down the creek bed towards a herd over the hills from us. As the hunter move down the creek I can see some or the horse are pancing and acting very impatient as if more eager to start the hunt than the men trying to remain calm of their backs.

The men have their bows strung these are mostly Osage orange bows or bois de arc they are called with most having a wrapping of sinew round the curve of the wood. Their quivers now in front of their bodies hold a couple a dozen arrows some of the men hold extra arrows in the last three finger of their left hand. I was shown these hunting arrows, which have tips of thin steel made from barrel staving or were trade points. The hunting arrow is a different design that the war arrow with the most noticeable difference is the nock is lined up with the plane of the blade tip. Some had three feather and some two feathers with a more noticeable opposing twist on the two than the three-feathered arrows. All the bows are short none coming no higher than a man's hip when placed on the ground. I have only used and seen longbows so these seemed short to me. But I was told they have the power to go though a buffalo.

The men mount their buffalo runners almost all are bareback with some only carrying a simple rope halter looped around the lower jaw of the horse the rope being about forty to sixty feet long this coiled rope is tucked under the loincloth. If a man is dismounted they will grab this rope so as to not lose their horse. Many men sit with the their robe around their waist some with skin shirts on and some with bare skin in the cold air it it perhaps a few degrees below freezing. Everyone is tense there is little talk movement is by hand signal, eyes and facial expressions. The men move out in silence.

We wait behind the hills, but the tension is too high and I sneak up the hill with some other boys leaving the packhorses in the ravine below. For a while all we can see are the buffalo grazing dark shapes scattered thoughout the valley. There are about six groups of fifty each and there is a separation of nearly a quarter mile before one sees another mass of dark clumps. A breeze blows in our faces and I smell the woolish smell of the beasts. It is late morning and many buffalo are sitting down with forefeet under chewing their cud. Movement from the opposite hills turns out to be hunters coming down from our left. Out of the creek bottoms rode several more at a slow walk and from our right down the ridge of hills were we sit a larger group of men ride. The outer line of buffalo catch sight of the hunters and start running towards our ridge line. The men below us charge forward to intersect the buffalo. The rest of the herd springs to its feet fol-lowing the ones running though their midst. But as the men from the left approach the herd they turns up our valley to our right. The men coming down he ridge flattened out over the mounts and intersect the front of the herd turning them left and I can see the first buffalo dropping. The men look like the legs are touching the buffalo so close they are to the beasts. They ride acoss the front of the herd turning them back to the opposite hills, which has cliff-like banks. The herd turns back upon the direction they came making a large U-turn with men ridiing on both sides on the the U in opposite directions and those that come down the hill riding across the front of the U turning them into the tail so that now the herd is running in a vast circle about a mile or more wide with the men strung out like spokes around the edge all the while firing arrows. While many beast from the outside sliding on the front feet and bellies and sides as they crash to earth in a puff of snow streaking the earth clean of snow making brown rents in the surface of white.

Around they go as the circle gets smaller and more bodies make brown rents causing some men to jump the prostrate forms. One man did so and his horse hit a depression full of snow throwing him forward his arrows scattering by his hand still clasping the long rope but a buffalo with an arrow in its side turns as the horse wallowed and hooked her in the side lifting her with a toss of his head and sliding her across the snow. A dark line appeared up her side as she struggles to their feet and a great mass of shiny material appear under her feet as she bucks and jumps spreading pinkness on the snow and soon it is evident her feet are tangled and tramping on her insides from which she manages to free herself whereupon she commenced a teetering trot about a hundred yards before the effects of the self-embowelment and bleeding fells her into a jerking jumbled pile that soon quivers into stillness another still dark form amidst the powdered plain. The hunter has run and leaped onto a passing hunter's horse his bow still intact in his hand. Soon both are shooting form the back of the horse the back hunter pulling arrows out of the quiver in front.

Around and around they go the hunter on the outer circle on their spotted their yellow their red their white horses with the blackness of the buffalo inside the hoop. More and more dark shapes drop sliding on sides and chests leaving one last dark mark upon their death. Bellows of anger and fear answered by neighs and trills of killing passion all with the echo of distance reaching my ears with a hallowed edge. Horses leap prostrate forms horse stretch their necks and strain to catch yet another wooly beast horses leap aside at swinging horns and charge again and again to the dark heaving sides of the beasts nearly twice their weight. Two more men become unhorsed but man and beast are soon joined again in the chase after both finish a wild skid on snow and mud the earth now churned from the hooves of fear the circle closing the white center shinking as the darkhoop fractures wobbles wavers and turns upon itself until only a bull stands legs wide sides heaving with shafts moving like the bones of wings shorn as he bellowed out his defiance at the beasts who ride around him the swinging and now impotent horns his bellow bass to the treble and soprano trills of hundreds of men women and now even children circling him and descending the hillsides to the bounty bleeding in the snow: shouts of joy, of life, of thanks, of unbounded happiness, of spirits soaring at the sight of warm robes waiting, snug moccasin, beautiful shirts and leg-gings, spoons of horns, hooves of glue, backs of sinew, to bind things useful and make bows strong, of elastic bags of paunch, heartskin, and bladder, to store, to canteen their water to bones of hoe, of knives, of marrow so rich and fat for pemmican and stew and to make children's bones grow strong and entrails all warm and rich with the life of sun and prairie still thick within, giving thickness to thin winter blood and richness to skin and bone and warm dense lean meat from tongue to hump, from rib to loin, from rump to shank it is all a guarantee of life to come of the everlasting circle of prairie and plains.

We all run leaping and sliding down the hill to the bounty below our faces are lit with joy and anticipation. The warriors are dismounted and moving among the downed to identify their kills waving to family. There are perhaps 300 buffalo on the ground. The bull has dropped his knees folding under him and he perched dead but still upright on a small hillock like a hub in the center.

The families reach their buffalo while some of the older women move down the valley to the edge of the river and begin setting up teepees. Most buffalo are turned over on their sides or back but a few dress the cows that have fallen on their knees by splitting the hide down the back and laying the hide flat on the ground still attached underneath the animal while they cut the meat off the bones and stack it onto the skins.

Travois behind dogs and horse are moved the yippy whining dog sound mixing with the excited happy voices of the people as they busy their hands. Laughter and shouts ring up the valley as the bellies of of buffalo are opened and steaming liver and kidneys taken out and bitten into and slices of meat cut off the hump and downed. The warmth of the prairie, the green grasses of summer past, the clean rain, The pure snow the crystal blue air are all before us in the warm embrace of the buffalo the living heat under our hand of a life past and life future for us the animals are destined to be part of us to cover us to decorate and to honor us these great beasts live on in our bodies and homes.

I found Eagle Hand and he has a cow turned up and opened up. He grins at me with a bloody chin his hand holding a large liver.

"You must eat so you do not get winter sickness. Here I put some bile on for flavor."

He sprinkles some greenish bile form the gall bladder onto the liver. I admit it is not fare that I relish although I have always liked liver, but not had it raw. I took the chunk he cut off for me for I have been trained since before memory to never refuse a host's offer of food. I close my eyes and bit into it and opened them in delight for the liver is mild tasting compared to beef and bile tastes like mustard and the warmth of the organ makes it seem cooked. Soon my chin runs with blood as do those around me the children's faces as well as hands covered in blood. An old women next to me dug out the eyes and began to chew on them offering me one when she saw me looking. I had fish eyes before they are chewy like sap of gum but these eyes looked too big for my appetite. Eagle hand took some boudin out of the first stomach and began chewing on one end of it he offered me the other end of it but I held up my liver that I was still eating. Another man came over and took up the other end of the boudin and they were standing face to face with the long gleaming steaming viscera hanging down between them. The chewed and swallowed as fast as possible and then the other man swallowing this leaned back and pulled the boudin out of Eagle Hands mouth they were whole not chewed. Finally grasping each other's shoulders they snapped the heads back and broke it off both laughing when they could use their mouths again.

These all have power! Eagle Hand said pointing to the people around us eating different parts of the buffalo. The kidneys help the aged the brains strengthen the warrior and the liver keeps the bones strong.

I knew the brains were also needed to tan the hides so I split the skull of the animal I worked on and scooped out the soft tissue onto the skin. This is my first fresh buffalo. I cut some meat from the hump. It is a dense meat with no fat visible in the meat yet it tastes rich and full and is very tender, more tender than any beef or lamb I've had. Soon I am amazed at how much I've downed. I have some salt with me, and that is all the meat needs. There is some fat next to the skin, but little within the folds of muscle. These beasts are big a ton or more and it amazed me how strong the arms of the women are in pulling off the hides which must a weigh nearly one hundred pounds with the layer of flesh still attached. Most of the meat is cut off the bones, but some cut the sinew in the joints and tie the legs to their packs thigh bones seemed the most numerous and always the tongue are taken even on the big bulls where the meat is left.

The only experience I had to compare was the butchering of sheep at my Uncle's. There was no ceremony no chase nor hunt no danger. I was killing an animal who knew not to fight and animal whose birth foretold its death an animal with a spirit bred for man not nature. It was a job with fresh stew as a reward. An occasional somber and non-religious event compared to this one. Yes many buffalo escaped and many did not and many died at once and many did not. But there can be no doubt in witness to the majesty of the these men as surpreme predators as lords of this land as a people whose footsteps are made with the skins and spirits of the animals of this land. These buffalo who died the rise above the plains in teepees their faces painted on homes, on clothes and on the skin of man while the skin and wool of the buffalo warms man even the bellow of the beast in turned into the boom of the drum.

These people, these strange new people whose tongue I do not know these people with sound of joy echoing up the down this valley this valley setting into the cooling of the night. These people have a life that was not in my imagination. Here there is no rent to pay no landlord no tax collector no king no one is demanding his due right now that assets are available. No singing in the pub nor dancing in the street can compare to the joy that I see. They have conquered. They are free. The old, the poor the crippled all eat, all dance and sing.

As we move down the valley to the river the flickering of yellow fire-light beckons from the hundreds of fires the still air filled with the smell of oak ash and roasting ribs, humps and buffalo fat. The valley thumps with the skins of the buffalo's ancestors getting louder at we near with loads of buffalo slapping on horseback or scraping into the earth on travois poles.

Several skins are on the path into the village where most drop chunks of meat and skins for those families without hunters. Women are cutting strips of meat against the grain and slapping half foot long pieces over the raised grid work of branches high above the dogs reach with smokey wet wood fires underneath. Tripods in and outside the teepees with iron pots and pauches fill with stews of hearts kidneys and delicacies of the fresh kill. Ribs and humps rest against licking flames. Stakes are being pounded into skins stretched in front of teepees. Dogs who are not feeding on the killing fields sit alert as chunks of meat are tossed their way. Already the howl of the wolves and whining yip of little wolves ring down the valley a night of feasting for all now begins.

To describe the variety of dishes cooking in the camp is difficult as there are so many pots with blood broth cooking there are humps the muscle from the hump cut from the spine and sewed up in a pocket being placed in earthen pits with glowing coals. This piece of meat is the most sought after for it has a strip of fatty tissue along its crest. Some are roasting the hump suspended from sticks over the fire. I saw one man eat the entire hump, which is nearly ten pounds of meat. Some are dipping chunks of meat in sizzling grease. One woman has dug a giant pit and lined it with fresh buffalo hide and she carries hot stones dropping them into the broth that filled the skin with water boiling as the stones are dropped in. It looks to be enough to feed several families. Another is boiling lung and corn in a broth and that I taste it and it is excellent. Stripped thighbones are arranged around most fires roasting to be cracked open and the marrow pried out and the crisp meat on the bone eaten with it. The marrow is also used to make pemmican. Everywhere I went people beckoned for me to try this or that delicacy. Only once that evening did I witness an act of selfishness and that was a young brave who was yelling at another over several robes. It seems he wanted the robes for trade and his brother wanted them for making robes, shields and other personal uses.

"Our people have always traded." Eagle Hand says coming up to my side while I watch the two men argue.

"I suppose fights like this are common," I said.

"No. This does not happen much. A man gets respect for what he gives away not what he keeps. I have seen more of this with the trading of whiskey and guns. Now that the American's are trading against the English whiskey is pushed by both sides. It does not affect my people for we do not trade with whiskey, but the Cree, Assinboin, Sioux, Cheyenne, Arikara and many of the tribes many times will trade for whiskey. Guns are given to one tribe to be allies with a group of traders and those without guns get driven out or killed so they are desperate to get guns for defense. As you see we don't need guns for hunting we need guns for defense."

There is dancing and laughter so Eagle Hand sits with me and tells me what the songs are saying. A young hunter is dancing singing his song with laughter:

Each twang of my bow
Brings down a buffalo
And now my belly is full

Each twang of the bow
Brings down a buffalo
And now I turn over my bowl

Each twang of my bow
Brings down a buffalo
And now I fill my wife.

He makes a mock charge towards his wife and there is great laughter as one of his wives sings back:

And my husband
Mounts me like a buffalo
Twang!

All erupt in laughter at the wife's song. Eagle Hand explains that when a bull mounts a cow he is so quick that if you blink he will be done and you will have missed it.

Dancing goes on all night the air is filled with the shouts of the winners in the many gambling games they play as well as the moans of the loser many robes not yet tanned trade hands that night. The grandmother stay vigilant in watchin the young girls who sit making eyes and smiling across the fires, the young men dancing and singing of their exploites that day to impress the girls, but the grandmothers are the ones to be making the lewd remarks and laughting among themselves.

I fall asleep to the song:

To squeeze my thighs
And draw my bow
My horse know where to go

We stay along the river for over a week everyone busy with hides and drying buffalo and pounding sinew and repairing bows and clothes with fresh sinew. I keep up my duties with watching the horse herds and I also start going out with boys younger than me shooting a bow. Eagle Hand handed me his bow telling me I must learn its ways. I have blunt tipped green ash arrows. I made some more by trading freshly cut ash runners to a man who had aged and smoked bundle of shafts tied in sinew. Using the hoofs of the buffalo long boiled in a iron pot I had glue to attach my turkey feather fletching to the shaft after tying each end of exposed feather spine to the shaft with sinew. I did both three feather and two feather arrows using opposite wing feathers for the two feather arrows thereby making opposing twists in the feathers. The knock I cut with a knife as I did a curving line along the shaft to increase the shaft strength in flight for the curved lines keeps the shaft from bending overmuch. My fingertips are soon sore as is my inner left arm for the snap of the bowstring.

I am soon shown that the shooting is not one where one spends time aiming, but rather one learns to shoot with your whole body following the focus of your eye and pushing the bow out with my left hand rather then pulling the string with my right. The repetition soon has me nocking and placing the arrows the same each time. By the second day I am hitting a rolling wooden disk wrapped in strands of dried marsh grass.

The day arrives when the crier calls out that all are to prepare to leave in the morning. We wake to the noisy chaos like our first morning out of the village only there is much more to load this morning with nearly every horse burdened including some of the buffalo runners of those who do not own enough pack horses. Grandmother is walking though calling on us to hurry as big snows are coming.

Two days later we are camped on the Little Blue River. Word comes back from the scouts that large parties of Sioux are on Omaha hunting ground northeast of our lodge village. The report comes from the Grand Pawnees. Medicine Horse sends another group of scouts out to further the ring of eyes around our group including scouts to find the other half of the village, which should be returning for the spring planting ceremonies.

CHAPTER XI

THE FLIGHT

THERE IS NO SIGN FOR love, as we know it at least in the romantic sense. The closest sign to it is crossed wrists that is closed fists in front of and above the heart a few inches out from the body with the right forearm pressed to the heart. It means embrace, fondness and liking there is no falling no ecstasy not even any lewdness in that sign although there are plenty of lewd hand signs. The sign for think means drawn from the heart. One holds the right hand with index finger pointing flat against the heart and moves the hand horizontally outwareds the to the right about a foot. For the people of the plains fondness and thinking come from the same place. It seems that these people think with their heart not their head.

Eagle Hand has an admirer. I've heard the women gossiping about it, that is I heard his name and I now know the lewd teasing laugh the women make when they are talking about attraction and they stop when Eagle Hand come near. Putting that together with seeing the woman who seems to walk by with wood and water and even empty hand several times a day over the last several days makes it obvious as does her flickering eyes turn on Eagle Hand when he is not watching her. The men, that is the young men spend their days trying to seduce or take the woman the women flirt and mostly avoid them but some like to be caught and go down to get wood or water alone and sometimes come back without either.

I am curious to know how this all works. It reminds me of teasing we got back in Dublin when someone caught one's eye or you were the object of such admiration. There being so many more women here than men unlike Dublin it seems that things work differently. It is the men who keep the village from being exterminated by their enemies and it is the men who are always killed first with the older women next and very young children next as they cannot be so easily cared for as captives leaving the girls as the most desirable captives. There are several women in this tribe who are captives and who ended up wives of men. They do not seem to be treated any differently to my eyes. The one women I know who is always treated badly is a Comanche women who does not yet know their tongue someone who doesn't respect the tribe enough to learn their tongue will always remain a captive and never a member of their tribe.

Coming from a society where we are oppressed by a people who place so much emphasis on bloodlines as if breeding is the sole criteria for all that is great in a person, it it curious to be amongst people where there is almost no concern for bloodlines. True the chief's son has more advantages than the village criers son, but both still have to prove their bravery and power to gain the respect of the people. Any man can rise to the highest respect of his tribe based on his deeds. Even being of the bloodline of of the enemy does not prevent one from rising in rank. One of the chief's has a Comanche wife who bore him a son and that son is treated like a chief's son. There are a couple of French trappers who have taken wives and they are part of the tribe as are their children are raised Skidi. The women have nearly complete control over the children until about age seven.

I sought out Eagle Hand to see what he had to say about this Skidi woman who seemed to have her arms crossed for him.

"Eagle Hand I'm curious how marriage happens with the Pawnees?"

He looked at me with a little smile. "You are too young for a wife. You have to show bravery but one cannot have a wife until one has gone out on a war path or has a skill."

"I do not wish to marry I wish to understand."

"Ahh! I see a star in your eye. You have another question."

"I see the Skidi woman look at you and wonder how courtship happens and then marriage?"

"You have been around the women too much, Irish." He laughs as he taps the pipe bowl against his heel. "Yes she is making signs to let me know she is interested. She comes from a good family and has two younger sisters she is much sought after for one will gain respect being part of her family and if worthy her husband will be able to take her sisters as wives when they become old enough."

"How old would that be?"

He laughed at me. "A white man question. A number makes it so, just like a name makes it real. It is not the number of moons or years of life for a girl but her first moon flow that is what makes her a woman."

"I understand that, but I wouldn't know which girl had her menarche in Dublin and I sure wouldn't dare ask her so that is why we go by age an age past the Menarche of most women."

You do not know when the girls of your village have their first moon-flow?

"Jesus, Mary and Joseph no!"

"Why is it hidden?"

"It's too private it's embarrassing it just isn't done."

Eagle Hand looked down at the fire with a sad face. "I do not wish to offend, for I do not know your ways. The moon-flow is the first sign of the great gift given to women of their creative power. After her moon-flow she has this great power this power to create life. To hide the greatest power on earth is beyond the understanding of I and my people and all the peoples that I know one these plains. All of the whte men hide this power of their women?"

"Yes all that I know of."

    moon-flow of our girls the crier runs though the village and announces it and a ceremony and celebration and gifts follow. She becomes a woman on that day and she begins to live her life as a woman from that day forward. She can be married after this event, but many do not marry for years after, but all know that she is a woman and she may be wooed. I have tired to think of a reason why the white man would hide the greatest power on earth for he does not hide the great power of his cannons or guns or steamships why does he hide the creative power of his women."

"I cannot really answer that for it is something I have lived with. I think it is because we fear sexual pleasure above all else and a moon-flow implies sex and if we don't name it like you say it doesn't exist. So how does courtship happen if a women is interested like this Skidi?"

"It is the white man believing that words or not words makes it so. How funny that he use his not-words against the greatest power on earth. Then Eagle Hand smiles and looks at me. I know your word courtship means woo but it is a twisted word for I understand it to mean like our council fireplace where chiefs and grandfathers sit for us it is not about king or courts of law. I like wooing better for it is more a dance of the body that starts a man and women on the path of joining. It is the spirit of our loins that makes our bodies dance for another and wish to join another. That is the most powerful force of wooing and that is what joins two different spirits of women and man together. But we have a custom that is part of the joining. The man must have the power and skills to provide the meat for his women and children and his women must have the skills to make the lodge, clothing and to grow and prepare the foods from the earth. She is the creator he is the protector, joined they are both stronger. The grandmothers help make him stronger and give him wisdom to provide and protect, so the spirit of the loins helps make a marriage but one does not join in marriage just for the loins. The young men answer the spirit of their loins in many ways without joining in marriage as do some of the young women but for women it is considered improper to have a child without a protector. Without a man in her lodge the child will be taken care of by the grandmothers but it is a burden to add to her lodge without bringing a strong hunter and protector. Such a woman could be in danger of being used by the warriors unless her family has strong warriors to protect her. So it is always best for a woman to have her man protect her. You ask how this happens: I tell you that if a man is interested he will make eyes with her and try to get her alone or talk to her at games and ceremonies show off in front of her and some will even try to play the flute to her although this is mostly funny since few can play a flute that pleases the ears. He will try to know her a little more that way but he knows much of her if he know her family so that is the most important knowing. He will usually have someone to talk to her father to see if he would approve the marriage and if the word comes back favorable or at least not negative for many fathers do not want to appear eager for they will lost some honor and position doing so. The father has such a position for he is the protector of the women in his family. The wooing man will have to leave a horse or several horses tied up outside her mother's lodge. If the horses are accepted then the marriage is appoved by her family. This is the story there are many more things that happen before the horses are accepted.

"So that it you give horses and you are married? She just moves in or is there a ceremony." Jack joins us as I ask this question.

Eagle Hand laughed at me again. "The man joins her family remember the mother owns the lodge and all that's in it. If the marriage fails the husband is thrown out the lodge we say they are *thrown away*. The young children belong to the mother and boys older than seven to their fathers, but the boys can stay in the mother's lodge and keep their father from the mother's family. The father does not force a boys choice for that is the way or our people to never force. Our lodges hold many families until it becomes too small that is were the couple lives. Many times the birth-mother and birth-grand mother of the wife live in the lodge as well as other mothers and maybe grandmothers. All these women raise the children all are mothers just as all the fathers and grandfathers raise the young boys to be warriors. There is gift giving and much teasing of the new couple, but there is not the running away ceremony like the white man has it is more a man joining the woman's family. It is adding two people to this large family and that large family then helps raise the children of these two people. White people have a large ceremony and little joining. I see all those lonely families on the farms and my heart is sad that those children have no village and have no culture. I fear what will happen to children raised in such a strange lonely manner."

"Isn't there a God that is prayed to for this marriage to take place? A blessing of the sacred union?" Jack asked.

"No God of marriage no. Blessing by the families and the tribe. A marriage is a natural strengthening for two people each will make the other stronger. The Spirits do not interfere in such matters unless the two are of the same clan and then the spirits can bring evil on all in the lodge and certainly on the children of the couple. Marriage is for children for keeping our tribe strong and making it stronger with more warriors. It also makes one's blanket warm on cold winter nights." Eagle Hand made the sign for copulation which is right forefinger extended the left hand is held in front knifelike and slanted palm towards your belly with thumb up and into the space between the upright left thumb and forefinger the right index finger is slapped the other fingers in the right hand are in a fist which is slapped against the left palm in a slapping sound like two people copulating hard. He laughed as he made the slapping sounds.

"We think marriage is only for procreation," Jack replied with a smile.

"What is procreation?" Eagle Hand asked.

"Having coitus only to have children," Jack replied.

Eagle Hand smoked his pipe and considered this in silence before he spoke. "If your men marry so young how do tthey have the skills to protect and provide."

Jack looked puzzled. "We do not marry so young we marry when we are older than many of your people."

Now Eagle Hand looked puzzled. "How do your people swallow the energy of their loins for so many years. I have not seen the white man lay with other white men like some warriors on the warpath."

Puzzlement turned to digust on Jack face. "Sodomy! That is a vile sin! We control outselves. It is sacred to only use our energy of the loins as you call it to produce a child."

Eagle Hand looked concerned. "It is twisted. Such a force cannot be controlled no more than you can control the wind. All powerful feeling and spirits can be controlled for a short time if a man is strong but he will be twisted and filled by the power of the loins if he denies it's truth for too long. Only death is stronger."

"That is the savage way! Us Christians deny such base deisires. It strengthens us in our denial!"

"This is never seen in any white man just as I have never seen then fast seek a vision nor cut off a piece of the flesh for the spirits nor have I seen them dance. All the white men I have seen take our women as their wives or trade to lay with our women. The people of the plains offer their blood, their flesh to the spirits but never do we give away to the spirits the power of our loins for to do so would be to deny our very life to deny life itself for no creature does such a thing it is a twisted act that turns inside itself. What medicine does such an act give you?"

"It gives us dignity it gives us control it gives us spiritual strength."

Eagle Hand considered this before he answers. "Even our very old still honor the spirit of the loins no one wants to lose the power of our loins. A medicine man may turn the power of the loins to other purposes and other may do such a thing but none deny the power as you do. I hear you denying that it exists and that cannot please the spirits."

"We will get our reward, our power in heaven," Jack replies.

"This is a fright to me for not one else has dared to try such a thing I wish to see what power this act grants you."

"Man cannot just go around mounting evey women in sight". Huffed Jack. "We get dignity in our denial."

Eagle Hand laughs. "All our young warriors would desire to do that, but I do not know where you have seen such acts. If we deny food to our bodies for too long we die. Why do you not have your woman use their mouth or the mouth-behind-that doesn't-make-babies if you do not want to make children or use the lonely hand if you do not have a woman."

Jack scrunched up his face. "That is disgusting. We do not do acts of sodomy and onanism!"

"You do the white man giving-of-bad-name-to-the-good-thing. A name does not change the good feeling. For I know white men have only one wife. We do not copulate with our women when they are with child, nor when they are nursing the child, but some of us have other wives some lie with other warriors, but we do not deny the spirit of our loins for it is too powerful. What animals do you see do such a twisted thing?"

Jack exhibited such disgust and was so offended that Eagle Hand changed the subject. Eagle Hand would go to great lengths to avoid talking about anything sexual with Jack after this for he did not understand what happened, but he understood it was greatly upsetting to Jack. I observed that Eagle Hand and the Skidi did not engage in a good argument like many of my people used to in the pubs. I had been used to the sexual talk especially in a joking way as it was constant especially with the women and even though I understood little of the words there were always many gestures use for emphasis. I think Eagle Hand thought it was like a religious taboo with Jack and brought on bad feelings. Anytime there was such strong feeling shown on anything but war or games I noticed that Eagle Hand and the Skidi would avoid such subjects. They had learned to fear talking about anything that another man feared for it would only bring bad luck to do so. Eagle Hand kept smoking but soon refused any further conversation no matter what the subject. I soon left as did Jack leaving him to his thoughts.

That afternoon riders came in much excited and there is a council held and much tension from the people. After several hours a crier walked amongst the tents his nose pointed up calling out to all in a slow cadence. Jack sought me out and explained "that half of the tribe had been located by scouts but some of their people were sick. They had found a Santa Fe caravan and had traded with them several weeks ago but now they semed to have the white man sickness that makes holes in the face. We are headed back to the village to begin our spring planting ceremonies but now there is such fear of the sickness that there is much fear among the group." Eagle Hand soons joins us.

"I do not wish to get this sickness," Eagle Hand states with a solemn face.

"We can head back to the Missouri and try to catch a boat up the Mandan village," Jack exclaims.

"What if the sickness is on the river?" Eagle Hand says concerned.

"I suppose it could be since the Santa Fe traders could have come out of St. Louis, but it seems early for them to be so far on the trail, they likely could have been coming form over wintering in Santa Fe." Jack pulls his ear as he thought this out. "I have it! I can travel back to the River and hail a keelboat or steamer and see if they have news. That way I won't catch the disease if it is coming from down river and, if not, I can return to get you two and we can take a boat up the river to your village."

"The Sioux are about. I do not think they will come this far south but if they have had a lean winter they will be looking for trade goods so they can get corn. You will be an easy target your gun and horse will buy lots of corn." Eagle Hand looks grave as he says this.

"Eagle Hand I can travel faster alone there is likely to be many traders and trapper setting out for the mountains this time of year. By myself I can make the river in three or four days I don't have to worry about travois or pack mules." Jack seemed very excited.

"I do not stop you only warn you. We will stay on the west side of the Big Blue for ten days. If you do not return we will travel west until we reach the Black Hills Then we will go around the hills and go north up to the Missouri which we will follow down to my village. That way we will avoid the Sioux and the Arikara the Cheyenne."

Jack stands rubbing his hand on his thighs. "I will ready my pack! I leave before first light."

Eagle Hand looks at the tent flap then at me. "I hear what you and other white men have told me about this disease. Some of my grandfathers have told of it. I do not know how it kills so many and why it has such a spirit for death. I have heard of tribes who flee it but the spirits follow and kill them. What I have heard is that only those in war parities who did not return to the village those who were given blanket warning to not enter the village they were untouched by the spirits of this sickness. There are some here who believe their medicine will protect them. They will return to the village. My dream's tells me that my medicine is not strong so I cannot return to the Skidi village nor to any Pawnee villages. My dreams tell me that I cannot enter any village except a white man village and that it will be longer than I desire before I return to my village. I must not enter the village of any tribe except my people and those of the white man. Eagle hand motions with his chin to the flap so I leave him."

We are up before light and see Jack off. We leave to journey further up the Big Blue River where there is more firewood and bark for our animals. We leave our lodge behind for it belongs to Medicine Horse wives. He has not returned so we are unable to say goodbye We are given some skins to make a lean-to. It begins to rain and by late afternoon it has turned to snow and the wind rises out of the Northwest closing our world into a stinging white swirling world one only four-horse lengths in front of us. The ridge opposite the river is gone the trees lining the bank in a long line turn into a single tree. I know the river is still to our right and that we are still moving north but there is no sign of it just cottonwood trees and willows first as dark forms and then suddenly ten feet in front of you. There is little sense of movement other than the up and down motion of the horse and mule mixed with the sudden looming blurry dark shapes. Many times we have to lead our horses and hold the long lead rope while we slide down the draw to view the bottom for one can not see it from above and the footing it getting too slippery to stay in the saddle on such inclines. We finally have to stop and erect our skins between two trees protecting us from the wind along with the hillside and the thick willows. The fire is a comfort as the wind howls above us with incredible ferocity and darkness descends upon us earlier than normal. We gather cottonwood branches for our hobbled Creature to feed upon striping the bark for him and stacking the naked wood next to our fire. The next morning blue sky appears in patches above us but the ground continues to swirl in whiteness. Sometimes the sun reaches us for minutes at a time before the wind driven snow blankets us. All that day and the next the wind blows and the snow swirls.

We stayed in camp for nearly two weeks as Eagle Hand felt the spirits had guided us to the camp next to the sacred circle. He spent several days in fast mostly by himself and seemed to be very focused on his dreams. The circle has in me the shivers but not of fear rather is the shiver of mysteries, the recognition of awe edged with imperfect understanding.

Eagle Hand explained the circle to me, but the nearest I can place it as a cemetery where the skulls are like our headstones. We bury each body individually and erect singular stones with words they arrange skulls of many who died some time ago and who had their flesh rotted off by weather and creatures where the bodies resided in trees or rickety poles. The naturally cleaned and bleached bones are then removed and these sacred cemetery circles are created as some type of link between the earth and spirit world.

The last of the snow is swallowed by the red earth and the glassine ice first jumbles and sometimes rumbles and sometimes makes cracking snapping noises until today the streams only make rippling gurgling noises. The skies fill with flocks of honking and squawking geese some dark some white all flying in precise V's Other crane like and swanlike flocks croaked, squawked and made strange trilling nosies looking at times serenely beautiful and they slowly pushed the blue crisp spring air down in long slow sweeps then glided on the gentle swells of springtime air such graceful ethereal dances can suddenly become sharp violent tipping and slipping thought the air as the birds make ungainly descents to some choice piece of water or open meadow where they noisily feed but always with sentinels watching with necks held high. The small oak and hardwood trees hold feathery surprises nearly every morning. It seems that some of these birds arrive at night for they are not there at roost time when the earth darkens.

Ten days have past but we stay on as we are sure the storm has delayed Jack. But at twenty days in camp I am uneasy, but for some reason Eagle Hand will not move. He seems to be waiting for something. I become confused and cross as he refuses to move and refuses to tell me why.

We pass twenty five days when there appears a reddish cloud followed by a long dark line appearing and disappearing between the hills to the south of us. As they come closer we can see they have wagons. This is a surprise to Eagle Hand for he says mule trains are the only way he had seen white men travel this route although he had heard of the two wheeled wagons that had been used the by the trader Sublette one year. This is a large party approaching over a hundred by my count and I really can't see how many men might be in the back of the wagons.

"Mr. Sublette had twelve wagons and two Dearborn's it was the summer of thirty when he bought those wagons full of supplies to the Popo Agie River in the valley of the Wind River Mountains. I heard about it from the Crows who trade with us. One man had a drawing on a hide of the wagons that's how I remember. This could be him again but some of the beasts pulling them are not mules they are cattle."

"Oxen it looks like," I reply.

As the line of men, mules, oxen, horses and wagons clops closer over the dried hard red hilltops I can see the men engaged in conversation. A stout fellow with a down turned thin mouth set in a fleshy face with sharp squinting eyes moving constantly he seems to be in charge.

This man rode ahead to greet us tipping his hat brim. "Morning Gentlemen. We are on our way to the Rocky mountains to try our hand at the fur business now you wouldn't be engaged in such business would you?"

"Not in the Rocky Mountains, my people are the Mandan and we trade on the upper Missouri."

"That's British and American Fur Company territory that is it's supposed to be just American or just Mr. Astor territory." I met Mr Astor in New York.

"I belive I saw you there, I said. I was working at the American at the time quite a coincidence to meet out on the prairie. I'm Git O'Toole and this is Eagle Hand." He dismounts and walks over to offer a gloved hand. A light complexioned man in his mid twenties trots forward.

"I'm Captain Bonneville and this fellow up here is one of my field captain's: Mr Michael Cerre." Mr Cerre rode over to us, and leans over to shake hands. "He has much experience in the Santa Fe trade and now he's trying his hand at the Rocky Mountain trade." Mr. Cerre nods and looks at us, but his eyes are soon scanning the horizon.

"Captain, I afraid we've not much to offer such a large party for hospitality," I say.

"Think nothing of it. We have little time to fumer la pipe, for these wagons move at the pace of the ox. But the men are mighty glad not to have to unload the mules nightly." He looked back at the long train. "We must make tracks. I apologize for our rudeness. Mr Cerre keep them moving we'll not be taking a nooner yet. Are their any Indians about that we should be wary of?"

"There are Skidi north of the Platte and we hear the Sioux are northeast of them but we do not know what lies to the west. The Skidi flee the disease coming from the Santa Fe trail. What news have you of sickness."

"None. All was well when we left Missouri. We left Fort Osage on the first of May and all was well on the Kansas when we met White Plume his people had no sickness and that was near a week ago".

A native comes riding up to the other man that Bonneville had nodded to in his introductions. He is still back near a hundred yards. The fellow is tall dark and seems used to command. The dress of the native was not one that I knew. I nod in his direction with a question on my face.

"Oh him. He's a Delaware. Good reliable men. They are without land at the moment waiting for the government to assign them some in the Indian Territory. They are eager for the hunt. They want to try their hand at chasing buffalo. We got 110 men to move. If they stop it's hell to get them going again so I bid you adieu". He nods his head to us. "You are welcome to join us at camp tonight."

"Thank you but we wait for someone here," Eagle Hand answered.

He rode down the line. We watch the train with all the men nodding, saluting and waving at they pass. Some look like seasoned mountain trappers and other like city boys. They are certainly taking more goods than just mules could have managed and it does seems easier to unhitch the oxen than to unload the packs off the mules each night. But on the creek just past us I can see the men trying ropes to lower and slow the wagons down the steep banks and then crowding around the wheels to push it up the other side. We had passed many creeks flowing from a westerly direction so it seems their progress will be slow until they reach the flat land by the Platte River.

There is a mixture of the two wheeled and four wheeled carts with the two wheel putting more stress on the animals up the steep banks. They have a herder driving cattle and sheep bringing up he rear with even a few calves.

I look at Eagle Hand as they pass up the far side of the creek bed. "Will we be joining them?"

"No. I did not see carts the men we seek will be on horse and mules."

I feel keen disappointment. It is now May 22nd and we have been waiting for a month along the Big Blue River. We expected Jack some weeks back. The weather has turned fair the leaves fill the trees the grasses grow green and tall and the birds sing in the defense of their territory with many busy tending nests. I take up my rifle and head up the hillside to west. After a short walk I came upon a strange sight at some distance. Tis a moving circle that slowly rolling across the earth in a lightly wooded area it looks like a large wheel as high as the burr oaks. As I move closer I see that it is birds. The earth is covered with bird's serveral acres in fact. Coming closer I see they are pretty birds maybe a pigeon. They walk along shoulder to shoulder feeding upon the earth and the rearmost birds are continually lifting and alighting to the front of the flock and thereby forming the circle of birds. The birds towards the front are continually picking food from the earth and those in the end march along with nothing to eat but remain in the march until they have no birds behind them and they lift off and land in front. I load my pistols with shot as my rifle in loaded with ball. I come right on to these birds and fire killing some and they don't change their march. They look at their dead and wounded companions beside them but continue moving forward and lifting off only when there was none behind them. I am able to slay thirty birds. These birds turn out to have the most tasty dark breast meat I have ever had. The legs are small so that I simply split the breast skin and popped the succulent breasts out. Wrapped in wild grape leaves and roasted with wild garlic greens it makes for a tasty meal.

The next day in the forenoon we see dust rising form the hills to the south of us. Going to the top of the ridge to reconitore we discern that it is a large party only there is no wagons this time. Coming closer we see that is a pack train with each man leading two pack mules one man comes riding from the rear and two confer and the rear rider turns back. Soon a blue-eyed fair skinned clean-shaven fellow with scar on his left chin is looking down at us. He has a slightly hooked nose and holds himself stiffly. He dismounts his fine horse and stand over six feet tall.

"Gentlemen, I'm Bill Sublette and that other fellow I's alongside is Robert Campbell. We're traders with supplies for the Rendezvous. I know most men white and Indian in these parts but I not seen you two afore. You don't look to be trappers" he said raising an eyebrow. He paused for us to explain ourselves. His eyes are keen and contantly moving as if he expects to see more men around.

"I am Eagle Hand of the Mandans People of the First Man and this is Git O'Toole of the Irish people. We are seeking passage to my village but the Pawnees who have sheltered us have taken the white man sickness from traders of Santa Fe and the Sioux are to the north blocking our way so we wait here. Yee I have dreamed. We wait for you."

"Well I already got two dozen downeasters that wouldn't hardly know a beavertail if it slapped them in the face Mr Wyeth's New Englander's party. I expect you two could be more handy in a fight than them. I been coming this route for several years now and some of the tribes have taken a right down bad feeling to me. But nobody joins unless they follow the rules and pulls their weight. You take your watch with your team and you take charge of two mules each which you load and unload the equipage and you follow my orders all right? We'll be goin' at round pace. You can fall in if you don't want to hold fast here."

I looked at Eagle Hand and nods to me. "Yes sir Mr Sublette!" I shout so happy I am to be moving further into the Far West.

"Just see me when we camp for your assignment, all right" Sublette says as he swings his horse around to the pack train.

I can't get the blankets rolled up fast enough nor do I make the kind of tidy roll that I like. I am doing this when I hear a voice behind me.

"Will ya be riding with that lumpy apishamore across this grand land?"

I turn to see a smiling Thomas Fitzpatrick.

"I'm glad to see you'll be cutting your stick with us young O'Toole. The Rocky Mountains are the grandest sight you'll ever see and the mountain air will make your limbs grow clean and tall. Twill be a grand ramble that you'll see. See me at my kit when we get to camp."

He turns his horse and falls in along the train.

Eagle hand got our mule packed and we are soon eating red dust as we make our way to the end of the pack. There are two rows of men and mules about fifty yards apart than at times blend into one when crossing one of the heavily wooded creek that comes out the west into the Big Blue I soon find out that the party totals 86 men including the Mr. Wyeth's 25 down easters there are near two hundred mules about a hundred horses and dozen oxen and a small flock of sheep.

An hour down the trail and from behind us out comes a singing Irish voice:

I've been a wild rover for many's a year
And I've spend all my money on whiskey and beer

And now I'm returnin' with gold in great store
And I never will play the wild rover no more

I sang back the chorus:
And it No! Nay! Never!

No nay never no more
And I'll play the wild rover
No never no more

A tall square jawed man in his late twenties with piercing sparkling eyes rides through the red dust. His eyes crinkle in at mischievous smile. Fitz told me we have another Irishman in the troop. He leans from this saddle to extend his hand.

"I'm Robert Campbell and I've five hired men and an interest in the these goods we are pack'n. Been in the business since the Ashley days back in '25. And where might you hail from?"

"The fair city of Dublin sir."

"County Tyrone tis for me, which I recently returned for a visit. But, don't hold my Ulster backgroud against me, he says, smiling. Tis to these mountains we head that I owe my life he says knodding his head west. Twas on my back and bleeding out the lungs back in '24 and one trip to the mountains and I 've not bled a drop more. Are you seeking health or adventure."

"Adventure sir."

"And who might you companion be?"

"Eagle Hand of the Mandan's. Eagle Hand came forward and clasped his hand."

"I must keep the end of the train tidy…welcome to the Far West lad I certainly recall my salad days when I saw the Rockies for the first time tis a grand feeling." He rode off to shoo some sheep that had strayed to graze up the hillside.

Later that day we pass Bonneville's men We slow in greeting and then Mr. Sublette puts us on double time for the rest of the day to make the greatest gap and ensure we would have fresh grass and firewood in being out front. We finally stop a few hours before sunset forming a large U with our saddles with the river at the top of the U. Some men set up tents. I am told the horses are to be hobbled and picketed within the U. We assist in unloading all the mules and unsaddling the horses. The Big Blue has widened into a nearly stagnant pond at this point, but there is plenty of grass for the animals and we set them out to graze with guard on the perimeter. Mr Sublette acts much like a military man. I leaned that he used to be the township constable in St. Charles Township near St. Louis. He has a brother Andrew assisting him and another brother Milton is a brigade leader in the Rocky Mountain Fur Company of which William is racing with this pack train to resupply with the goods he carries and he has another brother Solomon running a tavern near St. Louis called the Sign of the Eagle and yet another younger brother called Pickney who was killed several years ago by Indians so nearly all the Sublette are in the fur trade and none are with children or married. This Bonneville we passed today is a new competitor to the Rocky Mountain fur trade and is backed by capitalists from New York who want to challenge the Rocky Mountain Fur Company and the Hudson Bay company and even these Down Easters led by Mr. Nat Wyeth are out to enter the trade, but they are so green that Mr. Sublette took pity on them agreed to lead them to the mountains. I'm told that even John Jacob Astor's American Fur Company has recently moved their operation from their forts on the upper Missouri country to the Rocky Mountains to also challenge the experienced men of the Rocky Mountain Fur Company. We sought out Mr. Sublette to get our duties.

"Ah young O'Toole you and your partner are to be with the Rocky Mountain people Mr. Fitzpatricks mess he asked for it. He not part of my trading group, but one of the new owners of the Rocky Mountain Fur Company with my brother Milton and three other fellers all of them presently in the mountains. Nonetheless every man here is under my command and that's a fact. Each mess gets one tent. You two will team and stand yer two-hour watch in rotation with your mess. We will rise before the sun to turn out the animals to feed then catch them up and load and go. We'll make the Platte tomorrow. Fitz will issue you some flour from his mess and we'll be having a few mutton joints for feed. You'll get two mules to lead and are responsible for them and must take care of then first and if you don't you be in an unhandsome fix. If you fall asleep on watch you walk for the next three days and are fined five dollars and that a fact. We can't be losing our horses and mule and there will be plenty of Indians who will be scrounging hard to put their hands on em. Understood?"

We both nod our agreement. A tough man, but one I feel secure to be under his guard.

Each mess starts their fires susing scattered branches and over wintered sunflower stalks. We joined in Fitzpatricks mess putting our saddles and blankets near the fire and unloading our mule packs in a pile betwixt our saddles forming a wall around the fire We staked our animals on hemp rope twenty two feet long to a hickory pin two and half feet long driven into the ground that is attached to the a leather halter which has an iron ring attached to the chin strap and animals further out are hobbled about the forelegs. Fitzpatrick waves us over the fire.

"Well young O'Toole you've cut your stick with the best mess in the mountains. Look here those downeasters have bought some Eastern pemmican they call it noocake and it parched corn mixed with maple sugar tis a sweet pemmican not like the prairie pemmican but we've a fine mutton stew just set to boil with corn and fine roots".

The next morning in the gray dawn the voice of William Sublette rings out: "Up! Catch em up boys Catch em up." We catch up our horses and mules that are enclosed within the U of our camp and load the packs and are off. Double file in a line more than a hundred horses long with Mr. Sublette leading us, and Mr. Campbell bringing up the stragglers. There is no breakfast but some of the more experienced men were able to make some tea or coffee from the embers of last night fire while they wait for the Down Easters who fumble and chase their animals within their enclosure.

After a march of about 25 to 30 miles we reach the Platte River near an area called Grand Island. This is a river unlike those we have seen before: it is broad maybe up to one half mile wide in places shallow with many courses quite rapid in places and placid in others thick with a light soil and sandy color it is a light clay color, but devoid of rocks the swirl of the water is caused by snags and numerous sand bars. Thick stands of willows are on its banks and cottonwood trees fill the islands. In most places it barely reaches the belly of the animals, but I told that further along that it is filled with treacherous sand they call quicksand that will suck man or animal down in a slow enveloping grip that one cannot escape after a certain point.

There are still some broken high bluffs behind us angling to the southeast, but the land ahead is as flat as the ocean. This then is the beginning of the vast prairie or plains that I have heard so much about. It looks like one can drive a wagon across it with hardly a bump. The cottonwood trees make a hollow rattling sound in response to a light breeze, a mixture of blackbirds some yellow heads and some with bright red wing bars cluck and make grating-like sounds, but the vast grasses to the west seem to move silently like the prairie is the back of a giant caterpillar that is undulating without going anywhere. And the greens! Coming from the green island I possess a certain arrogance about the color, but tis green upon green here for in the distance one sees the deep dark green as if the grasses are mixed with coal-black then alongside such green is a luminous green filled with the yellow of the sun and next to the that is a green with a touch of gray in it, next to that sweeping across the top of a hill is a green with a purple in it so the colors of green grand prairie have claimed the entire rainbow for their own and it does not stop there for there are trees along distant waterways and a person's sight becomes a far different on the prairie for there are two places to see the prairie infinity even eternity itself if one is upon a sufficient hill. Parting grasses reveal twining vines hidden yellow flowers orange beetles yellow moths and a whole labyrinth of tangled greens with grasses thin and tall grasses small and wide tis a green jungle one parts under your hand and tis the magic of this land to this wee world going on underfoot while lulling you into thinking that the waving variations of green you see is the land of sameness.

There is also a thick crust on some of the land near the river that is sulfuruous tasting salt and water in the pools next the the river and has a most bitter taste to it. The Platte is our turnpike to the Rocky Mountains. We are on the right or south shore and we are to follow it for the next twenty some days. This is our first sighting of the pronghorn antelope and we see and hear many more wolves. Also the sandhill crane, the curlew and the great heron are seen stalking along the edges of the river and the cranes out in the fields eating insects.

The antelope or goat as it called are sometimes curious and occasionally approach us with a sheep-like bleating they make this high pitched wheezing snort when they are alarmed. Some of the men imitate the sound and bring then within fifty yards and shoot them and slung them over the saddle and we will eat them tonight.

Mr. Campbell rides beside me. "Git this here spot used to be a great buffalo crossing. I remember seeing endless herds coming up from the Arkansas heading to the Missouri. That was way back in '25 the year Ashley sold out to Jed Smith his partner and Jackson and Sublette. You know Jed Smith with his partners all sold out for $100,000 in '30 he was there from the beginning and he could have done anything, but he wanted to try his hand at the Santa Fe trade and after all the Indian fights we was in from here to the Columbia he gets killed by some Comanches while digging for water where the Cimmaron river was supposed to be. They never did find his body. Now the buffalo are rarely to be found here usually it is at least three more days west before we run into them. Best get your mess." He rode away with a melancholy look on his chiseled face.

I must mention the New Englanders insomuch that they present a certain almost soldierly uniformity that is at odds with the helter skelter appearance of the experienced mountain men. Each new Englander wears the coarse woolen jacket and pantaloons, a striped cotton shirt and cowhide boots and they all carry rifles not much used and a bayonet tucked int their broad belts which also contains a clasped knife use for eating and a small ax. Captain Wyeth carries two pistols as they call their leader and his brother John carries one pistol and the other brother Doctor Wyeth carries none.

We set up our mess with the fire going the tea on and our animals grazing. Mr. Ball one of the New Englanders joins our fire. A Mr. Smith now a westerner raised in North Carolina joins the fire as he is curious about Mr Balls experiences in Washington.

"Well Mr. Ball I hear you been to Washington visiting the old friends in all the halls of power."

"I have Mr. Smith I visited with President Jackson and he received me without introduction we had a nice visit. I then visited the House and saw my old college classmate Mr Choate and in congress Mr. Calhoun was presiding over the Senate with Benton, Clay and Webster present. I then spent time at the Supreme Court listening to Mr. Marshall of the Georgia versus Cherokee case a case that generates much interest and anticipation."

"Is that about gold? I know they discovered gold on Cherokee land it been many years since that happened. Got me a brother who sought his fortune but near got killed by the Cherokees. He blamed it on a man who went in to the Cherokee land ripping up fences and shooting injuns trying to get at the gold."

"No. No. The case is not about the gold it's about the land. The state of Georgia wants the Cherokee lands and the Cherokees being civilized as they now call themselves for they farm like us, live in log homes raise livestock and even have slaves. They also have their own writtern language and schools. They hired lawyers claiming their treaty with the federal goverement makes them a sovereign nation and not subject to the state laws. Georgia claims they are subject to Georgia law, although they won't let them sue any white men who destroys their land going after gold nor vote of course so it puts Georgia in a peculiar place."

"I've been given to understand that the American Government first role tis to protect its people?" I interjected.

"It is, but you must understand that it's not that simple Mr. O'Toole The Federal government is not blind in its protection. Us traders and merchants pay taxes...pay the tariffs that keeps the government going and we vote while the Injuns do provide us profit to us in trade they are not directly sending any money to the government. So you see the government must protect us first."

"Mr Ball has is jest right! Dem Injuns was fools to adopt white ways with their constitution and inventing their own letters and all. Done better to keept the savages ways and keep their warriors ready to fight off them gold diggers."

"Like the Creeks did?" Mr. Ball replied.

"How's that?"

Creeks stayed savage fought like hell and got wupped when some of them killed whites. The Federal government sent in troops every time they killed a settler and finally made then sign a treaty Indian Springs Treaty is was called. They are gone now not a Creek left in Georgia despite them fighting for General Jackson helping him win the battle of New Orleans. I expect win lose or draw in the Supreme Court the Cherokees will be gone in a few years too."

"You don't think the President and Congress can ignore the Supreme Court if the Cherokees win? It sounds like they have a strong case they have clear title to the land don't they?" I asked.

"First the case holds much interest because it appears thay have a strong case this is the first time the Indians have really used our legal system so it creates a delicate political problem of fairness. Still I don't think the court will rule for the Cherokees no matter how strong their case. Marshall is adept at coming up with a good legal reason to meet political needs. If Marshall was to oppose Georgia and everybody in Washington I don't think his decision will hold for Jackson will oppose it. Marshall is no fool of that you can be sure and you can be sure his legal decisions end up to the advantage of his court or of supporting Federalist policy."

"What is a Federalist? Seems they are the same as the conservatives in Ireland."

"I'd say your not far off young O'Toole They are the creditor-capitalists they are the merchants they are the large landowners they are the corporations they are the protectors of private property."

CHAPTER XII

JOURNEY UP THE PLATTE

Git O'Toole Journl

25 May 1832 Friday

The grass gets shorter as we move west and the land is stretched into endless-ness when one moves away from the Platte the trees disappear, the undulations of the earth cease, not even hills appear and from far beyond the eyes reach the wind comes. Today from the South it brings warmth but tis so strong that all movement must be with a lean to the wind the day is spent leaning the left with muscles sore from tensing to balance the wind. White Egrets herons and Brant geese fly but a foot off the ground staying within every crease of the earth to buy more energy from the wind. How far does the wind travel to be so strong so steady? It seems to rise most days hours after the sun is up and by eight o'clock is with us and it sets just before the sun unless there is a storm system coming our way from the west.

*Oh the giant clouds! There can be no clouds on all the earth like the prairie clouds, not even the sea makes such clouds. I had not imagined the sky so tall and could not have known its height but for seeing the reach of the mighty clouds of the prairie. There is nothing that man makes that will be anything but puny next to these clouds. Five maybe, six miles straight up they float. Nothing is more terrifying than the force of the lighting not even the sea prepared me for such a force. Unlike the sea one is planted solid but the grass whips and winds throw water across the surface or pummels one from above with balls of ice large enough to knock a man out and even a mule. There is nowhere to go even under the tent or lean-to feels frightful **one** has seen how the lighting of the prairie seeks out any lone tree any rise any challenge to the all powerful lighting. I saw a tree explode one night into near nothing with the stumps burning instantly like a fire had been lit under it for hours. I saw three horses instantly thrown and scattered like leaves by a bolt that struck near them. One sits tense in a tent hoping to be missed and jumping at each terrible crash as the lighting detonates.*

But when the clouds have passed and sun breaks though out of the west behind the darkness passing overhead there is no more beautiful sight nor smell that the prairie after a rain. The Prairie is glistening and every plant is lifted in the greenest thanks all sending out their own incense and birds flicking about in joyous song, the wind now calm and one stands on the cusp of violent darkness to the east and renewal and paradise to the west.

Tis a strange feeling to be amongst men who hail from the same soil but who have so little in common Mr Sublette now a practical westerner with southern origins has an air of gentility, a love or rank and an insistence on slavery; Mr Ball a New Englander is a more rigid man with a dislike of rank and slavery, but strangely more hopeful and Eagle Hand the true man of this land a man whose moccasins have long impressed this land whose ancestors have only known this land has few demands and no fear of the future, but all these men are men of courage all are men of vision they are my guides in this new land.

Eagle Hand Journal

30 May 1832, Wednesday

It is a new moon. The ponies will lift their heads to father sun and the rib bones of winter disappear. It is time to teach the young to hunt buffalo for the calves can be chased. The first berries ripen before the next moon appears. My people go on without me the doves sit on the lodge and coo and my ears are not there. How I miss walking between the lodges how I miss the smell of fresh buffalo stew touching my nose for the first light of day until darkness is lit by the fires within. How I miss standing on the hills to the north with the last light of day at my back and flicker of fires dancing though the many lodge hole of my village below. I listen to how the sounds of the night creatures make joy at the decending darkness the buzzing zoom sound of the hawk that hunts at night the whooing of the owl in the tree, the crick-creek of the cricket at my feet the high sounds of the the hoppers in the high grass and the rising howl of the wolves with the excited yips of the pups as they rise from their afternoon slumber the light touch of the wind on my cheeks and the heaviness of the night air like a robe over the earth. The distant shine of the mighty Missouri with its muddy smell with its silver reflections like a mighty snake it twists through our land and all us creatures get fat from her she quenches our thirst eases our burdens brings wood to our fires holds the joy of our children afloat brings many people to trade and every year brings the fat of the earth and the joy of the growing spirits so that our maize and our buffalo will grow and all the land will fatten. And it brings these many gifts with much force…it demands our fear our respect our awe for it is the mighty Missouri. Oh spirits of the Missouri how I miss you. Oh people of the First Man how I miss you.

It is like a war party the way we travel only we travel so heavy in so many ways. We carry more than a village and it is more like a village in mourning. There is no seeking spirits at night no dancing to please the spirits no honoring sacred places for it is fast hooves every day as if the enemy is at our heels, but no it is the front that pulls our reins it is trade that is the god of the white man. He enters this great land full of his many wonderful things and the he leaves the mountains with the skins of our brothers and always the white man is burdened. He carries his great guns only to protect his burdens he is never fleet, never light never hidden within the land. He goes bold he goes without the eyes of spirits of our land he goes over land sacred he goes over evil land he goes and goes and he is restless like the little wolf with an empty belly with the nose always searching and his belly always empty even after he devours the carrion of the land he still looks across the great prairie with green eyes that burn to eat and legs that won't stop and on he goes eating and eating. The white man keeps coming from across the Great River more and more little white wolves with the noses sniffing the land their tails wagging.

THE BIGGEST PRESENCE ON THE prairie cannot be seen cannot be ignored and cannot be changed. For two days the wind has been fierce. It come out of the south with no clouds driving it for there are clouds behind these winds we cannot see them and we can see for hundreds of miles, at least we can see anything as high as clouds. But the air is hazy and I think it is the wind. I can't imagine what engine drives this wind. I made the mistake of passing another man on the north and the sand driven downwind into my face and hands felt like a million little whips lashing me even the mules I led nearly jerked me backwards as they protested and their hides so much thicker than mine. I found myself leaning leftward in my saddle and became aware of it only when I passed on the south side a small embankment by the Platte and my body jerked further to the left. Conversation can't be had in such a wind. A man riding knee to knee with another man can't be heard without the use of hand signals and watching his mouth closely as the wind snatches the words and swallow them before they reach your ears. It is strange to see manes and tails at right angles all along the trail. I cannot hope to explain to one who hasn't spent two days in such a wind how it drains you not only of moisture but energy. I admire how the animals plod on ignoring it while I feel rising frustration and wishing it would stop for is makes my temper short, but I seem to be the only creature protesting all else accept it like they do the darkness that comes every day. I hope I will acquire their patience with age.

There are great flocks of shorebirds: plovers I am told migrating though. They circle the grasses in swift direction changing flights twisting one way then the other in unison and suddenly alight and seem to disappear into the prairie. I would not know that they are there without following the flight to the prairie. One of the men shot several and they make a dense dark breast meat like a wild duck only with more fat on it with a flavor more akin to the grouse or leg of turkey.

This night in camp we are ordered to not set any fires without digging a great circle round the fire ring for the old brown grasses lay thick under the carpet of small new green blades and the bulrushes by the Platte are still very dry and fear runs deep after yesterday.

Last night was a gentle northwest breeze the air warms the night and portents were good and pleasant. Most slept on the open ground around our dying fires, before sunrise the wind rose and this itself was unusual as early morning was the most pleasant times on the prairie with the calm colored air filled with the songs of the meadowlarks and the twittering of the swallows skimming the air for insects, but this morning only the hollow sounds of the wind greeted us.

The winds move to the north then northeast and at the hour of sunlight it was strong. We had just loaded all the mules when the cane and bulrushes north of our camp exploded into bright flames. The smoke rolled over our camp and shouts and hooves pawed the air.

"Form up Form up Get em out Damm! Move it!" Mr Sublette rode up and down snapping his quirt.

Soon at more than a trot and certainly not in two neat columns Mr Sublette wanted we are all scrambling west out of the path of the fire. The air is instantly distorted hundreds of feet above the fire and the flames look more orange than I ever seen before. Not yellow like a log fire but orange like the fires of hell and instantly a hundred yard swath of dried rushes are aflame. We had not gone a mile before we are once again enveloped in smoke and the animals turned white-eyed and then tried to turn in evey direction. Mules are kicking out and jerking their heads and horses circling in panic and it seems we are going to lose many animals and supplies and the same wind saves us by wiping the smoke clear of our area and sending it off to the southwest. When we are organized again we have to hold the animals at a trot so eager are they to get out of their area even if the smoke is gone.

The flames are now higher than the cottonwood trees on the islands in the river. The river is about a half a mile wide with numerous wooded islands and the water about three to four feet deep. The fire burns part way into the bulrushes and I would have thought it would race across all the dried rushes lining the river and islands but it only moves several feet out north into the river breaking into islands of flame and much of the the dried material out in the water remains unbrunt. What the fire did instead was devour its way into the prairie grasses to the southeast it did so at a much slower pace than the instant gulf it took of the bulrushes. The flames are laid low by wind and the fire seems to be fighting the wind to burn the prairie grass like a predator crouching and snapping with his ears laid back and then the wind breaks and the flames shoot up twenty feet in the air then the winds flatten the flames again. Yet the ducks swim out only fifty feet from the flames yellow headed blackbird chirp and fly over the flames like a fire is something these birds see every day. Some prairie chickens rise up in front of the flames and settle down in the path of the flames. Rabbits bounce across the prairie but did not seem in a great hurry. A hour later we can still see great plumes of white smoke looking like all world like a cloud touching the earth. No other clouds are in the sky. Mr Bonneville's party will be entering a blackened area following our trail.

That night are about twelve miles away from our morning camp and the clouds still hang over the prairie behind only now they are much further south. The sunset tinges the pure white clouds in a glowing pink and then purple color. It is like a pure slowly moving wall erected on the prairie behind us. It appears the hungry fire ate its way into the fierce wind. As the sun sets the wind is still blowing but beginning to die down the wind has been acting like a giant hand holding the flames down. As the wind died the flames reach skyward like they are tying to reach the stars. Millions of hungry orange tongues flick upwards like the demons of hell are raging to get at the heavens fireballs roll off the tongues of flames like a herd of angry dragons are howling at the black air above. A long line of jagged flickering orange lights the sky behind us. It is an unearthly sight as the nights are normally so black except moonful nights. It looks like one can see the curve of the earth glowing like we are on the edge of entering some terrible land.

The next morning I have the last watch and at the end of it when the gray light of day gives outline to the eastern grasses I can see several majestic stag horns and forms alert and watching us. I whispered to myself the Ox of the Deluge for it looks like the great black deer of Ireland now gone but seen in many drawings. I turn my head as one normally does which I know makes me visible and I am tired and forgetful. The stags see my movement and all have there ears cupped this way. I think it is hard for a person of the city to understand how long animals can remain alert and immobile. Of this never did I witness such alertness such tension and such focus from anyone or any animal in New York or Dublin as I have seen on the prairie like these stags. If I could walk with the quiet grace of a deer seen here I would be seen as a god. Five minutes maybe ten I wanted to see how long such a scene would go on. One doe dropped her head to feed when the noises from camp spooked them all in a few seconds there is only the muffled echo of the sharp hooves left in the cool morning air.

"Did you see the stags I inquired on entering the camp."

"Them ware elk. I watched on the sandbar in the river. Should be seeing buffalo right soon, I expect."

Loading the mules it always a difficult task except for the Creature for I get to talk to him and pet him and hear his snuffling noises and then grunting noises when I load him.

We are carrying 450 gallons of whiskey into territory where federal law bans it and Mr. William Sublette personally guards the whiskey or has his younger brother Andrew guard it. I am told William Sublette papers allowing him his trading licence for the season and allowing him whiskey for his boatman. Boatman on a muletrain in anther peculiar American form of laughing at inconvenient laws. Mr. Sublette has 39 employees and there would be near 12 gallons of undiluted whiskey apiece to drink on the boat trip which wouldn't take 60 days. Since Mr. Clark is the Federal agent in charge of these lands he should be enforcing these laws but it seems that he has a financial stake in such trade and the men tell me we would be at a disadvantage to the British traders of the Hudson Bay company if they couldn't bring whiskey in trade with the tribes

I find the Mr. Campbell has five in his employ and ten horses laden with goods and he seems to have some business connection to Mr. William Sublette although he is not formally a partner but he is bringing trade goods under Mr. Sublette license. They seem to be friends and Mr Campell is always in the rear securing and prompting any stragglers.

As soon as we leave camp the little and big wolves of the prairie who keep edging closer as we get near the packing out for the day these wolves race each other into the camp and scavage the fires and scattered bones of our meals nipping and chasing each other according to some rigid social structure. Some days I will see wolves out on the prairie all day long following us and they will stop at certain points and even whine like there is a fence and they will not cross it, but they are our constant companions and will always ring the camp in the grasses at night. This would not be something that would concern us and maybe even delight us were it not for the fact that many of the tribes in this parts will wear a wolf head and creep into camp especially to steal horses. It is common to see a set of ears in several places on one's watch and one can never known which is tribesmen and which it wolf unless they are very close to camp then it is sure to be a tribesman. Last night one of the men fired at a wolf thinking it was a warrior intent on horses. He roused the camp with his cries and shot and when it was determined it was a wolf he took much ribbing and hung his head at the deed. This is a fine difficult balance this job of doing one's night watch sitting alone between ridicule and death.

It is hot and the air is so much thicker like a fog, but it only shows as a distant haze and looks more like smoke than fog. My ass and inner thighs are sore from sweating all day. I am dusty and feel like I can barely breath. The sun beats on us all day and the wind is light meaning maybe ten miles per hour it is a hot wind out of the south. I'm beginning to think there is a vast fire to the south of us that feeds this south wind. I have my wool pantaloons on and my wool hat and a cotton shirt that cools me when I lift my arms. The wind will occasionally blow away the smell of sweat for I have reached the point where I cannot tell the sweat of man from beast. Seeing the Platte throughout the day makes me pine to feel her with my body. When the order comes to circle and mess tis none too soon for me. I hurry to unladen my animals and set them free after watering them. All are moving towards the water and I find many had reached it before me. I shed the now wet pantaloons and wool hat and soon I am in the running water of the Platte. Even that seems warm but dipping my head and letting the water run off my hair while a breeze riffles the surface feels so cooling. Nearly all the men had shed their dusty clothes and every pool of the Platte holds bobbing heads and whooping men.

I think there can be nothing better than to sit upon a rock wet and naked after a long day in the saddle and let the wind caress your body and cool you. Never have I felt such heat. The hot air is so thick it feels hard to swallow. The hot wind feels like it sucks the life force out of man and beast. The tops of the grasses dry from early morning dew to afternoons full of air distorted and waving before eyes as if the grasses are flames sending up heat from the earth. Us white men hide under the brim of our hats while the black sleek hair of the tribesmen reflect the sun the tribesmen and women coat their hair with bear grease. It is too hot for even mosquitoes, but flies seem to relish the tender skin of a sweating man where they land and bite a chunk and are off before your angry slap lands and they are clever to land on your back or lower legs. They seem aware of the face of man for one of the men tired riding backwards in his saddle to fool them but alas they stilled swarmed to his back. Ticks catch a ride from the long grass unto our pants leg and try to climb up towards our heads. I found that sitting the saddle with only a loin cloth makes it easier to detect them on your legs and one can easily dispose of them by picking them off. Tis more difficult with breeches on for they hide in the folds or walk on the outside where one can't feel them and one has to be alert in the blanket at night to detect them and toss them into the fire whence they will not return.

But tis a bit a paradise to sit here naked and feel cool with the water drying off your skin. Men are fighting for places and do so like the white herons fight each other for prime fishing spots so too we fight each other for prime cooling spots. I slip into the water several times to wet myself and would have done it longer but as the sun moves low the mosquitoes rise and begin to attack all the white succulent flesh. With much splashing we all leave the Platte running back to camp dripping and holding our clothes and rifles. Some of the mess cooks had already started and they look at all the naked men entering camp many with ginger feet and walking like long legged crippled birds and they have a great laugh.

Yesterday I heard an outcry from the bushes to one side and stopped as it sounded such a queer note. After listening for a few minutes followed by some silence a woman emerged for the bushes with a baby. She is the wife of one of the trappers in our party. There are several women and some children traveling with us. The next day she has the child secure in a deep basket hanging off the pummel of her saddle. The saddle is one that many women prefer if they use a saddle it is one of Spanish design with curved pummels front and back over a foot high using such a saddle they are able to rest their back against the back pummel which many a late afternoons I envied. One of these women is from the Flathead tribe or Salish and she does indeed have a sloped forehead and she carried her infant in a special basket with a board pressed into his head. It is truly amazing how tolerant these tribal children are as they hardly every cry or raise their voices, but the mothers are very attentive and seem to know what they want before the child makes it known.

I was able to meet Mr. Ball's leader a Mr. Wyeth who is from Clear Pond near Cambridge. He made some money in the family business of shipping ice from his pond. He is a man of great energy and though he knows as little as I about this trading and trapping business he seems a very intelligent and determined man. There have been three of his party who have decamped at night with horses and rifles when we reached the Platte most the remaining men sit around the fire and talk of what fortunes they will make trapping and how Mr. Wyeth has brought some trade goods as they have heard a man can make up the two thousand percent on trade goods in the Rockies. They talk about how they will make enough on beaver this winter to come back and buy trade goods and make two thousand percent next year.

Eagle Hand joined us after several days on the scout. I am glad to have him back at the campfire..

"The Arikaras will be moving north of us. My Arikaras friend Pachtuwa Chta was traveling towards the Black Hills near the Badlands. He is not with the tribe but seeking spiritual guidance. He believes his people will visit with the Pawnees this summer, but he does not like the signs so now he will return and he may be visiting my people. He does not like it that his people are traveling into land where the Cheyenne hunt. He says the Brules are north of us along the White River and the Cheyennes have killed some Crows so the Crows will be on the warpath in Cheyenne territory. These Arikaras are people who have tongues like the Pawnees. It is not good if they are leaving their villages. They have had many fights with the whites and the whites have been attacking them at their village. I hope we pass into the mountains before these people arrive for they are very angry with the whites and with the Sioux who attacked them with the whites. What news do you have?"

"You are the first scout with news. Other scouts have reported only buffalo and small party was sent out this afternoon for meat. The lamb is gone and we have been eating dried meat and small game. I have been thinking of the smell of roasting ribs all day. Mr. Sublete's slave got bit by a rattlesnake this morning and he put up a fearsome crying all day thinking he was going to die, but then it is declared to be only a glancing blow that struck his shin so it looks like he will be able to walk tomorrow."

We are joined at the fire by several men a mixture of trader's and trapper's and tyro's like myself. The talk turns to prospects in the mountains.

"Hear McKenzie finally got the Blackfoot trade."

"I'll believe it when I see it them rascals been killing near a dozen trappers a year ever since old Meriweather Lewis shot two of 'em they been sour on the Americans every since. Don't see how the King of the Upper Missouri got them to trade their furs."

"I'll tell ya how. He got old Jacob Berger to bring em in to his new fort he build on the Yellowstone named it Fort Union. Hear they near lifted Berger's hair before he got them to the new fort. Piegan's didn't belive there would be a fort there and they near tired of the long tramp ol Berger had to fast talk to keep his hair, ha, ha."

"Well I recken old John Jacob Astor buying out the Northwest Companies was a real smart deal since he got the clever Scotsman on his side. And now McKenzie got to be the only white man that could ever deal with them Piegan's. Course the Brits been selling them guns for years and I don't doubt they's smirking in their collars every time they see nother American scalp on the Blackfoot lance."

"McKenzie's been a busy man. Built a new fort by the Bad River guess old fort Tecumesh was built bad right near the edge and the river was swallowing the bank and the fort. Named the new one Fort Pierre Choteau."

"Hear the Blackfoot lifted old Dan Richards and Henry Duhern on Camas Creek this winter."

"That right and near 100 American Fur Company horses and plenty of supplies and trade goods, but old Astor can afford it if any can."

"I still say the best Injun trappers is the Crow and the Crees ain't too bad either, but they can't dress the skin like a Crow and they's women ain't as pretty as them Crow women."

"Well I'm agin this fort business seems like Astor's men intent on building forts all over this land ever since he bought out all the competition out of St. Louis. I swear this land going to be full of forts and it's goin to kill off the rendezvous. Doesn't seem right them putting up forts in Indian country. Makes the Injuns dependent on the forts especially given them whiskey all the time. Hell a blowout once a year won't bother 'em but not whiskey every day at the fort. Won't get any furs out of a drunk Injun. Seems like Astor got more money than sense, but I afraid money it all it takes to make it in America."

"I say its experience. The Rocky Mountain Fur Company...Fitz's crew are old hands at this business the Meek brothers, Henry Fraeb, Bridger, Gervais, Milton Sublette, Newell and that Iroquois Godin have stepped in nearly every part of then mountains and can smell beaver better than any group of men in the mountains except old Williams and some of the free trappers. I say them Rocky Mountain boys can out trap Astor's American Fur Company men any day of the week all Astor's got is lots of money and sharp manager in that Scotman McKenzie. And now we got those upstart Downeasters with Wyeth and Bonneville with his military ways. Course the British the Hudson Bay people they know how to cut any competition to the quick, but I expect the Federals will be keeping them in line now that Astor has forts near their territory...old Astor tired back in twelve to get a foothold in the British Territory with Astoria and I know he had backing back then and he'll have it now trying to take the Indian trade away from Hudson Bay hell everybody knows it was Astor that got Congress to end the Government monopoly of the fur business, the factory system, so he could expand into the Far West. But I don't know that these mountains have ever seen so many white men and it seems that the British have to trying to strip the country of beaver all along the American side of their territory and I'd say they done a good job of it. The only good country left is up in Blackfoot country and that means risking your hair and supplies."

"Ain't just the British competition has stripped nearly the whole Missouri up the jest past the Mandan's ain't hardly no beaver left and sure not nough fer a fellow to make any sort of living and that goes for the Colorado River too it's a shame when a rendezvous site don't even have any beaver left."

"Pierre's hole still has some so you might see some this year."

Tonight the stars shine bright with the big dipper over my head. It is cool tonight and I lie wrapped in my two blankets because it feels good to be all wrapped up under such brilliant sparkling skies and clean cool

mixed with the anger. I can feel a light breeze tickling my neck and within seconds the first the bear and then the bull are nosing the air. The bear edges sideways keeping up the roar The bull paws and bellows and moves his feet nervously. They both circle and the bear widens the gap between them until he is near another cut in the bank where an old watercourse has cut down several feet. Taking a last look at the bull he ambles down the course, but that cut circles around and I can see where it comes out about thirty yards down from the cut I am in. There is no way I going to wait for a wounded grizzly to find me so I run as hard as I can back towards my mule.

Huffing I arrive where I left the mule. No Creature. I look back no grizzly, but I have been told a grizzly can run as fast as horse for a short distance. I can only see about one hundred yards back to the last bend. There is a hole in the bank where the small cedar had been holding my mule. His tracks go down the sandy ravine. I trot after the tracks looking over my shoulder constantly. To my relief in a about a half a mile I spot my mule grazing atop the bank. He chews, his eyes on me as I approach he tries to run away but the rope is still attached to the small cedar tree and that is caught in the Y of another tree growing out the side of the bank. Mounting and turning the Creature he starts to move slowly then sniffs the air and takes off at a speed I had never seen him exhibit before.

After the relief of leaving the grizzly behind I felt another wave of relief that I didn't have to return to camp without my mule for I would not have heard the end of it from the men, especially the Downeasters who seem to jump at every chance they could to laugh at the misfortune of others maybe because they bring so much misfortune upon thenselve in ignorance of prairiecraft. Or maybe it is because they try to cover their ignorance with arrogance. They are only out here to make their fortunes as they say and the prairie is a mere impediment they have to get through in order to reach the beaver country.

The grasses become shorter and shorter as we move west and the land seems to be rising. Within an hour of sunrise the air begins to bend. This is a phenomena of these great distances and great vistas. Unlike the woods or city one can actually see the air on the prairie and I don't mean at a great distance or with a great amount of heat, but nearly every day that is not terribly windy one can see the convoluted waves of distorted air rising off the earth and all around in all directions from just above the grass tops.

Besides herds of buffalo and elk we are now seeing big herds of swift pronghorns. These animals are too swift to hunt by horse, but they can be lured in by their curiosity. If one puts up a flag a waits patiently in the grass many times they will slowly approach to see the fluttering thing is. They have the taste of goat and if one leaves their ribs to smoke over the coals for several hours it is a most excellent meal. Pronghorn like all wild meat is a lean meat with no fat so it must be cooked minimally with plenty of pink meat shown.

The days are sticky hot and the sun grows hotter each day. We pass the forks of the Platte and we cross the South Platte to the North Platte, which we now follow. Tiny black knats circle and hover over our heads and bite us about the neck, eyes and ears. Mosquitoes rise from the Platte in the evening and descend on us when we camp anywhere out the wind or on windless nights. Only a smoky fire brings relief and only if one makes a fire near the entrance to the tent. I have tried to bring coals into the the tent and cover them with green branches and that brings some relief, but the fire dies one is awakened by the pitched sceams of the little suckers seeking your blood. Only under a tight cover of the wool blanket is there protection. I notice the Delawares put liberal amounts of the bear oil on their skin and sometimes mud and they are chewing some plant and they do not suffer like the whites. Some of the whites have faces wholly swollen and even have their eyes nearly shut due to bites and a few have raw ears where it seems there is little skin left only raw looking meat like an animal has been chewing their ears. I have taken to caking my neck and face with mud which protects me until the mud dries and cakes off and a scarf around my neck keeps the mud on longer. I am laughed at as I have mud in the ears and I can't hear well. I feel like I would face a grizzly rather than the constant overwhelming assault of the these endless and persistent bugs that only a gallop will lose and then by magic they are upon you. Like they have watched you the whole time and see you are going at their speed and descend upon you. A cool dip in the Platte each evening is such a relief. I just sit up on the sandy bottom and dip my head underwater for as long as I can and splash away the hovering bugs.

We are upon the Chimmey and it is the ninth of the June. This is a tower of rock rising out the prairie about three miles south of the Platte. I am told the local tribes call it "Elk Prick" Even thought it is called rock when we get close enough to examine it I can see that is consists mostly of hard clay and soft limestone. Some of us climb it and we can see the flat green expanse we just traversed. The trees have almost disappeared except on the islands in the river and some of the streams feeding the Platte. From up the Chimmey is looks as flat as a green highway but in fact the ground around us is riddled with deep gullies some twice the height of a man and are impassible to wagons except down by the flat Platte River. The many hundreds of the flowers of the prairie are in bloom among the tangled grasses and butterflies flutter all around us for there are no honeybees except bumblebees this far from civilization. The meadowlark still sings as he did way back at the Missouri. Larger herds of buffalo are in the area and I have my first sight of the blacktail or mule deer. The animals aren't doing as well on this short dry grass.

We pass Scott's Bluff and I have my first sight of the bighorn sheep although I am told these sheep live all along the Missouri and on the bluffs along the river. This bluff is named after a trapper who was sick and left to die by his companions his bones being found the next spring by a supply party like ours. It seems he crawled for nearly sixty miles before dying. The name of the men who left him remains a dirty secret.

More fir and pine trees are evident in the draws of the increasingly rippled terrain the Black Hills appear in the distance so named for the dark looking spruce trees that cover the hills. These hills run form here far to the north where the headwaters of the Cheyenne and Bad rivers originate those rivers emptying into the Missouri around Fort Pierre Choteau country. Now we are entering the edge of the country where the fires no long burn the grasses being too short and sparse to support a fire yet the area abounds in buffalo, elk, mule deer, antelope and bighorns. This land is the hunting grounds of the Crow and Cheyenne tribes. We are back to the toil of rugged steeps and deep cuts and the mules balk after the easy-going of the flat prairie this past few weeks. The shoes of the horses are beginning to wear as the soil is no longer the black loam of the prairie or the sand of the Platte but rocky and many stoned.

We find wild parsnip along the water with yellow blossoms and my mule is delighted at his food especially the green tops. He stands staring at me with big brown eyes sometimes shifting form foot to foot his eyes never leaving me as I wash the parnips in the river. We put some in our stew made of buffalo, antelope, black tailed deer and one the large rabbits of the area. One of the other messes found two young grey eagles when cutting a tree and roasted them along with a badger. I tasted the eagle and it is a very tender and moist meat.

Our camp at night is now visited by dogs said to have come from the Crow they look wolf-like with shorter ears and the size of the pointer, they slink and sneak with ears back and tails tucked and are wary and watchful and will not allow one to approach, but will sneak near the fire when one's back is turned.

A curious event happened in camp this night. One the men calls himself a servant to the Lord and goes about asking some of the men if they have an objection to a man praying and if not he asks them to join him in prayer. It's referred to as a prayer meetings or revival by some the men. I had heard the singing and raised excited voices from our fires at night several times but this night I walked over to their mess to see this event, which seemed so unlike our Catholic ritual yet resembled our Celtic rituals from afar. I expected men like our Tinkers or Gypsies, but these men were done in the most humble way there was no colorful scarves or jingling bells or adroit moves. A clean-shaven yellow haired man in brown homespun hatless and standing in misshaped wooded shoes was before the fire eyes upwards speaking thus:

"…bleating of the lanb, it is welcome of the shepard, it is the fullness of glory, it is the essense of love it is being in Jesus, it is Jesus being in us, it is taking the Holy Ghost in our bosoms…"

He hugs his own chest and looks among the men circled around the fire with sad lonely brown eyes. He pauses, his face alights, his forlorn limbs liven his eyes widen like hands are upon his body.

"…it is being called to high places, it is eating, drinking and sleeping in the Lord! It is kissing the hand that smites it is being mighty and powerful and scorning reproof and scorning unbelief and scorning those of little faith and filling your breast in belief filling it with the might and righteousness of Christ."

Now his hands he raises, his body trembles, his feet move in short quick steps raising puffs of dust the whites of the eyes roll to and fro.

"…oh glory to be oh fill me Lord with thee thy power is me…"

He dances round the fire in short turning steps his body jerking is unpredictable ways. There are two Delaware tribesmen sitting calmly watching amidst several white men.

"…oh mighty, oh powerful smite mine enemies and reproof the unbelievers embrace the believers…"

The Delawares are signing and watching his feet. The man became fierce his eyes burning red his face aflame his body twitching.

"…We are one we conquer all, our might is right all are evil who impede our way for the Lord lights our way the Lord is Might the Lord is Right, the Lord is the way."

Several men join him dancing round the fire each speaking his own words so that a chorus of fevered speech rises like the high flames of a fire too hot. The dust of their feet is swept to the sky, in the swirl of the heat.

The Delawares sit impassive.

The Catholic ritual I'd been raised on had a measured stately flow. This American style of religion is new and not too different from what the Skidis did around their fires. It is this wild continent that brings forth such passion? Seems more like a resurrection.

Today June twelve we the reach the Laramie River it is a rapid river now in flood from the melting snows that originated in the mountains far the southwest of us.

Upon crossing the Laramie when are are in disarry four men appear on the distant hills. Mr. Sublette orders us into a surround and as we are arranging ourselves the four approach and turn out to be white men. Mr. Fitzpatrick goes out to greet them. He reports they are a party of 21 men camped not far down the Platte. They are of the Gant and Blackwell trapping expedition that had over wintered and the trapped the Rocky Mountains this past winter. I ride to their camp with Fitzpatrick and Robert Campbell.

Was it a profitable winter for you gentlemen? Mr. Fitzpatrick asked as he dismounted. The men seemed to know him.

There was a pause...It certainly was profitable for some! Said one man who looked with fire in his eyes at the others. This man was called Zenas Leonard who stood with two other men opposite the fire where the balance of his party are gathered they numbered eighteen.

Mr. Fitzpatrick looked from the three to the eighteen. Tis not to be a happy reunion for your party for you are all of the Black and Gantwell party are you not?

Mr. Gantwell returned to St. Louis with me this past fall and I'm sorry to report that his firm is bankrupt and dissolved. Have you any furs for your troubles this winter?

Mr. Stephens who appeared to be the leader stepped forward. We are in need of more horses, mules, powder and balls and some smaller items are you not carrying such supplies to the mountains?

Yes, and have you any furs to trade?

Mr. Fitzpatrick it appears there is little future for us without the means to recoup our losses so if you would please entertain a trade for I can only offer 120 beaver towards our stake.

They sat by the fire and Mr. Fitzpatrick had coffee brought and treated the entire 21 men to it while he worked out a trade with Mr. Stephens for what used to be Mr. Gantwell's furs. He had his men ride off with the furs to cache them to pick them up on the way out of the mountains.

Mr Fitzpatrick then announced to us that he was going to ride ahead and announce our arrival and to see if the American Fur Company was close. It seems to the first trader to arrive at the rendezvous goes the spoils for the people are eager to trade after a winter of work and will be in need of many items. Mr. Fitzpatrick has a fine full-bodied white steed that is easily the swiftest horse in our company and he leads another fine black horse upon which he packs his provisions, which he will also ride. Twas a glorious warm day with a dark blue sky. Mr. Fiztpatrick seems quite eager to secure the trade so he sets out late in the afternoon giving us assurance that he would rather do some night travel and that he knew the Crows where intent on the Cheyennes and so he would not have to worry about them and that the Blackfoot would not likely be this far east. He also stated that he had done this route alone many times before and that the moon was dark and no tribes would be traveling at night. It seemed a risky business to cross the country without the backing of a large company such as ours, but he seemed to have the utmost confidence in his horses to outrun any trouble he may encounter.

We settle into our camp for the night with the addition of the Gantwell men who tell of their adventures of the winter past. It seems that many of the men were new to the mountains and hoping to make their fortune this past winter and return flush to St. Louis. Now they all seem reluctant to return empty-handed and are easily convinced to attend the rendezvous and either join the Rocky Mountain Fur Company or possibly Mr. Wyeth's party to try to recoup their losses.

Mr. Zenas Leonard settles at our fire and begins to relate his adventures of his first year in the Rocky Mountains. He hails from a village in Pennsylvania. Most interesting about him is that he has a leather bound book into which he records his adventures. He seems quite proud of the book. We have buffalo meat appola that evening along with some river clams steaming in bankside greens.

"Let me tell you about our first buffalo hunt. Zenas smiled at us in a wry way. We were south of here and back near the forks of the Platte, but later in the season mid-July and we had made the Platte by way of the Republican River to the south. It had been weeks since our stock gave out and we hunted every day for anything that moved and there was not a day that enough moved to feed us. We had been eating our horses the past week and two men had stolen away with our best horses during the night, tired of a journey so poor for riches to come. A day after killing two elk we spotted two bull buffalo. Off we went in a mad chase not heeding the wind and the buffalo had a great start on us. We returned with one broken arm and not even a shot made. There was not a stick of wood to be found even if we had the meat we had no fire. But the next day we were lucky to come upon a large herd and we killed six of them but fired ten times that number of balls not having learned how crucial a proper shot was to down such a beast. From that day forward we were in the meat."

"It was on this very spot at the end of last August where we began our first season of trapping in the Rockies, he intoned as he looked upon a buffalo rib and peeled the pink moist meat off with his front teeth. We had seventy men when we left St. Louis in April and it was there that we split into four parties to trap. Our horses, guns, traps, saddles and even clothes were supplied by Captains Gant and Blackwell so first we were eager to pay that debt and then make our riches. I was with Captain Stephens and we began to trap the Laramies. It was there last fall that I first met Thomas Fitzpatrick. Him and three other men found us and walked into our camp one evening much to our astonishment for we thought the land devoid of white men. He was on his way to St. Louis and I must say I was angered at him for he refused to share any knowledge about the trapping business and we all knew him to be an old hand at such business. When Mr. Fitzpatrick left our camp Captain Gantwell accompanied him back to St. Louis and that was the last I saw of him."

"We followed this Laramie River right to the mountains from whence it flows, but the rock from whence it issues is too steep for travel so we had to ascend the mountain by the buffalo trail on the far side. We hit our first snow at the top and had frequent snow in the weeks to follow. We were to meet back here for the winter, but after trapping and doing well we could not get back the way the came as the snow was too deep. We were forced to camp in the valley of the mountains. We soon found that the cottonwoods up in that valley were not of the sweet variety, which can sustain a horse in winter. The grasses were thin the soil poor and the snow covered what feed there was. We had hardly a horse left by New Years Day. "Two weeks later we determined to pack out on foot to Santa Fe to trade for the some horses and we left four men two mules with most of our merchandise and beaver on this mountain except that each man carried nine beaver skins to trade in Santa Fe.

We followed a buffalo bull trail and had plenty of game at first and jerked some meat but soon left all the game behind and entered a plain and the snow fell every day. We had to make snow shoes to proceed and now we were out of food and it was too far to go back to game and unknown what lay in front of us towards Santa Fe. On we went and not a morsel of food appeared. We roastied and ate our beaver skins and then we had nothing. Mr. Carter a Virginian in our party dropped to his knees and declared "here I must die in the these forlorn mountains." But big Mr. Hockday prevailed on him and kept to the front and broke the snow for us."

"In such a state I could never have imagined a man to be. Going blind, every movement a tremble needing our rifles as crutches to stay upright and every thought mixed into a dreamy jumble that the made the simplest decision seem an act of Congress. In such a state we spot two animals not even able to discern what they were from a mere 70 yards. Mr. Hockaday and I had to sit and transform our rifles from crutches back to rifles all the while the terror that the animals would run off for we knew we did not have the strength to go much beyond where the animals were feeding."

"Crawling as much from the inability to walk as for stealth we came within fifteen steps of the animals, which we now could see were buffalo bulls. Mr Hockday brought up his rifle trembling and wavering and put it back down telling me that he could not see the blade on the end the the barrel nor hold it steady enough to hit the animals at fifteen paces. "I became our last hope and I raised, aimed and pulled. The click of metal on stone sounded in the wind. Nothing There I whispered in a most desperate hopeless tone. "Our game is gone" I said and I was expecting nothing less. To my amazement the buffalo raised their heads to the click of the hammer and looked around and then commenced feeding. It was a moment to get religion. I cleaned my flint off and aimed again and never had sound and smoke felt so good. My ball broke the spine of the animal. The men who could barely crawl rose from behind and shouting and whooping actually ran to the fallen beast. Tough old buffalo was consumed by every man starting with the life restoring insides, which went down without the pretense of the fire and it felt as if life itself was flowing back into me. That old bull gave us the strength to make it back to camp where the four men did not recognize us until we began to speak to them. This was in early March."

"And did you have a fine spring hunt after that?"

"Indeed we did for we found beaver aplenty and had a quantity of dried meat and hides enough that we built a wigwam and left it full of our traps furs blankets and utensils while we went to retrieve some furs we had hidden up in the mountains. Upon returning we found we had been robbed cleaned out of everything but the blankets on our backs. Moccasin tracks confirmed the thieves. The men were so mad that we set out that night to retrieve our goods with Mr. Kean being the most upset We came upon a camp of five fires on a moonlit night and though it was more men than we expected we moved forward. But before prudence could win an Indian dog set the alarm and we were forced to fire rousing three hundred Indians into a screaming rage. We were forced to retreat to a hill."

William Sublette had quietly come to our fire and was quietly listening to this story. His steady voice came out of the cool night air: "I expect they were mighty small Indians."

Zenas Leonard did not pause in his answer. "No sir same as you and I"

Sublette without a hint of a smile replied: I tote sixty Indians a fire, but I expect that's Pennsylvania math.

"Well now sir, Zenas replied it could have been less but we were only eight men having learned our lesson we left thirteen to guard the beaver skins and two mules. We fought from the top of the hill and no one on either side was hurt. Spying an opening we retreated in the dark and traveled back to camp where we made haste to leave the area. We cached what we could not pack on the mules and made our way back here, but not one of our other parties were here. That's when Mr. Smith and Mr. Fully went with me and we did some more trapping in the area. While doing so we had several encounters with bears and Mr. Stephens sent the rest of the men up the mountain to recover all the beaver pelts with the incentive of awarding them all rights in such pelts. That is how you found us, and that is the cause of the unhappiness I share with Mr. Smith and Mr. Fully as to our situation."

"Did you suffer from the bears?" I asked with my experience in mind.

"Mostly from great fright, but Mr. Smith was bit on the hand while beating a bear about the head his gun would not fire. I have found that the bears will rarely fight the face of man if one has the courage to stand up to them. They will charge to within five paces and stand and roar and if one does not retreat they will not attack I speak of the white or grizzly bear and I speak of the bear without cubs. Any retreat within striking range of the bear brings a certain attack. Firing without deadly aim only brings a sure attack."

Our journey continues in the rising foothills with more and more trees appearing and rocky outcrops and an abundance of game with antelope and bighorns everywhere. The nights are getting colder as the country gets higher. All the men of the Gant party now accompany us. The New Englanders have a doctor in their party a Mr. Jacob Wyeth a brother to the leader. This man is undoubtedly the sickest man in our party and he is treating himself with purges and bleeding himself all the time. It seems he has a frail Eastern constitution but he is treating himself with bitters and medicines he carries. I have been lucky to have suffered little and seem to be getting stronger the deeper we travel into the mountain country. We are four days traveling through the Black Hills and we have sight of the Rocky Mountains. Unlike the blue mountains of Ireland they are the most majestic, white capped, stone-topped line of mountains…truly one of the most majestic sights to awake to on a clear cold morning. The air improves one's sight as you ascend towards the mountains. We are slowed one day by quicksand, which requires a steady pulling pressure to escape and evokes much fear in some of the men.

We leave the Platte and cross a high barren hilly land devoid of any animals with tremendous winds and no water, but within four days come upon the Sweetwater River. This river has a sweet taste and clear complexion after very muddy alkali water we encountered for the last several weeks and of which many have complained of loose bowels.

The Sweetwater is a full, deep, cold river and one that we cannot cross with laden mules. I wonder how we will make this crossing. We are set to cutting the willows which are always dense along all the rivers of the Far West. We cut willows about an inch and half in diameter at the butt end and push them into the ground into a boatlike outline about fourteen feet long. A basketlike frame is woven with these anchored pieces being tied together with sinew. Buffalo skins are then sewn together over this frame and a low fire started under this structure to dry it. Melted buffalo tallow is run and rubbed into every seam and crevice.

When the boat is dry it is pulled up from the ground and turne d over, the sight of such a boat makes the New Englanders laugh for they are used to seeing large oceangoing wooden vessels. They express doubt as to its capacity and seaworthiness.

Mr Wyeth's party have been following Mr. Sublette direction but some of the New Englanders have been grumbling that they have mastered the art of prairie travel and have lately resented Mr. Sublette's rule. Seeing the bullboat built the New Englander's determine to build a wooden raft. Mr. Wyeth put his blacksmith shop on the raft, anvil, large vice bar, iron steel traps and even a cask of powder and has one of his men swim across and secure a rope on the opposite bank. Just as he is ready to launch his raft made of roped logs Mr. Sublette, ever alert rides up.

I tell ya handsome and straight that rope won't do, no sir, you'll find yerself in an unhandsome fix with only that rope, for it won't hold fast and I'd tote yer goods gone if'n yer ask me.

Well I'm not asking and we'll cross this river just fine as we crossed all the rivers of the Platte I guess we know about water.

That's an unlovely way to go about it but it's yer goods. Mr Sublette said as he reined away.

Halfway across the swift river the rope snapped and the raft caught the edge of a submerged tree and over it went. Mr. Wyeth lost his blacksmith shop and some of his trade goods and one of the Boone boys who was riding the raft dumped into the river, but makes it across after what seems a long while spent underwater. Before the raft overturned Mr. Wyeth was bragging of how he would sell his trade goods them move on to the Columbia and establish a profitable business in catching salmon, which he would ship back east in a ship that he had commissioned to meet at the mouth of the Columbia. Now some of his hopes are tumbling along the bottom of the Sweetwater River.

The bullboat which is a much larger version of our cockboat is the most amazing vessel riding as high as an air bladder on the the water and we are able to load horses and mules and supplies on it after putting some planks on the bottom and cross the river without any trouble.

We continue on with mountaintop snow in sight every day and sometimes we camp next to old drifts of snow and even had a few evening of light snow and one bad day of cold rain in which we made little progress as the earth is full of a sticky clay where it is nearly impossible to keep our footing and we risk broken legs with each step.

The snowcapped Wind River Mountains are the north of us as we continue heading west. We enter South Pass, which is a hilly high plains pass though the mountains crisscrossed with many horse and buffalo trails. Many tribes that use a major north/south route along the mountains use this pass to go west. Mr. Sublette is extremely alert and nervous as he is coming to the edge of Blackfoot country his avowed enemies.

In just three days we have gone from the sparse tufts of dry grass with bushes of wormwood and sage to the thick, verdant valley of the Colorado or Seeds-ke-dee agie (prairie hen river) as named by the local people. The Wind River Range towers over us to the northeast. My mule was so pleased he rolled on his back in the lush, soft green grasses and I thought it would be hard to catch up to bring him into camp that night, but he seemed extra alert staying close to my tent his ears scanning the darkness, his eyes keying to each sound his face a mask of concentration. It seemed something was about as I was getting used to my mules moods.

Horses and men appeared on the hillside and Mr. Sublette called up for everyone to catch up their horses and prepare for battle. Using a spyglass it is soon determined that they are trappers. Upon reaching camp we find the men are from the Dripps and Fontenelle trapping party one of the American Fur Company parties that has been trapping the Laramies this past winter. None of the six men are Drips or Fontenelle. They are camped about five miles away their being 13 more back at camp. They are new to the Rocky Mountain trapping and have not fared well not knowing the country. They came out of Council Bluffs the previous fall. There is another party of American Fur Company men numbering fifty and led by W. H. Vanderburgh who left Ft. Union up on the mouth of the Yellowstone and they thought we were of that party. They are nervous and glad to have the protection of such a large group as they say they have seen plenty of sign of Blackfoot around.

At about ten o'clock the camp is jolted awake to the crack of guns from the darkness around us, the zizzing of balls pass us in the darkness and swishing sounds of arrows which is even more unnerving in that one knows the bow wielder is likely closer than the man armed with a rifle and I am utterly unable to determine where the arrows are coming from so I fell to my stomach peering between two mule packs. I wait for the flash of pan and I fired at it and my fire draws arrows that thud into the earth around me they all sound like they narrowly miss me. The war cries from out of the darkness are answered by surprised enraged and even frightened cries from within our U-shaped camp the river is behind us. I hear shots from behind me and balls zizz over my head from behind as well. I feel cornered unable to move as it seems one is just as likely to get shot from the friendly men behind as from the unknown men in front. It seems that all respond to whatever is in front of them and there is no organized response to the attack. I feel lucky that the attack is not an organized rush. I slept with my pistols and rifle and having fired my rifle I lay my pistols on the ground ready to grab if I hear footsteps rushing me. I lay on my side pouring powder down the barrel, dropping balls out of my bag onto the ground fumbling, silently cursing myself for the clumsiness. I can hear and vaguely see the men of my mess loading and firing around me. I'm worried about my mule taking a ball as he is still staked near my tent and I can hear his outraged brays and thumping of his hooves such a big target he is for the balls crossing in the air.

After firing my third ball at what I had imagined was the last place to see a flash for I fired to the right of the flash assuming the tribal member was right handed. We hear the soft thudding of many hooves and taunting cries fading in the distance. Fearing a trap we all wait with hammers cocked trying to hear over our excited breaths. Soon a few men call out to hold fire they will scout and proceed with one covering the other to sweep the edge of our camp, getting bolder and bolder of movement until they are walking upright with noisy feet all about our perimeter. After a check it is found that there are only bruises from various falls taken in the dark with one slight bullet wound and no arrow wounds. No fallen enemy is found out in the darkness. Five horses are dead, 14 missing three wounded but most horses not tied down were chased into camp. I rushed to my mule and hold her neck to calm her so that I can run my hands over her to see if she is wounded. She stands blowing out her nostrils looking back at me as I cover her body with my hands and keep up the low chatter telling her to breath easy that all is right. She calms, but paws and stomps her back feet telling me she is upset and didn't like this fracas one bit.

In the morning the men discover some holes in the tents and one even in his blanket and that is the topic for today's trail along with more claims of men being sure they heard their balls hitting home and it seems that toting up the claims over a dozen of the enemy must have been wounded. No blood is found, but the tracks and marking on the arrows left are determined to be those of the Blackfoot, of the Gros Ventre tribe which many assumed were still far to the south visiting their Arapahoe cousins. All are extremely cautious today scanning the mountains towering, above us, and the willows at every creek we cross. The valley is narrowing into a mountain pass with the Wind River Range on our right and the Salt River Range on our left which we have to pass though to get to Jackson's Hole where the Columbia River or as some call it the Snake named after Merriweather Lewis; Snake being his name bestowed on him by the local tribes. We are to meet Fitzpatrick on the branch of the Snake, the Lewis River.

We have a tense ride through the narrow tree-filled valley. There is little talk and heads swiveling to and fro. Ahead of me rides a Frenchman called Jean the Jolly from the Red River area who spent the last several years trapping the mountains and has just visited St. Louis for the first time, meeting a brother who he hadn't seen since they were children. He always wears a bright red wool sash about his waist and a dyed red turkey feather in his hat and he is cheerful man given to bursts of laughter that causes him to throw up his arms and hands when he laughs. He is always going about to each mess tasting what they are cooking and making elaborate gestures about the quality of the food, but always laughing even if the food is not to his taste. Normally he is singing, but today he rides silent listening.

We are passing through thickets of brush and aspen near the trail and I am much vexed by the slapping of the branches from the mules ahead, yet afraid of being out of sight of Jean and he has lost sight of the pack ahead of us as the trail twists and turns and I see no one behind us. The Creature is very nervous and starts to balk and trys to turn on the trail. I fight the reins but he is determined and I begin to curse him and start to pull on his ears and he starts kicking and then I feel something is wrong. There is a tremendous roar a crash of brush in front of me. I look over my shoulder when I hear Jean scream. His horse is down and is screaming with all legs kicking. Jean is flailing with his arms and one leg his other leg is trapped. My mule is turning circles the pack mules have ripped loose out of my hands. There is a brown blur at the stomach of the horse. My rifle has been knocked loose and is on the trail but with my mule bucking I can't loose my hold to grab my pistols for I know I will be on the earth and that's the last place I want to be with a huge white bear swinging it's arms. There is blood flying everywhere the whole side of the horse is bloody. Jean is screaming and the bear leaps over the horse and swats at Jean. His screams stop in mid-scream with the swat from the bear. Jean is bouncing down the trail at me. My mule screams at the movement and races down the hillside though the thick brush. I can see nothing and have to close my eyes at the thick slapping branches. I duck holding on for I am terrified to be on the ground and would rather hurtle into a ravine on my mule than face that bear. My Creature runs screaming for I don't know how long until he strikes a tree, rears and I leap to the side and he rolls backwards.

He looks at me with a stunned look. I still have the rein in my hand. I talk and talk I'm calming him and then stoking him and I'm shaking and he stands and I can barely hold my foot still enough to catch the stirrup and he is shaking as bad we stand there in the silence of the woods with the clinking of the metal rings and the rattling stirrups and anything loose makes noise from our collective shakes. I can hear no roars, no gunfire and it seems like we are in another world. I wonder if I'm dead for there seems to be no sign of the world I was just in. I turn him back, but he refuses to take the shattered path of our entry and angles towards what would have been the end the pack train by following an old creek bed.

We come out on the trail. It is empty. No sound. I do not want to move forward up the trail, but it is obvious the train has passed. I now wonder how long we were in the woods for I have no sense of time. Slowly, cautiously we move forward and I know they are ahead as the Creature is sniffing the air and seems more and more eager to move forward. It is still the close brushy landscape with the brushes reaching higher than my head.

We come to the pack mules and horses tied to the side of the trail. My pack train is tied. When I tie the Creature he looks back down the trail like he wants to head that way but then looks at the horses nearby. The men are gathered by the scene of the attack. The horse is dead and exposed, it's white entrails shiny in contrast to the clumps of black clotted blood and the bright red of his exposed flesh on her serrated shoulders neck and ribs. The sound of slicing metal in dirt and clanking metal on rocks as several men try to dig a hole in the hillside. Jean's beige wool blanket is on the ground clean except for a thin curved line of darkness that has soaked though in the odd space above the shape of his shoulders and where the round off center objects protrudes. The blackish red line is in the shape of a smile. My head is filled with his head rolling towards me on the trail.

Good! We thought he got you too! Mr. Sublette said as he clapped my shoulder. "Are you all right boy?"

"I feel as if I met with a banshee and I can't get…Jean…his head it was so quick…I can't believe it's true…it could happen so fast."

"I expect he didn't feel a thing."

"He was screaming he was under his horse…the bear just slapped his head off…then he wasn't screaming."

"Is that how is was? Well it was a quick death."

"He had no idea. The bear just charged knocked his horse over."

She was a sow had cubs found their tracks she's gone. I better get the train sorted. Here have a shot you could do with a numbin' That's it. Ya don't have to watch it ya know.

I've watched plenty of dead at wakes I've just not watched the death of them come in a instant. I'll finish it. I need to do some of the digging for it could have been me.

When the hole is dug and twas difficult ground as it is full of chunks of granite. There is some awkward hesitation about moving him in. One of the women moves over him and tucks the blanket under the body and folds it from the top and ties it round. We lower him and I take his feet. We look down upon his form the round lump now on his right shoulder. One of the Frenchmen, his friend, is wailing and has dropped to his knees others sniff and cry some silently. I sob and feel disbelief as we shovel the dirt onto his form.

Later that day we reach the Snake or Lewis Fork and we move the supplies across the wide swift river. The shock of the cold water feels good on my body and I think how Jean will never feel the shock of cold water again. It is the fourth of July and we take nearly the whole afternoon doing the crossing Mr. Fitzpatrick does not show and we send men out in several directions to search up and down the green valley some even going north towards the Yellowstone country, but there is no sign of him.

The next morning we leave Jackson Hole and begin the steep ascent up the mountains that separates us from Pierre's Hole or valley where the rendezvous or trade fair is to be held. Some of the men have come down with Mountain fever and are woozy on their horses and not able to hold any food. We follow the heavily wooded creek up the mountain and I find the path so narrow I must dismount my mule. Mr. Wyeth's horse that he is leading loses its footing and tumbles one hundred foot down. Nothing broken, but it causes much fear as to puts a stop to those behind us as we rope the animal up who is much frightened and not very sensible about helping us.

Mr. Campbell rides up. "Git this is a beautiful valley knew the man it's named after Old Pierre he was the chief of the band of Iroquois we employed damm good men all of 'em and the best fighters and hunters. We were going down the valley heading to the Snake River to trap. The Blackfoot had visited us in camp the night before and they were following us. We went down a creek and came under a bank when they attacked us. Old Pierre hated the Blackfoot and he advanced too far and they killed him. So this is the hole where Pierre the Iroquois is buried as least his feet that is all we found when we came upon the Blackfoot camp several days later. I expect his feet been walking around these past seven years looking for the rest of him. Mind you watch the Blackfoot...I don't want to be burying a young ladd here...buried too many men already." He looked at me intently with his deep blue eyes. "I expect you'll enjoy your first rendezvous...these mountains have given me my health and a lot more. He nodded and walked his horse off."

We had scouts out but still no sign of Mr. Fitzpatrick. It has been 26 days since he parted company with us. Some of the men are worried that the Gros Ventres that we had an encounter with on July second were in the path for the tracks show them to be an entire village with women and children. Most tribes won't attack when they have women and children with them, but they will send parties out to steal horses and will attack small parties they are confident of overpowering. I wonder what has happened to Jack for he does not know the rendezvous will be in Pierre's Hole. If he is coming with a small party he might be in real danger. Possibly he made it to Fort Union on the Missouri by the Yellowstone outlet on the steamship the Yellowstone and will be coming down with the American Fur Company supply train.

When we reach the top the weather grows increasingly cold and violent and soon we are huddled in our tents and under lean-to's of pine as snow swirls aound us. The snow keeps falling all night until we wake with well over a foot around us. The the sun shines bright in the morning and the green valley of Jackson Hole lay behind us and ahead the lush green of Pierre's Hole.

CHAPTER XIII

PIERRE'S HOLE RENDEZVOUS

Git O'Toole Journal

July 8 1832, Sunday

The prairie and now the mountains have humbled me and they have taken my immortality and surely immortality is one of the most foolish things a man can possess. I'm told all youth have it and I am glad to be rid of it. Tis not the fact that there are men here who will rob or kill me for tis their land and tis a land ruled by those with the most power and this is a simple law to understand, but there are far more men of the prairie who wish me well and honor me as I stand before them that has never happened to me in my short life except among family and friends. The English rulers the merchants on both sides the the sea and even the American rulers do not honor me for all of them I am fodder in the their complex ambitions and fears. Here I am a greenhorn to the mountain and a young warrior to the tribesmen, but I am judged by my actions not my ancestry. Tis here upon this land of the Far West outside the United States where the true American lives this is the land of the free.

I cannot wake without knowing that this could be my last day. Did Jean have any feeling it was his last day. I don't believe so, he was afraid of a Blackfoot attack so he was not singing. My Da has told me that man of true strength can choose his death. I thought Jean a strong man, a brave man and man who took strength from living who enjoyed the daily rituals of life like food and who kept songs in his heart always so he seemed a strong man, but he seems not to have chosen his death. And he is gone utterly gone for I can feel no spirit of him and I have listened very hard and I can find no spirit either Catholic or Celtic so I wonder if it is just death, just this world just life all around us and them just death and that's all there is. That doesn't make life any less matter of fact it makes it more prescious, but it sure makes it harder to accept that Jean is gone, gone forever. I like to think of him as Jean singing in the other world tasting everyone's mess, but I fear not.

So I am not immortal anymore. One cannot travel these prairies and mountains without the sure knowledge an angry grizzly bear can emerge from the next bush and snap your neck like a twig or there is no place to hide from the bolts of lightning thrown by the prairie clouds above or that carelessness in crossing a spring river will mean the end of your days even getting a dinner of buffalo can end with a man lying smashed and broken on the prairie. So a man cannot go many days without facing these dangers.

Oh what a difference from living in the city. I've always wondered why the newspapers and daily talk is filled with death and tragedy in the cities and now it seems to me that if if man walks this earth thinking they are safe it feels unnatural and tis so in the real world so the men in cities try to remind themselves of this real world with their stories of death and some are living in more fear than men live with daily in the Far West.

Eagle Hand Journal

July 8, 1832, Sunday

These shiny White Mountains have heads like old chiefs and the spirits that holds much power. The nights are cool like our fall and the heat of the day is light and does not squeeze a man like the summer prairie heat. These great mountains make the water that fill the Mighty Missouri. I shall travel to the north were my river comes out of these mountains and I shall travel the length of the river past our eagle hunting lodges to my village and I shall tell all of what I see for I have heard of many places the spirits dwell along the river.

The rendezvous is the only celebration I have seen the white man do. They honor the gods of trade with a march through the camp and have have games and they council about their trade round the fires and then they drink their foolish water until they are foolish and helpless and that is the only time I have seen them helpless. But still they offer nothing to the Gods how can they be so powerful when they do nothing to the get the attention of the Gods. They do not seem to care if the Gods take pity on them. Maybe they are so powerful they don't need the Gods? That they can make so many trade goods is proof of a power, but they don't seem to command any Gods. This is the great mystery to me and I have many smokes over it.

The clouds come nearly every day and threw white fire to the earth, but no rain falls. I have never seen so many tongues of white fire strike the earth…is that how these mountains where carved? I tried to find where the fire touched the earth and could only find one tree, a tree already dead and now blackened by white fire split of the power of it. Surely not even the white man's cannon has the power of the cloud fire.

The Nez Percé is a people who do not trade with us for they are a mountain people. They have more horses than I have ever seen so many they are careless in guarding them and the Snake people get many horses from the Nez

Percé. The Iroquois are a people who have given their land to the whites and now many of men trod these lands with the whites. They are good warriors, but what will come of them is they do not live with their people. There is a Kickapoo and an Osage who hunt with the white man. But they are not going to their people as I am. They are going from their people. The Oasge tells me that the white man and many new tribes surround them like fences of the white man and the Sioux and the Pawnee prick at their weakness like vultures from the other side. Their food has been driven away onto the land of the Sioux and Pawnee. For them to eat is to be killed and so they stay and beg of the white man and implore the gods to pity them and bring back the abundance that the Gods once favored them with. He tells me that many of the men drink the firewater to lift the weight of the hearts, but he says that so many drink so much firewater that it saddens their hearts and robs them. He left his people for he seeks the honor of death before before that too is taken from his people. He does not wish to become old and sadden and die withered and helpless. He wants to walk proud in the land of the spirits and with all his strength.

SLIDING DOWNT THE STEEP SNOWY mountain takes considerable less time than ascending. The snow is heavy and melting off the boughs of the fir trees, but most of the men ignore the beauty of the contrast of being in snow yet being warm with the sun and heading into a lush green valley full of meandering streams so excited are they for the upcoming rendezvous. The Trois Tetons are quite visible and they are magnificent, as the French would say. They are so high they stay snow covered the year round. There are actually four peaks in a row with one smaller but tis the three that are named. I recall a statue with three breasts on it, but cannot recall who the goddess is. This sight is so much more Godly than a mere statue. Surely it is the three-breasted goddess who has made such a lush valley as this below her white tipped peaks.

After a final short ten-mile march we at last arrive at the rendezvous. Tis Sunday July 8, 1832. As far as the eye can see the valley is dotted with teepees and tents. I'm told there are lodges one twenty of the Nez Percé and eighty of the Salish and about sixty lodges of the Shoshone people and more than one hundred trappers of the Rocky Mountain Fur Company led the the four trapping captains: Milton Sublette, Henry Fraeb, Jim Bridger and Jean Gervais. Milton is the brother of William Sublette our leader. It appears the rest of Mr. Dripps and Mr. Vandenburgh trapping parties the American Fur Company people are here in numbers nearly equal to the Rocky Mountain people and there is quite a number of free and independent trappers many with their families and some mixed with the Snake or Shoshone people. I would say four to six hundred men and women and well over a thousand horses roam freely in this green valley with the thigh high thick grass full of curving creeks feeding into the the Snake fork of the Columbia River. Surely it is Eden after the dry high foothills of the Rockies. Mr. Sublette directs Mr. Wyeth to camp about a mile down this long narrow green valley it being nearly fifteen miles long and about two miles wide with the Tetons to our east and rough rolling hills to the west and distant mountains on the north and the south.

I'm told the rendezvous was started as a more efficient way to trap the Rocky Mountains. Supplies are brought out from St. Louis to the trapper instead of the trappers traveling back to get supplies. General Ashley pioneered this method. The other system developed first by the French and then the British and now imitated by the American Fur Company is a series of what they call forts but are really defensible trading posts within palisades. Mr. Astor American Fur Company bought out the Northwest Company and thereby took control of the Upper Missouri fur trade with their series of forts and are now busy building additional forts of which Fort Union on the Missouri/Yellowstone junction is the principal one of the attempted conquest of the Rocky Mountain trade along with Fort Pierre on the Bad and Missouri River and Fort Clark at the Mandan village on the Missouri. It seems the presence of the American Fur Company trappers is for them to follow the more experienced Rocky Mountain trappers into the fall hunt as they call the trapping season. This is what they call competition in America the richer men or companies use wealth to try to buy the knowledgeable man from competitors and he has so far failed to the lure the brigade leaders of the Rocky Mountain Fur Company into his fold so now he will steal their secrets by following them. The trapping seasons are fall and spring with fall the most productive as it is easier to get around before the deep snow. Many trappers will winter in some pleasant mountain valley when the snows too deep and the wind too fierce to travel the mountain streams. I'm told the summers are brief in these mountains.

The rendezvous supplies mostly come from overseas with England being a major manufacturer but even China supplies some goods like vermillion, which is much preferred by the plains tribes over the American Vermillion.

Late this afternoon just before darkness fell after nearly a month since he left us Thomas Fitzpartrick is found by two scouts on the mountainside of this valley tis not the same man he looks like a skelton his hair has turned white and he can barely walk without help and he comes to us with nothing but his tattered clothes on his back. After feeding him buffalo marrow broth with wild onion and ginger powder we gather round the fire and he tells us how he came to be in such a state.

"After taking leave of you on June twelve at the Laramie River I traveled the same route you all followed to get here. I made it though the Green or Colorado River valley and shortly after I entered the narrow valleys of the mountains west of the Green I spotted a tribe of the Gros Ventre ahead of me. He paused to sip his black tea."

"I thought they had not spotted me and I turned on my track only to discover that there is a small party behind me that I had not seen.. They see my attempt to escape and set to howling and yipping thereby warning the party in front of me and all close on me leaving me with only the very steep thickly wooded mountainside which I charged up with my valiant horse but was so steep that I had to let my other horse go. Up I go laying up the neck of my horse."

"When I look behind I see that the Gros Ventres have dismounted below me and there is a mass of warriors screeching and racing below me and of course I can hear the pop of rifles. The Ground is both very soft and full of rocks and outcroppings and it is soon evident I can't keep charging my horse up such terrain for it has nearly fallen on me several times and it was evident the Gros Ventres are closing the gap. I dismount taking only my rifle, shot powder and possibles bag. I slap my horse away with sad regret, but with the hope that my sturdy steed will be able to save my hair by distracting the Gros Ventres long enough for me to gain the summit."

"I turn and ran as hard as I could uphill for I had fresh wind and the men below had been climbing for some time. I the soon heard the whoops of joy and triumph and turned to see serveral men around my fine white horse. Panting now I redoubled my effort but when I came over a small rise where I was hidden from the men below I realized I had to hide for I would not be able to outrun so many men. I saw a large granite rock jutting up with a small hole under it. I ran up the hill to the next rise then turned back and jumped from rock to rock till I was back at the granite rock. I grabbed some dried grass and crawled in though the thorny berry bush growing at the base of the rock. I covered the hole with dried grass along with bending over the grass and bushes that grew aound the base of the rock. I could only hope that the men would rush by me in their excitement and greed to be the first to claim my scalp and in so doing cover up all traces of my trail. It was not long afore I could hear them whooping and calling to one another and hear the rattle of the leather fringe as they rushed by my hiding place. I was doing everything I could to hold my breath low, but I was still so winded that I felt as If I was drowning."

"It sounded as if the thump of my heart by was vibrating the rock above. But praise the saints those carnivorous voices faded until I was hours in silence. I was questioning ever leaving Ireland and that's a fact. A fine fix I was in. One the devils had come so close that I could see the fringe on his leggings. There wasn't a thing I could do as I waited for that devil to part the branches and reveal my poor self to the whole tribe. Thank the heavens he passed."

"Twas a gray day and hard to judge time especially so curled in the damp earth beneath a cold stone. It was hours after the voices faded that I dared stretch a limb and stir a leaf. The cold evening air filled my hideout and darkness gave me the courage to consider my position. I kept careful track of my rock that you can be sure as I slowly went down the mountain seeking my escape. But the saints weren't with me that night for I soon came upon the glowing embers of the Gros Ventre camp. They were a bigger party than I had considered. Slowly at first and then with more haste I made my way back to my rock having a fright of losing it in the dark. Back into it I went and worried my mind as the tracks I may have left, but there were tracks all over that mountain."

"A fitful fearful sleep did I have that night with jerkin' to every sound and mighty damp I was without my wool blanket. I knew the devils would be at me with the rising sun and soon I could hear them covering the mountainside not so loud as yesterday but calling back and forth and making their high pitched yips. But a chase without a running quarry is not likely to hold their attention. Soon they were all down in the valley having races with my horse and I was that proud it bested all their horses by a considable length. Back into the hole I went but when darkness fell I felt sure I could outflank their camp and soon followed a game trail across the side of the mountain till I was clear of them and then down to the valley and along the creek I went but little did I know that was the easy part."

"I had no food and did not dare fire my rifle for the Gros Ventre might be over the next ridge so I filled on June berries when my innards needed meat. The berries might fatten a bear but they don't stay long in a man. Ahh if that was the worst of it my hair wouldn't be white now would it?"

"Twas a tragic mistake I made. I used some rawhide, I did not have enough for my purpose and twisted some willows about some logs to make a raft for you see I had come to a river too swift and too deep to cross with me legs. Without a horse I had a great fear the Gros Ventre's would be sending scouts up the creek I was following so I wished to get across this water and thought is proper direction to Pierre's Hole. Into the cold swift water I went and I was nearly across but the current turned out to be stronger near the far bank and it took me round the bend then another and I am trying to hold my rifle and paddle with my hand and when the current brought me full into a boulder and flipped me backwards off the raft and I didn't know up form down and didn't want to be dashed on the rocks and the cold water had me in its vise…you know how the mountain water takes a man's breath right out of his chest if he bold enough to put his head into it, well I had my breath sqeezed just fine and it was all could do to make the fifteen feet to the shore once my head cleared the surface."

"A fine fix I was in for I had lost my rifle and had only my knife with which to cross two mountain ranges. I knew I couldn't use any of the trails without a rifle and I knew I would not be getting any meat and would be too weak to outrun anyone. June berries strawberries and the root of the Iris and onion and the inner bark of the pine which tastes like lemon syrup that was all I could manage to eat that day and the the days ahead. I grew more weaker and more confused as the days passed until I came upon a the carcass of a buffalo killed by wolves and so I scaped the remaining meat off and made a fire bow and cooked only the meat I was to have for the weeks of my wandering. I tell ya a man cannot live without his meat in the mountains and fine example of that I am."

"Godin here found me when I didn't think I could take another step but this marrow soup is putting the spine back in me so I'll be pulling the buffalo off the appola in no time. Of course a shot o' poteen would be mighty medicinal. As he said this his eyes lit for the first time and his face crinkled into a smile."

Mr. Sublette is the first major trader to arrive at rendezvous and the men are lined up eager for food, whiskey and supplies. Mr. Campbell has five mules full of trade supplies, but doesn't seemt to be a competitor to William Sublette in that he renders him much assistance. Mr Campbell has a brother named Hugh in dry goods in Philadelphia and Mr. William Sublette has General now Senator Ashley as a financial backer and buyer of goods and furs though the New York market so these men seem able and experienced men. Mr. Wyeth will be trying his hand at trading and the American Fur Company Mr. Astor's company will be trading here but their supplies which are supposed to have been shipped up the Missouri by steamboat to Fort Union which is near the where the Yellowstone empties into the Missouri up near Crow, Assinboin, Blackfoot and Cree territory their supplies which Mr. Fontenelle is bringing overland from Ft Union for the two American Fur Company brigades has not yet arrived and Mr. Sublette has refused to sell any goods on credit to the American Fur Company brigade leaders.

No one knows if Captain Bonneville will be trading and he hasn't arrived and isn't expected for a least a week or more as he is bringing twenty wagons. William Sublette says that he did that before and knows that is takes longer. He says that although there is less labor involved in wagons for one does not have to unload the wagons every night and reload then in the morning like the mules the delay in getting here late with wagons are more costly in lost trade. The inexperienced Black and Gantwell party appears to have only lasted one season in the business, but most of the men from that venture are here and will be employed by someone. There is also the Bean and Sinclair trapping venture out of Arkansas and they appear to still be solvent. And, of course the Hudson Bay Company controls all the North and Oregon Country and there are a few Hudson

Bay men here. I'm told that this is one of the biggest rendezvous ever seen in the mountains and certainly has the most trappers of any rendezvous. It looks like Fitzpatrick and company that is the Rocky Mountain men won't be having the mountain business to them selves any longer.

William Sublette has given financial backing to the Rocky Moutain Fur Company, but he is here to sell to all and at the greatest profit, as is Mr. Campbell. There are also a few small traders men who picked up supplies at Ft. Union or who returned to St. Louis with some pack mules and the tribes have many items to trade along with furs. Mr. Fitzpatrick brought four men with him and each with two pack mules they appeared a little lost as to what to do without him.

Ah the splendor, the color, the joy, the happiness of a trade fair. This mountain valley is glowing with every color of the cloth the world makes: green, violet, blue, red, black and olive colored cloth. Irish linen, violet bombazine chintz, blue mowmac calico, percale, yellow and scarlet flannel escalarta, rolls of linen, burlap, corduroy, fusteau. Brilliant shawls and scarfs flutter in the wind off the high lodgepoles and draped across the row of ropes: mandarin shawls belfa striped cotton cloth, Indian silk handkerchiefs, carrandan tunics, merino wool shawls, striped batiste, blue cotton and turkey red bandanas, indigo Florentine twill, white handkerchiefs, Sicilian silk tunics and even orange cotton shawls. But it is not just the fluttering colors of the world's cloth against the backdrop canvas tent, green grass and snowcapped Grand Tetons mountains in the clear crisp mountain air it is the strange minic of the city with rows and rows of tailored goods displayed by being pinned to the tent walls: green frock coats red flannel shirts, fancy calico shirts, Marsailles vests, suspenders, white woolen caps and hats, sattinet and linsey pantaloons, duck trousers, blue and grey cloth capotes and blue and green blanket capotes, country woolen socks, Kip shoes and green googles which I wish I had to protect me from the blowing sand and flies along the Platte. (They are priced at one beaver skin or $4 so I must try to trade for them.)

I am the cook for my mess and have been favored by some of the hunters with many varieties of meat and mountain fowl and foods. Camas root is an onion like root that is much in abundance out in the mountains especially west of here. I have also been bought dried salmon and find it excellent in flavoring stews and in frying greens in buffalo fat. The cook of the mess next to ours can't be found so the men pressed on me to fix them a meal after my mess is done. They settle around the fire and the exchange of news and discussion so often heard round the fires is the only way of finding out what is news outside the mountains.

"Heard that Black Hawk moved back across the Mississippi to his old stomping grounds...the miners and farmers are upset and they got the miltia together to chase them out, but he's a tough one and them local boys didn't get the job done. There wus whining for the Federal troops and sure enough the Federal boys was loaded onto steamers in St. Louis this spring to move Black Hawk off they got Winfield Scott to lead them."

"Well I expect if they hadn't found lead on his lands he'd still be there but then again those farmers seem to get the newspapers on their side: go squat on a fellars land and get your child killed then the politician's send in the Federal troops. I'd take an Indian any day over a farmer, but I expect those farmers will just keep rollin' west one outrage at a time then what the hell do we do boys? Shoot milch cows?"

"Pox will get the injuns before the mining companies and farmers do. I expect. Heard the Pawnees got it bad and they's dying fast...Knife Chief and his son Pitalesharo died and so did Iskatappe of the Grand Pawnees. Also heard the Commanches wiped out a good number of Pawnees down on the Arkansas. They's mighty good fighters but ya can't fight with dead warriors the Teton Sioux will go south to plunder what's left of the Pawnees. That's going to open up some mighty good buffalo country from the Platte to the Arkansas."

"I spent a bad winter with old Chief Iskatappe...I was with Jed Smith and Mr. Campbell workin for Ashley back to '25 I tell you that Pawnee corn saved our hides that winter now the pox got 'em. Old Hiram Scott was with us that winter and his bones are below Scott's bluff. Col. Boone was with us too Daniel's son, there are only a few of us left from that bunch.

Sublette was the one found old Hiram's bones picked clean by the wolves. He was with Jackson at the time…I believe it was twenty-seven when Hiram went under."

"Congress says they gonna cow-pox the Injuns to keep 'em from getting the pox. Sending doctors out of St. Louis this summer to start."

"I expect it's for show for the city women out east, I would't expect them doctors to step very far off their steamship to be scatching Injuns on the arm they ain't hardly a man in government wants the Injuns to prosper this pox business is jest a vote-getting scheme won't last out the year."

"We'll we got us a doctor out here…Doctor Wyeth."

"Why don't you ask him if he wants to de-pox the Blackfoot? Ha Ha."

"It ain't the Blackfoot that goin to be the end of us Rocky Mountain boys it's rich old man Astor and his cutthroats. This spring our brigade leader Bridger trapped in the west along the Snake and we had a fine hunt until we reached the Bear River when along comes Dripps and his American Fur men with hardly a beaver. They walked right into camp. Shoulda seen them pups gaping at the skins we hanging in the willow woods, hell musta have serveral hundred skins drying and tied in packs I expect that those flatlanders never seen so much beaver. They was trying to hire out our men behind our backs and questioning everybody and they was selling goods to the Injuns and even our hired men and worst of all when we went on the tramp them pork eaters dogged our trail the rest of the season for they didn't know where to find beaver. Mr. Astor is paying those men to be spies for they sure didn't bring any beaver out of the mountains. I expect they were there for our jobs. Now who's telling me thats fair? Who's tellin' me thats fair American competition? It just won't wash with me it won't."

"Well Rut you're a bigger fool than you look if yer expecting skill to win over money. Money don't have no conscience and once men get enough of it they don't have no conscience. A man who's growing money ain't above using you for fertilizer."

"Now you listen here Poliet, I seen more days than you and there good men in the world like the men running the Rocky Mountain outfit and they's no more skilled men in the mountains 'cept a few of the them free trappers than these Rocky Mountain men so I ain't about to sell a hide to old Astor and work for pilgrims."

"I expect you will once old Astor builds forts all over tarnation and buys our the Rocky Mountain boys."

"Why the polecat hasn't done a nothing for this whole business except follow the brave thinking men around and then either strangle them or buy them out. All that American Fur outfit is ruthless Eastern money."

"Now Rut I don't care to get you excited so we'll just see who's setting where in about two or three seasons."

The good feeling from cooking in the mountains is that everyone cleans their own kit and I have only the pots to deal with. I am able to ask many questions while cooking from the men that they may not have the patience to answer it they weren't waiting for their food.

Much of the trade here is not for dollars for few men have any dollars although there are signs in dollars rather it is truly traded meaning that men and women exchange one item for the another, but the St. Louis traders are interested in furs with beaver being the main item they seek although otter, mink, muskrat and other fine furs are traded as well as beaver castor or oil from the beaver. The prices I have written down are based on the net St. Louis price of three dollars to three dollars seventy five cents per pound for beaver skin which allows for a deduction of fifty cents per skin for shipping them back to St. Louis which is what Mr. Sublette charges to take to back. Of course the prices are higher in New York and higher yet in London. Muskrat brings the least amount and is hardly worth shipping at twenty cents each. Each beaver skin weighs from a pound to a pound and half with few of the two pound skins showing up today mostly due to the Far West being trapped for the past seven years and I told based on this rendezvous that the competition will be fierce this year so the skin size might go down as more traders brings goods out so the free trappers may get more goods for work if they manage to get good sized beaver and do a good job preparing the skins. Already the company trappers are being offered higher wages by some of the smaller competitors who want to lure away the experienced men so their new firms can get established. It seem that the companies with the most capital will fare the best and no one has more capital than Mr. Astor with his fur empire stretching across nearly the whole northern portion of America.

An experienced fur trapper can bring in from one hundred to two hundred furs per season if they have a good and knowledgeable brigade leader who knows the mountains well and knows how to avoid losing the furs and horses to local tribes and that would mean an income of nearly $300 to $750 for a season, but of course the free trapper has to pay for his outfit that is the horse, traps, pack mule and pay a camp assistant out of that income and hold on to all the furs until delivery. A good number of trappers have wives and these women work in the camps for they are more skilled than most men in dressing hides and can bring the trappers a higher price for a better dressed hide this is especially true of the free trappers and the French, but even man like Mr Fraeb of the American Fur Company has a pregnant wife and child of three with him.

Most of the company trappers get their outfit supplied and get a wage of two hundred and fifty to two hundred and ninety dollars for eighteen months of work or fourteen to sixteen per month. I been told that the Rocky Mountain Company trappers and the free trappers will get a little over a hundred skins per trapper per season, but the American Fur Company trappers who are new to the rockies get only a quarter of the that number. The Rocky Mountain people seem to have the best brigade leaders with one of the most admired being Jim Bridger who seems to have the most incredible talent of knowing every beaver stream in the rockies and being able to draw a map of nearly anyplace a person would care to travel in these mountains, but he has not a lick of education being unable to read, write and figure yet is one of the owners of the Rocky Mountain Fur Company. He speaks with a thick Kentucky accent which I have difficutly understanding.

The trapping season is based on when the animals have their thick winter fur and when the trappers can reach the streams. The trapping season goes from late August to deep snow, which is usually November. The trappers winter in some mild valley then trap from March though May travel to rendezvous and have a grand time during July. I have already been offered a job of camp tender, which most bridgades employ to cook and tend camp and clean furs. I still have my trade supplies and unsure whether I want to contract myself for so long. I really wish to have a horse.

The blankets are much treasured by the tribesmen and trappers the Hudson Bay blanket being the most favored but the American Mackinaw is sometimes traded. The blankets come in white, green and sky blue and sold according to the weave which ranges from one and a half points to four points with four point being the warmest and most expensive but there are some not rated by points but rather by color like the green and blue wool blankets that sell for ten dollars each or three beaver skins the same as the three point blanket. Hudson bay puts black stripes on the blanket indicating the number of beaver skins it takes in trade for the blanket.

Imagine a hardware store laid out on a white blanket surrounded by the greenest grass with the sweet scent of blooming yellow and blue flowers mixed with the smokey aromas of roasting meat. There is not a store in Dublin or New York no matter how bright the paint that can compare. In neat lines on the white blanket are bright oval fire steels, yellow bullet buttons, battle axes, packs of tinned rivets, copper soldering irons, sheet iron, kettles, bags of shot, rod iron, emery paper, white chapel needles, bastard and rattail files and brass wire.

The sun glitters off this hardware drawing one from far away and the knives always have a gathering of onlookers. What man can pass a display of knives. Wilson butcher knives, cartouche and scalping knives are easily the most popular knives buck-handle knives and fine looking green bone handle knives and cast steel butcher knives and even Masonic swords. By far the most numerous knives are the scalping knife. Mr. Campbell has a least a one thousand of them and about two hundred of the next most numerous knife the Wilson butcher knife. Seems one will doing a whole lot more butchering than scalping so the display is a mystery to me.

And what man cannot use a few number four fish hooks and some line for catching some trout. The wood screws and quires of sandpaper do not seem as useful to me but screw augers and metal frame and paper frame looking glasses and pocket compasses do.

What men cherish the most draws the biggest crowd and that is their weapon. Octogon brass barrel pistols glitter on a white blanket and rifles are displayed and stacked behind the clerks. I count over eighty Northwest rifles (English) but only 8 American rifles, Lancaster rifles. Confirming what Eagle Hand told me about the great demand for English weapons, but there are eight nicely engraved but expensive Hawken rifles from St. Louis that drew some looks but no takers. The Hawkens costs over five times what the Northwest rifle costs and about one and third what the Lancaster cost so it is easy to see why the British have the rifle trade over the expensive American rifles. Some American rifles might be of better quality but not five times better by any means. The Hawken rifle coast nearly twice as much as I paid for my Leman set and that includes my pistols with holsters and there are few pistols for sale.

My frugal Irish nature is being tested by walking amonst these goods I have decided I must have the green goggles for not only are they practical in keeping out the sand and dust they keep he glare of the sun off my eyes that are used to the gray skies of Ireland and I rather fancy the looks of them. I also fancy a looking glass for one needs such an instrument on these plains and mountains where much is beyond the naked eye. The Salish and Nez Percé have many beaver skins and I have determined to take Eagle Hand with to barter for it is well known that the Mandans are the most astute traders on the prairie. With some beaver I could consider a leather book with fine thick sheaves of white paper and even a spotted mountain horse could be mine as I have heard that they can be had for a blanket and a knife, but I don't know how to judge these stout shaggy mountain horses.

Walking about I come upon a man in front of neat tent with the acoutrements of a tailor sewing up shirts several which he had laid out. He had long delicate fingers that move rapidly and precisely in rhythm to his humming.

"I didn't expect to find a tailor in the mountains.

"I didn't expect to be here neither. It was a sailor that brought me here."

"A sailor that bought you to the mountains?"

"A sailor a preacher and a magistrate I sold a suit of clothes to a sailor on Sunday you see he was sailing that day and was desperate for he would be seeing his lady in Boston and he needed a suit. A preacher was watching my shop and he reported me to a New York magistrate who summoned me and fined me more than I make in a month. But then took pity on me and gave me three days to raise the money or go to jail. A man needs to use his time wisely and I did packing up my needles and awls and buying a horse. Not a man of religion myself so I though it best to be out of the reach of preachers. Be careful what you sow for the cities are full of men of malice who can pluck you with their laws, but I'm thankful I have my eyes and did not suffer the fate of Peeping Tom of Coventry for what is a tailor without his eyes."

"Yes I always wondered who was watching Peeping Tom to know he was watching Lady Godiva."

"Tis what all laws do, son they turn neighbor against neighbor they turn good men into demons. God made a law and if Adam hadn't turned in Eve we might still be in paradise but this here valley is mightly close and there are no demons here and no one sitting on top waiting with wagging tongues. Would you be looking for fine tunic or shirt."

"No my path twas a curious one I don't believe I have anything of interest to you to trade, only knife blanks awls beads and such."

"Look at this fine plaid domestic shirt I made it for a small Frenchman, Little Antoine but he took sick and went under before he could claim it. It yours on the prairie go on take it."

"But what is the trade?"

"No trade child it's on the prairie."

"No obligation them?"

"Yes son on the prairie means no obligation. For as you have noticed the prairie provides many fine things the buffalo being the linchpin of this land. You've had buffalo have you not? Study that animal for you will find all that lives here grasses, insects the very earth itself lives because of the buffalo. I think it will fit you fine. Put it on and give my eyes some satisfaction. Yes a bit big but you will fill our quickly."

"Thank you much sir."

"Oh don't thank me for it is the hand of Antoine that is still at play in this hole. I expect to hear his piping laughter echoing from the far trees where he's buried over yonder."

Wearing my new shirt I feel such a gift embolden me to trade for some beads to get a new set of moccasins. I pick our some cobalt beads from Czechoslovakia, candystripe and red and white heart beads from Italy and the Procer Padre beads from India as trade items. I need new moccasins and there is Crow woman living with a Nez Percé who is reputed to be the most skillful at making moccasins. When I get there she shames me into trading for a set of leggings and new elkskin shirt. How can one be charming and a sharp trader with just hand signals and a few words I will not ever know, but this woman with crinkles around her eyes and the ends of her mouth managed with her slender fingers to get me to trade for a whole new outfit using up all my beads some awls and some knife blanks. But she is so beaufifully and elegantly dressed that I can't resist and she fed me an excellent elk udder stew that is the most tender and tasty stew I have ever tasted. I am to stop back in three days time.

I should have waited for Eagle Hand but tis too late. I will need him to trade for a horse.

With the thousands of horses the tack is considerable: stirrup leather, martingales spurs, crambos, snaffle bridles, mule harnesses, roller buckles, harness rings, surcingles horseshoes and nails and more.

These displays are good for the practical man or for the working man of the mountains but the rendezvous is a time of celebration, relaxation, a time of games and a time to indulge in pleasure so the many men have brought food, foofaraw's and fancy fixing as they say. There are no farms in the mountains and tribes of the upper and lower Missouri raise corn not wheat so flour is a rendezvous treat and sugar a delicacy. A few man recently from the east cry foul at paying so much for flour and sugar, but after making the trip part of the way with the pack train I can attest to the work and time it takes to haul a barrel of flour so far with the constant risk of losing it all to attack, streams or weather. But there is far more brown Havana sugar than flour and I have seen a Salish trade for a whole cupful and fill his mouth with the sugar and then fall down as if dead drunk he could not be roused such was the effect on him and tis to be supposed that a people raised without sugar or honey have not the body to absorb such a tropical spice. The tribesman's have not learned moderation in imbibing in foreign sugar and liquor. They think it magic or spiritual that putting whiskey or sugar in their mouth will transport them to distant places although their bodies are decidedly planted hereabouts and do not seem as happy with the trip as the minds purport to be as judged by the sickness displayed afterwards

Rice can be had more reasonable than flour and dried peaches more reasonable than dried apples and raisins priced betwixt the two. Black pepper is at hand but no salt as salt is plentiful in the Far West. Young Hyson tea from Cathay or China can be had less the half the cost of coffee and that suits me fine as I don't have the bother of roasting those hard green beans and then grinding them all to get a cup of bitter liquor when I only have to pour some boiling water over my tea leaves. But the leaves most sought after are those of American tobacco: Cavandish is the finest quality. Tobacco is available in plug, carrot and twist tobacco. The cheapest seems to be the 6-twist tobacco. The upper Missouri tribes grow and trade a tobacco, but even they prefer the finer American tobacco. There are a few men who do some chewing but it is into pipes that most of this tobacco will go and pipes are sold and made mostly by the tribesmen in this area but the cheap clay pipes can be had at the river forts.

Mr Campbell brought 10 gallons of whiskey an he is using some of it to entertain a selection of independent trappers along with some tidbits of pilot and navy bread, which are crackers not bread on which he has put some tinned mackerel. He also has a small selection of spices such as Lexington mustard, nut-megs, cloves, ground ginger and pepper sauce. I tasted the whiskey, but it is the most raw burning flavor for is seems American's do not believe in aging for flavor or perhaps they do no wish to take the time when a profit can be made on raw whiskey. A good Irish whiskey I can sip on occasion, but not this whiskey. To rid my mouth of the bitter whiskey I cook some blueberries with a bit of sugar and put them over fritters tis quite good and restores my mouth. Fritters are a rendezvous treat. A cup of flour is brought mixed with water to thicken to make a batter and fired in bufflalo tallow to make the fritter.

With all the fancy colorful cloth to be had a man has to look presentable. I notice that men with Native wives keep themselves clean-shaven as it is universal on the plains for the men of the tribes to shave or pluck all facial hair and some remove all bodily hair. The first step to woo the tawny maidens in this camp is the shave. These tribe women seemed to be disgusted by hairy faces so the razors and cake shaving soap are much in demand, but below that clean face the men will likely be wearing a new cotton checked or plaid domestic shirt perhaps with a marsailles vest over it and red flannel scarf tied about the waist and maybe a pair of satinette pantaloons with his head topped with a clean white wool hat into which he has put a red cock feather and his hair might have an ivory comb in it. His neck might be tied with a black silk handkerchief and his chest rattling with dark blue cut glass beads mock garnets Carnelian fine beads, blue snake beads, red striped agate beads, amber or yellow beads.

The valley is truly a land of peacocks as all the men become resplendent, colorful and showy and they walk in front of the maidens.

There are many fetching women around my age walking about in groups admiring the trade goods. Instead of the white powder that women wear on their face in New York these women favor rounds of vermillion on their upper cheeks which in themselves are much more prominent being higher and sculpted giving these women a very handsome cut to their faces. Many of them part their hair in the middle and this part is also red. Not one but many earring hang from their ears and many braclets and sometimes shells and bells are tied to their clothing so one can hear the rhthymn of several women walking before one sees them. Tis pleasant to hear the music of approaching women and then see their laughing excited faces. The men use many more colors and designs on their face and bodies than the women.

I watch a young snake women this morning a wife of a trapper named Adam she is kneeling, sitting upon her heels and scraping a hide staked to the ground. She wears a deerskin dress belted at the waist with the rawhide cord, sleeveless with fringes about the shoulder and along the hem, which is tucked betwixt her thighs exposing her knees and a bit of her thighs. As she works the hide she rises sliding forward putting her weight on the scaper until she is stretched forward then her actions starts over again. But most of these women will only give a man a very brief glance, for it is only a warrior's place to look a man whom he challenges straight in the the eye. Her eyes stay down and not in submission like some of our women, but from respect and habit.

What rushed into my mind watching this woman was that one rarely sees American city women doing such physical labor and if one did there would be the most lowly of women such as servants or women on a farm. There are women here who dress finer than others but no women who do not work unless they are unable. This woman I watch is maybe four years older than myself. It seems to me that I have observed that a white woman would not long let a man watch her without responding in either annoyance or coyness unless she is quiet old. This Snake woman seems unconcerned about my study of her for she is surely aware.

The men wear beads to impress and tempt women who admire them as the men try to talk to them. One advantage of signing is that it requires the attention of the woman's eyes that she would have normally averted while she talks with her voice. To watch the sparkling excited eyes of these women was they watch a man's hands talk to them gave me much pleasure, but I am too afraid to try my hands with them myself being painfully aware I have no horse, no beads no fine fabric and do not have the dress that a woman could read my exploits no scalp sewn in my shirt no painting of wounds nor of horses or plunder captured no sacred animal as a protector just my rifle, my pistols and my inexperience.

Seeing all these goods has brought a fever to my blood, as markets are apt to do. I have my journal and blank book Mr. Catlin gave me but don't know when I will be able to procure another so the leather covered blank books are tempting me for I envision them filled with a flow of black ink powder and tis a wonder that I have even found lead pencils and red ink powder for drawing and emphasizing.

Mr. William Sublette has arranged a grand parade with all his men dressed in the most colorful sashes and handkerchiefs of every color and some adorned with hawk bells, which jingle with each step and he even has a band of sorts with penny whistles, skin drums and fiddles. Men fire their rifles in the air, horses dance with the full array of tack and he is tossing sweets and tobacco to the onlookers as his parade weaves in and out of tents and teepees. Men are juggling sitting backwards ont their horses standing on his horse with feet and hands and dancing and singing. It is quite a spectacle.

After the parade the chief of the Nez Percé gathers his people and gives a speech to them telling them to honor all agreement to not to get angry to not to steal. It is amazing for quite a number of men have bought horses from them and every day the young Nez Percé horse tenders return to the new owners their horse out of the vast grazing herd.

Today the Salish and Nez Percé camp is full of excitement for all the men have spent the morning painting themselves and their horses and we are to see a grand spectacle and afterwards there will be games played by all. When we all assemble they trot out en masse in a long line to the distant hills and line up with war lances raised feathers fluttering in the wind. The chiefs raise their lances and a tremendous war cry rises from one end of the line to the other and the whole line moves forward with plumes of dust shadowing them. The line then breaks into several groups, which then interweave like a series of snakes then reforms into a single line some of the warriors break out of the line into a full charge towards us, some of the men disappear behind the horses hanging onto the manes others are on their backs with legs hooked up around the neck and they shoot arrows at our feet as they pass. Several young men about my age ride past with two horses side by side and leap from one horse to the other at full gallup and then stand and jump from one horse to the another.

A lone rider races up with a nearly white horse. He is naked, his face painted white and his body red with with white strips. He slows the horse to a gallup and dismounts with fluid straight legged swing off the horse his legs hit the earth striding and he runs behind his horse charges and leaps over the rear of the horse onto the rump of the horse and then pushes off with his hands and swings his legs around like a open scissors and faces backwards on his horse. All laugh and clap while he keeps a very straight face and rolls backwards and does a handstand and he rides away with his arms flexing to the motion of the galloping horse and his sex flopping and waving at us. All are laughing.

Rotten Belly a Nez Percé warrior rides by completely hidden behind his horse and then rides standing atop his horse shooting arrows at our feet. The Lawyer, Red Crow and Red Beard all follow him doing the same. They wheel and several trappers lay plugs of tobacco on the ground and each warrior swoops in a full gallup and sweeps down picking up the plugs with Red Crow missing his and Rotten Belly wheeling to pick his up before Red Crow can turn his horse.

They race back to the line of the lances they have pitched into the ground. Pulling them up as they gallup wheeling and charging a painted skin hung in a willow frame and swaying on a rope from a tree branch lance after lance plunges in followed by the younger warriors who let their arrows fly with all going though the hoop and the young ones racing to retrieve the arrows holding them up for the owners to grab as they race bay. They all pull out their rifles they carry acoss their back or chest and raise them firing into the air and racing off across the hole. Then the trappers mount up and there is a mixed melee of horsemanship and horse races while the New Englanders stand watching this all with mouths agape. The mountainman are showing the corncrackers some fine and outrageous riding and they are loving every moment of being able to show off with riding and shooting skills.

A lone rider comes over the hill the horse is at a smooth walk. A very tall rider, but then it is a rider with a very tall head and then it is a rider with a stack of parfleche cases on his head no not his, her it is a grandmother and on hair streaked with gray balance ten parfleche cases the cases all manner of color and design. Her neck moves with the movement of the horse and children run alongside screaming and waving their hands. When she passes the line of painted horses races by all the riders hidden on the opposite side but as they pass two warriors swing underneath and rise up the opposite side. After one last charge in front of us, all the tribesmen wheel and dismount and form a long line as does the trappers with William Sublette in the lead and the Chiefs in front of their men. The first chief steps up and grasps the hand of Sublette and raises it as high as his head and holds it in that position while he says a short prayer. The chief goes down the line and pays his respects to each of us and followed by the rest in order or rank. This takes over two hours, but all of us have met and clasped our hands to each other. Pipes are produced on both sides and circles are formed on the earth with Sublette, Fitzpatrick and the leaders of the trading and trapping brigades sitting with many chiefs of the tribes. After the talking and smoking all are in good and high spirits and the games are organized.

I move to an area where a circle has been made in the earth. Two trappers are grappling to throw one another down or out the circle and the men and tribesmen are all yelling and betting. Horse races are being arranged and the hoop and pole game is being played by young warriors and women are playing a type of dice game and every game involves betting with the tribesmen and women being most insistent on betting. Even the men shooting at sticks on the ground bet on each shot.

Eagle Hand comes up and motions me to follow him. We come to an area where the ground has been trampled to dirt by the horses and branched smooth. It is about ninely feet long and nine feet wide. A man is trundling a wooden ring about ten inches in diameter along and letting is roll free while two men run along each holding a piece of wood three foot long and four inches in diameter. They throw after this hoop and throw before the hoop stops. The man whose stick comes closest to the ring after it falls wins the game. People are lined up on both sides laying out beads robes and even guns and powder in their bets.

Eagle Hand placed and then won his bet without a word to me and then he spoke. "This is a game the tribes on the Missouri play, he said. I see you have been trading that is a fine shirt."

"Thank you I have new moccasins leggings and elkskin shirt being made."

"Who is making it for you?"

"The crow woman I cannot say her name. She is married to the Nez Perce"

"I know her. She makes the finest but you must understand that clothes speak before the man and we will be going though lands where the enemies of the Crow live. She must make your clothes speak Mandan and you must have this on it. He pulls out the scalp of the Cheyenne."

"I felt confused and he responded to my face."

"It is the Cheyenne you killed at the Skidi village. You did not think the scalp important but if you walk into your village with the crow skins on would not your people laugh or shun you?"

"Yes they would."

"If you were a blue-seizer would you not wear the yellow strips you earned on your arm?"

"Yes I would."

"With pride and honor?"

"I would."

"This hair is your yellow stripes, I will have it put on your shirt and you can wear it with pride for you for you are young for wearing such a honor. Only time will tell if you are a great warrior and if the spirits honor you for a man needs both for success in life. I will go and with your word I will put this hair on your shirt and have her paint of your deed."

"Yes you have my word thank you."

I watched him stride off his strong lean legs flexing. My heart is filled with joy and shame: joy at how grand my shirt will be and shame that I do not deserve it for I do not feel brave only lucky and shame I'm wearing it when other braver men do not have such a shirt, but joy that the shirt will make me feel more the man of the Far West for I so want to be part of all this but I feel small and ignorant to all these wise and tough men.

As the day wears on more and more men and tribesmen go the tent with the whiskey barrel the hollow wood as the tribesmen call it and the small camp kettles are nearly all being used and passed around. Now there is dancing round the fires, which are ringed with willow appolas sizzling with buffalo meat or holding ribs upright.

The men line up at the whiskey tent:

"I'll be having twenty dollars worth of John Barleycorn for my mess, heres my beaver.

"One beaver full of arwerdenty for I have a powerful thirt from being chased the year long by the Blackfoot."

"I believe that panther piss is just the medicine for what ails me."

They are passing round the horn and getting on the horn while the camp kettle goes round. The bragging and stories start rolling out. I move closer to group of trappers none of whom I know. I want to listen to see what I can learn but I am spotted.

Why don't ya punch up that fire pup?" A balding, brown haired man with close set eyes is looking at me. It takes me a few seconds to understand he means me and what he wants. "Dere some fat wood behind this here tent," he says at my silence. I walk behind the tent to a pile of branches and bring them about.

"You look too young to have your skelp locked on tight this yer first ronnyvoo."

"Yes sir."

"Sir! Why that just sours my milk. Tain't never been no sir. Last man that called me that I fotched on the side of the head. Whar's yer diggings pup?"

"Born in Ireland, Si—came out with Mr. Sublette."

"Trader or trapper?"

"Trader."

"Yer not a fils de bast are ya?"

"All the men laugh."

"Ya got any baccy, pup?"

"No, don't like the taste."

"If yer durst to stay out in these mountains little chile you find a good chaw will make you feel right pert."

"How 'bout eau de vie?"

"Poteen? Er whiskey? No I prefer porter."

"No porter out here. Looks like you been buying some fooforaw you a tender for Sublette?"

"No I worked in New York at a hotel."

"A greenhorn? Yer gonna haf to put some bark on ya is yer wants to avoid catching a galena pill and losing that curly hair to hungry Injuns. Are you on yer own hook?"

"No I'm traveling with Eagle Hand and another fellow that ain't showed yet he's a preacher."

"A sky pilot. Don't need no puritan palavering all over us niggurs and chasing our robe warmers away. Gimmie some more of that baldface, coon. I swar by hook, I'll not have sky pilots at the ronnyvoos. That fellar shows up here you better tell him to keep his trap shut."

"I ain't ever met a sky pilot who could keep his beanhole shut seems they natural born to naybobbin likes yous born to squeeze that kettle tween yer fingers. Past the panther piss."

"I don't shine to any sky pilot they's for robbin a man of his spirit and that the real job they do no matter what words they throw about they make me feel real squampshus like. Somethin ain't right about men makin' a living with words that don't even make a man laugh leastways some of the politicians make a joke or two and I don't shine to them either. They why I knowed that der preacher book they tote is fraud don't have a single laugh in it and that ain't human and ain't no God who made humans made that book cause he made humans with laughter. I toted it up and I ain't ever living in no world without laughter and I take the trappers oath on that for I see too much dying and the onliest medicine for too much dying is laughter that and some John Barleycorn now git that kettle or'r here!"

"I hold fast to what old Duff says and toss in that if'n those preachers wus truly in the hand of the Lord they wouldn't be alwus be flipping and levying and takin' our labor fer their livin' Seems that if'n a man's got the ear of God and doin his work God ought to been at least feedin ya. It's first rate disgusting how they never fail to hold their hat out."

I slink off as they get to arguing the demerits of sky pilots. Maybe it is good Jack didn't show, but I bet the rascal has found some tribe to preach to and that's why he's not here.

I pass a couple of men snoring face down on the ground. The sky is turning purple and the drums, laughter, high-pitched yells and gunfire all mingle in a racacous sound from all over the valley. I come upon a cirlcle of Nez Percé women dancing surrounded by a big crowd of trappers. There brown calves are flexing and flashing with each light step they make to the drum and their united soprano voices drown out all other rendezvous sounds. Some wear dresses tied with hundreds of bells and shells and the chinging and ringing is music added to the drums and voices with each step. They are not all uniform in their steps each dancer keeps the rhythm but retains an individual style such as little cross steps or back steps I like that for it reminds me of my people who seem incapable of doing any activity as a uniform group which the British seem to excel at. The Irish love social gathering but can't seen to agree on anything. I get the feeling these people accept their individuality whereas we seem to keep striving to act in concert as a group and generally fail. Ah if only we had these people as neighbors maybe we would have our own country or a least a land ruled by several clans.

The dance goes on for some time and then the trappers begin hallowing and holding up beads, colored cloth, knives and even rifles. The women move over to their husbands and while looking at the gathered trappers the husbands talk to their wives and point at the trapper and one by one the women move over to the trappers and are earnestly trading. The husbands hang back until the trades are completed and then move up to take the goods from the wives and the trappers and wives begin moving off among the tents and beyond the fire.

I move on it is not yet full dark, the evening star is out but the big dipper is not yet visible. The distant sounds of yelling, gunfire and laughter contrast with the moans, the huffing and panting sound in the longer grass between the tents. I see the shine of trapper showing buttocks that have been too long covered with buckskins moving to all different rhythms. I smile to myself at such a sight for they now look quite funny and not at all brave. I hear the giggle of women and some naked women run across my path chattering and laughing and bouncing while being chased by a trapper with glowing white parts. All around it seems are short quick desperate movements of heads of white skin of shiny brown skin or soothing slow movements brown hands moving languidly over white skin or white hands moving over and filling with damp glowing brown skin some are coupling like horses with full breasts swaying as the day turns to night. I find it more amusing than arousing.

I walk out beyond the tents. I smell horses and head into the smell. Whininying pawing snuffling and sniffing sounds come out of the darkness four-footed forms stand watching me as I make my way deeper into the herd. The hollow clomping of hooves sounds as the skittish move off in the darkness. I heard a familiar snuffling noise behind me and turn as the wet nose does the tapping nudge at my shoulder and the Creature turns his head to get his ears rubbed on my shoulder and a contented expulsion of air flubs his lips as I rub his ears and he leans into to me. It gives me such pleasure to scatch him.

Today I have my new clothes from the Crow woman. Truly she has the finest hand of any person alive. Eagle Hand has directed her well for I have a green horse on it and locks of hair run down one side and the fringes are so very fine. Tis the softest thing I have every worn. It is a bit warm in the daytime sun but I am so proud of it that I ignore the discomfort. I note that many women flick their eyes towards me and I feel a new swelling in my breast and find myself eagerly watching their eyes as I pass. Tis a vanity, but I can no more resist it that some of the men can resist whiskey. I spent most of the afternoon walking around and pretend interest in many trade goods but my swollen chest compels me to buy the green googles and I put them on to try to them out and it makes the world seem a different place. I have them around my neck as I stop to admire some bows.

"She fancies you, you know."

Mr. Smith from the Wyeth party is nudging my side as we look at a bow made from the horns of a bighorn. The grandfather who made it sits smoking a pipe and the two girls around my age giggle and peek from inside the teepee and then come out and offer to trade for the old man. They know a few words of English.

Great power. Though buffalo. Never miss She smiles saying this with long fingers.

Her hair glistens in the sunlight her eyes sparkle with mischief she has long batting lashes and delicate expressive fingers that go thought the motion of shooting the bow. She moves so lightly in her bare feet as she picks up the bow holding it up for us to admire. The bow is beautiful as it is covered with a rattlesnake skin on the belly and polished on the other side. There are other bows made of the ribs of buffalo. All are fastened in the middle with an interlocking cut and glued and wrapped in sinew.

"Grandfather says Great Spirit power. Says only for warrior."

She looks at the scalp locks on my shirt her mouth curls into a proud smile her head come forward and her eyes rise to mine as she makes a languid blink with her big lashes. I impulsively lift my beads I have over my neck and step to her and put over her neck. The old man grunts, she beams her sister giggles. I feel embarrassed and feel sudden fear that I have offended. I look at Smith with a question in my eyes.

Gifts are always all right kid. Grampa here has been eyeing yer pistols, but I sure wouldn't go the whole hog and give em both for the bow... its right down good bow and I expect a powerful one but I tote yer gots the moon for fer the Mountain Lamb.

"That is her name?"

"Yes lass"

"Mountain Lamb" I say aloud with wonder in my voice.

She looks at me her head tilted in a puzzle. I feel embarrassed. I extend my hand and point to my chest and say Git. She smiles and takes my hand and it is warm liquid power that flows out of slim strong hand. My hand lingers and she quickly withdraws it and her eyes shoot over to her grandfather.

Smith lays a carot of tobacco on the man's blanket. The old man nods. I take out two awls and a needle set I have in my possible bag and hold it up for her to see and then press them into her hand just so I feel her soft skin again.

"Well now I expect her fast on tradin' yer gonna have to trade fer the bow as you got no horse and that's what it will take for the girl and ya traded for her I expect yer're too young to go with the ranchera. The bow's gonna be a whole lot less trouble if I was to make a projector. Is it the bow boy?"

"Yes sir…it's a fine bow and I have two pistols and I need to learn the bow."

"Some men swear by their rifle but if yer set on a bow then we better get arrows and case too. Smith touched them and pointed to my pistol."

"Lay ere down on the blanket boy. Put some powder down and a bag of balls"

The old man smiles and reaches for his pipe. We all sit and the Mountain Lamb answers the voice of her grandmother from within the teepee. I watch her bend to enter and she looks over her shoulder and smiles at me, and hurrys inside to the scolding voice of her grandmother. I keep glancing up at the entrance while the ritual of the pipe is performed.

I feel eager to show Eagle Hand my new bow, but I do not want to leave without seeing Mountain Lamb again. I keep looking back as we walk away but her pretty face does not show.

Eagle Hand approaches me. He has excitement on his face.

"You traded for a bow. It is beautiful. Come I will trade for a horse with a Nez Percé. These horses are hard to find on the Missouri. I will show you horses that can outlast all others. He stops and holds up his hand. They aren't as fast as a horse like Fitz's but if you stay a good distance away from your enemies they will never catch you not even big American horse for these horses can swallow all the wind the prairie can make. "

We come to herd of horses and a man is standing staring at the horses. Without looking at us he steps along with us and we walk among the grazing horses.

"That one!"

Eagle Hand nods at a gray horse with brownish red spots all over its body. I saw some of these horses in the parade. I remember one with red robe cut and decorated with beads and wearing a face hood. The horse had feathers coming up betwixt its ears a beaded chest shawl and its tail was tied in red string and feathered. This one looks like that horse. The horse looks at us and as we approach and can nearly touch it, it canters off and stops to look at us. The man holds up his hands to us, and walks over talking and holding out his hand. The horse watches him with her head turned back along her body raising it and stomping her back feet when the man touches her. He slips a rawhide rope round her neck and leads her back to us.

She is a mare but she is bigger in body and head than a nearby stallion of the same color. She is fifteen hands high her ears are nearly as large as my mule and her nostrils are set wide on her face and she has a sparse mane and tail. Her chest is broad with sturdy wide-set front legs.

I have never seen such a horse up close. Her ears are very attentive and expressive turning independently to different sounds and then very upright and focused when she is spoken to. Her wide set eyes are very serene and intelligent looking. Some of the other horses nearby are the same gray with the light-gray almost white spots. There is something very pleasing about this animal. Eagle Hand has a blanket over his shoulder. He hands his blanket, his knife and a bag of balls and powder over to the man and then wraps his rawhide loop into the mouth of the horse over it's lower jaw, leaps onto the horse in one smooth motion fitting very nicely as the barrel of the horse is deep with high withers and that makes for a nice seat. He smiles at us, wriggles down and turns the horse around two times and then trots off, the movement of the horse is the smoothest I have ever seen. I am full of envy but nearly out of trade goods and I feel I cannot usurp the Creature and my feeling for the Creature soon quells my envy.

CHAPTER XIV

THE BATTLE OF PIERRE'S HOLE

IT BEEN NINE DAYS OF doin's as the men say and the public whisky is sold and most of the goods gone and what wasn't Mr. Campbell sold to the American Fur Company men as their supply train did not show. All are restless to catch up and move out and most of in debt and need those beaver plews to dig themselves out the cache of debt from whiskey, women and fooforaws.

Eagle hand trades for another mule and it is not fit to ride but seems an excellent packer. He gives me the Creature since we seem made for each other. We are now mounted with a pack mule. We have been talking to Fitzpatrick as he is planning to trip in a northerly direction and we thought it better to travel with the protection of a larger, more experienced group in Blackfoot country. The other Rocky Mountain brigades are to try a new country to the southwest and avoid the American Fur Company trappers at the same time. We know that if we can get north to the Missouri River and as far East as Ft. Union where the Yellowstone empties into the Missiouri we have a good chance to find another party to travel down the Missiouri or even get a keelboat to the Mandan village next to Fort Clark.

It is July 16th and Milton Sublette and Frapp the Dutchman are eager to explore the county to the southwest and never having trapped it before and have set the morrow for their leave taking of this rendezvous. The free trappers lead by Mr. Sinclair will accompany him out of this range of mountains along with the downeasters that is what is left of Nathaniel Wyeth's group which is only eleven men and they are headed for the Pacific. Some of the Nez Percé will take the same trail until they reach the other side of the mountains.

I find out that Sublette and Frapp will only be going about eight or ten miles down the valley the first day so that the mules and horses can again get used to packs and men. I want to see the Mountain Lamb again and find that she is going back to her village so I ask Milton Sublette if I can ride out the first day with them as I want to get my mule ready for the trail again. But when I tell Eagle Hand he thinks it is not safe as there has been a lot of Blackfoot sign reported by the scouts. He says he will come with me and try out his new horse. Fitzpatrick will not be setting out for several more days.

We ride out many hours after sunrise, as it seems everyone is having difficulty with their animals, some running bucking the packs others running with a packs under their bellies while the animals try to kick it off. There is much cursing and laughter. I watch amused and try to help as I don't have any responsibilies.

Once under way I see that the Mountain Lamb is riding near Milton Sublette near the lead. I ride up beside them and and she gives me one glance over her shoulder and pays me no attention. It must have been obvious to Andrew Sublette Milton's younger brother moved up beside me and began to speak.

"She's right mighty handsome. Umentucken Tukutsey Undewatsey."

I looked at him and he is looking ahead. "She certainly is that I reply. Do you know her and is that her Shoshone name?"

"Yes I expect I'll know her better this winter."

"Puzzled I ask are you staying at the Snake village?"

"Maybe a visit but the last visit my brother had with the Snakes he nearly lost his hair."

"I though the Snake were friendly."

"They are if yer a big enough force. Milton got hisself stabbed over a woman by a chief this winter. That was another tribe and had to be left behind to recover Joe, Do ya know Joe Meek other there?"

"I've met him."

"Well now Joe stayed with Milton their fast friends until Milton recovered and that took forty day and when they were makin' their way to find the rest of the brigade they come on a band of Snake on the Green River and the warriors set to screaming and so Joe and Milton raced straight on to the village and leapt off their horses straight into the medicine lodge. No killing can go on in a Snake Medicine lodge. Vexed those warriors they did. Those scalp sniffers came in long the teepee wall watching Milton and Joe sitting their silent like they was lost in thought. The Snakes were talkling behind their hands and they was passing the pipe and talking about what to do with my brother and Joe. What the Injuns didn't know was they both speak Snake."

"Why didn't they speak to them?"

"Most of the men wanted to kill them. So they just sat there looking unafraid which is the best way to deal with any Snake. But there was this old chief called Gotia who talked about letting them go. But to no avail for as the sunset a decision was made and it was death to them both, set for sunrise. Decision made they filed out to eat and get ready for the next big day. Old Gotia was the last out and he made a sign to them to be quiet and he would return. They sat there silent for hours in the dark not wanting to arouse the guards outside the teepee. Next thing they hear is horses whinnying and shouts and everyone running to the horse herd south of the village. Old Gotia appears in the flap and motions them out. He leads them acoss the creek to the willows where the horses are being held: it is Mountain Lamb that hands Milton his reins. Milton said when he touched her hand holdin' that rein he know he had to touch it again someday."

"How long ago did this happen?"

"This summer jest before the rendezvous. She must of felt the same way for she got old Gotia to bring her here to the rendezvous. Thay's married now. I better check the rear…someones always havin' trouble the first day out."

I slumped my saddle. The Creature ears turned back and then flattened and his head went down neck out. Married! I looked back. Eagle Hand is talking to Mr. Godin and does not notice me. I want to leave for I feel the fool. She is maybe two or three years older than me and Milton must be twice our age. I stare at the back of Milton's head to trying to figure out what it is he has. He has the eye for the ladies as they say and I thought that would be obvious to the Mountain Lamb. And he owns several horses and I can see he has been generous in bestowing beads on her and she a new bright red blanket round her shoulders in the cool morning air. He likely gave her the fine horse she if riding and the knife at her waist as well. I will be doing work for some years before I have enough to give all that away.

"Bird Woman was snake too Eagle Hand says as he follows my eyes to the Mountain Lamb."

"I didn't even hear him ride up and was not in a talking mood."

"Who was this Bird Woman I ask with some disgust in my voice."

"You know her as Sakakawea that is her Hidatsa name."

"Oh…with Lewis and Clark."

"She was a captive a slave purchased by the Forest Bear or Charbonneau along with Otter woman for his wives the Hidatsa's captured her when she was ten years old. She had a gentle nature like the Mountain Lamb.

"She's dead?"

"Yes she was given to much sickness for I think her body needed the clear mountain air of her people the Missouri air was too heavy for her gentle nature. She moved away from her village the year before her death. Charbonneau bought some land in Missouri and took Bird Woman and her two children with them. He did not last, but half a year and sold the land to Big Red to Clark and the Forest Bear his wife and infant daughter moved back her to the Hidatsa village leaving the boy with Clark who put the boy in a Catholic school. She came back to our village wearing the fine clothes of a White Women and was much envied by the other women in our village. The end of the next year she died after being sick for some time.

She had no family at the village to care for the girl and Charbonneau was not a patient man who could care for children. The trader Luttig took the infant girl to St. Loius and Big Red took her. Toussaint the boy is now here in the moutains as a free trapper.

"Was she handsome like the Mountain Lamb?"

"Yes but most Shoshone women are handsome and they do not have the fast tongues that the Hidatsa women have."

"Was she the only women who went with Lewis and Clark?

"There were other women who traveled with them, but none as far as Bird Woman. She did not want to go, the Forest Bear was hired as speaker for Lewis and Clark and he would not go without her for he was not a man who can bear setting up a teepee and traveling long without the comfort and care of a woman. Forest Bear spoke enough Snake tongue that he did not need her for her words, but he had to tell the Captains so that they would allow her along. It does not take words to buy a horse from a Shoshone who has likely just stolen is from the Nez Percé does it?" He smiles

"No. One holds up a blanket and knife and points."

"Telling them not to steal horses that would take many tongues. He laughs with a hand over his mouth."

This is a sliver of a moon, but it shows the white of the Grand Tetons behind us and the black of the forested slopes around us. I feel confused about the Mountain Lamb. I want to talk to her more to be her friend for I feel some special bond with her that I can't name, but now tis all dashed for this marriage business takes her away and I cannot even be her friend. She will ride over those Mountains and I will only have the image of her brown shining eyes looking at me with those slightly downturned eyelids that are pinched at the corners looking at me while laughing she will take the warm powerful touch of her hands and most of all she will take that slightly crooked smile over those full straight teeth away from my eyes. To her I'm just a nice kid she shared some time with to me she is mystery and promise who will ride over the Rockies as the sun rises tomorrow.

The mules and horses do not think one day is enough time for them to become eager for the trail. More kicking and braying, but my Creature is eager to go looking over his shoulder at me with impatience as I put the borrowed saddle on him as if to say let's make some tracks. But the men are more organized and all formed up much earlier than yesterday. Eagle Hand and I walk along the line forming up saying our good-byes. A cry arises form Godin who set out in advance. I look's like there is buffalo coming down the mountain pass with part already on the prairie about two miles distance. Those with looking glasses pull them out to survey.

"Doesn't look to vee buffalo," Mr. Fraeb remarks

"Men and horses it is I expect it is Fontenelle finally getting to the rendezvous," Mr. Sublette remarks as he squints.

"Vell there is no one to rendezvous vith except company men now," Mr. Fraeb said

"Them's not trappers," Milton Sublette stiffens as he says it.

Glassing them with my new glass it is evident that only about a quarter of them are mounted and it seems a bigger goup than what the Fontenelle party would be, this party numbering 150 to 200. After steady glassing I can see they wear feathers, but none of us can indentify what tribe. The distant tribe seems to hesitate at the sight of us and the approach of the two men we sent out to them. They unfurled a white flag and a greatly decorated man likely a chief with blue and scarlet robe rides out to meet them.

"If they are Blackfoot there will be trouble Antoine's father was killed by Blackfoot and they are a treacherous lot the kind to show a white flag and then to murder us all at night." Mr. Sublette says as he glasses the parties moving together.

I watch through my glass. The chief is alone and rides with his lance in one hand and holds up a peace pipe with the other. The two men approach near him I see smoke from the Nez Percé gun and the chief slumps and the report of the weapon reaches me just as Antoine rips the blanket off the chief knocking him to the ground. Smoke erupts all along the line of men waiting for their chief. As the reports reach us we all tense and all talking stops as we wait for Antoine to fall as he is behind the Nez Percé who turned his horse and fled as soon at he shot the man. It is hard to believe that Antoine has not been hit for the line of men is covered in smoke from all the shots and out of it rode a couple dozen men after Antoine arrows fly thought the air and arch past him. He is racing holding up the robe and sceaming. Some of the men giving chase are firing at him, but they are several hundred yards back and firing from a galloping horse which leaving aside the distance is a pure waste of powder and ball but there is still a slight chance like lighting that he will be struck so we watch with tension rifles ready for the two or three minutes is takes for the two men to reach us, but well out of range of our rifles the small band of avengers turn back.

"Blackfoot! Blackfoot! A whole village of Gros Ventré," Antoine sceams amid flying clods, as he races past us trying to stop his horse.

"You two! Back to Pierre's Hole and tell them the vhole Blackfoot village is about to attack us. Form up in a line. Take off those packs and make a fort. Bring the horses back in those villows. Mr. Vyeth take charge of your men behind those packs. The rest of you who have some Injun fighting behind you form up behind me." Henry Fraeb barked out his orders.

As we watch the whole Blackfoot band breaks up and scatters but out of the aspens emerges a mounted band of warriors perhaps fifty who trot out to greet us. They spread out in a long line and we all move behind our saddles and cock our rifles. When more than about a quarter mile distant they check their advance and turn into a stand of aspen cottonwood and willows by a beaver dam on the creek. This puzzles us a little until we look to the north to see the dust of a large party of coming from the rendezvous. A cheer goes up. The Blackfoot are now doing what we have just done: taking off saddles and piling up fallen timber to make themselves a fort in the willows. More of the tribe moves forward into this fort and some retreat into the mountains whence they came. The warriors move forward and fire at us while hiding behind trees. Some of our men fire back at them, but I see no use wasting balls at such a distance for I had fired my rifle back at Lancaster at some split wood at various distances and found that at a quarter mile my ball wouldn't even penetrate soft pine so even if I could hit some one at that distance I would only likely bruise them but is seem both sides love the sound of firing and they keep it up without one person being hit.

Everyone not firing moved quickly behind trees and saddles with not one person in command. William Sublette and Robert Campbell lead the traders and are giving them orders. Rotten Belly is conferring with a circle of warriors and a pipe is being passed. Little Chief and Old Gurgueo of the Salish assemble their warriors and talking and whooping. We have perhaps 400 from those two tribes and other trapping brigades of the Rocky Mountain Company with Jim Bridger and Thomas Fitzpatrick and even the American Fur Company men so we go from being outnumbered to outnumbering them about three to one within half a hour. What a surprise to think you have a superior force only to see a force twice you number ride in before you can launch your attack. Of course we are far better armed than that Blackfoot for I can see that only about half carry rifles and, all of our group are stocked up with ball and powder for the winter hunt.

Glassing them I see the Blackfoot are digging in many of the women is busy digging along the edge of the fortification with others bringing fallen branches and logs and any opening are being closed with lodge skins. Soon they will be quite secure in their trench and only a head shot low to the ground will be able to reach them while they are looking out.

William Sublette is flush in the face he rides up quickly dismounting his six-foot frame moving aggressively towards us.

What have the devil holed up? I hear they act like they want to make peace but when the sun goes down they will have all your scalps, horses and supplies. As he says this he strips off his shirt and walks back and forth in front of us his face flush. Now the enemy is near and I tell you if we do not show a bold front here and now before our winter hunt our prospects in the mountains will be blasted! Shooting from here will do no good and will not show a brave front. Boys here are the Blackfoot who have killed so many of your friends no doubt they been prowling about for days waiting for a chance to attack us waiting to find us unprepared and who even now dare us with a show of force. They may have been the ones to taken some of our horses and shot at you that night on the Green river. We will never be stronger than now so now is the time to stike a blow! Some of us may fall but we die in a good cause for whose life or property will be secure if the, foe be encouraged by refusing their challenge. Here is a dram for all. Take from the barrel boys it will give you extra courage.

All gather round the whiskey barrel with some gulping is out of their kettles. Some of the men keep up a contant fire while others mill about talking and drinking and then go over to fire from behind the packs. This goes on for a hour or more. Mr. Campbell smokes with the Salish and speaks to them in a similar tone telling them the white men are going to attack their enemy and they wish them to be brave and follow. Impatient William Sublette comes rushing back amongst us.

Now is our chance and now is the time. I go now to strike a blow. I will go to the left flank and my brother Milton will lead the attack on the right and my brother Andrew will be with me. Let us strike a blow for our security for our property for our future. Come let us strike a blow for our fallen friends. Now is the time. Let us be done with this troublesome Blackfoot band.

William Sublette mounts his horse while Mr. Campbell speaks in sign and some words to the Salish in much the same tone for his is a great friend of the Salish chief. William's brother Andrew and Mr. Sinclair the leaders of the free trappers along with Mr. Phelps and Mr. Kean also free trappers join William and then Mr. Campbell mounts. William's brother Milton mounts and 13 men including Zenas Leonard, Joe Meek and Smith of the free trappers joins him and most the of the rest of his trapping brigade.

Fitzpatrick stays to direct the Wyeth forces and the Nez Percé The Wyeth man are easy to direct for they have not fired a shot and did not look inclined to commence. They are sent to guard the horses and make a corral for them and the making the corral seems to please them immensely. The

Nez Percé and Salish are much inspired by Willam's speech and display and move towards the fort as the spirit takes them firing and forming and reforming into bands under various warriors some riding out past the fort taunting the Blackfoot or just riding past and shooting others rush into the willows fire and return but all perform their attacks individually Fitzpatrick can do little to direct them only inspire them. Some of the American Fur Campany men who do not want to take directions form Fitzpatrick or any Rocky Mountain man but also do no want to appear cowards fire from behind the packs with a few moving closer from their protected positions to fire on the front of the fort most are hundreds of yards out but the effect of so many guns all firing is tremendous in the noise and smoke it generates and the Blackfoot respond with a cracking of fire out of the woods. I look about to see which force I can move with, Eagle Hand is already ahead with the Salish. William Sublette is waiting as Mr. Campbell mounts to join him. Mr. Campbell spots me as he turns his horse.

"Git mount and come with us we need another horse and rearguard."

Excited and nervous I ride off with twenty men who go whooping and sceaming and I must admit one cannot help but get your fire going at such sounds. We go wide to one side all the while there is tremendous amount of fire going on much to relief of the men for we all feel it will better our chances of getting close. We stop at a thick stand of willows and tie all the horses. William, his brother Andrew, Mr. Campbell and three other men hunch over and move towards where they believe the fort to be. It is tall grass and willows that I follow them though keeping the horses in sight for I want a sense of where we are having lost my sense of where the fort is. When we get to the point where we see smoke rising up from the fort I stop. The men drop to their knees and crawl. I watch them go until they are gone from the tall grass and then I watch until the bushes hide them from me. They seem to be moving quite fast and are easy to detect at that speed, but I guess they aren't trying to sneak up on deer or buffalo and they are experienced fighters.

The firing rose and fell in volleys and balls are striking to my right and some are zizzing over my head. I couldn't be from the fort tis the wrong angle. Tis our side that the fire comes from! I am a couple hundred yards to the side of the fort, but the firing smoke has drifted to surround me on a very gentle breeze. I fret whether I should be in sight of the horses and then fret that I may be mistaken for a Blackfoot hiding in the grass for I can hear some men yelling to my right and I want to be near our forces instead of by myself.

I crawl forward to have a view of the fort for I cannot stand to be sitting there with balls flying over my head and not see and not be able to shoot. I crawl to a stand of aspen and get behind a tree that is forked and is large enough to cover my body. I have a white wool hat, which is not really white to tis rare for any cloth to be white only the rich business men in cities can afford to wear white. This hat is nearly the color of aspen bark so I raise it slowly up on my rod and it draws no fire. Not certain how far the Blackfoot are I had crawled on my belly and could not see nor did not dare look above the thigh high grass and brush I had slithered though. I keep the hat on the stick and push the stick into the soft earth and I slowly peek around the side of the trunk. The firing is still going steady, but none of the balls are coming in my direction just balls zissing over my head and making smacking and cracking sounds as they hit trees and brush. After a bit I feel secure enough to put my hat on and peer through the crotch of the aspen. I pull my glass out of my possible bag and slowly lift it up there being no sunlight penetrating the trees to give me away. I glass until I detect skins hanging betwixt the trees. I slowly glass up and down the base of those trees. I see occasional movement but get no clear view until a face blackened with red streaks across the cheeks and around the eyes appears the whites of his eyes lit up against the red and he looks more demon than man and I nearly jump back thinking he can see me as well as I him I have a hard time keeping him focused but I can see him sight down his barrel and it looks to be pointed at me. His face is gone behind the smoke the report is blasting my ears and above my fear I hear: "I am shot oh God take me to my brother!" I look though the glass again and just catch another face and the rifle being fired and another cry goes up in the long grass. None of our men have fired yet and it seems they are being hit. The voice I heard was very close to the fort it seems our men are nearly upon the logs of the fort, but I cannot see them. The Blackfoot know there are men there now and many rush to fire into the tall grass. Now fire erupts from the tall grass with three rapid shots in a row. I see the smoke and know their position. I am still too far back for effective shooting so only in my glass am I able to see the Blackfoot so well. When sighting my rifle I can only see movement not the face I saw in my glass. I bring my rifle up to fire even though I know I am unlikely to hit anything, but I hope to confuse the Blackfoot. I see the red face and fire at it and he disappears behind the skin.

Watching for movement I'm ready to fire when I hear voices behind me. I determine tis not English voices, but whether twas Blackfoot or Salish I cannot tell. I know that Sublette expected others to follow them in the attack, but it seems few were inclined to do so.

Another shot and a large *tha-wop* echoes from the grass. No cry this time but one of our men is surely hit. This is followed by another *tha-wop*, and some cursing and two rifles respond out of the grass.

Movement in the grass catches my attention and I level my rifle. A back of a man appears with a rifle slung over it he is hunched over and moving towards me. He is dragging a man, a limp man with blood all over his chest. It is Andrew Sublette. I rush forward to help. I see that it is Sinclair who is bloodied and his eyes are wide open and I think it a strange look as I grab his arm to help pull him. He is absolutely limp I have never felt a man so limp his body moves as if it is liquid over the ground.

Phelps is wounded in the thigh and is crawling back this way. "Sinclair here wanted to be taken to his brother," Andrew says as he drops Sinclair's arm.

I hold the other arm. I look down at Sinclair. His upper chest is bloody and I am surprised I don't hear a sucking noise for it looks like his lung has been penetrated. I look at his eyes and they are still staring. With fear I move my hand to his eyes and when I nearly touch them and they do not blink. His chest does not rise. I drop his arm. His arm makes a wet thud on the earth.

"I'm going back to help Phelps. If you find his brother tell him."

I feel a sudden need to find his brother and stand just as a ball smacks a aspen about four feet away. I find myself flat on the earth. When no more hit I move my head around and my eyes rest on Sinclair's moccasins. One is untied. They are new moccasins they are even beaded so he must have been proud of them. I don't know how long I hugged the earth staring at Sinclair's moccasin but Andrew comes back with Phelps who has a ball wound in the left thigh and I now have a man alive to look at. Tis an ugly looking wound that passes though the front of the thigh and out the outside. There is too much flesh on his thigh to be able to press down to feel if the thighbone is broken, but if not broken surely it is bruised for the ball went though his flesh and looked to pass very close to the bone.

Andrew is huffing and seems loth to return as the firing is fierce and the air is full of balls and it is a dangerous place to turns ones back as he describes it. It seems the firing where Mr. Campbell and William Sublette were has stopped. I crawl down the path of beaten grass to see if I can get a look and am met by the backside of Mr. Campbell. He is dragging William Sublette who has his right arm around Mr Campbell's neck and his left is all bloody is across his stomach Mr. Campbell drags him backwards. I want to assist but I can see there is little I can do as Mr. Sublette's left shoulder is injured with what looks like a ball hole that comes out his upper back.

Andrew looks alarmed.

"Are you going to make it Bill? He asks anxiously as he looks at the wound."

"Damm right! I'm just too weak to keep fighting. They got Kean a ball in the forehead dropped at my side he did and without a sound," William said with a deep sigh.

Smith comes crawling up he has a wound in the side of his foot. All of our party is now out of the fight with two dead and three wounded with Mr. Campbell and Andrew Sublette being the only two to escape untouched.

Several of the Nez Percé men lead by Rotten Belly come up and examine the men and ask where they have been and then they move forward towards the fort each making their own path. The firing is still intense from our men in front of the fort but much slower from the Blackfoot side. Two of the Nez Percé men retrieve Kean's body. He has a neat hole in his forehead with little blood aound the edge and otherwise he looks healthy but his staring and bulging bloodshot eyes are difficult to look at.

I pick up Mr. Campbell and William Sublette's rifles as Mr. Campbell helps Mr. Sublette to his feet and Andrew takes Phelps on one shoulder and Smith limps back using his rifle as a crutch and the Nez Percé drags Kean. We all move back to the horses with the mood somber. Mr Sublette's wounds are to his left wrist with one bone broken by the ball and the left shoulder where the ball pass out under the shoulder blade. He is very thirsty and empties his water bag upon reaching his horse. We assist him onto his horse and then the other two wounded men. The Nez Percé flops and ties Kean to his horse which present the unsightly spectacle of his shattered skull to our view and it is not bloodied much but his brains leak out with each bounce of his head with each step of his horse and I'm afraid there will be little left by the time we reach the main force. I am leading his horse so I can't help wincing with each step and would of walked the horse except all the men gallop being eager to get back to be doctored and get some whiskey to dull the pain. We leave the Nez Percé men behind to fight on. Why I feel so queersome about Kean I can't eplain for I know the man to be dead, but I feel a strange urge to keep all his parts intact for burial.

Milton Sublette is still down along the creek fighting when we come back. But there are two dead Nez Percé men laid out and the women are tending to them by painting them and gathering blankets and weapons to send them off in the next world.

Most of the Salish and Nez Percé are moving around the entire perimeter of the fort trying to find a way to assault it but the Blackfoot firing keeps them back. The men at our emcampment have ceased to fire and are busy watching the action from behind the packs. Over the hill the New Englander's are still busy building, a corral there being two carpenters among them and a blacksmith they are constructing a very strong corral I believe they think we are to make a siege of it.

Milton Sublette comes riding back along with Joe Meek and Zenas Leonard followed by the rest of the men several have wounds and two more bodies are slung over saddle. Sinclair's brother rides up leading a horse with a wounded man laid up against the horses neck. Sinclair looks at some of the men that rode off with his brother and their eyes turn away and his face shows alarm.

"Whare is he?"

Phelps laying on a blanket knods his head off his right shoulder towards the dead men laid out.

"He asked for you he said bring my brother...I heard him..."I am shot take me to my brother." But he was dead by the time we got him back to the horses. He died quick I'm sorry sir."

Sinclair's brother looks at me hard then he looks at William Sublette being tended by Doctor Wyeth then at the wounded men and finally his eyes to over to the two dead bodies about twenty paces away. His eyes rise and he looks off as he speaks: "I would a thought ida been me: he was braver a better shot and he had more sense...I expect I better look so I can get to believing it believing always takes the most doin in matters of death. Thanks boy."

After Sinclair kneels by his brother, Milton Sublette spoke, his eyes on Sinclair. "Rut took a ball in the head the drunken fool. He rolled a log all the way to the edge of the Blackfoot fort with them blowing chunks of that log all over but not touchin' him. He skat behind a tree and peered up though the crotch of it and they plugged him clean in the forehead. We tried to reach to body for he was only ten foot from the fort and they dragged him in whoopin and sceechin'. Won't be no body left to do any believin' over for poor Rut."

It is now late afternoon and the firing has slowed down to occasional shots. Mountain lamb and the other woman are out gathering sticks and wood for the Blackfoot have stopped firing and most believe they are out of balls and powder. Most of the Salish and Nez Percé have moved within fifty yards of the fort and are kept away only by the arrows flung at them. They are taunting the Blackfoot trying to get them to come out and fight and trying to pick off the men shooting arrows for it is more difficult to fire a bow though cover of the fort without exposing oneself. The women move close to the warriors and begin to pile wood around the fort.

A loud voice began to speak from the fort in a bold comtemptuous tone, but the words are lost on us and it takes a while to make all quit firing at the voice so his words can be understood. One of the Nez Percé with us told us he is saying that there is a village of 400 in the mountains behind us and right now ready to attack our camp. The alarmed voices of the trappers and traders all start asking questions at once.

"Camp? That's our camp in Pierre Hole!"

"No they mean here."

"This ain't no camp all our supplies and horses back at camp with only a couple dozen men!"

"But we're here so they's going to attack us here."

"Don't be a fool there ain't no plunder here. Hoss let's ride I ain't losing my winter outfit."

"Attack at the camp! Back at the camp! Blackfoot attack!"

It was chaos with turning horses men running to the corral and other men looking blank and confused and soon most of the men are making dust across the valley leaving a small guard her with the women and our tribesmen myself included. Even some of the wounded ride back.

The sun is behind the peaks and soon darkness settles. Eagle Hand makes his way back to our camp as do several Salish. They bring back more bodies and look to have ten laid out. We start a fire below the hill out of sight of the Blackfoot fort.

"They're gone! A voice called from the willows."

"Gone? How can that be, didn't you fellars have a watch on em?"

"They're gone every last one."

"Well don't stand there with the gapes ya old coons, let's have us a look."

"Et de dam Pied Noirs!"

We cautiously move through the grass and willows towards the Blackfoot fort, our rifles held ready. Some Nez Percé and Salish run past us with high steps whooping and when they breach the fort the rifles begin to lower and we all run forward.

Entering we can see tis a flimsy affair. There is a trench dug round the perimeter and the walls are mostly skins, blankets cedar and willow branches with saddles on the ground. Looking to the rear of the fort one finds a tragic sight: Dead horses. There must be twenty-five horses shot up. There are still a few towards the back tied up. One of the Salish has a rope on a big white American horse.

"Whoa! Tell that chief that's Fitzpatrick's horse. This is the band he musta run into."

Some of the dead horses are horses taken from us at the nighttime attack on the Green River. Some of the men gather round something on the ground. I thought it a Blackfoot I wanted to see what they look like up close. I rush over. A dead man. He is on his back his eyes, his insides and his sex is gone, large slashes up his thighs and his tendons cut and a dozen arrows pinning him to the earth. It is Rut Certainly he was dead when they dragged him in there but they didn't want him to have a good journey to the other world where he will now crawl blindly without the pleasure of any bodily sensation expect pain. The Blackfoot understand hell to be purely a bodily experience. For them is seems the other world is a good place so they must cripple their enemies who enter it. For Rut will never taste the victuals or virgins of that world.

We found several dead women and some children but no warriors. Our revenge was not to bury them. I wonder what happens to those that are eaten by vultures and wolves. I'm told the Blackfoot always carry off their dead but they missed these. The men seem disappointed in not having more dead Blackfoot and making claims for many more Blackfoot dead that what we had suffered which is for seven trappers seven Nez Percé and fifteen Salish and nearly as many more with wounds is each group. Including the Blackfoot shot off his horse there is six Blackfoot bodies.

The New Englanders are digging a grave in the corral as we don't want our dead dug up and multilated later. The earth of the corral is so trampled that it will be difficult to find the graves. The Salish and Nez Percé are digging their own holes in the corral. Oh the crying sounds the women make are the most mournful sounds I have ever heard They begin on a high pitch and waver downward but it is the passion of their cries that pierces one's soul and the depth of their sorrow seems to have no end as does their tears. Their bodies heave and convulse at the knowledge of this end of their loved ones. I myself cannot get over the demarcation: one moment voice and vitality and the next utter stillness. Tis no wonder all the peoples of the world need stories of heaven and other worlds for it certainly seems impossible that such a force as life could be extinguished utterly and forever in a instant, although that is what my eyes have seen over and over again for all creatures. Tis easier to believe in ghosts and souls as the energy that runs us all for without them the world seems a more lonely and cruel place.

The wolves will feed tonight and already during the light the vultures circled.

I look at Eagle Hand who stands beside me. "It shivers me to think of that," I say.

"It is the way of the world and it is one of the fears we share with the white man."

"Being eaten?"

"Yes all things are eaten in death and we try to cheat the teeth of the wolf and the beak of the vulture we can never cheat the many leggeds and

THE BATTLE OF PIERRE'S HOLE 363

the invisibles so our bodies are taken in little bites all are eventually eaten in this world."

"There is a people across the water the Egyptians who preserved the bodies of their kings by taking out the internal organs and filling the bodies with magic fluids and wrappings and put them in a place of stone so that the bodies do not get eaten."

"Ha! A foolish way to live. What would happen to the earth if all things did not die and return to the earth. It would fill up and the whole earth would die and all would be silent. The white man does not understand that death happens to make life."

"We believe that we will someday return to paradise where there is no death."

"That may be but such a place cannot be of this earth for the spirits and all things live by death and struggle such as we saw on this field today."

"But that did not have to be. With peace all these people would be alive."

"Peace? The Blackfoot are enemies this is their hunting ground the trappers take their animals how can there be peace. If the Blackfoot let the trappers on their hunting land they will not leave until the animals are gone."

"Maybe they could share and everyone could live?"

"If a wolf family allows another wolf family into their territory for peace as you wish when luck turns bad both families starve. No the wisdom of all animals is to keep their hunting lands for without them they are no more all lose when they share for lean years always come."

"Look at our cities we have many different people living in peace could that not happen here?"

"Do you see wolves geese and buffalo living together?"

"No."

"Your cities look like that to me unnatural as you name it. I have seen that there is much stealing and killing in your cities. Your people live by books of paper by enforcers and by jails for they do not know how to live like a village they do not know how to fit into this world. They come from different villages and most are forced to follow leaders they do not repect and rules they do not understand for they talk much of justice and freedom. I believe the white man's heart is so broken that he keeps building things he is like the man you told me of that pushes the round rock to the top of the hill only to have it roll down again and and he must keep doing this. Stand on a hill and look down at New York or any American City and it is like watching ants moving in and out of there village both so busy and both so unknowing of all that surrounds them so intent on building their mound. All around them the world goes on as it has since before my grandfathers walked the earth and it will keep going on and keep ignoring the white man even as the white man keeps piling up the grains of sand that makes up your cities. The white man sits inside his cities and looks with fear to the world outside and he talks of courage but then he stays in the cities in fear of the outside and lives in fear of each other and so reads and talks much courage. Inside the rooms, which they must pay to live in and pay to keep warm, they talk of freedom. They talk of equality but the big law of the land says that only men who own the earth can vote and that men can own other men. To me that is not civilized for man to own the earth or another man. From such a people I know that peace does not mean peace it means they want to build something or they want to trade. Only the very strong can have peace and few remain very strong. Peace may be in this garden of your first man but peace is in my heart because I know that it is not to be found in this world and I know that I will die. It does not matter how many grains of sand are moved death waits for us all. The white man does not fight for honor he fights for trade for land for things and he fights because other men tell him to fight and only white men of the mountains who live with us live with honor, freedom and courage and these white men are not liked in your cities and they do like your cities. I have learned that the white man of the cities talks much of the things he does not have: freedom, courage and honor."

"Eagle Hand I do wish to have courage I wish to be just, I wish to be strong and respect all around me and I fear death."

"Tis a grand vision." Thomas Fitzpatrick has been listening to us. "And one I have lived and the best years of my life have been on this grand prairie and mountains but as that Englishman Thomas Malthus writes the world is getting more and more people and so only trade and agriculture will be able to support so many people and that means that this grand life of hunting and livin' off the land will end someday for it can only support a few people per acre of land. Git you know how Ireland is nearly burstin' at the seams with every square of land taken."

"Yes, but look at the history of Europe its filled with disease and mass wars and and look how this land has little disease and the wars are skirmishes this is paradise next to Europe."

"I've no argument with you there but trade breeds greed and greed will take all that we see and I hope to be gone before that happens."

"Git you are young," Eagle Hand said, "your heart is strong your vision keen and if you see a people who live on and of this earth you might become a man of this earth. The white man tries to live too far above the earth in his building. I will take you to my people so that such a world may stand before you for you have only seen a part of this world. Let us go sing for our brothers who are now fighting in the spirit world."

We went over to the circles of Nez Percé and Salish who are singing and wailing and dancing and drumming around the finely wrapped warriors about to be lowered into the earth.

"Oooohhheeeeeeeeeyaaaaaa!"

It is not the words that are sung is it the pure feeling and words only cover such feeling so we all let our bodies make the sounds.

Into the earth upon which we trod will go these brave men into the earth where she will begin tentative nibbles and become more voracious unitl the skelton that carried these brave men across the earth lies exposed and for a long time defiant at the mouth of mother earth but she will have the bones too and from them will rise another man though the mouth of the buffalo and another man and another man but never again this man.

William Sublette is nursing his wounds as well as several other men including Rotten Belly who took a ball in the shoulder as well. The Salish had battle with another Blackfoot tribe just before rendezvous and came to the rendezvous with about twenty wounded and they have now taken on another twenty some wounded. They claim eight scalps in the previous fight. I must say that the taking of scalps seems more efficient that my ancestors habit of taking heads. My Celtic ancestors made these little round holes around round the entrance to the houses and these they would fill with heads they took in battle. There was no doubt you were entering a warriors house going though such a doorway. As anyone knows in taking heads are messy affairs that take a long time to tolerate what with their stinking ways. Drying and tanning a scalp takes little effort and attracts only attention and not flies and and other undesireable creatures so I must say that is seems a great improvement and certainly more truthful in ranking a warrior than the stripes given to American soldiers.

Milton Sublette waits a few days with us for the attack by the larger village of Blackfoot, but there was no sign of them in Pierre's Hole so he again turned to the southwest taking the Mountain Lamb with him. She gave me a brief smile and flick of her eyes as she rode out of Pierre's Hole.

Part of Mr. Wyeth's team decide that they had enough of the mountains and wants to return to civilization as they call it and along with Mr. Stephens and Mr. Foy of the Gant and Blackwell firm and the two grandsons of Daniel Boone they set out not wanting to wait for William Sublette's larger party. The seven men set off three days ago though Hobart Canyon. The Blackfoot were waiting. Down the slope they attacked with a terrible din and Mr. More from Boston was thrown from his horse fortunately he was not hurt and rose to his feet and there he stood with sceaming

Blackfoot bearing down on him. He did not move a muscle as a warrior rode up to him and split his head open crumpling him to the valley floor. Foy dismounted and seeing Mr. More's predicament he rushed to him too late and thus is was too late for Mr. Foy to retreat and down he went with a crushed skull. Mr. Stephens fired and held them off and took several wounds the rest escaped keeping the Blackfoot at bay with a steady fire as the Blackfoot claimed scalps and goods. Mr. Stephens died today and the rest are now content to wait for William Sublette to heal so that they can return with him to St. Louis.

CHAPTER XV
DOWN THE MIGHTY MISSOURI

Git O'Toole Journal

August 17, 1832, Friday

Last night whilst looking at the very last of the day, disappear into the blackness of the west I saw a piece of a star burn across the sky. Twas very low and set against the last faded blue and purple of the sky and so it seemed to me to be nearly within reach and I expected it to hit not a mile away but I do believe it burnt itself up for it did not burn but a brief moment before my eyes and I would have seen it if my eyes had not been fixed as they were in the sky. I don't know that another soul saw it and twas a splendid sight from afar but had it lit upon the ground it would be a horrible, wreckage.

Tis my birthday. Thirteen years and surely one of the luckiest lads alive for I am in the heart of the Far West of this splendid land a land new to me and home to many men, men who have no idea of the ocean I have crossed of the green island from whence I came and of gloom that hangs over my dear homeland. I come from a lovely but hopeless place and feel badly at times I did not stay and fight against the hopelessness fight to drive the invaders from our lands but tis a mired state and my Da and uncle Bres have put their hopes in my breast and the breast of my dear brother Deny where ever he may be and so here I stand in the Far West a land far far from the tribes of Ireland far from the yoke of England or any hand of power for no ones owns this land even though America claims it and tis the most glorious freedom any man can stand under even though though there is danger but there was danger in the city and rules upon rules. I may not be a trapper but I am a mountain man for I have made the journey and I have lived the rendezvous and met the men who are trappers. My journey is yet long and dangerous but Eagle Hand has accepted me into his village and I will go and live the life of a Mandan and learn how to use their bow and hunt buffalo and be a warrior. Up to the Missouri to Fort Union where we may find Jack. Then follow the Missouri until we are out of Blackfoot country and into Crow country and then when we leave Crow country we will be closer to friendly country.

The Sioux may be roaming the friendly country so we will have to watch our step every- where we go. We will be traveling though the Blackfoot mountains the whole way to Fort Union. So I will see further mountainous country and learn more about the Far West.

I feel so free so surrounded by all these brave men of the Rocky Mountain Fur Company. And I have more confidence in my rifle skills than I thought I would at this point. I love this country and this life it is the life for me even with the danger there is anyways danger in life. But the freedom I didn't think was even possible. The Pawnee village experience showed me what village life can be like and how free it is. Eagle Hand is right once my duties are done I can learn with my new bow and look forward to calf hunting and then buffalo hunting.

AS WE LEAVE PIERRE'S HOLE some miles to the west I stop the Creature and look back on the green valley in the early morning mist and I look hard for the short stubs of Pierre feet parting the lush grasses and mist as the feet of the Iroquois chief walks up and down the valley looking ever looking. Oh poor Pierre there is a song that follows the feet of poor Pierre…of course it's a rollicking roguish stomping song with the banging of the skins and sceaming of the fiddle:

Oh poor Pierre
He's only a quarter there
Oh poor Pierre

He is two feet below
The three breasts
For the Blackfeet
Have taken the rest

Oh poor Pierre
He's only a quarter there
Oh poor Pierre

He cannot kneel to pray
For there is not way
For the Blackfeet have
Taken his body away.

Oh poor Pierre
He's only a quarter there
Oh poor Pierre

He can only run and run
And cannot ask the way
For the Blackfeet have taken his mouth away.

Oh poor Pierre
He's only a quarter there
Oh poor Pierre

He walks runs and jumps
Up and down
But nowhere is his body to be found

Oh poor Pierre
He's only a quarter there
Oh poor Pierre

So if you see two feet
Running in the hole
Below three breasts
Then you know

It's poor Pierre
He is the Iroquois chief
Who has his own two feet

Oh poor Pierre
He's only a quarter there
Oh poor Pierre

We leave the dance and dash of a trade fair unlike any that I have seen in the Irish countryside not for the wildness of it all, but for the strange mixture of cultures from men college educated to unlettered men men from sophisticated cities to wild areas of places like Kentucky to villages west of these mountains to proper New England man with collars buttoned and men with nothing but a scrap of skin and women, women who work like men and take their pleasure like men and do everything but fight like men but I wouldn't want to test that with them and most of them as handsome and natural as can be.

We ride west below the crags of the hootsholes as the Salish call them and out of Pierre's Hole. The valley widens as the Tetons fade. We can see mountain ranges ahead to the west and there is always a range to our right. Across a tributary of the Snake and onwards towards the Salmon we go in the heat of late summer but it is only flies that bother us in these mountain valleys. We reach Camas creek on the second day.

"I wonder where the bones or Dan Richards and Henry Duhern are?"

Christian Shotts stood near me. He is one of the men Fitzpatrick agreed to hire from William Sublette pack train one of five men our of that group who decided they wanted to try trapping in the mountains. We stood watering our animals.

"Met Richards in St. Louis two years back when he was signing on to the Company. Now he's gone and I'm standing on the selfsame creek whar he was scalped. But I always wanted to try my hand at this trappin' maybe some day if I keep my hair I can be an independent trapper like those fellows at the rendezvous."

"What did you sign for?"

"Eighteen months at sixteen a month cause I ain't got trappin' brigade experience.

You sign on?"

"No I'm a mess cook for my keep and some trade goods until we reach the Missouri then I headed down the Missouri to the Mandan village."

"By yerself?"

"No with Eagle Hand."

"Way I hear it ya can expect Blackfoot and when you get past their lands you dab in the middle of Crow country. Me I'm staying with a big a trappin' party as I can."

"I don't think it's any more dangerous that you an your buddy out there during the day setting your eight traps on a stream."

"I expect I'll be might nervous at that, hope I can hit the caster with my stick. Ha! Expect we better pasture these animals."

"I'll stay here a bit my mule is fond of standing up to his belly in the water never wants to go any deeper but on a warm day he sure loves to cool his belly and if he can find the shade of a tree I imagine he'll stand there all day until he gets hungry of course."

Today we turn northwest and follow the Lemhi River valley at a good pace in order to reach our trapping grounds and the talk is that we want to create as much distance from the American Fur Company brigade headed by Vandenburgh and Dripps as possilble for tis feared that their strategy is to follow us to learn where the trapping streams are. That is why Milton Sublette headed far to the southwest as well. Our last word was that the American Fur Company supplies had arrived in the valley to the east of Pierre's Hole where Bonneville was building a fort that is near the Green River valley.

The land of the Lemhi River which lies along a northwest/southeast axis is a most barren land with tufts of dried grass and sage everywhere and other aromatic bushes that gives off the most incredible smell after a rain which it seems is always brief and capricious as to whether the cloud will let its water go whilst passing over you and then only enough to wet the leaves and dampen the earth. The hills and beyond to the far mountains on both sides gives a most grand spectacle whilst camped along this clear stream with trout visible and mule deer coming to peer down from the hills in the cool evening as well as great carnivorous and carrioneous birds who soar from the cliffs about us.

We move quickly for there are few beaver although the men are eager and ride off sometimes to the distant mountains to trap a creek which they check in the early morning and sometimes we are leaving with trapping parties still out but our trail is big and cannot be missed. We arrive at the Salmon a large fast river one of the big mountain rivers that one is best careful crossing for the rocks are loose many times slippery and the current will sweep you in a flash if your feet are upset. The Creature detests such streams stepping in and looking back at me as if to say *do I have to?* He will go back and forth and knows we must cross but cannot bring himself to do so until nearly all the other are across and I myself start across with a long rope attached to him. Most times he will then come with ears back and darting eyes.

Reaching the Salmon we are on the edge of Nez Percé land the land of many horses but this is as far west as we will go for now we turn back to the direction Eagle Hand wishes to go. Fitzpatrick caches their goods taking only what they need for the fall hunt as they call it. He will stop to retrieve the goods after the hunt. We are to start trapping the Big Hole River valley which means all the little mountain streams that run into the river the trappers will follow up in search of beaver and tis us they will go for the mountains are steep and sometimes the beaver builds their dams quite high where the aspen is plentiful. It is August and at these heights the nights are quite cool and above us the leaves are turning golden but the quaking aspen still rattle with leaves all about us. Tis a soothing rattle that these heart-shaped leaves make and the valley is much changed when the evening mist creeps about the low greenery and the air is still and the Aspen quake no more and only the gurgle of water close and the roar of the distant struggle of water with rocks marks the night that is if the whip-poor-will does not call when the sun falls and the paint does not roar in distant crags nor the little wolves howl when they rise from their dens yes sometimes the nights can be busy and noisy place but sometimes there is utter stillness not even a bird for there are few here compared to the prairie.

We move towards Blackfoot land and will pierce the heart of their mostly untrapped lands untrapped by white men that is. Towards the three forks of the Missouri we move with many valleys in between. Tis the richest of all land out here in beaver country because it is lands most vigorously defended. Fitzpatrick's Rocky Mountain brigade is risking it because the Rocky Mountains are covered in competition this year with the American Fur Company putting one hundred ten men into the field and Bonneville seems to have nearly that many again and there are serveral smaller new independent parties like Nathaniel Wyeth trying to establish themselves.

The lands of the Blackfoot have rarely been trapped for they mostly trade with the Hudson Bay Company and do not let the American trappers onto their hunting grounds. One might say that these men are risking their lives for fortune but the talk I hear has been about competition certainly from an Irish perspective there is no greater spur to get a man moving that the threat of loss not of his life but of his place and possessions. Tis pride prodding these men and my Ma would be making tsking sounds with a shake of her head and saying the men were going to get into trouble for surely the road they were taking would have a turn in it. Our direction brings to mind the Irish saying: *In every land hardness is in the north of it softness in the south Industy in the east and fire and inspiration in the west.* Certainly tis true in America that the Industry resides in the east and I have ridden though the fire and glory of the Far West and now we are moving to the north and land of the Mandan lies to the north. What hardness will mean I cannot fathom but I shall be keen to it.

Fitzpatrick rides to my side with a twinkle in his eye. "I've told you of how I acquired a child of my own."

"I did not know that you had a wife."

"I do not but this summer past I was with Jed Smith on the Santa Fe Trail for I was late in getting supplies and had some difficulties in financing in St. Louis so Jed and the others assured me that I could get my supplies in Santa Fe and then turn north to the rendezvous which was in Cache Hole. You've met Kit?"

"Carson?"

"Yes. That's where he signed on that is at Taos, which is north of Santa Fe. We lost Jed Smith somewhere on the Cimarron. He and I went ahead of the wagon train to find water and split. We never saw him again. His pistol and equipment turned up in Santa Fe with some Mexican traders who claimed they traded for it with some Comanches. It was in that country on a Friday that I came upon my foundling. He—"

"Oh Friday! Yes I met Friday in St. Louis."

"Why yes you did. I have forgotten so much has happened since then." He shook his head now covered with white hair where it was black when I first met him.

"He is Arapaho?"

"Yes and that tribe are related to the Gros Ventre's that we battled at Pierre's Hole. I left him with the Priest in St. Louis for schooling and to learn our tongue. I have word that the Arikara tribe made an attack on Bonneville's train before he reached the Green River. I have never known them to be so far from the Missouri. They were the tribe that I had my first battle with just after I joined Ashley's expedition. Are you sure you wish to go the the Mandan village for I'd be happy to have you in our mess the men say you are a right smart cook and have the hang of flavoring the meat?"

"Tis a promise I made and a wish to be fulfilled for Eagle Hand was there when my brother Deny did not show. He filled my heart with stories of his village and the land of the upper Missouri. I've not yet acquired the American need for a fortune for me this land and these free people tis fortune enough. My rifle, the Creature with a good blanket meets my needs. Tis a grand adventure here in these mountains with you and I shall return with you indulgence but I've a burning desire to live among these people for I am still a lad and find joy in following my curiosity tis not something I can find the words for but my promises have been made and the shadow of my Da would not permit me to reconsider a promise."

"Tis grand to be young. Do you know the motto of the Fianna?"

"Yes from Uncle Bres! *Three things we live by: truth in our hearts strength in our hands and fulfillment in our tongues.*"

"All right lad well may St. Columba guide your way to the peoples of the upper Missouri. I will have some letters for you to take to Fort Union and will scibe them before we part."

We leave Big Hole and Beaverhead and Jefferson Rivers, trapping up and down them and we have not had any sign of the Blackfoot. We leave the Madison River and are upon the headwaters of the Missouri.

Tis an unsurpassed beauty in the air within these valleys autumn as I have never felt the aspens and cottonwoods are turning brilliant yellow the icy dew greets us many mornings and the mountain air so clear tis like we are looking through diamonds The faint hue of a rainbow just hidden from our sight but I feel is there and I strain to see it. The elk are whistling and buguling and the mule deer bucks find boldness is their search for does and the bighorns seem to watch us form every peak and the buffalo are succulent from a summer of lush mountain grass tis paradise before the first fall of snow.

The Missouri. Tis a mountain river here with a clarity speed and smallness not imagined back in the state of Missouri. How very amazing to come upon a river here that flows northerly and will stretch a long way to the east and turn above the Mandans to the south and then turn again east and end up feeding the Mississippi although is seems the Mississippi feeds the Missouri for surely where they meet the Missouri has more might and the Mississippi is a mere arm of the mightly Missouri and but for a perferences of some long ago Frenchman the Missouri might be the name of the river that empties into the gulf. I have traveled a couple a worlds away from St. Louis and yet here I am upon the very river that serves her and yet vast lands lies to the south with rivers unvisted: The Republican, the Arkansas, the Canadian, the Red, the Rio Grande and the Pecos and rivers to the west the mighty Snake and Columbia upon which I have touched and which flows to the Pacific and rivers to the north that feed the great Arctic lands atop the earth. Tis a far far vaster land than my mind ever imagined.

North, up the Missouri and into the very heart of Blackfoot country we go quickly efficiently with some fear of being followed not by Blackfoot but by the American Fur Company brigade. Today where the Dearborn comes into the Missouri one hundred twelve men under Mr. Vandenburgh catch up with us. They have been tracking us and trapping behind us since they left the Green River with their supplies. The Rocky Mountain men are very accommodating to the unwelcome visitors but they grumble amongst themselves. Now the trappers are to turn south again back up the Missouri and now we are to turn East down the Missouri to the land of Eagle Hand the land of the Mandans land that lies far to the east of us but starts in the heart of the land of the Blackfoot and flows into the land of the Crow and finally passes though the land of the Hidatsa distant cousins of the Crow and into the land of the Mandan.

"Git we are moving out smartly today no nooning just dried meat for we have these American Fur Company men dogging us. Follow us and steal our knowledge will they? Follow they may but our knowledge they'll not have. We have twenty packs of beaver and they five with twice the men and ther will be no more beaver taken in this country." Mr Fitzpatrick said his face reddened in anger.

We move quickly all that day and for three more days and then it seems the American Fur Company men caught on we were in a land barren of beaver.

Mr. Fitzpatrick came to my mess that evening.

"Git, we'll be turning up the Missouri to the Gallatin and making our way back to the Salmon where we'll winter. Now tis the time to separate if you're still of that mind but know we are in the heart of Blackfoot land."

"Mr. Fitzpatrick my mind is set, but I'll be missing your company sorely. God willin' I be back for these Mountains are a magical place and the company most dear. Eagle Hand and I along with Moses Harris will be moving to Fort Union where we'll be out of the hands of the Blackfoot."

"Well lad that will be it then may the saints watch yer hair and may ya find yer brother and friend and I've a feeling we'll be meetin' again."

"And a great joy it's been here in the mountains and meeting you."

Tis a misty gray morning with a slight breeze but a deep chill in the air It feels so good to feel the warmth of the Creature about my legs. I hug his neck and scatch him while waiting for Eagle Hand to complete his round of hand clasping. Mr. Harris walked around and around checking his packs saddles and even his rifle and seemed to ignore all leave-taking. He just stated he was off to the men and they seemed to accept it.

Black Harris so named because of his nearly black face a Welshman whose true name is Moses Harris. He is an independent trapper that has come into camp on the upper Missouri. He usually traps alone. He is much admired and always gets the best price for his furs as they are the best dressed and some of the biggest beaver. I remember him at rendezvous as one of the men who had a high time with the whiskey, which made him tell stories and laugh often. In camp here he is quiet in his conversation, polite but not given to say too much. He has some business at Fort Union and decided he would accompany us. He has coal black hair and skin like a burnt roast. He rode and packed with a mule and took a liking to the Creature and said that I was starting our all right by attachin' to a mule for they were better than a dog at sniffing out trouble.

To the north we rode to the south the rest went up the Missouri. The American Fur Company now tired of the chase and with few beaver has decided to strike out on their own and turn towards the Madison. We trapped some of the streams in the area. The American Fur Company men are moving towards the heart of Blackfoot country.

Moses rode a mule and rode with the stirrups set high that his knees are near his hands and he rode a bit hunched over with his eyes always squinting and flicking and he'd wriggle his nose and sniff the air every few minutes and always slowed to a slow walk on every rise of land with most times him stopping and when his eyes had cleared the rise he set his mule and gazed the land and his mule would stand at attention sniffin and working his ears and then Moses would make a little hop in his nearly flat Indian saddle and his mule would set forward if satisfied. If it wasn't' satisfied Mr. Harris would start talking to mule asking him what those flop ears are hearing and if he was nostrilling a bear or injun. The few times that this happened that day Eagle hand would dismount to add his senses to the mix. Once is was a white bear or grizzly down in the hole in front of us turning over rocks and logs. The other time it happened we weren't able to see what the mule was fixed on. That made for a silent uneasy riding for the next hour. The Creature seemed quite curious about Mr. Harris mule and would watch is closely and raise it's head sniffing on those stops and stand very alert and shift between watching the mule and the countryside around us. Near noon Harris began to speak.

"I ain't telling ya what to do but I burn my meat at the nooner and leave off a fire at night. Some vittual at night and move off a ways from the dying fire to sleep, but I tote too many doin that fer too many a year and tote the Blackfoot are keen to it. Man can get a long ways from his nooner fire. If yer twos are of a mind to."

"We both looked at each other and nodded our assent."

"He didn't look at either of us and his eyes was scanning and I wasn't sure he saw our nods but he kept looking and started speaking. "Back in 27 I opened the New Year by making out on snowshoes from the Great Salt Lake back to St. Louis. Bill Sublette need to get back to order the supply train for we had a great hunt that fall."

"You took horses across the mountains in the winter? I asked."

"Aint nary a horse could make it. Took an Injun pack dog. I spect it is near fifteen hundred miles. We returned in late June with forty four men in our pack train and one cannon."

"A cannon?"

"A present from General Ashley a four pounder it was pulled by a two mule cart over the Rockies and down the steep rocky canyons to Bear Lake goin down is a mite tricker with wheels."

"Taking a wagon that far must a been a feat."

"Not nearly the feat of Jed Smith reaching the Pacific that year. They lost seven animals and nearly lost one man coming across the desert. But it was a bad winter with plenty o' blizzards and bad for some trappers for we lost eleven men to the Blackfoot that winter. Up yonder creekside we can sizzle some of this elk looks like the air is pushing down from that bluff keep the smoke low and confused."

I gathered some firewood *two fingers thick and sappy wood* according to Moses for he explained that he wanted the fire hot and fast just like he liked his women then he laughed with a nasal *hey hey hey*. When I brought my bundle of branches back he had his glass out and was burning some dry moss and whittled tinder in his hand. I love to watch how the sun is turned into little red-white dot that explodes tinder into flames for is always seems magic to me and confirmed the power of the sun to me. Eagle Hand cut thick chucks of red meat off the haunches of the hindquarter of the elk we had tied over the back of one of the pack mules. We tied the mules off to the trees and they grazed with saddles and packs on. A clear mountain brook swished beside us. The scent of pine was in the air and the day clear. I ground the peppercorn on a flat rock and crumbled salt betwixt my fingers and rolled the meat with the spices and then speared them with willow appolas and pushed them into the red earth next to the gray and glowing branches. Oh the glorious smell of wild meat sizzling to tis hardly a smell to such fresh meat once it is separated from the hide for the hides carry fermented forage smell to them but the flame brings out a smell like wet hay smoldering from the meat and that odor means the most satisfying fullness will soon fill our bodies.

I don't know that I ever felt such happiness such fulfillment such freedom as I feel today with the still clear mountain air the clear cold water rushing by my feet the freshest more tender meat sizzling in front of me with the cool night air to look forward to for the kind of deep sleep that one can only feel outside and heading down one of the greatest rivers of America to a whole new world that I can't yet imagine at the Mandan village. As we ate our lunch Moses eyed me and began to talk.

"Git you'll be having first watch tonight I have some mightly fine Mandan tobaccy and you're certainly welcomet to puffin some this evening for that will be the only fire we will keep. I find It keeps me alert and I know Eagle Hand will have some he said looking at Eagle Hand who is busy eating elk off his willow and he smiles as the juices run down his chin."

"Tis a fine night for me to indulge I'll not let you down on me watch for can be sure I'm a bit of a worrier and may be up imagining Blackfoot crawling though the grass."

"Alert is alive in this here country. I make my camps careful and I walk around them to see how a man might see them if he was to sneak on us and I say you do the same for it is a habit that's kept me alive for then you will know where to watch you will know where a clever fellow will be crawling and you can put your mind to every tree and tuft so you know where something doesn't belong. I'm not one to be trusting others with my hair so you best be doin things the way that's' kept me from going under for I'm not one to put trust in pups. He said while eating and did not look at me and his voice was firm."

"We have traveled from New York and I now sleep when Git has the watch Eagle Hand said with his eyes scanning the rocky ridges above us."

"Expect you learned some sense with Eagle Hand here."

Two more days we traveled no danger did we encounter despite having seen some fresh tracks of the Blackfoot our first day out. We are nooning on a mule deer that Eagle Hand had taken with his bow when we heard the beat of hooves. We clenched our rifles and moved behind tree trunks and it was curious because it was only one horse we heard and it was in a hurry riding without caution and when man and beast appeared from over the ridge on our trail it is a hatted man so we knew it not to be Blackfoot. He rode in and and did not slow and did not hail but dismounted and quickly entered our ring so that I felt like taking a step back. I did not know him and my companions did not hail him by name. He announced that he was an employee with American Fur Company is on his way to Fort Union with news.

"Vanderburgh is dead! Blackfoot! Ambushed us on the Jefferson his horse went down pinned him but he got a shot off but they tomahawked him as he wus drawin' his pistol they was in a little gully that we jumped our horses over on the way to the trees. Shot at us from behind. Killed the Frenchman right off his horse. There was only six of us and we had to save ourselves. Oh it wus terrible they hacked his arms off first the arm that drew the pistol then the other oh he screamed terrible but they was swarming over him cutting him up so we got away. I can't get over the sight of im sittiing there with no arms sceaming. We had to split our brigade. Some still followed the Rocky Mountain outfit then lost them and we wus taking a shortcut to find them. Why didn't they they just tomahawk him in the head. No they just kept cutting away. We came upon some buffalo killed and he set out with six of us to scout the area. The Buffalo was still warm and moccasin tracks all around we thought it was only seven or eight of 'em a small hunting party. There was even a herd of buffalo still grazing in the valley so didn't think there could be too many Injuns around. We headed to a dense stand of trees up river and that's when we crossed the gully hell that thing could hardly hold a jackrabbit how could it hold a hundred Blackfoot. A half a dozen come out the trees and we shot at them then the gully erupted with Blackfoot. He wus sceaming of us not to run and then he was just sceaming it wus a terrible scream from a man who never screamed. I got lost ran on and on then the next day came upon a trapper from the Rocky Mountain outfit he set me straight on my directions and told me they had a battle with the Blackfoot too! Jim Bridger took two arrows in his back as he rode up to the chief to parley. Chief didn't trust him when Bridger cocked so he grabbed the barrel and knocked Bridger off his horse and and braves filled the air with arrows. He got away but three trappers were killed. Are ya headin to Fort Union?"

"Yes we are but were not busting though the country like you," Moses said.

"Well I aim to put miles between me and the Blackfoot if they can kill a man like Vandenburgh man was a West Pointer they can kill me. I expect I'll need a piece a meat if yous can spare some."

"Why here take a stick it's a long way to Fort Union don't know that that horse will make it the way your driving em."

"Horse will be dead if the Blackfoot catch me. Thank yee much."

Off he went leaving us uneasy.

"I expect he will clear a path ten mile wide in front of us. We best be careful for if thay scalp him they might be waitin' on us." Moses said as he scanned the skyline.

We came upon moccasin tracks the next day a small party of five and they had circled around the tracks of the trapper but continued to the east. We had snow the night before and the country was rugged and rocky with narrow passages and so it made one mighty uneasy for there was no choice, but to go ahead into the defile where leveled rifles could await and a rain of arrows could descend. The animals could sense our fear and were beyond alert to touchy. We began to traverse a narrow path high on a rocky ledge. I dismounted to recover blanket that had worked loose on the pack animal. I heard a protesting haw and over the Creature goes on the cliff. I was scree loose rock below down I went to see how the creature was and it was tense for a while as he was still on his side and finally he got to his feet and he did not like the loose rocks as we clawed our way back to the trail. That was a relief to have the Creature be all right.

We continue that way the rest of the day and camped without a fire that night. The ghosts of our breaths return to us each night and stay with us till the sun is a couple hours high. The mountaintops behind us are covered with snow the leaves have fled from the frigid air making warm beds under the trees but the green of the pine and firs still dot the cliffs, bluffs and hillsides. We are going east following this mighty river. I ride with the Creature who is learning to be a good alert mule by watching Moses and his mule. The Creature had me at the grizzly attack and now I trust her more than a horse. We are in a land where no one had sure claim, but Blackfoot, and Crow contend. We leave the mountains behind us but massive bluffs and spires of clay like castles greet us sometimes shining like diamonds in the morning or evening sun as it reflects off the thouasands of gypsum cyrstals imbedded in the clay. The trees grow smaller each day until they become rare with only an occasional cedar tree clinging to the ravines and cottonwoods only appearing where the river enters the Missouri but for long stretches there is nothing but unbroken rolling beige brown and broken green prairie. Bighorns, antelope, Mountain goats, mule deer, wolves and elk peer down at us from the keeps of clay castles above us. Massive grizzly tracks imprint old mud now seeming rock. We find old war lodges old campsites old tracks of men hunting buffalo and each other. Some days the distant hills are black with buffalo other days not a sign of life. The sand bars of the Missouri are covered with brant and and ducks the low honks the high-pitched honks and the laughing honks fill the air night and day. I watch flocks pass at night overhead under the full moon of August.

We come over a rise of hills with more hills to our left and the round clay hills across the river and we see the plains around Fort Union covered with teepees and the wide Missouri below the fort. We shot our rifles to announce our approach and several shots answered.

Eagle Hand and Moses look to the fort with hunger in their eyes for both have beaver to trade I have some too having gone out with the trapping parties and they kindly teaching me how to set the large heavy traps by scenting a fresh cut stick above the trap with castor oil for the gland of the beaver. It is not the fort that holds so much interest for me as the teepees around it for they are of of design I have not seen before.

We move towards the main gate, which faces the Missouri. "W. W. and V. for me Moses said as he smiled"

I looked at him with a questioning frown.

"Whiskey women and vittuals ya pup. Might do you good to take a shot and forget yer troubles."

Upon coming to the gates eyes appear in a little peep door and the large gates swing open Standing there smiling like a just swallowed a possum is Jack.

"Jack!" Both Eagle Hand and I called in unison.

"Well I thought the Missouri would ice before you fellas show up. I see you both have your hair he said with a big smile and affecting a Far West accent."

We introduce him to Moses and we shake hands and then Moses is off to deliver his letters and I give him Fitz letters to deliver. The fort is a fine affair with large almost elegant house at the rear with paint on it. The trading post is to our left as we enter the big gates and the smith next to it. There is another set of large doors about thirty feet inside and an opening in the wall about chest high into the trading post it seem they can take trade with the inner doors shut and thus prevent entrance into the main area of the fort. To the right within the double doors is a place for horses. Both sides of the inner fort are lined with building some look like lodging and some storage. In the center of fort is a stone well and a large wooden press used to bale the plews of fur and a very tall flagpole. There is a walkway high on on the inner wall in which one can circumnavigate the interior perimeter of the fort interrupted on the northeast and southwest corners of the fort by large overhanging stockades. The upper wall and stockade have numerous slots cut into it for for wielding of rifles and I see the barrel of a cannon on the stockade near the front gate. The stockades protrude out so there is a clear line of fire down two sides of the walls the two stockades providing defense for all four walls. A thin man with a city hat come out of the northern stockade we move to the center of the fort. He waves at us. I squint at him. Tis Mr. Catlin the painter he hurries down to meet us upon recognition.

"Why it's the young Irish explorer Mr. O'Toole."

"Mr. Catlin are you manning the cannon up there?"

"Why no it is my studio. I've some splendid painting of the Blackfoot Cree and Assiniboin!"

"There are Blackfoot here?" I asked with uneasiness.

"Certainly you have nothing to fear All are on their best behavior Here they are at there most honest...they are in the pure simplicity of nature. It is astonishing to be so near tribes who have not yet been corrupted by cities and civilization."

"We had several battles with the Blackfoot."

"You've been in battles?" Jack asked in a surpised and hurt voice. Before I could answer he proudly proclaimed "I was on the first steamboat to reach the Yellowstone River I boarded it after I left you and Eagle Hand We made it to this fort for the first time and we visited Fort Pierre on the way. Mr. Catlin was on it and so was Rabbit Skin Leggins and No Horns on His Head remember we met them in St. Louis seeking God's word. Amazing that they had to walk 3,000 miles seeking God's word and then ride back nearly to their land on the first steamboat to penetrate this country surely God has a hand in that."

"Jack is quite right I rode all the way up the Missouri the River of Sticks for I have never imagined so many logs, trees why it was a raft of them at times but we shuddered and roared and puffed and toiled for three months and look at us now her in the middle of the Far West in perfect harmony with nature. Come now we must introduce you to Mr. McKenzie and the other guests. Did you know Mr. Sanford the subagent to the Mandans was on board He and his slave left us at Fort Clark He is engaged to Emilie Chouteau who rode with us as far as St. Charles and her father Pierre was with us till we arrived at his new fort called Pierre Chouteau oh we had quite a celebration with wine and whiskey and some fine meals at the christening. Mr. Laidlaw had just finished the fort before we arrived and a splendid place covering over two acres I believe Mr. Mackenzie is in the trading room."

Passing though the inner gate we turn left and step up to a long sparsely furnished room with a rough wooden floor and a fireplace on the far end. To the left upon entering is a waist high counter and beyond it the trading room rull of shelves of goods a rainbow of colors form bolts of cloth stacked on the shelves. The floor was covered with kegs containing foodstuff spices and in the far corner gunpowder. Tack rope quirts hung from the ceiling. In the back two men dressed in black are conferring.

"Mr. McKenzie! Pardon but some dear friends have arrive from the Rockies I met them back in St. Louis. Mr. Eagle Hand of the Mandan and Git O'Toole recently of Ireland."

"Mr. Mckenzie a tall dark man with thick expressive brows raised them as he appraised me. "A bit young for a trapper aren't you?" His dark eyes fixing on me.

"I'm a camp tender and I'm headed to the Mandan village."

"Well let's see what you brought to trade."

"We have some beaver to trade."

"You get in some beaver trapping too ladd".

"Yes I did."

"I traded for some more balls and powder and awls and needle sets and some blank knifes."

"Eagle Hand traded for more balls and powder."

"You gentlemen haven't had your nooner yet have you?"

"No we haven't," answered Eagle Hand

"Sit down at a table for a nooner something you too haven't done in a while."

"I make it the 18 of December that I last sat at a table to eat in St. Louis and today is August 25th."

"We will have buffalo hump today the best part of a buffalo. We have potatoes and gravy and creamed corn."

We go into the house which has a palor and go to the dining room where we are served our meals and a great meal it it with silver and napkins better than eating with a knife.

I go out and get the creature's saddle off and and take the load off the mule and get the animals some hay. We are leaving tomorrow for we are anxious to get on the trail.

Some Blackfeet Indians come to trade bringing otter and beaver skins and I get a chance to observe them closely. One woman that comes to trade has her nose chopped off. This is a Blackfoot custom if a woman is not true to her man. They have rather large noses and are tall and the women paint their chin red with vermillion and the whole of the cheek as well as the cheekbone. One of the men has a beaded stripe down the arm of the skin with blue and white beads in a white cross pattern. There were shells affixed to his shirt and an ermine fur collar, in his hair he had feathers from birds of prey with a grizzly claw in the center. His face is painted black and indicates a recent heroic deed. He is the most finely dressed the other have beaded skins and not much else besides a choker of beads and earing. I believe that they are the Piegan tribe of the Blackfoot.

I wander out of the trade building and go into the courtyard where Eagle Hand is talking to an Indian I think he is a Cree. They use words and sign and I can't follow the words.

When he leaves I ask Eagle Hand what that was about.

"The Crees are enemy to the Blackfoot and have to live among them here and they despise it. The Assninboin are also enemy of the Blackfoot and they are here too. Everyone is on their best behavior."

"Are we leaving tomowrow?"

"Yes it is best if we leave while the Blackfoot are occupied here and they are surrounded by enemy. The Piegan are here and I hear the Bloods are at the three forks of the Missouri and the Gros Ventre are just getting back to their village so now is a good time to leave."

"Before sunup so the Piegans don't get any ideas to come after us. I think I will see Mr. Catlin's painting if he is not with a subject."

I head over to the blockhouse to see Mr. Catlin.

Mr. Catlin is occupied finishing some painting.

"Come in Git."

"I'm just finishing up some painting."

"I see you have the painting of the man I just saw down at the trade house. Same clothes too. And you painted some women they are plainer than the men."

"Ah but they paint their face much brighter than the men."

"Do you roll up the painting up when you are done. How do you transport them? You have so many?"

"Yes I take is off the frame and roll it it up and so far I've been lucky with transport but it will not last and I will have to get a pack mule and travel that way."

"Did you paint some Crees?"

"I am a fast painter and if they are here I will get them painted."

"Git will you dine with us tonight."

"Yes I will, I will see you then."

I go over to the stable to see the how the Creature is getting on.

He has hay in his mouth and gives me a whinny and has those big ears pointed towards me. I go over and rub his ears and the flubbing of the lips happens.

I stay in the quiet of the stable for an hour thinking about how far I've come and how far I yet have to go. I'm glad the Blackfoot are occupied but that doesn't mean small parties are not out looking for intruders to their hunting land. I trust the creature even more now that I have seen how Moses treats his mule. They are better than a dog at sniffing out trouble and I will ride the Creature and if I need a pack mule in the future I will get one.

It's time for dinner and so I head over to the house and we are having elk ribs tonight with sweet potatoes and white beans in a red sauce spiced with chilies. It is an excellent meal. They sure do set a good table at Fort Union.

The moon is half and glowing I am up on the walkway to see the stars and moon for I can't stand now to be cut off by trees or building from the stars and moon I don't know how I lived in New York with all the tall buidlings but after sleeping on the praire for so long I need to see the night sky and see where the moon is. People live with hardly ever seeing it in the cities and I can't live that way anymore. I need the open spaces of the Far West as my playground and here I will record what happens for the rest of my life. It may be settled like Mr. Catlin says, but there will still be open spaces to live out here and that is where I will live. August is a magical time in the Mountains with winter coming and the trees are the beauty of the mountains and aspens are a magical tree and it is too bad Ireland doesn't have any aspen to be part of the magical trees.

The moon is set and it is blackness except the Milkyway glows on the edge of the sky. Time to head to the Mandan Village and sneak out of the camp of our enemies. Before the gathering of the firewood happens we will be out of the Fort. The gate is opened and out we go in the cold morning air, but I have the Creature's warm body to keep me warm. I scatch her withers and leave in a thin Indian saddle that I traded for I have my stirrups lower than Moses. We head to the east on the north side of the river the side the fort is on. The south side is full of willows and brush and clay hills and the north side is flat and passable. Jack is coming in the spring as he thinks he has enough preaching to do here with all the tribes that come to Fort Union. He can stay at Fort Clark and it may not have the dining table that Fort Union has but it will have to do.

We adopt Moses methods and will noon with a fire and have no fire at night as there is few downdrafts to hide our smoke and the smell will carry for miles. We will adopt this method until we get to Minnetaree country. We past the Yellowstone as it enters the Missouri.

We see no one all morning and the nooner is by the cottonwoods by the Missouri. Hot and fast is our fire we have some of the muledeer left and we roast that.

"Eagle Hand how does it feel to be on the Missouri and be headed home."

"Too long have I been away and too far I have been. I cannot even tell my people most of what I have seen for they will think me a big liar and if you say the same they will think the same of you. I have seen this before from those that returned from the east. I have to put that out of my mind and live the life of my village. I know that the white men will come and will settle this land there are too many of them not to and like you I will enjoy the life that I have as long as I have it and then I will live the life of living with the white man. I only hope that the buffalo is left alone and not killed off like out east for that will reduce our tribe very much and I do not wish to see my people like the tribes of the east that they moved to the west begging and living off of whiskey for that is no life that is slow death. Every day a little death and life becomes one long slow death living with the whiskey because all else is gone."

"I am with you I will stay with you as long as this lasts and then I will find something to do maybe guide pioneers to the west along the Platte or something involving this great Far West I will be involved in."

"Enjoy every day because the end will come sooner than you think."

We were both lost in our thoughts about our freedom and this is what this life represents is freedom.

"They still have their village and the horse and the stories and rituals and the bow and the games they still have much of what makes a tribe strong if they spent their time strengthening the tribe instead of the the daily death that whiskey brings."

"It's sad to see a whole tribe like that drinking their self pity instead of doing the acts to strengthening the tribe."

We put out the fire and checked the straps and the Creature doesn't want to go. I tell Eagle Hand someone if coming or there is bear around. We tie the animals up and crawl to the top of the cottonwoods to view the praire and soon we see a family group of Assiniboins going by headed to Fort Union. After they are gone the Creature consents to go and we are on the trail again. The afternoon passes without incident and we find some cottonwoods and willows and after checking out all the possible entrances I take the first watch and Eagle Hand sleeps and I know now that he sleeps. I watch the stars and the half moon which has a glow of some clouds around it and I see a few shooting stars and watch the shapes that are now familiar to me around the campsite while covered in my wool blankets but mostly I listen for the Creature to alert me to anything going on. Maybe some day in the Far West this won't be necessary but I considerd it time well spent and time to think of this all being gone like Eagle Hand thinks and even if it is there will be wild places for people like me to wander places that trade can't take place. The mountains for one will be the last places settled.

I wake Eagle Hand for his watch and I think I had the easier watch since I had no sleep to leaden my head. Good night Eagle Hand and I

396 JOURNEY TO THE FAR WEST

snuggle down into my wool blankets for the air is warmer here than in the mountains even though we are a high elevation.

The tea is going and and a small hot fire is burning and and buffalo stew is on. The clouds are low in the east and so the day lacks the warmth of the morning sun. We have our stew and linger on our tea while I let the animals out on the prairie to graze. Them it is time to catch up and load. We have trade goods and our blankets and meat and Eagle Hand's mule carries it all and it seems to be learning from my mule to nostril the air and slow down before every rise in the land to scout what may lay ahead.

We talk between hills.

"Eagle Hand if your tribe succumbs to the whiskey and begging and the buffalo are gone from your lands do you think we could roam the Far West and live the life of trapping or some other trade so that we could still live this way."

"Yes Git that would be my choice too. I cannot stand by and watch my tribe become what so many other tribes have become. It won't be quite as free as it is now. For if one can keep your hair you can go anywhere and travel anywhere and travel though anyplace. With settlement there will be many places we cannot travel and the game will become scarcer and they will be a time to pay to lodge somewhere may come to the Far West. I hope not in my lifetime, but if it does we can find some trade that will allow us to live the free life we live now. For this freedom we have danger, but it is still freedom and few men have experienced it and the trappers all have a taste of it even those employed by the outfits know the feeling of freedom that this life offers. There is only one other place to find that freedom and that is in a village the trappers don't believe that but you do as you have lived the village life and you know that there are few rules and much freedom. You will learn our ways you will buffalo hunt and steal horses and be a warrior if that is your path and the stew will always be on in the lodge. You may even marry and have children of your own and you can help the village have a future for your children."

"I like the mountains and the life of the mountains."

"Yes it is a shorter life than the praire meaning the winters are long and the snow deep and life if difficult. Sometimes it is July before the Mountain passes are clear and then the snows of late August and September begin. The Rendezvous is a marvelous event and we should attend another one. With all the competition the mountain will be trapped out and the rendezvous will end. We must make sure we attend another one maybe in the Green River Hole."

We rode on until the mule stood snorting and earing back and forth and I asked bear or Indian. I concluded bear and sure enough there were berry bushes on the praire and we made a long way around the bear, as the Creature can't stand to be near bear after our last experience.

The black birds are flocking up and the shorebirds that are left are in flocks that touch the wings into the Missouri was they flit back and forth over the water with the changing color of the flock as they change direction. The ducks and geese are still local and flying in low flocks to feed on what I don't know as it is all prairie away from the river possibly bugs in the grass.

One more bear sighting as the bears are getting ready for winter and feeding continuously. This one the Creature wouldn't go around and we had to wait a half hour for the bear to move out of the way.

We had our nooner and ate the last of the buffalo, as it was only some we were given. I took my bow out and went in look for game. I got a shot at a doe mule deer buck but my arrow was deflected by a twig of a tree Eagle Hand saved some dried meat that he had smoked the last two fires and so we will have some meat for tonight and tomorrow.

I made one last try and shot a brant geese with my arrow and got my skins wet getting it. We have fresh meat for our nooner tomorrow.

We camp in willows for the night and I take the first watch. It seems the moon is higher in the southern sky tonight than it was last night. Tonight a paint or cougar is about and the mules are not happy to be hobbled the cougar has the most awlful sound. Luckily it is on the other side of the river and the sounds only goes on for half an hour and the animal is silent.

Eagle Hand is up before sunrise and the animals are out grazing and the tea is going and the brant is on for breakfast. A dense dark meat with no fat typical of wild meat. The buffalo has the most. Deer have very little more in the Mountains than on the prairie. The brant has none. Eagle Hand stewed the meat as it would be too dry to bake it on willow sticks with no fat and we have only a little buffalo fat.

After catching up the Creature does not want to go and so we tie them up in the willows and find that a party of Blackfoot are coming though with horses. About ten men and twenty-two horses. They have been riding all night and I am worried that we had a fire and cooked some food and they may detect it. They are painted up in black and red paint and ride bareback and switch to fresh horses wherever needed.

The sun is one finger up before we are clear to proceed. We pack the mule and decide that maybe we should wait to let the animals loose for grazing.

The morning was without any Creature comments and we proceeded well. We nooned with dried stew meat. I hunted at noon but the deer were bedded down for the day and I had made one last sweep and came upon a yearling in a ravine that was eating and I shot from behind the wind being so loud that the mule deer didn't hear me and I shot him in the spine and dragged him back to camp where we ate the liver and the heart and the rest we left of the insides and I skinned him and pulled the hair off the skin for later when it got cold and we could fill our moccasins with the warm hair. I tied the deer over the back of the Creature.

That night we found some old lodges and stayed in them for the night and a good thing for is rained about four o'clock.

For breakfast I got up first as I wanted the loin of the deer, which is inside the back a long muscle that runs on either side of the backbone and are the most tender part of a deer. I pulled the meat out and butterflied the

steaks and seasoned them with a little powdered ginger and salt and pepper and then apploa them to willow sticks for breakfast. I let the animals
out at sunrise and sleepy Eagle Hand was just getting up.

"Git good loin that is the most tender meat. Just think some people
have their deer processed by a butcher back east and we know the most
tender part by butching our own. I have a saw blade and will cut the ribs
off for the nooner".

Two bears this morning and one that won't move so we have to take
the prairie the long way around. We are following the river. The right of
us is generally cottonwood in the ravines and where the rivers enters the
Missouri. To the left is prairie. We are headed east.

We had mule deer ribs today at our nooner. And they were good and
we had a steak from the shoulder. This afternoon we came upon a small
group of buffalo.

Eagle Hand you want me to shoot one with my rifle or should you
shoot one with your bow and we will stay quiet.

Think the mule can keep up. Why don't you shoot a calf with your
bow. We still have deer meat and won't need a whole buffalo. That bow is
powerful enough that if you don't get close enough it will still do the trick.

Creature you want to go buffalo hunting? The Creature could hear
the excitement in my voice.

Sneak up on them using the ravines and them run the calfs and find
one and go to the right of it and get as close as you can and shoot behind
the ribs and wait for it to go down.

I sneak up real close using the ravines and the bufflalo just looked at
me when I rode out in the open and soon a cow started running and the
rest followed and sure enough the calves fell behind and I picked one out
and got the mule to ride as close as possible and he did and twang went my
bow and the arrow disappeared into the calf and I followed it until it fell
and rolled it over and started taking the good parts out of the insides. The
liver was real good and I shared it with Eagle Hand. Now we had plenty

of meat and the pack mule was full of meat. I packed the hindquarters of the mule deer on my mule and we finished that first. I had my first bufflalo hunt with the Creature

That night I had a scare I had sighted the whole camp site like Moses said to like I was attacking the camp and I had memorized all the tree and hills and hilllocks and I was on watch first and found a set a ears that didn't belong there. So I stared at is a while and if you stare too long in the dark things disappear from your sight meaning you lose sight of them. So I thought it was sneaking up on us and I almost woke Eagle Hand unitl I let my eyes go round and round the ears and that is the way to keep things in focus in the dark and I finally saw the ears turn back with the half moon shining on the back of the ears. That is how the night can play tricks with your sight and how hard it is to spot people sneaking up on you.

The next morning we had the last of the deer meat stuck on willow sticks and the sticks stuck in the ground next to the fire and the heat of the fire roasts the meat and we just unstick the stick from the earth and turn it over and roast the other side of the meat.

After we catched up the animals it started to rain and the Creature wouldn't go and I couldn't tell if it was bear or Indian so we stayed and about half an hour later a group of fifteen Crows ahorse came though and we watched from the edge of the willows as their faded outlines in the rain slide on by. Whether they were after the horses or a raiding party of their own we wouldn't know.

That day we nooned in the rain and the wood was too wet to fire so we had some hump meat raw and it was good to slice it thin and eat it.

The rain stopped before night so we didn't have wet blankets that night.

Buffalo hump for breakfast with fat next to it the best meat on the prairie. A day after a rain smells so good and the day is so fresh and clean like the earth was washed and now it smells good and clean.

Today the Creature wouldn't move and and we had to go back to a ravine and hide because we though it Indian and we waited there for a hour and no one showed and we decided it was a bear and the Creature needs to learn to speak to tell us which is which. I think the Creature is more afraid of bears than than Indians. And we are the opposite.

At the nooner we had buffalo loin also called backstrap. With some wild onions and and roasted wild turnips that I had saved.

"Eagle Hand what do you think of George Catlin painting the Indians before they are civilized?"

"He is doing it for a sense of freedom for himself but the painting is for the white man and trade. He sees a way of life that has disappeared from the east and he think it will happen in the Far West and he wants to document it for the white people to see what they missed. He should try village life he would like it."

"Do you think there will be more painters coming to the Far West?"

"Yes because they can see what happened to the eastern tribes and they will have the same idea as Catlin to come out to document what may happen here."

"What do you think of the painting and how they differ from yours."

"That's amazing how he has depth to his paintings and we don't. I'm not that good of painter so I can't follow him but I bet Four Bears could."

We continued on without incident that afternoon. That evening we came to a set of lodges like we build on the prairie in the snow. Eagle Hand insisted that we hide the animals and so we took them to the next ravine and the Creature hee hawed for a while and didn't like not being around us at night. We just got in the lodge and we hear horses and voices and we waited and then Eagle Hand signals that I go out and look and I poked my head out the bottom of the door and I see four horses and a fire in the next lodge. I tell Eagle Hand. The horses are Indian. We sneak out of our lodge and because it is dark I can't see the twigs on the ground and have to move very slowly and feel with my feet to make sure the earth is clear of twigs and branches as I did not want to step on one and break it and alert the Indians. It took us an hour to work our way out of the ravine by feeling with our feet. We loaded up and traveled all night and rested during the day the next day.

"Eagle Hand are you married?"

"No my wife was killed by the Sioux. She was tending her crops and a small band of Sioux surprised her and another women and scalped them and killed them. That is why I did the interpreting work for the seizers and traveled to the east."

"Did you have any children. Yes the child was with her and was captured she is a girl and I miss them both very much. The lodge is still there and the grandparents still live there and I will too when I return and you will live with me as my guest."

"Eagle Hand I'm sorry. Is there a chance to get a war party up to recover the girl."

"No the Sioux are too powerful and we would have to go against the whole village to recover one person and we don't have the warriors to do such a task. We are only eighty some lodges."

"Would you marry again you are still young. Are you in your twenties?

"I am twenty two. And yes I would marry again, but at this time I do not feel the need to for I still mourn. I would like to have a son. My time with you has shown me what it would be like to have a son and teach him how to find his path in life."

"I don't know if I want to marry or just be a roustabout and travel the Far West and find adventure."

"That is your choice or you could become a warrior and marry and have a warm bed at night. Remember a warrior has great freedom to go as he pleases and as his dreams directs him if he become a war chief. Four Bears is our war chief and he is an excellent one. He will be interested in you since you have a scalp. When you are a little older you may come along like the Pawnee young men who tended the horses and fetched the wood and did the biding of the warriors. That is how you learn."

"I would like that and like to learn the warrior way and learn to be a good buffalo hunter."

"You have taken the first step on that path with your calf kill."

"I will have to trade for a buffalo horse or steal one."

"Steal one may be your better chance as the horses for trade may not be fast enough to make a buffalo horse although we do get some good trades."

"Do you guard the crops when the women work there."

"No we do not. There are usually young men hanging around flirting with the young women. The crops are located down on the flooded river land. That is land that floods every spring. The crops are the women's work. They know the ways of the crops and if we know there is enemy around and or suspect it we send a guard down or the women don't go down to the crops that day."

"Eagle Hand how many more day will it take us to reach the village?"

"Six or seven more days and we should be there."

"Will I be taking the horses outside the palisade."

"Yes and you will do the bow games with the other young men. You will learn our language and learn the sign language better. You can do the calf hunt with the Creature, but you should find a buffalo horse and trade for it and begin training it. You will be one of the few to ride a mule and it may not be fast enough for warrior work although I now see their value as a warning system for they are better than a dog and Moses is alive in

Blackfoot country as a trapper due to his mule and that is the real value of a mule is in enemy territory. I may have to get me a riding mule for warrior work."

We nooned on some chunks of the rear quarter of the buffalo Good lean steaks cooked pink. We took off in the afternoon after a morning of sleeping and then nooning.

"Git we are now in Crow country and have been for the past two days. I think it was Crow that used the lodge huts. It takes a long time to walk at night without breaking twigs with your feet. Now you know how long it takes to escape. We were lucky they stayed in the lodge and had a fire and food or they would have spotted us."

The Creature had one stop on a hill. Is it a bear or Indian? I ask and the Creature turns her right ear backwards to listen to me and then does a whinny when I say bear and we know that it is a bear in our path. We take the prairie the long way around. We have been following a trail cut in the prairie next to the cottonwoods that line the river and there are berry trees that grow in the cottonwoods and patches on the prairie.

We set for the night in some cottonwoods near the river. I had bought some hooks and line at the rendezvous and I baited it with some deer meat that was going bad. Sure enough I caught two catfish and we stuck sticks in their mouths and roasted them and picked the meat off the bones. I put ginger power on the fish and black pepper and a little buffalo fat on the belly. Succulent catfish was a good dinner with some wild greens.

The night was quite except for a shooting star that landed nearby. I marked the spot and will see if I can find it in the morning.

Breakfast is buffalo calf haunch. I went out to find the falling star and it was further than I thought but I had it lined up with two trees and find it I did and it is nothing more than a burnt piece of rock that looked like it melted. I showed it to Eagle Hand.

I have seen these before not often when I was a child and a bow and arrow maker brought one in that he had found out getting arrow shafts from a green ash tree.

It has iron it it that he tried to use for arrow heads but there is too much rock mixed with it to make metal arrow heads. It's amazing such a small thing can make such a bright light and it is falling pieces of rock not stars that we are seeing in the sky.

We are on the edge of Crow country and now the country is contested country between the Mandan's and the Cree. The calf is cut into strips of meat for stew. We are on a beautiful bend of the river with sumac trees all red. The river is lovely and getting wider and wider as we come down it. Soon in a few days we turn south and follow the river south to the Mandan Village and I will live the village life that I dreamed about and learn all about the life of the Mandan tribe and be a warrior and buffalo hunter.

Today we saw many big horns on the cliffs on the right side of the river. That is what my bow is made from the horns of the big horn. It is a strong bow as the arrow nearly went though the calf that I shot. The horns are heated and uncurled to make the bow. We cross the river on a sand bar and go up to my waist when the sandbar ends. We are now on the right side of the river.

Tonight's watch was uneventful and the moon seemed to be higher in the sky tonight.

Buffalo stew for breakfast with wild kuddi or potatoes that I had gathered last night. It is cloudy and raining this morning. The rain turns to snow and the Creature refuses to move and so we wait and watch to see what is coming for the creature indicated that it was Indian. We wait for fifteen minutes and sure enough a group of Sioux, fifteen of them walking their horses in the snowstorm and it looked like a painting with the faded Sioux walking though the storm.

We waited for an hour and then left when the Creature said it was all right to leave.

We noon on a creek that ran clear over rocks and the water sure was good as was the tea. We finished off our buffalo calf and Eagle Hand went hunting and came back empty handed.

The Creature gave us the all clear and and we had clear sailing all afternoon until we found another creek that empties into the Missouri and we are surrounded by green ash and cottonwood trees and some long green grass which the animals loved.

The next morning we both went hunting and Eagle Hand shot a doe mule deer and we had about thirty-five pounds of deboned meat. We had loin and liver for breakfast along with green tea for me and black for Eagle Hand. We also smoked the ribs for our nooner today and we will roast it at noon.

Three times we had to stop for bears they are feeding on berries and getting ready for winter. The Creature is deathly afraid of bears and will not proceed if there is a bear. Luckily for us she won't if there is Indians ahead either. So the bear waits are worth it due to the Indian warnings. We nooned on ribs and roasted deer heart.

We are turning south tomorrow for the river is now south of us. One day and half and we should be at the village. The moon is getting bigger and is moving towards full with it over half tonight.

Breakfast is deer steak and roasted prairie turnips that I had stored. The Creature knows we are getting close and the day is without any bears although we see big herds of elk.

Tomorrow we should reach the Mandan village and our journey is nearly over. From New York to the Mountains to the Mandan village what a journey it has been. A peaceful night in, which we had a fire as we are close to the village. The Moon is three quarters full and will be full soon.

Before sunrise Eagle Hand is up and the tea is brewing and the meat is sizzling.

We figure after our nooner we will be there.

"I will be good to back to the People of the First Man We should shoot a couple elk to take to the grandparents. I don't know how they are doing on meat without a hunter there. They will be glad to see me and I them. The grandmothers will be happy to have a guest to care for."

I see there is elk up ahead do we sneak up on them or run them and bow shoot them. I like the meat better if the animal is not run with the exception of buffalo, as that seems to make no difference. When we are done with breakfast we will take the shoreline up the elk and shoot two for meat for the lodge.

It took us about a hour to get up on the elk and we each picked one out and shot it and gutted it and skinned it and loaded it onto our animals. I took a rear quarter for the Creature and walked her and so did Eagle hand with his animals.

We walked and skipped the nooner as Eagle Hand was too excited to eat and soon we come over a hill and saw a village.

That is the Minnetaree village ours is very near A couple hours later and there sat the village sorounded by a palisade tucked up against the cliffs of the Missouri with a bend in the river below the village. We fired our rifles and several fired in return and the young men rode out to greet us. We are still walking our animals. They are asking Eagle Hand all kinds of questions that I don't understand, but I will for I will learn their language and their ways and grow to become a man in this village and live a life of freedom and know what that word really means. Perhaps I will fall in love and marry and perhaps not but I will follow the warrior's way and I will learn to dance my story and sing my story. So all know what happened and I don't have to depend on someone else to tell my story. I will learn to hunt buffalo and learn to paint my face and I will learn to shoot my arrows from under the horse's neck while I hide behind the horse. Oh how I wish this will all last and that the Far West remains the place of wild beauty, freedom and danger for it is the danger that makes a man and that is what we face here. Here the Blackfoot no longer are my enemy and the Sioux become my enemy. I hope to steal a great buffalo horse that has training so I can contribute to the family meat supply. I want to hear the winter stories that are only told in the winter. I want to watch and participate in all the dances I want to learn all the games. I even want to know how they grow the food and how it differs from our methods.

We are entering the palisade and people are surrounding us and greeting Eagle Hand. I get some flicking of the eyes as some young women see my scalp lock on my elkskin shirt.

We get to the lodge and I unload the meat for the family and the grandfathers help me and sign me a greeting The stew is on and I am hungry and grandmother fills my bowl with buffalo meat and beans and corn. My long journey has ended and I'm home.

Git O'Toole Journal

September 6, 1832, Thursday

After all the talking and walking and riding I have reached the place that Eagle Hand put in my mind last year. I don't have to pay for lodging, but I will have duties to learn the bow, the language, the dance and the customs of the Mandans. I will have duties with the young men of my age and I don't expect any trouble from them when they see my scalp lock.

Will this be the place of freedom I imagined it to be? I will be learning the Mandan ways but I will be living the Mandan life of freedom. After my horse duties I will spend time with the young men as we practice our bows and I learn their language. The Mandan's enemies are the Sioux and yet they are related to the Sioux so it is a variation of the Sioux language that I learn.

This land is now feeling like my land now that I have traversed a fair chunk of it and met people from many different parts of this country. Ireland will always be strong in my mind but she faded some in the adventures I had in this Far West. The freedom from so many people and to be surrounded by animals most of the time brings with it a sense of freedom of being one with nature and of knowing nature. Nature in Ireland was in isolated patches and with the animals owned it is like they were domestic animals rather than the wild animals like the elk I saw on the Platte that night.

The Ohio the Mississipi the Missouri the Platte the Sweetwater the Snake the Salmon the Lehmi the Big Hole the rivers of the Far West and I have traveled them all. For this journey it was the Platte and the Missouri that I rested my warm body in the most and had the most influence on me.

On November 23, 1831 I stepped onto the banks of the Raritan River and started this journey. It is not quite a year later and my journey has ended and yet another journey starts this one not in rivers traveled or distance but in learning the skills to live with a free people. My journey ahead is a cultural one and one of skill and bravery. I wish to become a warrior. A life based on giving and helping others and on dreams and visions so very different than the life I have been brought up in. My richness is decided by my skill as a hunter and how much I give away to guests and those in need. Instead of accumulating wealth for myself the tribal way is to gain respect and honor by giving it away in feasts.

Have I found freedom? Have I been living a free life? Have I found life itself?

You who read this will have to decide that for after I have written this it is no longer mine it is yours. It is a story that lives in your hearts. I'm starting on a new journey for this one is over and I have reached my destination. I will always have a new journey and it will be written for my family, friends and strangers to read.

Eagle Hand Journal

September 6, 1832, Thursday

A long journey to the white man's land and and even longer journey back to my village and to grandmothers lodge. Buffalo stew with colored maize and climbing beans in the green ash bowl. I will now turn over my bowl in my lodge.

It is strange to come with so much knowledge and not being able to impart it. But that is the way of truth for it must to linked to what one sees.

I do not know the power of the white man and I understand his spirits even less and the power of them, but I know the white man is powerful and many and I shall not forget it. Maybe the white man comes and settles this land and moves us further west or maybe the cow-pox comes and makes us one village. I don't know our future and I know some of them are not good and could mean the end of this life I love.

Git is like a son to me and my heart is glad that he has chosen the Mandan life when he could be trapping or a mess cook in the mountains that he clearly loves. With first blood so young he will do well with us and he is beginning to understand our way of life better after the Pawnee village life. If he learns our language, life will go well for him. Now he will see what freedom really means. He has too much city in him and thinks about freedom as a concept instead of living a life of freedom. One cannot be free with many trade goods and that is what most white men want. To have a bigger lodge to hold more things and enslaving oneself to pay for the things that is what lack of freedom is. Do what one loves and free oneself to get on a horse and ride the trails and learn about other people. Find a life where one doesn't have to pay for everything to live. Pursue what makes you happy and you will have more than most in life.

It is sad coming back to a lodge empty of wife and daughter, but so fulfilling to see grandmothers and fathers. There are women who wish to marry here, but I am not at that time yet. I have other journeys to follow.

To sit in my chair and face the east and smoke my pipe in the lodge is peaceful and relaxing. Git is not a big smoker but he will share the pipe with me. Someday he will have a tribal name and will go by that. I am looking forward to watching him learn our language and customs and become a warrior if that is the path he choses to follow.

The eagle catching camps will soon form. It is a solemn affair to catch eagles. The trap is put on the western slope of a butte. The trap is only entered with a west wind. A Hole is dug in the ground or a depression is selected that has an area to sit in so that the hands can reach above the brush pile on top with a rabbit as bait that enabled the man to reach up and grasp the legs of the eagle when it lands to eat the rabbit. There is one man to a trap and fasting is require to trap eagles as well as a sweat lodge to ensure success. Old Wolverine is the sacred bundle that is honored in praying for success. A clan member may make cuts on the skin to please the spirits for success in eagle catching or the member may be suspended by cuts in the chest or back from a sapling in the cold fall weather to ensure success. The tail feathers are all that are taken and the eagle is killed with a twine around the neck and the sacred bundle holder Old Wolverine was given the rest of the eagle. These stories you will find in the next book Evening of the Mandan Tribe.

My journey is to get over my sorrow and to lead Git forward in the Mandan life and teach him all that I know and make him a good hunter so that the lodge will have plenty of meat and the grandmothers and grandfathers will be happy. Join us on our next journey living the Mandan way of life in "Evening of the Mandan."

ACKNOWLEDGEMENTS

THE PAWNEE PORTION OF THE book was taken from *The Pawnee Indians* by George E. Hyde

Fitzpatrick's brush with the Tribal Members and his wandering in the mountians was taken from *Broken Hand The Life of Thomas Fitzpatrick Mountain Man Guide and Indian Agent*.

Information on Bill Sublette was taken from *Bill Sublette Mountain Man* by John E. Sunder

The sign language information was taken from *The Indian Sign Language* by W. P. Clark.

The Mandan farming information was taken from *Buffalo Bird Woman's Garden* by Gilbert L. Wilson. Irish history and celtic rituals was taken from *An Atlas of Irish History* Second Edition by Ruth Dudley Edwards. Celtic rituals was taken from the *Dictionary of Celtic Myth and Legend* by Miranda J. Green. Celtic life was taken from *The Celts* by Gerharo Herm. The information on Druids was taken from *The Druid Way* by Philip Carr-Gomm

The book *Mandan Social and Ceremonial Organization* by Alfred W. Bowers proved invaluable in understanding Mandan life and stories. The book *The American Fur Trade of the Far West* by Hiram Martin Chittenden filled in the details about certain people and where they were at certain times.

Thank you for reading my book before publication: Rick Berg, Lee Fortin, Dick Goette and Randy Benson.